D0672919

Three for Hire

REVENGE OF THE MESCALERO APACHE

Dan Burle, Sr.
2015

3.

DAN BURLE, SR.

Wasteland Press

www.wastelandpress.net
Shelbyville, KY USA

Three for Hire:
Revenge of the Mescalero Apache
by Dan Burle, Sr.

First Printing – April 2014
ISBN: 978-1-60047-947-2
Library of Congress Control Number: 2014934354

Printed in the U.S.A.

0   1   2   3   4   5   6   7   8   9   10   11

Other Books by Dan Burle, Sr.

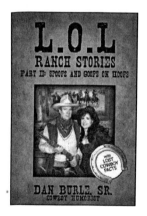

Dedication

This book is dedicated to my three brothers: Ray, Bob and Ken. Our parents had to put up with the likes of us four boys who enjoyed pulling pranks on our mom. We wouldn't do it to our dad because, even though he had a big heart, we could get our behinds whacked, if in his opinion, there was no humor in the pranks.

Even though none of the pranks were harmful, they sure created a lot of excitement in the ole household. I remember the time we found a nest of three baby mice in the backyard. We boys scooped them up in a box and took the box inside and set it on the kitchen table. Then we told mom to turn off the vacuum cleaner and come to the kitchen to see the nice surprise we had for her. I'm here to tell you that I had no idea that my mom could scream so loud. It dang near broke our eardrums.

Christmas was always a great time around the household. We always had a tall Christmas tree with lots of big ornaments on it, and that was a good thing for us. You see, our parents would always buy us plenty of toys at Christmas.

However, it seemed like every other year they either forgot or weren't paying attention. One of the gifts Santa would leave underneath the Christmas tree for us rascals quite often were toy rifles that shot corks. Well, we had two natural targets, the big glass ornaments that we "accidentally" shot off the tree and broke (I use the term "accidentally" in the loosest term possible), and my mom's behind, which was a "fairly easy" target (I use the term "fairly easy" target with all due respect) when she bent over to clean up the mess.

One thing for certain though, we had a good home and we were really well taken care of. All four of us enjoyed watching the old Westerns on Saturday mornings and to this day, we all enjoy everything "country" and everything "cowboy". And what's even better is that, we all get along.

So Ray, Bob, and Ken, enjoy a Western on me.

Disclaimer

This book is a work of fiction. Names, characters, places and incidents either are the products of the author's imagination or are used fictitiously, and resemblance to actual persons, living or dead, businesses, companies, events, places, or locales is entirely coincidental.

Author's Foreword

Imagine that you and your family own 300 acres of land in the country, 30 miles outside of the nearest city. It's been in your family for four generations. Your grandfather and your father were born on this land. You and your brothers and sisters grew up on it. Your father, as his father did, gave you and your siblings a piece of it on which to build a house and raise your family.

You can remember your childhood growing up. It was wonderful: you had family picnics along the stream that ran through it, you played childhood games on your family farm, you had your own horses and rode the trails your grandfather made for riding, you and your family worked the ground and grew vegetables in the garden, and you hunted the woods and fished the lake. It was a wonderful life.

Then out of nowhere, the land next to you became incorporated and a subdivision was built and then another one and yet another one. Then a grocery store and other retail businesses went up.

And finally one day it happened. The government said, "We are buying your land from you. You have no choice in the matter. We need it for the common good". Eminent Domain was what they called it. It was also called "Compulsory purchase" which was the power of the government to acquire rights over an estate in land, or to buy that estate outright, regardless of the willingness or otherwise of its current owner, in return for recompense.

How would you feel? Would you fight for it by taking it to court or would you just say, "Fine, it's yours, we'll move on".

Chances are, you would fight for it.

As I studied and organized my historical research for this Western novel, I discovered so many facts about the indigenous peoples of the Americas which seemed to evade my education over the years as I journeyed through grade school, high school and college.

I knew only the Hollywood version of the so-called redman, Indian, hostile and savage. I was not made aware of the real plight of the courageous first inhabitants of North America, who were aptly named the "Native" Americans.

The Native Americans were on this continent centuries before any white man ever set foot on it. They found unprecedented ways to live and survive with nature, and be a part of it.

Everything they ate, every piece of clothing they wore, every tool they made, every dwelling they lived in, came from the very sacred land they called home. They didn't only live with nature, they were part of it; like melting snow becoming one with the land.

When the Native Americans looked around and saw what was there, they knew there had to be a higher being, a creator that gave them the substance by which they lived and survived. To them, he was known as the Great Spirit.

Then the white man came. They wanted land, and they wanted more land. They desired the furs from the animals and the precious metals from the earth for their own purposes and many for their avaricious desires. All of this was at the expense and detriment of the original inhabitants.

The European whites systematically moved the natives from the east to the west through laws, treaties, land grabs, wars, and broken treaties. They couldn't survive with the redman and some Native Americans felt the same way about the white man.

The Native Americans who resisted the treaties were gathered up and forced onto reservations. They were treated like lowlife, no better than dogs. The whites brought death and destruction and lethal diseases while many natives fought back to no real satisfying end. The great buffalo herds were destroyed which ultimately ended their way of life. The natives were stripped of all dignity, self-reliance and worth.

Many chiefs, respected warriors and their tribes fought valiantly for the survival of their land and their way of life, chiefs and warriors like: Cochise, Mangas Coloradas, Victorio, Sitting Bull, Crazy Horse, Gall and Geronimo.

Others like Red Cloud of the Oglala Lakota Sioux, and Spotted Tail of the Brule Lakota Sioux knew that there was no future but for the way of the white man. If they didn't cooperate with the government, they would not survive. They eventually gave up like most. They grew weary of battle. They could not fight any longer. The spirit of "fight" they once had, departed from their very souls. In our days, the fight would cost us money in court; in their days, the fight would cost them their lives.

There was a wise chief who lived in the Northwest. His name was Chief Seattle (born 1780 – died June 7, 1866). He was the chief of the Duwamish Tribe in the state of Washington. The city of Seattle was named after him. He was a prominent figure among his people; and he, like the Oglala Lakota Sioux Chief, Red Cloud, pursued a path of accommodation to white settlers.

History reports that Seattle wrote a letter in 1855 to President Franklin Pierce when the government endeavored to purchase and pay the Duwamish for land occupied by this Northwestern tribe.

There remains a controversy behind the real existence of this letter since the original has never been located. In fact, it has been described by a historian as "an unhistorical artifact of someone's fertile literary imagination".

Whether the letter was really written by Chief Seattle or not, it undoubtedly demonstrates the wisdom and understanding of the fate of the Native Americans.

Here then is the questionable letter to President Pierce from Chief Seattle.

THE GREAT CHIEF in Washington sends word that he wishes to buy our land. The Great Chief also sends us words of friendship and good will. This is kind of him, since we know he has little need of our friendship in return.

But we will consider your offer, for we know if we do not the white man may come with guns and take our land.

What Chief Seattle says you can count on as truly as our white brothers can count on the return of the seasons. My words are like the stars – they do not set.

How can you buy or sell the sky – the warmth of the land? The idea is strange to us. Yet we do not own the freshness of the air or the sparkle of the water. How can you buy them from us? We will decide in our time.

Every part of this earth is sacred to my people. Every shining pine needle, every sandy shore, every mist in the dark woods, every clearing, and every humming insect is holy in the memory and experience of my people.

We know that the white man does not understand our ways. One portion of land is the same to him as the next, for he is a stranger who comes in the night and takes from the land whatever he needs. The earth is not his brother, but his enemy, and when he has conquered it, he moves on. He leaves his father's graves and his children's birthright is forgotten. The sight of your cities pains the eyes of the redman. But perhaps it is because the redman is a savage and does not understand.

There is no quiet place in the white man's cities. No place to listen to the leaves of spring or the rustle of insect wings. But perhaps because I am a savage and do not understand — the clatter only seems to insult the ears. And what is there to life if a man cannot hear the lovely cry of the whippoorwill or the arguments of the frogs around a pond at night?

The Indian prefers the soft sound of the wind itself cleansed by a mid-day rain, or scented by a piñon pine: The air is precious to the redman. For all things share the same breath — the beasts, the trees, and the man. The white man does not seem to notice the air he breathes. Like a man dying for many days, he is numb to the stench.

If I decide to accept, I will make one condition. The white man must treat the beasts of this land as his brothers. I am a savage and I do not understand any other way. I have seen thousands of rotting buffaloes on the prairie left by the white man who shot them from a passing train. I am a savage and do not understand how the smoking iron horse can be more important than the buffalo that we kill only to stay alive. What is man without the beasts? If all the beasts were gone, men would die from great loneliness of spirit, for whatever happens to the beast also happens to the man.

All things are connected. Whatever befalls the earth befalls the sons of the earth.

Our children have seen their fathers humbled in defeat. Our warriors have felt shame. And after defeat they turn their days in idleness and contaminate their bodies with sweet food and strong drink. It matters little where we pass the rest of our days — they are not many. A few more hours, a few more winters, and none of the children of the great tribes that once lived on this earth, or that roamed in small bands in the woods will remain to mourn the graves of the people once as powerful and hopeful as yours.

One thing we know that the white man may one day discover. Our God is the same God. You may think that you own him as you wish to own our land, but you cannot. He is the Body of man, and his compassion is equal for the redman and the white.

This earth is precious to him, and to harm the earth is to heap contempt on its Creator. The whites, too, shall pass — perhaps sooner than other tribes. Continue to contaminate your bed, and you will one night suffocate in your own waste.

When the buffalo are all slaughtered, the wild horses all tamed, the secret corners of the forest heavy with the scent of many men, and the view of the ripe hills blotted by the talking wires, where is the thicket? Gone. Where is the eagle? Gone. And what is it to say goodbye to the swift and the hunt? The end of living and the beginning of survival.

We might understand if we knew what it was the white man dreams, what hopes he describes to his children on long winter nights, what visions he burns into their minds, so they will wish for tomorrow. But we are savages. The white man's dreams are hidden from us. And because they are hidden, we will go our own way.

If we agree, it will be to secure your reservation you have promised. There perhaps we may live out our brief days as we wish.

When the last redman has vanished from the earth, and the memory is only the shadow of a cloud passing over the prairie, these shores and forests will still hold the spirits of my people, for they love this earth as the newborn loves its mother's heartbeat.

If we sell you our land, love it as we have loved it. Care for it as we have cared for it. Hold in your memory the way the land is as you take it. And with all your strength, with all your might, and with all your heart – preserve it for your children, and love it as God loves us all.

One thing we know – our God is the same. This earth is precious to him. Even the white man cannot escape the common destiny.

These are precious words worth pondering, whether they were really written by Chief Seattle or not.

Discover what I learned about the plight of the Native Americans and some of the causes for what has been described as savage behavior and just maybe we will be closer to understanding why they fought so hard to resist the life that the government forced on them.

Enjoy this exciting Western (historical fiction) and the third episode in my *Three for Hire* series. Now saddle up pardner for a wild ride in the Old West.

Dan Burle, Sr.

Fictional Characters

Jesse Caldwell, and sisters Ruth and Mary
Scott Johnson, and his father, Mathew
Thomas O'Brien
Elizabeth O'Brien
Jeanie and Jennie O'Brien
Josh O'Brien
Janice
Lilly Shannon
Colonel Jonathon Baxter
Sergeant Tyrus Owens
Sergeant Jake Miller
Corporal Josh Taylor
Corporal Ben Allen
Corporal James Pendergast
Yellow Wing
Lone Wolf
Lawrence Williams
James Freidman
Red Feather
Running Deer
Desert Flower
Swift River
Young Eagle
Golden Sun
White Cloud
Spotted Feather
Josephine Wagner
Pops
Mr. and Mrs. Bannister
Meta
Willy Kincaid, Jed Kincaid
McDaniel family
Josephine
James Brent
Will Franklin
Andrew Goodson
Phil Osborn

Table of Contents

PROLOGUE

Drumbeats of war!
Homesteads raided!
White men scalped!
Bluecoat vengeance!
Bloodthirsty retribution!
Tribal villagers slaughtered!
But why?

It was about the land. It was always about the land: the virgin soil desired by farmers, the abundance of undisturbed precious metals sought by prospectors, the lush grassy prairies required by cattle ranchers and sheepherders, the great quantity and variety of animals available for fur trappers and traders, and the wide vast open ranges and flat terrains waiting to blossom into new towns and railheads overflowing with potentially overwhelming prosperity for the adventurous and audacious entrepreneurs.

It was all there for the taking; or so the white man thought. Manifest Destiny was their warranted justification for moving West and confiscating the land from the original inhabitants.

But the Native Americans saw it another way. After all, they were the first occupants of North America numbering as many as ten million people and hundreds of tribes at one time or another throughout the country.

They were self-sufficient, proud of their self-reliance. They didn't just live off the land, they lived with it. Nature was everything to them. They hunted the wildlife for food and clothing; they ate berries and nut crops, and found many uses for plants and herbs. They even made their homes from buffalo hides, tools from animal bones and rocks, and weapons from branches and stones.

The government created treaties with the Indians and gave them land to separate the white man from the redman to avert deadly clashes. But then the westward bound pioneers wanted more land and so the government unilaterally rewrote treaties or just disregarded the existing ones.

The white man continued to force the Natives to move from their birth places and sacred grounds and seek out new safe havens. Tribes were eventually forced onto reservations only to live and barely survive like dogs with no dignity. Their spirit was broken, their self-worth was shattered, and their pride was destroyed.

While many of the Native Americans gave up all hope, some refused to live like mangy diseased animals in virtual natural cages on the reservations and consequently decided to fight until the end for their sovereignty and self-worth. Some wanted revenge; revenge for many reasons: broken treaties, broken promises, ungodly living conditions on the reservations, slain family members, massacres in their encampments by bluecoats for no apparent reason, and total annihilation of their way of life.

The sadness, the despair, the misery and the stripping away of their self-esteem was just too much to bear for the spirited and strong-willed. These were the ones who became known as renegades and they created mayhem throughout the Great Plains and the mountainous and barren regions of the Southwest.

Throughout the great land of North America, there were many tribes: the Cherokee, the Sioux, the Shoshones, the Osage, the Choctaw, the Comanche and many, many more. Some of the tribes were friendly and some were hostile.

But of all of the hundreds of tribes that existed throughout North America, through works of graffiti which were hand painted and carved on stone walls in remote desolate caves, and through descriptive tales of woe orally passed down from generation to generation by tribes on the receiving end of relentless terror, it is told that none were more ruthless, more cruel or more merciless than the Native Americans known as, the *Apache*.

In 1879 to 1880 a disturbance with renegade Apache was getting out of hand in the New Mexico and Arizona Territories. The governors of both territories, Lawrence Williams of New Mexico and James Freidman of Arizona, met in Santa Fe to discuss the horrible Apache raids on small towns and homesteads which were occurring in their territories. Neither one had answers as to why the renegades were wreaking death and destruction while kidnapping white women and children: the wives, mothers and sons and daughters of hard working ranchers and settlers. Were the women and children being slain or were they being held as hostages? No one knew the answers.

The governors sent out posse, and even had assistance from the U.S. Cavalry to search out and capture or kill the renegades and free the hostages; but all of this was to no avail. The death of ranchers and townspeople along with the kidnapping of women and children became unbearable.

In a desperate eleventh hour attempt to put a halt to the kidnappings and killings, and having nowhere or no one else to turn to, both governors took a train to Washington, D.C. in August of 1880 to meet with President Hayes to ask for the immediate assistance of more troops from the U.S. Army.

Unaware of and oblivious to the horrible circumstances occurring in these two southwestern territories, Hayes invited them into his office and asked them to pull up two chairs in front of his desk, and to be seated. Hayes sat down as well and lit up a cigar before he asked the obvious question,

"What can I do for you today, my friends?"

Hayes listened to what the two governors had to say and flat out categorically rejected their request. The governors were taken aback and were downright shocked at President Hayes' response.

"Gentlemen, from what you have told me, I don't believe at this juncture, that more troops are the answer. It sounds to me like you're putting the buckboard before the horses."

"What do you mean Mr. President?" Governor Williams asked.

"What I'm saying gentlemen is that I concur that you have a serious problem. However, I believe you must first establish the root cause of the problem and then after its unearthing, well then gentlemen, we can take appropriate action."

"No disrespect intended Mr. President," the Governor of Arizona responded in a slightly condescending fashion, "but just how do you recommend we go about finding the cause of the problem, sir?"

"No disrespect taken governor, but I just might have a solution for you if the clandestine project I have working right now pans out for me, like I think it will."

"Can I ask what that is, sir?" The Governor of New Mexico asked with great interest.

"Yes you can but I can't give you a direct answer yet," President Hayes replied. "I can only inform you at this time that I have three men I hired for my project who could be just the men you need to resolve your problem. They are close to winding up my mission."

"Who are they?" The Governor of Arizona asked.

"I'm not going to give you their names now but I will tell you this. They are brave and courageous men who are not afraid to look danger in its very face. They are sharpshooters and marksmen of the highest caliber. They're trustworthy, loyal, and devoted to their country and true patriots. One is a retired trail boss, cattleman, and rancher from Austin, Texas, one is a retired Texas Ranger living in Dodge City, Kansas, and the third one is a Civil War hero who was wounded at Shiloh. He is a Kentuckian.

Like I said before, I'm not going to give you their names right now."

"OK sir, how should we then refer to them?" The Governor of New Mexico asked.

Hayes then stood up from his chair, puffing on his favorite smoke, a big fat Cuban cigar and turned around and looked out of his window onto the lawn of the White House.

The two governors looked at each other and then back at the president waiting for a response.

President Hayes then turned back around, took a big ole puff from his cigar, looked skyward as he blew the smoke away from his face, stared at the two governors for a few seconds and with a big ole grin on his face, proudly said,

"I call them the *Three for Hire*. That's all you need to know. When they complete their mission for me, I'll approach them and inquire if they are interested in going on a new mission for you.

I'll tell you this, gentlemen, you'll have to pay them out of your own funds for their assistance. If and when they discover the source of your problem, then we'll talk about the possibility of employing federal funds.

However, rest assured that you'll be hiring the best. I speak from experience.

Now governors, I suggest you continue to fight on with your current resources and I trust that you will keep me apprised of your situation on a regular basis.

Godspeed gentlemen."

CHAPTER ONE:

Colonel Baxter's Personal War

It was the year of 1876. Colorado had just become the 38th state in the Union on August 1st and its white population was expanding ever so rapidly with homesteaders, gold seekers and squatters. But just south of its border was an unsettled hidden natural haven, unknown to most white men and only familiar to a few Native Americans.

To the white man, it was the middle of September. But to the Native Americans, it was known as the time of the "Hunting Moon".

The Native Americans' calendar year differed significantly from the white man's calendar year. The Native Americans' year began in the welcomed spring months because that's the time when lush new green plants sprung up around the countryside and new life was born in the animal world on the Great Plains and in the natural beauty of the undeveloped wilderness. Thus it symbolized the beginning of a new year.

Their monthly calendars also differed from the white man's. It was "moon based" and coincided with events in nature. For example, January was often called the "Strong Cold Moon", February was known as the "Snow Moon", March was known as the "Buffalo Calves Drop Moon", and April was called the "Planter's Moon". Names of the moon months would vary by tribe.

And so it was in 1876, the season was now changing in the high elevations of the Southwest. On the Indian calendar, it was known as the time of the "Hunting Moon", mid-September and then soon would come the "Falling Leaves Moon" and then the "Beaver Moon". The fall chill was pervading the air on the southwestern short grassy Plains and in the rugged mountainous countryside. The temperature for this time of the year was running below normal and Mother Nature saw her family of wildlife preparing for an unusually early winter.

Just as the beaver in Southern Colorado and the Northern New Mexico Territory along the shallow narrow tributaries and small clear flowing streams began patching up their lodges and gathering food for the long hard winter, so too the Native Americans in the area were sending out many hunting parties to do the same: gather tepee and wickiup food for the winter and collect extra hides for warm winter clothing.

Tucked away, below and just south of a large mesa in an unusually grassy range in Northeastern New Mexico Territory near the Cimarron River, was a small Mescalero Apache Indian village. This peaceful encampment had been hidden and in place for almost three years. Very few knew about its existence. Fresh flowing water for cooking and drinking, fertile bottom land, relatively speaking, for growing and harvesting, and excellent hunting grounds for protein and hides made this a perfect location for long lasting survival.

It was three years before, on May 27, 1873, that President Grant established the Mescalero Apache Reservation by signing an Executive Order. It was established near Fort Stanton (built 1855) which was a U.S. military fort constructed in the New Mexico Territory. The fort was built to protect homesteaders and settlements along the Rio Bonito during the Apache Wars which commenced around 1849. Kit Carson, Billy the Kid, and the Buffalo Soldiers of the 9th Cavalry all lived in the area.

It was shortly after the Executive Order was signed that this particular band of previously nomadic Mescalero Apache Indians headed north to escape the reservation life. They discovered this hidden paradise and subsequently lived in peace and harmony with nature.

They lived in a few portable tent-type lodges called tepees which were made up of a few poles and buffalo hides. However, most of the village dwellers lived in huts which were known as wickiups in the American Southwest and West, and wigwams in the American Northeast.

Tepees were mostly used by the Native Americans who roamed the Great Plains following the great buffalo herds for food, clothing and such. They were easy to assemble and just as easy to break down. In fact, it was the women of the tribes who were in charge of setting up and breaking down the tepees. They could be put up and taken down within an hour and they were architecturally as sound as a rock. They could withstand very high winds on the Plains.

The basic structure of the lodge was a three wooden pole tripod system. These were the heaviest poles of the tepee. Once they were in place, lighter poles were positioned to help round out the shape of the tepee. Then a final pole, which had two large units of stitched-together hides by strips of leather, went up. The hides were rolled around the structure, one to the left and then one to the right. They came together on the opposite side of the tepee and then were connected and stitched together, as it were, by many small wooden pegs.

The next step was to secure the outer shell to the ground with wooden or metal stakes that went through loops attached to the shell. The bottom of the outer lodge cover did not touch the ground, just the loops did. There was an important reason why the outer shell did not go all the way to the ground.

After the outer shell was secured in place, there was a rope attached to some poles on the inside of the tepee about four to five feet off the ground that went all the way around the tepee. What followed was another large piece of sewn together hides attached to the rope and then attached to the ground about six inches from the outer cover leaving a space between the outer and inner shell.

This was a key factor in the construction of the tepee to keep the inhabitants from being smoked out when they built a campfire inside the tepee. With the outer shell being about six inches off the ground and the inner liner going all the way to the ground, this allowed airflow to take the smoke from the campfire out through the opening left at the top of the tepee. It acted as a natural chimney flue. This was an ingenious architectural achievement which was used by Plains Indians for centuries.

On the other hand, wigwams and wickiups were more permanent structures which took about three days to construct. They were dome-shaped structures with a great deal of variation in size, shape, and materials. The materials used were based on what was available from nature in the area. Whereas tepees were constructed by women, wickiups were built by men.

They were generally eight feet high at the center and approximately seven feet in diameter and contained a fire pit. Long fresh poles of oak or willow, maybe two to three inches in diameter, were driven into the ground. These poles which formed the framework were arranged at approximately twelve inch intervals and tied at the top. A hole was left at the top for campfire smoke to escape. The roofing and siding were made of grasses and hides. A hide was suspended from the entrance for a door and could swing in or out. The door generally faced east toward the rising sun. These structures were very comfortable during the winter months. Maintenance was fairly easy and would be handled by the tribal women during the year.

In the last couple of years, some Kiowa Apache escaped from the reservation in the Indian Territory (later to become known as the Oklahoma Territory on May 2, 1890) and found their way to this small little tucked-away village hoping to live the rest of their lives in dignity. They were accepted by the Mescalero with open arms. But the runaway Indians' desire for freedom and self-reliance put this secret peaceful village in horrible jeopardy. Unbeknownst to the reservation refugees and the hidden band of Mescalero Apache was that the U.S. Army, led by a bloodthirsty colonel from Fort Sill, was hot on the trail of the escaped Kiowa Indians.

The colonel's name was Jonathon Baxter. He was a tall thin man about 6'1" and he wore his prematurely gray hair at shoulder length. He was a protégé and close friend of George Armstrong Custer. He later even mimicked Custer's flamboyant dress wearing a wide-brim cream colored hat similar to the one Custer would sport on occasion.

Baxter was an only child and grew up in a small town in northwestern Pennsylvania called Titusville which was only about 12 miles from the Allegheny River. At that time, the main industry was lumber.

Baxter's father was well-off and owned and operated one of the largest sawmills in the state. They lived in a modest cabin which really upset Baxter. His father had a lot of money and was one of the well-to-do in town but he was very frugal and lived below his means mainly because he was a Quaker and he had a commitment to simplicity in his life.

Baxter resented living like a pauper and it angered him deeply especially knowing that they had the means to live better. However, there was nothing he could do about it but just complain every once in a while. He never understood his father's parsimonious behavior and the ways of the Quakers. He felt like being well-off was a good thing and living high was even better.

When the Civil War began in 1861, Baxter joined up on the Union side in Pennsylvania and before he knew it he saw action.

Baxter first met up with Custer and his 2nd U.S. Cavalry division during the First Battle of Bull Run which was fought on July 21, 1861 in Prince William County, Virginia and which was considered a victory for the Confederates. It was the first major land battle of the Civil War.

Custer had just been commissioned a second lieutenant. The Army commander Winfield Scott detailed both Baxter and Custer to carry messages to Major General Irvine McDowell. Neither one saw much action at Bull Run.

After the First Battle of Bull Run, Custer and Baxter were assigned to the 5th U.S. Cavalry and they both served through the early days of the Peninsula Campaign in southeastern Virginia which was fought between March and July of 1862. It was there they participated in their first major battle but the North retreated and the Confederates claimed yet another victory.

Baxter also fought valiantly side-by-side with Custer in Custer's Michigan regiment at Huntertown and East Cavalry Field at the Battle of Gettysburg. Both of these men were fearless and were not afraid to look death squarely in the eyes. They charged on their trusty steeds with their swords raised high into the air leading their regiment into one of the bloodiest and deadliest battles of the Civil War.

Baxter was grazed by a stray bullet in the left arm but that was not about to stop this courageous soldier as he continued to advance valiantly toward the enemy with abandon, side-by-side with Custer.

And so it was, during the rest of the War, Custer and Baxter were inseparable and fought shoulder to shoulder until the War came to an end in 1865.

Following the Great War Between the States, many enlisted men went on to make careers out of soldiering in the U.S. Army. They were sent out West to fight long and blood-splattered battles with Native Americans.

As settlements quickly sprung up across the West due to gold rushes, the quest for cattle grazing lands, and the transcontinental railroad's completion in 1869, clashes with Plains and Southwestern Indian tribes reached a final phase.

The military had its orders from Washington to clear the land of free-roaming Indians for the safety of whites and put them onto designated confined lands known as reservations. However, the stiff resistance of well-armed and battle-hardened warriors of Native American tribes in the West and Southwest resulted in the bloody Indian Wars of the 1870's and '80's.

In 1873, Custer was sent to Fort Lincoln in the Dakota Territory. Custer requested Baxter to join him and so Baxter did being extremely elated that Custer wished his presence. Both Custer and Baxter now had new ambitions, to claim fame and glory by encountering the Lakota Sioux and the Northern Cheyenne in Wyoming and Montana and restricting them to their designated reservations.

It was just one month before Custer and the 7th Cavalry headed to the Bighorn in '76 that Baxter was showing off his riding skills to a bunch of new recruits and tenderfoots. Custer was looking on with delight and was enjoying watching his friend Baxter demonstrate brilliant horsemanship to a group of greenhorns.

On that day, Baxter got just a wee bit too sure of himself and grabbed two fairly trained stallions to do a little trick riding known as "Roman riding". In Roman riding, the horseman stands atop of two horses, with one foot on each horse. It is one of the oldest forms of trick riding and goes all the way back to the times of the Roman Empire.

Well everything seemed to be going great until ole Baxter decided to do something down-home stupid and attempt to jump over a five foot rail fence. The horses leapt in an uneven fashion and Baxter was catapulted through the air and landed cockeyed on his left leg resulting in a serious compound fracture.

Custer himself thought it was whimsically hilarious until he discovered the extent of Baxter's injury. The compound fracture of the tibia, the larger of the two leg bones located below the kneecap, and the fibula, the smaller of the two leg bones located below the kneecap, rendered Baxter helpless for several months.

When it happened and while he was in unbearable pain, Baxter had visions of ole "sawbones" going at him, hacking off his left leg just below his kneecap. He had witnessed the screaming horror of the painfully wounded during the Civil War lined up like sheep going to the bloody slaughterhouse and having their limbs sawed off and sometimes gruesomely hacked off by less than proficient white coats who, brashly but questionably, called themselves surgeons.

"No sawbones is hacking off my leg!" he yelled out in excruciating agony. Custer wouldn't have it either; so the field doctor set the bones the best he could and put a splint on his leg.

Then he loaded Baxter up with laudanum, a drug to alleviate his pain.

When it came time for Custer to lead the 7th Cavalry to the valley of the Bighorn during the Summer Campaign of '76, Baxter was frustrated because his leg injury prevented him from joining Custer. In mid-May, with his leg still in a splint but healing nicely, Baxter was ordered to Fort Sill in the Indian Territory to be second in command at the fort. His orders from Washington were to help recapture Indians who had escaped from the reservations. This was the first time in years that Baxter had been separated from his friend, Custer.

On January 8, 1869, Major General Philip H. Sheridan, who led a campaign into the Indian Territory to stop renegade bands of Indians from raiding border settlements in Texas and Kansas, staked out a site for Fort Sill in the southwest portion of the Indian Territory.

The garrison was first called "Camp Wichita" and was referred to by the Indians as "the Soldier House at Medicine Bluffs". Major General Sheridan later named the fort, Fort Sill, in honor of his West Point classmate, Brigadier General Joshua W. Sill who was killed during the Civil War. The very first commander of the fort was Brevet Major General Benjamin Grierson and the very first Indian agent was Colonel Albert Gallatin Boone, grandson of Daniel Boone.

Unlike other U.S. territories scattered around the country, the Indian Territory later to become Oklahoma, had no organized government. Therefore, Army posts like Fort Reno, Fort Supply and Fort Sill were the most significant federal and legal presence in a wide territory. These forts had many responsibilities: they provided protection to Indians and civilians alike, dealt as mediators between the Indians and Indian agents, and protected the various Indian tribes against intrusion by the settlers who became known as sooners.

Sooners was the name given to the restless settlers who entered Unassigned Lands (situated in the center of the Indian Territory) in 1885 before President Grover Cleveland officially declared "the land" open to homesteaders on March 2, 1889 with the Indians Appropriation Act of 1889. The sooner name was the designation which derived from the "sooner clause" of the act, which specified that anyone who entered and occupied the land prior to the opening time would be denied the right to claim land.

It wasn't until mid-July that Baxter heard of Custer's demise at the Battle of the Little Bighorn at the hands of the Sioux and the Northern Cheyenne. From then on he was determined to make "the redskins pay, no matter what tribes they were from". That's the type of revengeful person Baxter would become. His hatred for the Injuns loomed large before but now it was in the realm of uncontrollable rage, the rage of a near madman.

In early October of 1876, Colonel Baxter took about 600 men, 30 wagons, 20 pack mules and two Gatling guns on a long journey, heading west from Fort Sill, on a mission to recapture the Kiowa and a few other bands that escaped from the reservation. Their orders were to round up the strays and bring them back. If they came across any other tribal encampments, then they were to round those Indians up as well and take them to the reservations in the Indian Territory. If any of the Indians showed resistance, orders were to kill them and destroy their encampment. Women and children were not to be harmed.

The soldiers traveled about 25 miles a day from sunrise to just before sunset eating dust from the dry New Mexico Territory terrain. In the evenings they would unsaddle their riding horses, unhitch the wagon horses and grain them just before they tethered them to a picket line, a thick rope tied from tree to tree or wagon to wagon. Then they would pitch their canvas tents, build their campfires, cook their meals, and then relax the rest of the evening.

The bright orange and blue flames of more than 30 campfires illuminated the campsite as the familiar aroma of burning mesquite permeated the cool crisp air of the new fall season. This was the lazy and relaxing part of the day for the tired saddle-worn soldiers and it was the time of day they enjoyed the most as they laid or sat around the campfires, staring into the almost hypnotizing flames thinking about their families or loved ones they left behind.

Then there was always someone either playing old Civil War tunes on his harmonica or another strumming his trail worn guitar while packs of coyotes could be heard howling out in the distant shadows of the moonlit night on the vast open range of the southwestern Plains.

Colonel Baxter had a group of five soldiers he would invite into his kerosene lantern lit oversized tent each night to play a few hands of poker. This was a tight knit group and they were on a first name basis even though their ranks varied. There were two sergeants and three young ambitious corporals. Their names were Sergeant Tyrus Owens, Sergeant Jake Miller, and Corporals Josh Taylor, Ben Allen, and James Pendergast. All were Union soldiers during the Civil War and had joined up in their home state, Pennsylvania, at the same time becoming good friends while participating in several important battles during the War years. The Province of Pennsylvania became the second state in the Union on December 12, 1787. Delaware was the first on December 7, 1787, just 5 days before Pennsylvania.

During the Civil War, the state of Pennsylvania played a major and critical role for the Union. The state provided a huge supply of military manpower, raising over 360,000 soldiers for the Federal armies (more than any other Northern state except New York) of which most fought in the eastern theater.

Pennsylvania also served as a major source of artillery guns, small arms, ammunition, and armor for ironclad United States Navy gunboats. The Phoenixville Iron Company, located in Phoenixville, Pennsylvania by itself produced well over 1,000 cannons for the Union forces.

Pennsylvania was the sight of the bloodiest battle of the entire Civil War, the Battle of Gettysburg, which was fought on July 1-3, 1863. This battle became known as the "High Water Mark of the Confederacy" and the "Turning Point in the War", ending Lee's invasion of the North.

The casualties (killed, wounded, captured and missing) at the Battle of Gettysburg were listed in this way: the Union, 23,055 and the Confederates, 23,231, for a grand total of 46,286.

All of the men in Baxter's clique served at Gettysburg and survived the great battle and the Civil War and decided to make a career out of the U.S. Army.

Sergeant Tyrus Owens

Tyrus grew up around Pittsburgh, Pennsylvania where the Ohio River meets the Monongahela and the Allegheny Rivers. He always talked about what became known as the Great Fire of Pittsburgh which occurred on April 10, 1845. He was only 10 years old at the time but he recalled the fire "like it was yesterday".

It was a warm but a very windy day. Just before noon, a lady by the name of Ann Brooks (Tyrus didn't know how old she was) who worked on Ferry Street for a gentleman by the name of Colonel William Diehl, left a newly stoked fire unattended. The fire was built to heat wash water. A spark from the fire ignited a barn nearby. The local fire department responded but their poor equipment was not able to put out the fire and the flames spread to other buildings.

The winds carried sparks and embers around the area and buildings began going up in flames like they were kindling. Between 2:00 and 4:00 p.m., the fire began to march from building to building, block to block, residences to businesses, not distinguishing between the poor and the well-off but turning everything in its path to rubble and ashes.

Tyrus' family was on the top side of the middle class but on that day, like so many, his family lost everything. Tyrus remembered the way the city looked the day after the fire, April 11th. He said it looked like "a city of smoldering rubble and a forest of brick chimneys".

The fire destroyed as many as 1,200 buildings and displaced 2,000 families and about 12,000 individuals from their homes. The cost estimate of the damage ranged from five million to twenty-five million dollars in damages.

On that day of April 10, 1845, the Owens family lost their family clothing business and their living quarters, which was on the second floor above their business. They went from being well-off to having nothing. Tyrus and his family did their share to help clean up and rebuild the town earning money only for food and board. With no other future to look forward to, he was happy to enlist in the U.S. Army years later and eventually make a career out of it after the Civil War.

He was an adventurous sort of guy and always loved challenges. Some people who grew up with him said he always liked to live on the edge.

Sergeant Jake Miller

Jake Miller's family lived just south of York, Pennsylvania about thirty miles east of Gettysburg. His family was poor and didn't have many material goods. They lived on a 120 acre farm where they raised a small herd of crossbred cattle for beef consumption.

His family also raised a few chickens for the local market and had layers to sell eggs to neighbors. Jake learned hard work at an early age as most did who grew up on a farm. When he turned fifteen, he went to work for a neighbor who was well-off. They were tobacco farmers and made good money for their crop.

Jake was paid very well for his labor. He was one of the best workers on that farm. Because of his work ethic, the owner of the farm would invite him to his house on occasion for dinner. The house was the size of a huge plantation house, two stories tall and very plush on the inside.

Ole Jake made a promise to himself that someday, he would own a farm with a lot of acreage and a huge two story house sitting right in the middle of it. However, he had to put his dreams on hold when Lincoln sent a request for a volunteer army to save the Union. Jake grabbed his rifle, packed a few clothes and headed to the nearest recruiting station.

Corporal Josh Taylor

Josh Taylor's family lived in Harrisburg, which is the capital city of Pennsylvania. Before the first industries appeared in Harrisburg, it was a scenic, pastoral town, typical of most of the towns of that day. It was small and surrounded by farmland on all sides.

In the year 1812, the state legislature selected the small town of Harrisburg to be its state capital and in 1822, a very impressive brick capitol building was constructed by local laborers, and workers from all around Pennsylvania as well. The building cost $200,000 to build. At the time when Josh was growing up, there were no factories yet in Harrisburg, just small businesses and blacksmith shops.

Josh's father was a tall and burly-built, well-respected blacksmith in town. He had more business than he could handle. Josh, who was tall but with a thin frame, was taught blacksmithing by his father at an early age but he hated the hard work. Standing next to a scorching hot forge, constantly working the bellows to keep the fire hot, the smell of burning coal, breathing in the dark smoke that blackened his face, and pounding a heavy five-pound sledgehammer on glowing red-hot metal over a one hundred-pound anvil was just not his cup of tea.

The shock to his joints caused by pounding metal on metal against the anvil with a five-pound sledgehammer all day long finally gave him such a painfully sore elbow that it took literally months to heal. At times the pain in his elbow was so great that he couldn't even lift a cup of coffee.

He worked with his father until the startup of the Civil War when he happily joined the Union Army to get away from his father's blacksmith shop.

Corporal Ben Allen

Ben Allen grew up in a small rural area in Crawford County, Pennsylvania. In 1862 it became known as Hydetown. It was classified as a borough, which in the U.S. Commonwealth of Pennsylvania was a self-governing municipal entity that was usually smaller than a city.

When he was growing up in this small community he attended a rural school. It was there he heard the white man's side of the story from the schoolmarm about who Crawford County was named after and the fate of that man being tortured and killed by Indians. He never heard the Indian's side of the story in school because his teacher had a bias since her grandmother and grandfather were both killed by Native Americans years before.

The entire chilling story goes this way.

Crawford County, which was previously part of the Allegheny County, was created on March 12, 1800. It was named after Colonel William Crawford (September 2, 1732 – June 11, 1782).

Crawford was a brave American soldier and a land surveyor. He worked as a land agent for George Washington. He bravely fought in the French and Indian War (1754–1763) and the American Revolutionary War (1775–1783).

The Munsee was an Indian tribe which roamed Pennsylvania and areas of the northeast. There was a prominent missionary among the Munsee whose name was David Zeisberger (April 11, 1721 – November 17, 1808) He was a Moravian clergyman (a Christian) who preached Christianity among Native Americans. He established communities of Munsee (Lenape) in the valley of the Muskingum River in Ohio and in Canada.

The Moravian Church was a Protestant denomination. It put a high premium on Christian unity, personal piety, missions and music. The church's emblem is a picture of a lamb with a flag of victory, symbolizing the Lamb of God. The lamb is surrounded by the Latin inscription: "Vicit agnus noster, eum sequamur", which in English means: "Our Lamb has conquered, let us follow Him".

In 1772 Zeisberger led his small group of Christian Munsee to the Ohio Territory. His plan was to isolate them from the conflicts of the approaching American Revolution.

However, in 1782, the unthinkable happened to a group of 96 of Zeisberger's Christian Munsee. Some Pennsylvania militiamen, in search of Indians who had been raiding settlements in western Pennsylvania, came across a group of 96 of Zeisberger's Christian Munsee and rounded them up in the village of Gnadenhutten, Ohio.

The Munsee truthfully pleaded their innocence; but the militia took a vote and decided to kill all the Munsee Native Americans, including the women and children. The killing became known as the Gnadenhutten massacre also known as the Moravian massacre. It happened on March 8, 1782.

The Native American massacre by the Pennsylvania militia was horribly brutal. They brought the Munsee, a subtribe of the Lenape to one of two "killing houses". One of the houses was for women and children and the other was just for the men.

There the militia tied up the Munsee Indians, stunned them with mallet blows to the head and proceeded to scalp them with fatal scalping cuts. On that day, the militia murdered and scalped 28 innocent men, 29 innocent women, and 37 innocent children. They then piled all the bodies into the mission building, burned it down, and then torched the entire village. Two young Indian boys, one of whom had been actually scalped, escaped and lived to tell of the massacre.

Ben Allen did not learn of this massacre in school. However, he was taught about the fate of Colonel William Crawford and his execution at the hands of Native Americans.

Crawford was leading an expedition against the Lenape Indians at Upper Sandusky, Ohio in Wyandot County along the Sandusky River when he and many of his men were captured by the Lenape and Wyandot Indians.

Even though Crawford had not been at Gnadenhutten, he and his men were brutally murdered in revenge for that massacre. They were first ritually tortured for about two hours and then burnt at the stake. This execution was widely publicized in the U.S. It served to worsen the already strained relationship between the Native and the European Americans.

Ben Allen lost his mother and father at an early age. His father was killed in the Mexican-American War and his mother died of consumption. He grew up living with his uncle who was quite a shady character and had very little money. They had just the bare survival necessities.

When Lincoln sent out an urgent request for volunteers after the attack on Fort Sumter, Ben was one of the first to join up from his county.

Corporal James Pendergast

James was a mischievous little trouble maker growing up in a village known as Slocum Hollow which later became Scranton, Pennsylvania. Slocum Hollow and the surrounding area had been inhabited by the indigenous Lenape tribe. In 1778, Isaac Tripp, who was known as the area's first white settler, built his home there.

Most of the settlers in that area came from New England in the late 18th century. They gradually established mills and other small businesses in the Slocum Hollow village. The area was rich in anthracite coal and iron deposits. Anthracite is a hard, compact variety of mineral coal that has a high luster. It has the highest carbon content, and the fewest impurities of all coals. Some of the uses of anthracite coal in the 1800's were for heating homes, smelting iron, and used in fireboxes of steam locomotives.

Two brothers by the names of George W. Scranton and Seldon Scranton moved to Slocum Hollow. Their purpose for moving there was to establish an iron forge but instead they focused on manufacturing pig iron using a blast furnace.

In 1840 they founded the Lackawanna Steel Company and it was once the second largest steel company in the world. Around 1845 the company began making rails for the Erie Railroad in New York state and eventually became a major producer of rails.

The name Lackawanna came from a Lenni Lenape Indian word meaning "stream that forks". Scranton sits on the banks of the Lackawanna River.

In 1851, the Scrantons founded the Delaware, Lackawanna and Western Railroad (DL&W) to transport iron and coal products from the Lackawanna valley.

Scranton, Pennsylvania became a borough on February 14, 1856, and a city on April 23, 1866, directly after the Civil War.

Ironically, while the Wild West was still going strong but the railroad was making progress across it in the 1870's and '80's, the first electrified streetcar (trolley) was established in Scranton in 1886, giving it the nickname: "The Electric City".

James Pendergast worked for Scranton's steel company smelting ore and making rails. It was arduous and tiring work being close to that extremely intense heat. One could easily get overheated and seriously injured working around that hot liquid metal.

James learned to hate the work and never got along with many people. He was short-tempered with a "short fuse" and often got into fights with his co-workers. Oh, he was making good money alright but he was working extremely hard and long hours doing it, and it just put him in a seemingly perpetual bad mood. He had promised himself that someday, he would find an easier way of making a living.

Like Baxter's other poker buddies, James signed up to be a Union soldier at the startup of the War Between the States.

MOVING ON

Colonel Baxter would not allow his troops to drink any kind of liquor while they were traveling and on duty away from the fort but he himself kept a hidden stash of several bottles of the finest Tennessee sour mash for himself and his card playing pals. Each one of Baxter's poker playing cronies seemed to carry more cash with them than your average enlisted soldier. Many outside of their circle wondered, yet no one ever asked, where they acquired their unusual wealth and supply of gold coins; the ones at the poker table always kept it to themselves.

It was about 9:30 p.m. and the group was on their 7th hand of 5-card draw poker.

"Your deal Ty," Baxter said.

Tyrus picked up the deck and shuffled the cards and then dealt out five cards to each player. Jake, sitting directly to the left of Tyrus, said,

"I'll open for 5," as he tossed 5 one dollar gold pieces into the middle of the table.

"Reckon I'm in," Josh acknowledged, as he also leisurely pitched five coins into the pot.

"Me too," Ben followed.

"In," Baxter said.

"Deal me in," James repeated.

And finally Tyrus threw in his 5 bucks and said,

"Dealer's in."

"How many cards you want Jake?"

"Hit me with two sarg."

Just as Tyrus was about to ask Josh how many cards he wanted, they heard the hooves of what sounded to be three horses galloping up hard to Baxter's tent. One rider jumped off his horse, and then he yelled with a redskin accent,

"Permission to enter, Colonel Baxter."

"Who is it and what do to want?" Baxter yelled out in an angry tone being quite agitated since they were right in the middle of a poker hand and he was holding a pair of black aces.

"It's your scout, sir. This is Yellow Wing. I have important information about an Apache encampment."

"Well then, come on in scout."

Yellow Wing, a Shoshoni scout for the U.S. Army, proudly wearing a U.S. Army issued blue shirt, entered the tent and breaking protocol for an Indian scout, casually saluted Colonel Baxter while the others stopped playing and looked up at the scout. Baxter did not salute back.

"Well, what's all the excitement about, Yellow Wing?"

"Sir, I find hidden Mescalero Apache encampment about two suns ride from here, below big mesa near Cimarron River. Trail tells me that escaped reservation Indians in camp with Mescaleros."

Baxter then laid down his cards face down, stood up quickly with his eyes wide open almost bulging out of their sockets. It was similar to how Custer reacted when his scouts told him that they found the Sioux encampment along the Little Bighorn.

"How large is the encampment?" Baxter anxiously asked.

"Many wickiups, about 50, 60. Some tepees. Saw three hunting parties leave camp at first light. Took much food and many ponies. Means they will be gone three to four suns depending on success of hunt."

"Which way did they go?"

"They ride opposite of morning sun."

Baxter looked at the group and said, "West, they headed west. That's good."

"How many are left in the camp?" Tyrus asked.

"Many women, children and old men. Also maybe 40 to 50 warriors."

Baxter couldn't contain his excitement.

"This is the news we've been waiting for men. We can take that encampment with ease. Now, let's finish this last hand and call it a day. I have a lot of planning to do."

And so they did, while the scouts tied up their horses and chowed down after their long hard ride. After the last poker hand, everyone gathered up their coins and left the Colonel's tent except Baxter's closest friend, Tyrus.

Baxter learned many of his battle tactics from Custer and that was what he wanted to discuss with Tyrus.

"What's you got cooken in your mind, Jonathon?" Tyrus asked.

Baxter took a few seconds to roll a cigarette before he answered as he appeared to be scheming. He always kept a pouch of shredded Kentucky tobacco tucked into his left uniform shirt pocket with rolling paper. With his left hand he cupped the paper with his fingers and, with his right hand, he meticulously poured the tobacco out of the pouch spreading it evenly across the paper. Then with his teeth, he pulled the pouch string shut and tucked the pouch back into his pocket. He then rolled the paper into the shape of a cigarette with both hands, licked the edge of the paper from end to end, sealed it, and then licked and twisted the ends shut. He could roll his own in a matter of seconds.

After striking a match and taking a long draw and blowing it upward into the air with a sense of extreme satisfaction, he looked at Tyrus and said,

"Here's what I'm thinking, Ty. I learned this from Custer. We need to advance within several miles of those savages the day before, and then execute a surprise attack early the next morning while they are still sleeping in their wickiups. That way we can wipe out every one of those useless redskins and torch their encampment and let it burn to the ground."

"You don't mean kill all the women and children too?" Tyrus questioned.

"Some Ty, maybe not all."

"But sir, our orders are…"

"Don't you go telling me what my orders are, sergeant, I know what they are. But there needs to be some payback for the slaughter at the Little Bighorn and I intend to be the one to settle the score."

When morning arrived, and after a hearty breakfast of biscuits, beans, cured ham, red-eye gravy and thick morning Joe that left them with a mouth full of coffee grounds, the soldiers broke down their tents, loaded up their canvas covered wagons, saddled up their horses and headed northwest. It was a two day journey, across the rocky and dusty New Mexico Territory and the prickly pear cacti and mesquite laden terrain, to the Mescalero Apache Indian village.

Baxter and his regiment were well aware of the infamous reputation of the Apache, who were fierce warriors, experts in guerilla warfare and highly skilled horsemen. Baxter called the Apache, "Tigers of the human species". But based on the information from their scouts, the soldiers figured they had the upper hand because of their sheer numbers. And if things got out of hand, well then they would go to work with their Gatling guns.

The ability of the Apache in battle became legendary. It was also spoken in the frontier and on the prairies of the open ranges and mountainous terrains that an Apache warrior could run fifty miles without stopping and travel faster than a troop of mounted soldiers.

They came from the far North and settled in the southernmost part of the Great Plains and the rugged Southwest around the year 850 A.D. There were ten different distinct divisions of Apache tribes that made up the Apache Nation: they included the White Mountain Apache, the Aravaipa, the Chiricahua, the Western Apache, the Cibecue, the Tonto, the Jicarilla, the Kiowa, the Mescalero, and the Lipan Apache. Amongst themselves, Apache Indians actually were called the Dine, which meant "the people" but all the other tribes referred to them as the Apache, which meant "the enemy". They were labeled this because they frequently made enemies with their neighbors.

At times they would trade with other tribes for meat, hides, pottery, blankets, corn and such. But they were mostly known for just taking what they wanted. The Pueblo Native Americans called them "Apachu", which also meant, "the enemy".

Apache were fierce warriors. Their warfare techniques were said to be unmatched and extremely vicious. The very name "Apache" struck terror into the hearts of the Pueblo Indians, and later the Spaniards, the Mexicans and European white settlers. Bloody, brutal raids were carried out on the white settlers for food, horses and cattle. Apache claimed they raided for survival and pure necessity to provide food and sustenance for their families when wild game was scarce.

For food they sent out hunting parties to harvest buffalo on the grassy Plains, elk and deer in the woods and mountains, and antelope on the prairies. The women of the tribe would hunt berries, nuts and dig up edible roots, and plant seed for maize and squashes. On occasion the women would also hunt small game like rabbits.

They dressed in animal skins, made footwear from animal hides, war paint from berries and plants, tools from animal bones and stones, and weapons from branches, sticks and stones. Everything they had, everything they owned, absolutely everything, was from nature.

The Mescalero Apache were primarily a nomadic mountain people. They originally did not call themselves Mescalero. Rather, they referred to themselves as Shis-Inday, meaning, "People of the mountain" or Mashgalende, "People close to the mountains". Neighboring Apache tribes called the Mescalero, Nadahende, "People of the Mescal". They called them this because a plant named "mescal agave" was a staple food source for them. They relied on stored mescal for an important food source in times of hunger and scarcity of other food sources. In 1550, the Spaniards realized the importance of mescal as a food source to these people so they named them "Mescalero". The name stuck.

The versatile succulent mescal or agave plant looks like an overgrown aloe vera plant or a yucca. It was primarily used as a food source. The Mescalero would roast it to consume as a food. However, the sap was also collected and fermented as a mild liquor that, when distilled, produced what the Mexican vaqueros came to enjoy and called, tequila. Other tribes used the sap to treat wounds, rashes, chapped lips and sunburn.

Life for the Apache, as well as other Native Americans, improved when the horse was introduced to North America. In the late 1600's the Pueblo Indians in New Mexico raised large herds of horses from horses left in the area by the Spanish when the Pueblos drove the Spanish out of their land and back to Mexico. It was the Pueblo Indians who introduced the Apache to the horses which became the new beasts of burden and the new means of hunting wild game for food and to traverse the land during battles and raids.

Before the horse, dogs were used as their beasts of burden and packers. Dogs alone could not carry much weight on their backs. But when they were set up to pull a travois, they could haul over 100 pounds.

A travois was a frame structure that was used by indigenous people, mainly in the Great Plains in North America, to drag loads over land. It was made from branches and was in the shape of an elongated isosceles triangle. There were two long branches, maybe six to eight feet in length, which would cross at the top of the dog's back and then would spread out maybe three to four feet behind the dog. It then had smaller cross sections which supported the load. The dog would drag the apparatus like a sled. When the dogs broke down, they were eaten. This was a practical approach to life on the Plains; don't let any meat go to waste. Horses later became the beasts of burden.

Baxter's forces were now on their way north in the eastern New Mexico Territory on the fringe of the short grass of the Great Plains. The trail was rocky, dry and dusty but the cool temperatures made it bearable for what would have been an otherwise miserable trip northward.

The rocky terrain caused many wagon wheels to collapse and even a few axles to break. This dramatically slowed up the movement toward the Apache encampment which irritated Baxter to no end.

In the meantime, the unsuspecting Mescalero Apache had sent out three final hunting parties to prepare for the winter. The hunting parties were made up of family groups and relatives who were hunting to gather food for their kin.

One of the hunting parties, which numbered six, was led by a warrior called Lone Wolf. He was 33 years old and a striking figure. He was tall for an Apache, standing at about 5'11", had a muscular frame, classical Apache facial features, and long jet black hair. Some say he was a spitting image of the warrior Cochise (1805 – June 8, 1874), Chief of the Chokonen band of the Chiricahua Apache.

Lone Wolf (El Lobo Solitario in Spanish) earned respect as a brave young warrior and was regarded by all members in the encampment as being a very wise man and leader.

He was born in Southern New Mexico where the Mescalero Apache were originally from. He was given his name by his father who spotted a single wolf on a hillside when he stepped out of his wickiup the evening his child was born.

Lone Wolf grew up in a close family group. He was the son of the warrior called Red Feather and his mother was named Running Deer. In their family group, Running Deer had a half-sister, by name only, who was white. She was not a blood sister. The Apache gave her the name of Golden Sun because of her blonde hair. Golden Sun, whose real name was Josephine Wagner, an orphan traveling with a family of German immigrants, was a lone survivor of a raiding party massacre on a wagon train on the Santa Fe Trail and was forced to live with the Mescalero, or die. She had no choice but to choose life. They treated her well even though she was a captive.

Golden Sun taught the Mescalero children how to speak English while she learned how to communicate in Apache with her captors. When Lone Wolf was a young energetic boy, he picked up the English language quickly and became bilingual, speaking fluent English as well as Apache. He became very proficient with a bow and arrow at an early age learning adept hunting skills from his warrior father, Red Feather.

Golden Sun accepted living with the Apache and eventually became fond of their ways. When the Mescalero left the reservation and moved to their hideaway village in northeastern New Mexico Territory, Golden Sun happily traveled with them, as well. She eventually married a warrior ten years her elder by the name of White Cloud.

As the hunting parties would leave camp, they would ride to the top of the mesa and look down on their village and ask the

Great Spirit to care for their encampment while they were gone and then they would pray for a successful hunt. Conversely, when they returned, they would again ride to the top of the mesa, peer down on their village and thank the Great Spirit for a successful hunt and ask for many blessings to make it through the winter moons.

As they turned their horses toward the west and headed to their hunting grounds, no one knew the ill fate that was about to befall on their peaceful encampment; for Baxter's bluecoats were trotting their steeds northward, four abreast, and just a few hours away from the Mescalero encampment.

When the well-equipped, well-trained cavalry was only three hours away, they stopped to make camp for the night. Baxter's plan was to bed the troops down early, arise before sunrise and attack the village while the Mescalero were still sleeping in their wickiups. If things would materialize the way he planned, it would be a slaughter of biblical proportions, and that's just what the bloodthirsty Baxter wanted. Payback was only hours away and he could hardly contain himself.

On this chilly fall night, the night before the raid, he broke out his sour mash early and gathered his poker playing buddies together and boasted about the upcoming slaughter. Ty reminded him that they were not to harm women and children.

"Yeah, yeah, Ty, I hear you," Baxter said in an already drunken condition. The other cronies just laughed as they had no feelings one way or the other about tomorrow's outcome.

As the sun began setting over the New Mexico high country, the chill in the air became quite uncomfortable. After all, the elevation in this area was just beyond 5,500 feet above sea level and the air cooled down quickly when the sun disappeared from the western horizon.

While the soldiers lit campfires outside their tents, just three hours away from their destination, the unsuspecting Mescalero Apache had started fires in fire pits in their wickiups. Some families were visiting other families sharing ancestral stories like they so often did with the young ones.

Many of the elders were reminiscing about their past hunting exploits while they talked and laughed about their grown children now supplying food and furs for their families just as they did many moons ago in their youth.

Baxter's buddies played a few hands of poker and then he called his officers into his tent for a planning meeting. Baxter already had the plans in his head so his officers said nothing and just listened. They knew Baxter's attitude toward the Injuns and they also knew that he had been drinking. This was not a good time to disagree with the boss less you wanted to be court-martialed for subordination or even worse, "mistakenly" shot in battle by "friendly" gunfire.

Baxter began to lay out his plans to his men.

"OK gentlemen, listen up. Here's the battle plan. We know that our escaped reservation Indians are in this village. We also know that many Apache warriors have stayed in camp. These Apache in this village have escaped the reservation life for years even though they were all informed a few years ago to report to the reservation. As far as I'm concerned, they are no better than the escapees we trailed. We were told to bring back everyone to the reservation, unless we met with resistance. Gentlemen, I can tell you right now, we met with resistance. Does anyone have a problem with that?"

They each looked at one another and said nothing. Ty wanted to speak up but had already been verbally reprimanded a couple of days ago for his opinion, so he said nothing.

Baxter then reiterated the question in a raised voice,

"I said, does anyone have a problem with that?"

"No sir," they responded.

"That's more like it. Then here's the plan. We will leave in the morning at three o'clock sharp. That will put us at the encampment at about 6:00 a.m. just before sunrise. We'll leave the wagons here but take the two Gatling guns and ten pack mules with ammunition. When we approach the camp, we will position ourselves this way. The Gatling guns will be positioned about 100 yards apart from each other. We will fill in the gap between the guns with soldiers on horseback and then have soldiers flank both sides of the Gatling guns. According to the scout's information, this will put the savages between us and the Cimarron River. The river runs south but from an east to west direction. We'll spread out the troops so that the redskins can't run to the left or to the right. And if they try to cross the Cimarron, feel free to use them for target practice. There will be no escape route for them.

When I give the orders with one shot fired into the air, I want the Gatling guns to begin spraying the wickiups with a barrage of bullets. Hopefully, no women and children will be hit," Baxter said in a facetious and sarcastic tone.

"The guns will go through two straps of rounds each and when they stop, we will charge the village on horseback with our pistols drawn, killing as many resisting damn savages as we can.

We need to leave some women and children alive so it looks like we followed orders to not harm them. After we gather up the survivors, I want every tepee and wickiup torched to the ground, and their dogs, horses and livestock shot. By the way, we'll come back and get those hunting parties on another day. Are there any questions?"

No one said a word.

"I'll take your silence as a 'no', so let me pour you all a glass of my finest sour mash and let's toast to Custer's revenge." And so they did.

Three o'clock a.m. came before they knew it and the troops saddled up chewing on beef jerky for breakfast as they made their way north. Baxter sported his extra-wide brim white hat and a red silk scarf wrapped around his neck. His shoulder length gray hair, white hat and red scarf made him stand out in the crowd. He was as spiffy as his ole friend Custer ever was but contrary to the results at the Little Bighorn, he was determined to make this the Mescalero's last stand.

Three Shoshoni scouts led the way to the encampment riding just in front of Baxter. The anticipation was great. There were mixed feelings amongst the troops about how this whole situation was being handled. Most knew that this was a revenge battle and a potential massacre that could put a black mark on the U.S. Army for years. Nevertheless, they had their orders from Baxter and they had no choice but to follow them.

When the scouts informed Baxter that they were only a half a mile away from the encampment, Baxter passed the order along to dismount and walk their horses the rest of the way. They began to spread out in their planned formation being led by the three scouts and forming a virtual half-moon formation around the encampment. They stretched out from the east to the west banks of the Cimarron River.

When they were all in place he quietly passed the order around to remount. Then Baxter looked at Tyrus and said,

"We caught them sleeping Ty. Now let's finish it!"

With that, Baxter unholstered his brand new Smith & Wesson .45 Schofield pistol, raised it into the air at arm's length, held it in place for a few seconds contemplating his victory, and then pulled the trigger. Within a second, the cranking of the rapid-fire weapons began. The deafening sound of two rapid-firing Gatling guns echoed off the wall of the mesa across the Cimarron while spraying 400 rounds per minute in a random fashion as continuous flames, easily seen in the predawn early light, shot out from the rotating barrels with the unceasing flight of each bullet.

The bullets hit the wickiups sending their material flying in all directions. The Indians inside were laying low not really aware of the seriousness of what was taking place until some were hit and wounded while others were killed instantly by the flight of incoming deadly projectiles.

What followed was horrifying. First the deadly silence, then the familiar sound of a bugle charge, followed by Baxter raising his saber and yelling at the top of his voice,

"CHARGE!"

The Mescalero Apache men, women and children, ran out of their wickiups only to find 600 bluecoats charging them with drawn pistols firing at them like they were scampering animals. Hundreds of shots echoed back from the wall of the mesa and across the Cimarron. The sight and smell of black powder smoke filled the air as women and children screamed frantically while they ran for dear life toward the river.

Many warriors took up their bows and arrows and rifles and fired back to no real avail. Most of them were cut down immediately because of the overwhelming numbers of charging troops. When the soldiers spent their last bullets in their 6-shooters, they unsheathed their sabers and went to work, drawing blood with each wild swing of their long blades.

It was a bloody massacre like no one had ever witnessed before. It had a disgustingly evil way about it because it was so one-sided and there was no chance for the Mescalero to peacefully surrender.

When the shooting, the bloodshed and the mayhem ceased, only a few soldiers laid dead and wounded. But that was not the case for the other side. Every unsuspecting but fearless warrior left in camp was brutally slaughtered and many helpless women and children were caught in the crossfire and accidentally, along with purposely, slain as they hysterically ran for safety.

The massacre lasted only fifteen minutes, and then it was over. By now the sun was appearing on the eastern horizon and what was left of this hidden haven in the first daylight on this partly cloudy chilly morning was a morbid scene of human carnage and destruction.

When the smoke cleared and silence descended upon the encampment except for the wailing of the surviving women and children, Baxter ordered several soldiers to round up the survivors. Then he ordered others to light up torches and burn down the village. The previously serene Indian village took on the horrid appearance of a virtual hellhole.

In the meantime, as ordered, several soldiers reloaded their pistols, rode around and unconscionably shot and killed every living animal in camp.

To Baxter and some, this was a great victory and a successful payback. To others, including Tyrus, it was a sickening display of unimaginable cruelty and unbecoming of civilized behavior.

Unaware of the wrath and butchery inflicted on their tribe, the hunting parties were on their way back to the village with their packhorses set up with travois to haul back their wild game. They were on the opposite side of the mesa and with the north wind blowing at a near gale force at their backs that morning, they could not hear the repeating sounds of gunfire or the desperate screaming cries of the helpless women and children coming from their remote village.

As Lone Wolf's and the other hunting parties reached the top of the mesa and looked down into their village, what they saw was insufferable. Dead bodies around the encampment, burnt wickiups smoldering on the ground, and complete annihilation of their peaceful community.

The soldiers were riding out of the encampment with the surviving women and children herded like cattle on foot, following the mounted troops. Behind the women and children were six bluecoats on horseback. One was wearing a large white hat and a red scarf and had shoulder length gray hair. Lone Wolf figured he was the one in charge.

31

Lone Wolf gave out a loud scream and quickly turned his horse around to race down the mesa and after the soldiers. Two warriors in his hunting party ran their horses in front of Lone Wolf's horse stopping him in his tracks. One shouted,

"Use your head Lone Wolf; their numbers are too great. Save your anger for another day."

When the soldiers were completely out of sight, the hunting parties galloped down to the village at full speed to see if anyone was still alive. When they all arrived, they jumped off their horses and started combing the area, walking toward where their families' wickiups were located.

It was agonizing to witness the carnage around them. Lone Wolf found his father, Red Feather, in the middle of the encampment slashed to death by a bluecoat's long blade. He was a peaceful man but it appeared he fought valiantly. He died with his knife in his hand.

Lone Wolf then found the remains of his friend and English teacher, Golden Sun and her husband White Cloud in a collapsed and smoldering wickiup. Their charred bodies were riddled with gunshots. It appeared that they both took bullets from a Gatling gun at the outset of the surprise attack.

Then he discovered his 23 year old brother's body lying there with three bullet holes in his chest. His cold hand was still clutching his bow.

Lone Wolf never did find the bodies of his mother (Running Deer), or his wife (Desert Flower), his sister (Swift River) or his 14 year old son (Young Eagle). He could only assume that they were captured by the bluecoats and on their way to an Indian reservation.

The rest of the warriors in the hunting party found similar results regarding their own families, some killed and some missing. In the late afternoon, before the sun had set the warriors gathered up their dead, buried them that night, and piled rocks over their grave sites as was their custom. Then they rode off and never looked back.

The eighteen warriors from the hunting parties, rode west and then turned southwest toward Old Mexico. They camped out near a small stream, gathered dried branches and logs for firewood and then built three campfires to keep themselves warm. They brought meat with them which they harvested during their hunting trip; so they were able to eat a good meal. The weather was cool enough to keep the fresh meat from spoiling.

After they ate, they sat around the campfires and discussed what their next move would be. Lone Wolf took charge at the request of several of the warriors. For now, everyone went along with the idea.

With really nowhere to turn, they all decided to search for the Apache, Goyaale or named by the Mexicans, Geronimo, and join up with his band of renegades. They were out for revenge and knew that Geronimo and his band were capable of inflicting the type of revenge they were after.

Lone Wolf said of Geronimo, "He has old wounds, old hate, he will help us."

In the meantime, the survivors of the attack were marched on foot, miles away, over rocky and dusty terrains, counting as many as 95 old men, women and children. They had very little warm clothing on their backs. However, they all eventually made it alive to the reservation in the southwestern corner of the Indian Territory where they were given food rations and heavier clothing to survive the winter. They knew that their traditional way of life was shattered forever.

Their only consolation was that they would now be given food and clothing by the government and they would, at the minimum, have the essentials for living out their lives in some semblance of peace and comfort.

At least, that's what they thought.

CHAPTER TWO:

Renegade Bands Raid Homesteaders

His name was Goyaale "one who yawns". The Mexicans were the first to call him Geronimo. He was born on June 16, 1829 to the Bedonkohe band of the Apache, near Turkey Creek, a small tributary of the Gila River near the present day Clifton, Arizona adjacent to New Mexico. Back then the area was claimed by Mexico.

His grandfather, Mahko, was the chief of the Bedonkohe Apache and said to be a peaceful man. Goyaale's father was Taklishim and his mother was Juana.

After the death of his father, Taklishim, Goyaale's mother took him to live with the Chilhenne band and he grew up with them. At the age of 17, he fell in love and married a young woman by the name of Alope from the Nedni-Chiricahua band of Apache. They had an idyllic life living amongst nature and their people while enjoying their three children together.

But then, tragedy struck. It was on March 6, 1858, when Goyaale and some of the other men from camp were in town trading. Four hundred Mexican soldiers from Sonora, who were led by Colonel Jose Maria Carrasco, attacked Goyaale's camp outside of Janos and brutally slayed the Apache in the camp. Goyaale would discover that among the ones killed were his wife, his children and his mother. This horrifying loss made Goyaale hate all Mexicans the rest of his life and to seek revenge for his loss.

At the time, Goyaale's chief was Mangas Coloradas, or Dasoda-Hae (means "He Just Sits There") (1793 – January 18, 1863). Mangas Coloradas was the Apache tribal chief of the Eastern Chiricahua Nation. Their homeland was vast. It stretched west from the muddy banks of the Rio Grande to include most of the present-day rocky mountainous region of southwestern New Mexico.

ABOUT MANGAS COLORADAS, AN IMPORTANT APACHE CHIEF

Mangas had a nickname given to him by the Hispanics. In English it meant "red sleeves" or "roan shirt". Some say he received this name because of the color of the fabric of the red sleeves on his shirt. Others say that it was because his sleeves were covered with the blood of the Mexican who murdered Juan Jose Compas in 1837, who was Mangas Coloradas' predecessor.

In the 1820's and 1830's the Apache tribes were at war with the Mexicans. The Mexicans wanted the land of the Apache and attacked them without conscience. The Apache fought back ferociously with raids on Mexican ranches and settlements and they killed and mutilated many Mexican soldiers. It was retaliation and vengeance. It seemed like a never ending vicious cycle. When the Mexican authorities placed a bounty on Apache scalps, Juan Jose Compas was killed and scalped for money. This infuriated Mangas Coloradas and he went on the warpath against the Mexicans.

Furthermore, because of their hatred of the Mexicans, the Apache gave the Americans safe passage through their homeland when the United States went to war against Mexico.

Once the United States occupied the New Mexico Territory after the Mexican-American War, Mangas Coloradas signed a peace treaty citing the Americans as the conquerors of their despised Mexican enemy. *The enemy of my enemy is my friend.*

But that peace did not last long. As in so many stories of the Old West, the discovery of gold was the catalyst that broke unstable peace treaties, made enemies of friends, brought on vengeance for the butchered, and changed the landscape from fields of green to pools of red.

In the early 1850's, there was an influx of gold miners into New Mexico's Pinos Altos Mountains. This is what eventually led to a new conflict between the Apache and the Americans. Small fights broke out during the 1850's but things really came to a head in December of 1860 when thirty miners launched a surprise attack on a small Apache encampment on the west bank of the Mimbres River. Historians report that the miners killed four Indians, wounded many others, and captured thirteen women and children. It was after that, Mangas went on the warpath and conducted raids against U.S. homesteaders and their property.

In 1862 after recovering from a bullet wound in his chest, Mangas became tired, drained, and weary of war with the Americans. He was now contemplating another peace treaty with the U.S.

In January of 1863, he decided to take the first step toward a new peace. He met with military leaders at Fort McLane, in southwestern New Mexico Territory. Mangas rode into the fort under a flag of truce to meet with Brigadier General Joseph

Rodman West (September 19, 1822 – October 31, 1898), a future Reconstruction senator from Louisiana.

Immediately, armed soldiers took Mangas into custody. On that day it was alleged that General West disregarded Mangas' intentions of peace and gave the following execution order to his sentries:

"Men, that old murderer has got away from every soldier command and has left a trail of blood for 500 miles on the old stage line. I want him dead tomorrow morning. Do you understand? I want him dead."

On that night, Mangas was tortured, shot and killed "trying to escape". The following day a barbaric act of crudity was manifested when a U.S. soldier cut off the head of Mangas Coloradas, boiled it, and sent the skull to Orson Squire Fowler (October 11, 1809 – August 18, 1887), a phrenologist in New York City.

The murder and gross mutilation of Mangas only served to augment the hostility between the Apache and Americans which continued for another 25 years.

BACK TO GERONIMO

Mangas Coloradas was the father-in-law of another famous Apache chief, Cochise. Cochise married Dos-The-She who was Mangas Coloradas' daughter.

History has it that Chief Mangas Coloradas, sent Goyaale to his son-in-law, Cochise to solicit help and warriors to wreak revenge on the Mexicans. Cochise was one of the most famous Apache leaders. In his own language he was called "Cheis" which meant "having the quality or strength of oak".

Mangas thought Cochise could help Goyaale with his retaliation on the Mexicans. It was around this time when Goyaale was in a battle with some Mexicans that the Mexicans subsequently gave him the name Geronimo.

Whether the story is true or not, this is how it goes. They say it was on the feast day of Saint Jerome. In the aforementioned battle, ignoring a deadly hail of bullets, Goyaale repeatedly attacked Mexican soldiers with a knife. What followed became the controversy of the origin of his new name. Some historians say it was the appeal by the soldiers to Saint Jerome (Jeronimo) for help. Others say it was the mispronunciation of his name by the Mexican soldiers. There are other stories as well. No matter what it was,

Goyaale would forever become known as "Geronimo" to both the Mexicans and the Americans.

After the death of his family, Geronimo would frequently attack and kill any group of Mexicans that he and his followers would encounter.

In his later years, he would remember the unforgettable slaying of his family in this way which became a section of a biography on his life as an Apache:

Late one afternoon when returning from town we were met by a few women and children who told us that Mexican troops from some other town had attacked our camp, killed all the warriors of the guard, captured all our ponies, secured our arms, destroyed our supplies, and killed many of our women and children. Quickly we separated, concealing ourselves as best we could until nightfall, then we assembled at our appointed place of rendezvous - a thicket by the river. Silently we stole in one by one, sentinels were placed, and when all were counted, I found that my aged mother, my young wife, and my three small children were among the slain. There were no lights in camp, so without being noticed I silently turned away and stood by the river. How long I stood I do not know, but when I saw the warriors arranging for a council, I took my place.

Geronimo's revenge was brutal and long lasting for this slaughter. It is said that a governor of Sonora claimed in 1886 that in the last five months of Geronimo's wild career, his band of 16 warriors slaughtered some 500 to 600 Mexicans. Geronimo admitted many Mexican killings in his autobiography in 1905.

I have killed many Mexicans; I do not know how many, for frequently I did not count them. Some were not worth counting. It has been a long time since then, but still I have no love for the Mexicans. With me they were always treacherous and malicious.

Geronimo's hatred toward the Mexicans ran deep and continued to the end of his life.

However, he also begrudged the Americans moving west and robbing the Apache of their homeland. For this, he also conducted raids on Americans and carried out brutal murders of innocent homesteaders.

Lone Wolf had heard the story of Geronimo losing his family at the hands of the Mexicans. So just as Geronimo sought help for retaliation on the Mexicans from Cochise, Lone Wolf sought out the help of Geronimo for the revenge on the white-eyed bluecoats. He wanted to make buzzard bait out of every single long blade toting bluecoat he could, especially the flashy dressed Baxter he would come to call, Long Gray Hair.

Before Lone Wolf and his warriors could travel far, they had to take care of some basic survival issues; food for a long journey and weapons and ammunition for protection. They only had six long-guns between them and the rest had bows and arrows. Lone Wolf felt it was necessary to equip all of his warriors with repeating rifles.

So the first stop on their journey was a well-known trading post not far from their destroyed village in a town which would soon become known as Springer and would become the county seat of Colfax County in the New Mexico Territory from 1882 – 1897. It was near the Cimarron Cutoff of the Santa Fe Trail. They didn't have anything to trade for food and guns so they would follow the traditional way of the Apache; raid the place and take what they needed for survival.

Lone Wolf, unlike some of the other warriors traveling with him, did not want revenge on all white men. He was taught different morals growing up around and being taught by Golden Sun. The only revenge he wanted was to inflict harm on all soldiers, and especially the soldiers who destroyed his village, killed his father, brother and others and marched off his mother, wife, sister and his son to the reservation.

As they sat around the campfire the night before the raid on the trading post, Lone Wolf laid out his plans to the other Mescalero.

"We will break into the trading post just before first light so that we will inflict no harm on anyone unless we are forced to. I wish not to take any lives, just food, long-guns, ammunition, and warm clothing for the cold moon coming on."

A young Kiowa warrior known as Spotted Feather, who was one of the escaped Indians from the reservation at Fort Sill, vehemently disagreed with Lone Wolf. He hated all white men and had an urge to kill as many as he possibly could. Just as Geronimo had rage in his heart for all Mexicans, Spotted Feather had rage in his heart for all white men.

"I see no reason to leave any white man live when he crosses our path. They should all die. They destroyed our people and our way of life. They must suffer for this wrong."

"No, Spotted Feather," Lone Wolf yelled, "we will not harm anyone unless we are forced to. You are Kiowa, all others here are Mescalero. You will follow my ways or be cast out like an unwanted sick buffalo calf from the great herd." Some of the other warriors had feelings in their hearts similar to Spotted Feather but said nothing.

During the night, Lone Wolf wrestled with his feelings as he laid there staring at the stars on this clear cold night and listening to the distant lonely wails of the Mexican gray wolf. His head told him he wanted revenge on all white men but his heart told him something different. He was taught Christian morals by Golden Sun. Plus his father was a peaceful and wise man and had taught Lone Wolf about the battles one faces all of his life, inside one's head and his heart.

Red Feather named his son Lone Wolf for two reasons. One because he spotted a single gray wolf on the hillside the evening Lone Wolf was born. But secondly, he knew that there would always be a "battle" inside of the Apache between two wolves because of the dealings of the white man toward the Native Americans.

Lone Wolf remembered the wise words of his father.

"A single warrior has the choice to choose the one wolf he will live with. It is his choice alone. Both choices have consequences. One wolf is the 'evil' wolf. It is anger, resentment, lies, killing, and revenge. The other wolf is the 'good' wolf. It is peace, hope, truth, love, joy, and forgiving. The wolf that wins is the one you feed."

Lone Wolf would struggle with his choice for years feeding both wolves but trying to starve the evil one. On this night, the good wolf conquered the evil one and he smiled thinking about it, as he slowly drifted into a deep sleep while the light of the campfire dimmed and finally gave way to the dark of the night.

The Apache warriors awoke when the first light appeared in the eastern sky. Frost was on their blankets and the chill was almost unbearable since they had inadequate provisions to protect against such conditions. They needed warm clothing for immediate relief from the cold and more food for now and their upcoming long journey.

Without hesitation, they threw their blankets on their horses and quietly made their way to the trading post. Behind the trading post was a small single room cabin where a man and a woman lived who owned and operated the post. Renegade Indians in the area were peaceful to them since they generally were able to provide a continuous supply of basic survival needs and jugs of the Indians' favorite drinks, mescal and rye.

When they rode up to the post, Lone Wolf had three braves watch the small cabin while the rest went inside to pilferage the place. Lone Wolf told his band that he wanted no shooting unless they were threatened.

Unfortunately, one of the three Indians who was watching the cabin was the Kiowa warrior, Spotted Feather. He was holding a rifle while the other two had bows and arrows.

The other Apache were running in and out of the post with supplies and placing them on two travois they set up on a couple of horses. One Apache was tying the supplies down with rope he found in the trading post.

When all their needs were loaded, they mounted their horses. Just then, an unarmed man came running out of the cabin shouting,

"Stop, stop you thieves!"

Lone Wolf shouted, "NO" when he saw Spotted Feather aim his rifle toward the man.

But within a split second, the rifle was fired and the man fell, face down to the ground. A woman then came running out of the cabin, screaming at the top of her lungs. Spotted Feather wasted no time, aimed, pulled the trigger, and she fell lifelessly on top of her husband's body.

Spotted Feather raised his rifle in the air and screamed a victory cry as the Apache all quickly rode off toward the south.

Lone Wolf was sickened by the event.

After riding hard for about two hours straight, circumventing small towns, ranch houses, and other trading posts, they found a place to hide and rest amongst some boulders. It was then that Lone Wolf jumped off of his steed, ran over to Spotted Feather and pulled him down off of his horse. They both drew their knives knowing that this would be the fight for leadership of the band and a fight to the death.

The fight began and it was fierce.

Spotted Feather lunged at Lone Wolf and gashed Lone Wolf's arm just above the elbow drawing blood. Lone Wolf lunged back but missed Spotted Feather. Now all the rest of the Apache circled around the two fighters, enjoying the fight and yelling out battle cries. It was hard to tell who was rooting for whom.

The fight continued for several minutes as they sparred each other both drawing blood with slashes of their knives. Then Lone Wolf charged Spotted Feather and wrestled him to the ground. They continued to roll around on the rocky terrain until Lone Wolf was able to roll on top of Spotted Feather, pin Spotted Feather's knife hand to the ground and quickly thrust his eight inch blade into Spotted Feather's chest.

The fight was over. Spotted Feather lay dead from a stab wound through his heart. The other Apache became very quiet as Lone Wolf pulled his knife out of Spotted Feather's chest, stood up, and wiped the blood from his knife on his own buffalo hide trousers to serve as a reminder and a warning to anyone else who cared to challenge him. No one did that day.

The group eventually dug a shallow grave with their knives and buried Spotted Feather and finished covering the hole with large rocks. There was no Indian burial ceremony for this undesirable Kiowa warrior.

They took a few minutes to chew on some jerky and eat some biscuits they stole from the trading post. No one said a word. Then they mounted their horses and continued to move southwest in search of Geronimo.

Lone Wolf's band of now seventeen Mescalero warriors searched out Geronimo for a few months. They traveled over the mountainous region of the New Mexico Territory keeping clear of trouble and dodging U.S. soldiers at practically every turn.

On occasion they had to raid general stores, trading posts and ranches during the wee hours of the morning for food and to swap out for fresh horses. They were always able to do so undetected and avoided getting into skirmishes.

They traveled through the New Mexico Territory, parts of the Arizona Territory, and Old Mexico, running into small bands of Apache along the way, who were on the run from reservations but who did not have an ounce of fighting spirit left in their under-nourished bodies. Rather they just possessed a desire to live with nature and not on a reservation.

One day Lone Wolf's band came across six fugitive Lipan Apache, who were far removed from their Texas homeland. Lone Wolf raised his hand and in Apache language spoke first,

"Greetings my friends, you are Apache but from which tribe and what land?"

"We are Lipan Apache. Our homeland is Texas. We escaped from the reservation. We will die before we go back. We were treated well by the Great Father but we cannot live in captivity like caged animals. Where are you headed?"

Lone Wolf said, "We seek out Geronimo to join his band. We will ask for his help to bring revenge on bluecoats who massacred our village and stole our wives, mothers, and children. Have you heard of Geronimo's whereabouts?"

"Some say Geronimo is hiding out in the Robledo Mountain range in Dona Ana County, south central part of New Mexico Territory, northwest of Las Cruces. Others say he is hiding out in the mountain range south of Apache Pass in Arizona Territory.

"Do you wish to join our band?" Lone Wolf asked.

"Our fighting spirit is like a leaf in the wind. It has flown from our bodies; but our will to survive and live with nature is strong. We will go our way. May the Great Spirit protect you and all Apache."

With that, both bands were on their way and rode off in different directions. However, two days after the bands met, the Lipan Apache met an inauspicious fate when they came across a rancorous group of no-good Mexican scalp hunters up from Old Mexico and were overtaken by repeating rifles and gruesomely scalped for bounty. Their bodies were left to rot in the sun and were feasted on by a pack of hungry, mangy coyotes. What flesh remained filled the bellies of scavenging buzzards.

In the meantime, Lone Wolf's band met a few more renegade Apache. This time they were in luck. These renegades knew exactly where Geronimo was hiding out and they led Lone Wolf's band through a narrow mountainous passageway in the Ojo Caliente Reservation area which was in the southwestern part of the New Mexico Territory.

Lone Wolf introduced himself and his warriors to Geronimo and they agreed to join forces in a few months at Geronimo's hideout in the Chiricahua Mountains. Geronimo convinced Lone Wolf to conduct raids on Mexicans first, then Geronimo would help Lone Wolf seek revenge and conduct raids on American soldiers. Lone Wolf agreed and began his trip to the Chiricahua Mountains with his band of Mescalero.

Geronimo had just arrived a couple of weeks before Lone Wolf in the vast territory of the Ojo Caliente Reservation, from his hideout in the mountain range to the south of Apache Pass which was the Chiricahua Mountains in Arizona Territory. That area was the home of the Chiricahua Apache. Apache Pass was a level area between the Chiricahua Mountains and the Dos Cabezas Mountains and was the site of many clashes between the Apache and the whites.

The Apache resented the intrusion of the white-eyes on their homeland. But the white man needed access to Apache Pass, which was a natural southern route from the east to the west, because of the flat terrain and the most precious commodity, water. In fact, in 1858 the Butterfield Overland Mail (stage coach) began service between St. Louis, Missouri and San Francisco, California, using Apache Pass. There was a stop off place built of stone on the east side of the pass near a spring where they could fill up on water. Cochise allowed this to happen.

However, Lt. George H. Bascom (1837 – February 21, 1862) set the stage for an eleven year war with the Apache and Cochise from 1861 – 1872 when he tried to arrest Cochise near the spring for a crime he didn't commit but was committed instead by another raiding Apache band. Cochise despised the false accusation and thought this was a betrayal since the Apache allowed the Americans safe passage through their homeland years earlier during the Mexican - American War (April 25, 1846 – February 2, 1848). The Spaniards and Mexicans were the first enemies of the Apache since they desired and fought for the Apache's homeland. So since the Americans won the war with the Mexicans and parts of Apache homeland were acquired by the United States in 1850, it ushered in a brief period of peace between the Americans and the Apache. However, Bascom's actions promptly ended that.

A battle ensued and hostages on both sides were taken and executed. Some of Cochise's relatives were among the slain hostages. This began a long war between the Americans and the Apache.

The war between Cochise's Apache and the Americans ended with a treaty which was facilitated between Cochise and his only white friend, Tom Jeffords (January 1, 1832 – February 21, 1914, and General Oliver O. Howard (November 8, 1830 – October 26, 1909). However, Bascom's actions left a residual anger for many years even after Cochise's death in 1874.

The treaty that was signed around September of 1872, provided for a Chiricahua reservation (1872 – 1876) in the Dragoon Mountains on the west to the Peloncillo Mountains on the east. It also included the Chiricahua Mountains and ran south to the Mexican border. Cochise agreed to move his people there. Tom Jeffords became the Indian Agent. However, after Cochise's death in 1874, Jeffords lost his influence with the Chiricahua Apache. The U.S. Government decided to move the Chiricahua to the San Carlos Apache Indian Reservation in 1876. Half complied and the other half, led by Geronimo, escaped to Mexico for now.

The San Carlos Apache Indian Reservation (1872 – 1884) was established on December 14, 1872 by an Executive Order of President Grant. The plan was to concentrate at San Carlos many different Apache subgroups (Coyotero, Chiricahua, San Carlos, Tonto, Yuma, and Mohave) who were often hostile to each other. The Americans did not fully understand the differences between the bands. Washington thought a "one-size-fits-all" approach would save money, free up more land for the whites, and enable the Apache to be controlled in one location. This was resisted by many Apache.

Conditions there were horrible and it would later be described as an inhumane prison. There was always a shortage of food and water and the land was always dry and dusty.

Lieutenant Britton Davis, Third Cavalry, described it this way, "Rain was so infrequent (at San Carlos) that it took on the semblance of a phenomenon when it came at all. Almost continuously dry, hot, dust-and-gravel-laden winds swept the plain, denuding it of every vestige of vegetation. In summer, a temperature of 110° in the shade was cool weather. At all other times of the year flies, gnats, unnameable bugs, - and I was about to say "beasts of the air" - swarmed in millions. Everywhere the naked, hungry, dirty, frightened little Indian children, darting behind bush or into wickiup at sight of you. Everywhere the sullen, stolid, hopeless, suspicious faces of the older Indians challenging you ... that unspoken challenge to prove yourself anything else than one more liar and thief, differing but little from the procession of liars and thieves who had preceded you."

And then Asa Daklugie, a Chiricahua Apache gave this account of San Carlos:

"San Carlos! That was the worst place in all the great territory stolen from the Apache... Where there is no grass there is no game... Nearly all of the vegetation was cacti; and though in season a little cactus fruit was produced, the rest of the year food was lacking. The heat was terrible. The insects were terrible. The water was terrible... Insects and rattlesnakes seemed to thrive there... There were also tarantulas, Gila monsters, and centipedes... Apache experienced the shaking sickness."

Between 1872 and 1874 a number of Indian Agents came and went. Many were corrupt and sought to line their own pockets, selling food and clothing that were meant for the Indians, and kept the money for themselves. The Apache living on the reservations, were supposed to be fed, given seed to plant, clothes to wear and housed by the soldiers. Instead, those soldiers and their commanding officers would sometimes brutally torture and kill the Apache for sport.

When the government became wise to these horrible deeds in San Carlos, they changed Indian Agents. They hired a man by the name of John Philip Clum (September 1, 1851 – May 2, 1932) to restore law and order and a sense of civility to the reservation. Clum arrived at the San Carlos Apache Indian Reservation on Tuesday, August 4, 1874. He was 22 at the time about to turn 23. Clum stayed on as the Apache Agent until July of 1877. He later became the first mayor of Tombstone, Arizona Territory after its incorporation in 1881.

Many Chiricahua Indians from the Chiricahua Reservation continued raids into the Mexico states of Sonora and Chihuahua. Governor Pesqueira complained bitterly about the raids. This caused General Crook to figure out a way to force the Chiricahua onto the San Carlos Apache Indian Reservation.

When Cochise died on June 8, 1874, Thomas J. Jeffords, the Indian Agent in the Chiricahua Reservation eventually lost his influence with the tribe. In 1876 he was relieved of his duties and on May 3rd, Clum was ordered by the government to move the

Indians from the Chiricahua Reservation to the San Carlos Apache Indian Reservation.

Out of more than 1,000 Chiricahua, only 42 men and 280 women and children accompanied Clum to San Carlos. Many went deeper into Mexico and others went to the Ojo Caliente Reservation in the New Mexico Territory.

In April of 1877 Clum was ordered by the Interior Department to move the bands of Apache from Ojo Caliente to San Carlos as well. Luckily, Lone Wolf's warriors were already gone from the site.

During Clum's tenure at San Carlos, he treated the Apache as friends. He came up with a unique system. He established the first Indian Tribal Police and Tribal Court, forming a system of Indian self-rule.

It was Clum's Tribal Police who captured Geronimo at Ojo Caliente on April 21, 1877. They surprised Geronimo, seized his rifle and threw him in shackles. This was the only time Geronimo was ever captured at gunpoint without a shot fired. He, along with 452 Chiricahua of which 100 were Geronimo's men, were taken to San Carlos.

This was an embarrassment to the military since they were not successful in capturing Geronimo themselves. The military also disagreed with Clum's methods of treating the Apache. Over a short time, Clum's feuds with the military escalated. Clum became frustrated with the feud. He was also dogged by the uncaring Indian Bureau administration toward the horrible conditions the Apache were forced to live under.

Totally fed up and discouraged with the situation, Clum left his post as Indian Agent at noon on July 1, 1877, nearly just three years after he arrived. There were different stories about the events relating to Geronimo's departure from the reservation after Clum left. Either he was freed by Clum's successor or he escaped from San Carlos Apache Indian Reservation. Whichever was true, Geronimo then headed south to meet with Lone Wolf and the Mescalero as he had promised.

They met south of Apache Pass in the Chiricahua Mountains and then headed south to the Sierra Madre mountain range and conducted more raids against the Mexicans in Sonora and Chihuahua, brutally murdering Mexicans every chance they got.

Lone Wolf and the Mescalero participated in the raids but Lone Wolf saw the rage of a demon in Geronimo that he himself did not possess. Geronimo would kill not only Mexican soldiers but enjoyed murdering Mexican women and children as well.

One night Lone Wolf got into an argument with Geronimo and said,

"Your way is not my way. I promised to help you seek revenge on Mexican soldiers but not on innocent women and children."

"You are a woman and a coward," Geronimo said in anger.

The tension then became great.

Lone Wolf stood up immediately in an aggressive manner followed by his band of Mescalero. Geronimo and his warriors also stood up and several drew their knives.

Lone Wolf raised his arms outward and said. "Wait, there is no need to fight amongst us Apache. We will go our way and you go your way."

Geronimo said, "Fine, then leave now."

"We will leave at first light," Lone Wolf said.

On that night, the two bands separated about one hundred yards from each other and kept sentries on guard to protect against one another.

Lone Wolf and his band of Mescalero left at sunup as promised. They headed back north to hide out in the Chiricahua Mountains until Lone Wolf would determine their next move. Lone Wolf had many hours on the trail to think about their future. He was growing weary of traveling miles and miles in unknown territories and would wonder where their next meal would come from. As was happening with many Indians who had escaped life on the reservation, the revengeful spirit was fleeing from his body.

In the mountains and near Apache Pass they would continue to come across many bands of Apache who left the reservations. Some were battle weary and others continued to be aggressive toward the white man. On occasion, they would come across covered wagons that were burnt and vulture-picked dead mutilated bodies of white families rotting in the mountainous passageways.

About a year went by and more Mescalero who escaped from their reservation met up with Lone Wolf's band. Over time, word got out amongst the Mescalero Apache where Lone Wolf was hiding out. The secret was known only to Mescalero. Lone Wolf's band grew to 30.

Where they stayed was well hidden and the land was rich with fresh water and wild game. Several natural springs in the wilderness provided water for the abundant wildlife. White-tailed and mule deer, mountain lions, golden eagles, bald eagles and many other animals and birds inhabited the Chiricahua Mountains. The Mescalero built an encampment of wickiups and began to survive day-to-day with no plans for their long term future. But this type of living could not go on forever for there were no women or children in their camp.

Then one day in the summer of 1879, things would change. Three young Mescalero Apache who escaped from the reservation at Fort Sill rode into Lone Wolf's camp with horrifying news. When they slid off their horses, Lone Wolf fed them and then they spoke.

"Lone Wolf, we come to tell you what a bluecoat by the name of Baxter is doing to our people."

"Who is this Baxter that you speak of?" Lone Wolf asked.

After the Apache described Baxter's appearance, Lone Wolf said,

"Ah, you speak of Long Gray Hair, go on."

"Lone Wolf, we bring you distressful and disturbing news from the reservation. The government has reduced the shipment of food to the reservation and our tribe of women and children are starving. They have also quit supplying warm clothing for the winter months and many are getting sick and dying. There is uprising amongst the old and very young men and fights are breaking out; soldiers are torturing and killing anyone who becomes aggressive."

"My family, what about my family?"

"We bring you sad news about your family, Lone Wolf. Your mother Running Deer and your wife Desert Flower have starved to death. Your sister Swift River died from white-eye disease and your son Young Eagle was tortured and is near death."

Lone Wolf stood up and yelled out, "NOOOO!"

"I will revenge the bluecoats and the ones responsible for this to my dying days. Vultures will fatten up on the ones who are to blame," he shouted as the other Mescalero stood up and raised their guns in the air as they continuously yelled and shouted Apache battle cries.

Some of the other Mescalero were told that they too had lost family members through starvation and disease.

When things calmed down, Lone Wolf had time to think. First he asked the escapees,

"For what reason did the government decide to starve our people and torture and murder our women and children?"

"We do not know, Lone Wolf. Baxter, the one you call Long Gray Hair, was made in charge of the reservation twelve moons ago and things began to change for the worse then. He and his men who surround him, there are a handful, began treating the Mescalero and other tribes like animals. We did nothing to deserve this type of treatment. One day we were taken care of, the next day we became dogs."

"We will think about our revenge on the government, the white man, the bluecoats and Long Gray Hair. We will think about it, pray to the Great Spirit about it, and then we will act swiftly.

I will promise you this, there will be revenge!"

At that point, Lone Wolf could not help but feed the "evil" wolf inside of him. In fact, it was uncontrollable. It was something he didn't think about. It just happened.

He also kept pondering the reasons why the government turned against the Indians on the reservation so. There had to be a reason. But what was it? What he heard from the escapees seemed extreme, the worst he had ever heard. None of this made sense to him or his warriors.

For two suns, Lone Wolf sat in his wickiup and contemplated his next moves. On occasion he would take a walk down to the stream, sit on the grassy bank and reminisce about his wife and son, his mother and father, his sister and brother, and his friend and English teacher Golden Sun.

The memories of his deceased loved ones brought overwhelming grief which was almost impossible to bear.

He thought about growing up in a Mescalero village with his sister and brother and mother and father. He thought about how his mother and father taught him how to live off the land and survive on the Plains and in the mountains. They taught him what foods he could eat and not eat and how to make his clothing.

Apache relied on hunting of wild game and gathering of cactus fruits and other wild plants. Hunting was a part of their daily life. They hunted deer, jackrabbits, coyote, javelina, fox, beavers, buffalo, bear and mountain lions; some for food, some for clothing. There was no fishing. Eagles were hunted for their feathers. They preferred the bald eagle feathers.

Lone Wolf was taught at an early age that certain animals were believed to be unclean and therefore could not be eaten: prairie dogs, snakes, turkeys, and fish. His father taught him how to move through the woods quickly but quietly to harvest wild game for their family. All Apache were taught how to hunt at an early age.

His father taught him the technique of greasing his body with animal fat to mask his scent so that the animals he hunted would not pick up the human scent and be spooked. He was taught how to make Apache foot-hold traps to catch large animals and deadfall traps to catch rabbits and eagles.

Lone Wolf's father and the other elders taught the young ones the ways of the Great Spirit and various tribal ceremonies. The ceremonies were called "dances". There was the rain dance, a puberty right dance, the sunrise dance for young women, a harvest and good crop dance and a spirit dance.

He was taught how to plant seed and raise corn and squashes and how to make jerky from the meat of large game. His father taught him how to break green horses in the river and how to make weapons for war and weapons for hunting. These were all things he looked forward to teaching his young son.

He remembered taking gifts to his father-in-law to ask him for his daughter's hand in marriage. Her name was Desert Flower. He was struck by her natural beauty. She was slim, average height, had long straight black hair, high cheek bones and her heart was as pure as the new snow on the highest mountain peaks.

Lone Wolf remembered how nervous he was on that day. He was a young man at only eighteen years of age. He brought the gifts of two horses he trained, and some deer skin clothing his mother made for the occasion. He was extremely happy when Desert Flower's father said,

"These are good gifts. You may have my daughter's hand in marriage."

Three months later he and Desert Flower married.

Lone Wolf remembered the short prayer his father recited at the wedding ceremony.

My dear children

I promise you this. The warmth from your hearts will comfort you on cold days. The rain and snows from the heavens will not be of concern since you will be sheltered by the other. Your companionship will see the disappearance of loneliness just as the sun fades in the western sky and new happiness will be born each day as the sun smiles at you from the eastern horizon.

May all your suns and moons bring you complete joy and happiness as you travel through your life's journey together.

And may the Great Spirit give you a never ending basket of its natural possessions of food and clothing all the days of your lives.

Go my children, live long, prosper, raise your family and teach your children as we have taught you, the ways of the Apache.

Lone Wolf also thought about his friend Golden Sun who taught him how to speak English. She was a kind and gentle person with a heart of gold. She was a Christian and taught Lone Wolf and some of the others the ways and prayers of her religion. Lone Wolf's father told him that when he came of age, he could choose what he believed. But he always said this,

"There is only one Great Spirit who created all things on this earth. He created it for all men, for their pleasure and survival. Treat the Great Spirit's creation with respect as you respect your father and mother."

All these things were great recollections and brought happiness to his heart for a few hours. But when reality collided with those wonderful memories of the past and the past succumbed to the present, he realized that all of those things were snatched away from him like a thief in the night by the white man; his mood changed and the "evil wolf" inside of him overpowered the "good wolf" and revenge overtook his soul.

So after two days of praying to the Great Spirit, Lone Wolf called his band together.

"Hear me my brothers. This is my decision. We will raid ranches and homesteads in the New Mexico and Arizona Territories and steal their women and children just as they stole ours. We will take the hostages and hide them in the mountains. Their fate will be determined later. From this day forward, it will come to be, that the white man will feel the pain they inflicted on the Apache."

On that day and forever more, Lone Wolf and his band of thirty Mescalero would become known around the Southwest as "Lone Wolf's Renegade Apache".

And so the raids began, one right after another.

THE SILVER CITY RAIDS

Silver City was located in the southwest corner of New Mexico. This area had been home to Native Americans (namely the Apache), Hispanics and white settlers for many, many years. Silver was discovered there which brought a wave of prospectors in the 1860's.

The town of Silver City was founded in the summer of 1870 shortly after the discovery of silver at an area called Chloride Flat. The discovery of silver ore was just west of the farm of Captain John M. Bullard and his brother James.

It was Captain Bullard who laid out the streets of Silver City. It started as a tent city as most newly established mining towns did. But unlike many tent city mining towns, it did not become a ghost town but instead, a permanent town.

Captain Bullard never lived to see his town grow to permanence since he was slain during an Apache raid on February 23, 1871.

As was true with many newly established towns in the Old West and especially in mining towns, the violent crime rate was extensive during the 1870's. In 1874 Harvey Whitehill (September 2, 1838 - September 14, 1906) was elected sheriff of Grant County. Silver City was the county seat.

Whitehill arrived in town from Ohio during the time of the Apache Wars in the mid-1860's and he took part in those. In 1875 he solicited the help of a notorious hired gunman by the name of "Dangerous Dan" Tucker (1849 – unknown). Many of the town folks disagreed with Whitehill's decision since Tucker rode with another famous outlaw by the name of John Kinney (1847 – August 25, 1919) who organized a gang which committed acts of robbery, murder and cattle rustling.

However, Whitehill's decision proved to be the right one for that wild time period as the two set out to tame Silver City, a small frontier mining town. Shootouts with outlaws, confrontations with trouble-making miners, and several legal hangings began to bring law and order to Silver City.

In April of 1875, Whitehill went down in history as being the first lawman to arrest William Bonney who would later become known as Billy the Kid. He would again arrest Bonney in September of the same year. But the arrests were for minor offenses. The first was for stealing cheese and the second one was for stealing laundry.

Whitehill would later tell people that Bonney was a likable young man and that his two thefts were due to necessity, since his mother had just died there in town, rather than him being a criminal of sorts. His mother was buried in the town's Memory Lane Cemetery.

In 1878, "Dangerous Dan", who had worked for Whitehill since 1875, was hired as the first town marshal.

There is an interesting story that would later develop. In 1882, a year after lawman Pat Garrett killed Billy the Kid in 1881, Garrett ran against Whitehill for sheriff. What was ironic was that Whitehill was the first sheriff to arrest Bonney and Garrett was the last. Garrett, who was not well liked in the area, lost to Whitehill.

Lone Wolf thought Silver City was a good place to start to make a statement and get the revenge he was after for his cause. After all, it had good population growth with prospectors and families homesteading around this silver mining town. But there were great risks involved because of the better than average lawmen in that town.

However, Lone Wolf was brave and fearless as were all Apache; so the raid would go forward at midnight, during a half-moon phase in October of 1879, which aided in both cover but gave off some light for a successful foray.

Since they scouted out ranches and discerned which ones had families, they knew exactly where to strike. And strike they did, hard and fast, charging into ranch homes with rifles and spears in hand yelling and screaming to create a chaotic scene, during the dead of the night, beating the men of the families within an inch of their lives and riding off with their women and children as hostages. They also pilfered food, blankets and winter clothing for themselves and the hostages if they were going to let them live. They would do this on all future raids.

Lone Wolf had no intention of killing the men of the homesteads unless he had to for self-defense reasons. But one thing for certain, the men were going to be beaten because at times, his revengeful spirit, the "evil wolf" inside of him, was just too enraged for him to control.

On that night, Lone Wolf's renegades raided three ranch houses and took away three women and eight children as hostages. They rode off to their hideout in the Chiricahua Mountains.

When the news hit the streets of Silver City the next morning, the town was horrified and in shock. They thought that the Indian raids by Apache in the area were things of the past. "What does this all mean?" the rumbling cries around town went and "are the women and children who the Apache stole still alive or were they murdered?"

The sheriff and the marshal formed a posse and sent a telegram to the nearest U.S. Army fort for help. But by then, the Apache were long gone and covered their tracks like only they knew how.

When the renegade Apache arrived at their secret hideout in the mountains, they separated the grown women from the wailing children. The women were placed in a wickiup with a sentry, next to Lone Wolf's wickiup. The children were placed in a wickiup on the other side of the encampment with their own guard. They were given food to eat but nothing like what they were used to. They were also warned by Lone Wolf,

"Hear me now; what I tell you is true. If *one* of you tries to escape, then the coyotes will fatten up on *all* of your remains."

The terrified hostages did not think that this was an idle threat. The women knew the horrible ways of the Apache. They knew an escape attempt was not wise.

After one week passed and plans were made for the next raid, the Mescalero renegades ventured out further from home. It was a three day journey to a town toward the west. This time it would be in the Arizona Territory.

THE TUCSON, ARIZONA RAIDS

A few months after the startup of the Civil War in 1861, Tucson, which was part of the New Mexico Territory at that time, was the western capital of the Confederate Army. Mesilla of the New Mexico Territory was considered the eastern capital of the Territory.

In 1862 a Union volunteer force sent from California, called the California Column, drove the Confederates out of what is now

Arizona and New Mexico. They journeyed over 900 miles from California traveling through Arizona, New Mexico, to the Rio Grande and all the way to El Paso, Texas between April and August of 1862. They were a force to be reckoned with.

All of what is now Arizona was part of the New Mexico Territory until 1863 when it became part of the new Arizona Territory.

Tucson was the capital of the Arizona Territory from 1867 to 1877. It was incorporated in 1877, thereby making it the oldest incorporated city in Arizona. Like other new towns in the Old West, law and order did not prevail at first. Plus, Apache had their way with raids in the early years. That's why Fort Lowell was built in 1873 just east of Tucson, to protect settlers against Apache attacks in the area.

In 1882 Frank Stilwell, who was implicated in the murder of Morgan Earp in Tombstone, went to Tucson with Ike Clanton, Hank Swilling and another cowboy to kill Virgil Earp at the train depot. Virgil and the others in the Earp family were on their way to California. Wyatt along with Warren Earp, Doc Holliday, "Turkey Creek" Jack Johnson, and Sherman McMaster accompanied them to the depot in case of trouble. And trouble there was. Stilwell and his men were waiting to kill Virgil. But the ambush did not materialize as planned. Stilwell was gunned down on the tracks. Wyatt would later brag that he was the one who killed Stilwell.

Lone Wolf and his Mescalero renegades took a major risk traveling over one hundred miles to Tucson to raid homesteaders and steal their women and children. Before they left though, they parleyed with another famous Apache chief, Victorio.

ABOUT VICTORIO

Victorio (1825 – October 1880) was a fierce Apache warrior and chief of the Chihenne band of the Chiricahua Apache. In his 20's he rode with Geronimo and other Apache leaders. He eventually became the leader of a band of Chiricahua and Mescalero Apache and would come to fight against the United States Army. Between the years of 1870 to 1880, Victorio and his band were moved to and left at least three reservations.

Victorio and his followers left the San Carlos Apache Indian Reservation in the Arizona Territory permanently in late August of 1879. He would lead a guerrilla war across the southwest and northern New Mexico. Unhealthy and deplorable conditions in the San Carlos Apache Indian Reservation were the causes that led him into combat. His warpath would become known as Victorio's War.

Victorio had a sister who was a famous woman warrior by the name of Lozen, or the "Dextrous Horse Thief". She was not only noted for being a skillful warrior but she was also a prophet and an outstanding medicine woman.

Victorio is quoted as saying, "Lozen is my right hand...strong as a man, braver than most, and cunning in strategy, she is a shield to her people."

BACK TO THE TUCSON RAIDS

Victorio was more familiar with the Arizona Territory and fort locations than Lone Wolf was and after hearing from Lone Wolf about his families' fate, Victorio and his warriors agreed to accompany Lone Wolf on their raiding parties.

On their way to Tucson, they stole two buckboard wagons in the dark of the night from a small tent-city silver mining camp. Gunfire was exchanged when the miners heard their wagons being driven off by Apache but no one was wounded or killed on either side.

They made it to the outskirts of Tucson in two and a half days. Lone Wolf then sent out four small search parties to locate possible ranches that could be raided that would yield hostages. He told them to return to their hideout location in two days.

There were four ranches discovered just outside of town that were good to raid. Victorio and his band of Chiricahua took a wagon and would hit two of them and Lone Wolf and his renegades would do the same. After the first raid by each group, the women and children were to be taken to their hideout outside of town and guarded. When all the raids were completed, they would ride back to their mountain encampment together and then discuss the next raids.

Once again, Lone Wolf made it clear to everyone that he was not interested in killing anyone. He was just interested in taking women and children hostages. But his message fell on deaf ears as far as Victorio was concerned. Victorio was like his friend Geronimo. He was out for blood, mutilation, scalps, and the death of all Mexicans and Americans alike.

The first ranch that Victorio's warriors raided was the Lane's Cattle Ranch with a family of five living in the main cabin. There was a small bunkhouse behind it housing three ranch hands better known as cowboys. Victorio had eighteen warriors with him.

In the dead of night, the warriors snuck up on the cabin and the bunkhouse. When Victorio gave the signal, eight stormed through the door of the bunkhouse yelling and screaming and with stone tomahawks and sharp knives, they went to work cutting up and beating the three cowboys to death, mutilating them and then scalping each and every one of them. Blood was splattered everywhere. It was a horrid scene. The cowboys never knew what hit 'em.

Simultaneously, Victorio and six warriors stormed through the front door of the cabin, screaming as loudly as they could. The man of the house, who was sleeping lightly, heard the Indians just before they broke through the door. As he was reaching for a shotgun, the door flung open and Victorio shot the head of the household with his rifle, five times. One of the warriors immediately ran over to him and scalped him right in front of his wife and three teenage girls.

The woman and the three girls were screaming loudly and crying frantically. The warriors slapped them around, grabbed them by the arms, dragged them outside and tossed them into the wagon like they were sacks of flour.

Lone Wolf's ranch to raid was about a mile away. It belonged to a family of four. They were the McDaniel family, immigrants from Ireland. A small two room cabin housed the small family.

Lone Wolf led the way as he kicked open the door and stormed into the cabin. Three warriors ran for the man of the house, beat him and then tied him up. The woman of the house was screaming to high heaven and was immediately slapped out cold by one of the Mescalero. The two young boys were scared out of their wits but were relatively quiet and then thrown into the wagon with their mother. No one was seriously harmed as Lone Wolf and his renegades rode off to their hideout nearby.

It was now about 1:30 a.m. and each group, Victorio's Chiricahua and Lone Wolf's Mescalero, had one more ranch to hit. While they did that, two Mescalero and one Chiricahua stayed guard over the hostages. Victorio never told Lone Wolf about what happened at the Lane Ranch. Lone Wolf assumed nobody was harmed as he had ordered.

With only about four hours of darkness left, both groups immediately went to their next target. Once again, Victorio's murderers went to work butchering and scalping the men on the ranch with such brutality it was not fit for visual consumption. Yet it was witnessed by the two children and their mother. The children were a boy and a girl under the age of ten and they cried profusely while the brave mother tried her best to console them.

Lone Wolf's group was able to gather up three children and the lady of the household with no trouble. Her husband was out of town on business and would have no idea what had happened to his family when he would return home about three days later.

After the Apache met at their hideout outside of Tucson, they waited until nightfall, about twelve hours later, before they loaded up the women and children into the wagons and began their long journey back to their mountain encampment traveling only at night time. Once again, Victorio never told Lone Wolf about the brutality he and his warriors inflicted on the families and Lone Wolf was none the wiser.

Before heading out on the trail though, all of the mothers and the children sat around a few campfires the Indians made to keep everyone warm. Some of the younger children were cold, hungry, scared to death and crying. They were all fearful for their lives. After all they were surrounded by Apache who they were taught were brutal savages and had no problem in torturing, mutilating and killing white men. To make things worse, the Apache talked to each other in their own language and the stress of not knowing what their conversations were all about weighed heavily on the captives.

One lady who was terrified yet angered at the situation jumped up and shouted at the top of her lungs in what she thought would be a futile but dangerous act,

"Do any of you savages speak English?"

Everyone stopped what they were doing and turned and looked toward the lady. Some Apache picked up their rifles, cocked them and aimed them toward her not understanding what she said and what she was going to do next. The lady became startled while the other women became alarmed and feared for that brave woman's life. Just then Lone Wolf in Apache ordered,

"Put your long-guns down, my brothers, I will talk to her."
Lone Wolf walked over to her and said,
"I speak your language, what is it you want?"
The woman was surprised that one of the Apache actually spoke English and began to calm down, then she asked,
"Why is it that you took us away from our homes? We didn't do anything to deserve this. What is it that you want? Are you going to harm us?"
"Your fate is yet to be determined. You ask me why. I'll tell you why; revenge for your government and your soldiers stealing our women and children and making them live like dogs and then starving them and torturing the young men who rose up against the conditions. Look around woman. Many warriors you see here had family members lose their lives on the reservation in what your government calls the Indian Territory. I, to whom you speak, lost my mother and father, wife and son, and brother and sister at the hands of bluecoats. My anger is great toward your people. My warriors' anger is great as well."
"But we are blameless, we here had nothing to do with your loss."
"Our families were innocent too. Yet your people massacred my village people and stole innocent ones. That's all I have to say. Now tell these others do not try to escape. For if one of you escape, the gray wolves will feast on all of your remains. Do you understand woman?"
"Yes, I do. But I beg of you, please spare us."
Lone Wolf then turned around and walked over to a campfire and sat down to meditate. The conflict between the wolves inside of him was great. When the sun began to set, the Apache loaded up the two wagons with the women and children and then headed for their hideout in the Chiricahua Mountains.
It came to pass that Lone Wolf and Victorio would raid ranches around two more towns in the next few months and a couple of more the following year in 1880 around Tombstone in the Arizona Territory, and Las Cruces in the New Mexico Territory. All and all, they would have raided 16 ranches and took 16 women and 42 children hostage.
Never in the history of both territories were so many women and children stolen by Apache. No one knew if they were still alive or if they had been slain. All of the towns, the settlements, and

ranchers and homesteaders were in a state of panic over the recent events and were afraid for the lives and the well-being of their families. They didn't know who to turn to. The U.S. Army was having no success finding the thieving Apache or locating the hostages. Posse from local and surrounding towns were sent out to no avail and overwhelming panic was setting in around the countryside.

The citizens of the New Mexico and Arizona Territories turned to and put pressure on the governors of the territories to get answers and results. There was a citizens' uprising. They demanded answers and they wanted them now.

At this point, the governors only had one person they could turn to, the President of the United States, President Hayes. But in reality, what could he do?

CHAPTER THREE:

Territorial Governors' Desperate Plea for Help

The citizens in the Arizona and New Mexico Territories were in an uproar. Nothing seemed to be getting done about the Apache raids on innocent folks. So many husbands and fathers had lost their families. Women and children had been snatched up from their homes in the dark of the night and some ranchers, cowboys, and family men had been killed, scalped and mutilated by Victorio's savage Apache warriors.

The homesteaders and ranchers were desperate. Now they were going after the governors of the territories. The message to them from the citizens was "If you don't do something soon and get our women and children back, we'll send you out of the territory on a rail and take the law into our own hands."

The pressure was now unbearable. The Southwest was wild enough. More lawlessness would be like taking two steps backwards as they tried to bring law and order to the Wild West. So the governor of the Arizona Territory sent a telegram to the governor of the New Mexico Territory.

Lawrence Williams
Governor of New Mexico Territory
URGENT
The U.S. Army and the several posse have lost the trail of the raiding Apache who kidnapped our women and children and killed some of our men. My citizens are about to become vigilantes. If this happens, lawlessness will once again prevail in the territory. I cannot allow this to occur. I would venture to state that your citizens are reacting in the same manner. Since we haven't heard anything from Washington, D.C. yet about any plans to help us, I suggest we take another train trip to Washington to plead our case once more. We should not leave the president's office until we get a promise of help. Need to hear your opinion on this matter soon.

Yours truly
James Freidman
Governor of Arizona Territory

The telegram from Governor Freidman was rushed over to the New Mexico territorial governor's mansion by one of the men working in the telegraph office. When he knocked on the door of the mansion, a staff member answered.

"How can I help you?"

"I have an urgent telegram for Governor Williams."

"Thank you, I'll take it to him," the staff member said as he began to close the door.

"Wait a minute sir. The governor might want to make an immediate response," the telegraph operator offered.

"Well then come on in and sit in the parlor and wait to see if he wants to respond immediately."

So he did while the aide took the telegram to the governor's office.

The aide knocked on the governor's office door and waited for a response.

"Come in," he shouted.

The staffer opened the door, walked over to the governor's desk and said,

"Sir, this is an urgent message from the governor of the Arizona Territory. A telegraph operator is waiting in the parlor to see if you want to respond directly."

Governor Williams quickly grabbed the telegram and began reading it. When he was finished, he paused for a while and thought for a few minutes. Then he said,

"Tell the telegraph operator that there will be a response and to wait until it's completed."

Governor Williams then referred to his schedule for the next couple of days and weeks ahead. There wasn't anything of urgent importance planned for the next several weeks so he composed this telegram to the governor of Arizona Territory, Governor Freidman.

James Freidman
Governor of Arizona Territory
I received your telegram. I am in agreement with your suggestion for I too am receiving increased pressure to resolve this issue. Please contact the White House to see when the president will be available to meet with us. I have nothing pressing on my schedule in the next few weeks. I am available to leave here at any time during that time period. Let me know at your earliest convenience.
Sincerely
Lawrence Williams
Governor of New Mexico Territory

The Governor of the Arizona Territory then contacted President Hayes in late December of 1880 and asked if Governor

Williams and he could have another meeting with Hayes to discuss the Mescalero raids on the homesteaders in their territories and the kidnapping of their women and children.

President Hayes wanted to coordinate the governors' meeting with his famous *Three for Hire* so he checked his schedule and the willingness of the *Three for Hire* to participate in another project.

Everyone agreed that January 15, 1881 would be a good date to meet. However, Hayes brought in the *Three for Hire* a day early to discuss some of the issues going on in the Southwest and to see if they were willing to risk their lives once more for their country. He also made it clear to them that he was not the one who was hiring them but instead it was the governors of the New Mexico and Arizona Territories and that the three would most likely be dealing with the likes of savage Apache.

The *Three for Hire* were brave and fearless men who would look danger straight in the eyes, and they were sharpshooters of the highest caliber. They all came from different backgrounds and all had their own different aspirations in life.

JESSE CALDWELL

There was Jesse Caldwell, a retired cattle drover and Texas rancher. Ole Jesse was born on June 14, 1830 in the area which became known as Austin, Texas, which was named after Stephen F. Austin, the so called "Father of Texas".

Caldwell was no stranger to the harsh treatment of homesteaders by Native Americans. He grew up in an area traveled by the Comanche and the Lipan Apache who followed the great buffalo herds but also raided settlements for food, cattle and horses. Both tribes were extremely hostile to the white settlers.

When Caldwell's father died, Jesse took over the operations of their large cattle ranch. Not only did they raise their own longhorns, but they also gathered up strays that were roaming the flatlands during the Civil War years.

It was on March 2, 1866, one year after the Civil War ended that Jesse Caldwell and his vaqueros and cowboys gathered about 2,000 head of their longhorns and drove them up the Shawnee Trail to the railhead in Sedalia, Missouri. There the cattle were loaded onto railroad cars and shipped to the slaughterhouses in Chicago.

From 1866 to 1879, Jesse drove Texas longhorns on those dusty and precarious cattle trails to the railheads in Missouri and Kansas every other year. During those drives, he and his drovers fought off rustlers, vigilante groups, irate farmers and ranchers, and Indians along the way. He demonstrated leadership skills and bravery that was second to no one.

The destination of his very last drive was Dodge City, Kansas where he met up with the other two of the *Three for Hire* in a historical incident that changed his life forever. He had aspirations to get into politics after his last cattle drive. His hero was Congressman Davy Crockett who was killed at the Alamo in 1836 when Jesse was just a kid living on the family ranch in Texas. However, his ambitions had to be put on hold for the time being.

THOMAS O'BRIEN

Thomas was one of two sons of immigrants who purchased a small cattle ranch in rural Pennsylvania in the 1840's after they arrived on a ship from Ireland. In October of 1861 while Thomas was visiting with a friend in Ohio, they both decided to sign up with the Union Army.

Not long after that date he found himself heading to the Pittsburg Landing on the Tennessee River. He and many more soldiers, under the command of Major General Don Carlos Buell arrived at Pittsburg Landing during the evening of the first day of the Battle of Shiloh which took place in Hardin County, Tennessee on April 6th and 7th in 1862. It was the bloodiest battle to date in the Civil War.

Thomas was seriously wounded during the second day of the battle and recovered from his wounds in a hospital in Cincinnati, Ohio.

He later met a young lady named Elizabeth and they were wed. They went on to have a son and twin daughters and lived in Scott County, Kentucky until they decided to make a bold move. Thomas wanted to get into the cattle business. So on July 10, 1879, he and his family loaded all of their belongings into two covered wagons and headed west.

Their destination was Dodge City, Kansas. Well things did not quite work out the way they expected. Thomas was involved in that incident in Dodge City with Jesse Caldwell.

From then on, Elizabeth would discover that her husband Thomas had a wild streak for excitement and daring that she was not able to tame.

SCOTT JOHNSON

Scott Johnson was born on September 15, 1846 in a rudimentary sod house just outside of what is now called Fort Worth, Texas. His maternal and paternal grandparents were all Scottish immigrants.

His father, Mathew Johnson was a blacksmith and had a booming business in Fort Worth over the years due to the importance of Fort Worth to the cattle trade. Fort Worth became a stopping off place for drovers along the dusty and sometimes muddy paths of the Chisholm Trail as the Texas cowboys drove their longhorns to the railheads of Wichita and Abilene, dodging Indians and rustlers along the way.

As a young boy and later, as a young adult, Scott worked in his father's blacksmith shop. He was a hard worker and he sweated over those blazing burning coals in the forge and pounded red hot steel for years before he decided to go out on his own.

He always had aspirations to become a gunsmith since he loved working with steel. He also enjoyed target shooting as well, which became his after-work hobby.

Before the age of twenty, he headed east to join up with a major gun manufacturer to learn the gunsmith business. After perfecting his skills, he moved back to Texas and became a Texas Ranger at the will of his father and the governor of Texas.

After a few years as a Texas Ranger, he retired and set out to fulfill his original dream, to become a gunsmith. He had ambitions to open up a shop in a town that would support a new business; he found that town. It was the booming cow town of Dodge City, Kansas. There he would meet a young lady and start up a serious relationship.

Everything was going as planned in Dodge City until gunslingers arrived in town and changed his life forever. On that fateful day he met up with Jesse Caldwell and Thomas O'Brien, and the rest is history.

WASHINGTON, D.C., JANUARY 14, 1881

It was a frosty and frigid morning in Washington, D.C. There were 3 inches of snow on the ground compliments of the first major snowstorm of the new year. The *Three for Hire* had arrived in town the afternoon before and stayed at a plush hotel which President Hayes suggested and paid for.

They arrived at the White House at nine o'clock on the morning of January 14th in a carriage which was dispatched by the president. Hayes was doing some paperwork when a staffer opened the door to his office and said,

"Mr. President, there are three frontiersmen in the lobby to meet with you. Their names are..."

Just then Hayes interrupted and smiled as he said,

"Are they wearing cowboy hats?"

"Yes sir they are."

"Well, for crying out loud, don't just stand there, bring them in."

"Yes sir."

When the three walked into the president's office, everyone was all smiles. They greeted each other like old friends and the president then asked them to sit down. There was a lot of lighthearted conversation first and a little reminiscing about the three's previous involvement with the president regarding a secret society that had threatened the very existence of the Union and even the president's life.

After they concluded the small talk, President Hayes became serious and got down to business very quickly.

"Gentlemen, I really didn't inform you about this next assignment when I sent you a telegram and asked you to come back to Washington. It's because I really don't have all the facts and details myself. I called you in a day early to inform you of what I do know though.

There is a disturbance in the New Mexico and Arizona Territories involving renegade Apache. It seems that Mescalero, led by a warrior they call Lone Wolf and assisted by a renegade known as Victorio, who was killed in October last year, have raided settlements in the two territories and brutally killed, mutilated and scalped men on ranches, and kidnapped their women and children."

"Where did these renegades come from?" Jesse inquired. "I thought the Apache were all on reservations."

"I suppose they left the reservations," Hayes responded.

Then President Hayes continued,

"I don't understand their reasons for leaving because the government is giving them all the food and clothing they need to live a good life on the reservations. Plus they even get government funds to purchase provisions at the Indian reservation trading posts. We supply them with tools to work the ground and seed to plant. I don't know why they are becoming so discontented. I just don't get it."

"Are you sure that everything they are supposed to be getting, they are in fact actually getting, Mr. President?" Thomas asked.

"Now that is a good question, Thomas. I can't really answer it with 100% certainty. I can only assume that they are," Hayes said. "Maybe the governors can shed some light on that subject."

"By the way Thomas, what does your wife think about you going on another mission?" Hayes questioned.

"She's sort of getting used to it, sir."

"Really?" Hayes asked with a dubious tone in his voice.

"No, not really," Thomas acknowledged. "She's always concerned about my safety, of course, but she also knows about my adventurous spirit and for some strange reason, she puts up with it, at least for now."

Then Hayes continued,

"One of the reasons why I wanted to meet with you first is to inform you that you will not be working for me on this project. You'll be working for both of the governors. They will also be the ones bankrolling you and paying your salaries.

The other thing I wanted you to be aware of is that you will be eye to eye with the most ruthless Native Americans in this country, the Apache. I know you have already heard of the exploits and killings of Geronimo. Well, this Lone Wolf guy sounds like he's cast in the same mold. Have any of you ever faced Indians before in your travels?"

"I have," Jesse said. "I faced them after crossing the Red River into the Indian Territory, driving cattle up to Kansas. We had a few run-ins along the way with renegades but no real trouble that we couldn't handle. Most of them just wanted some beef for their tribes. Many times we just cut a few steer out of the herd and left them for the Comanche and Apache. That seemed to appease them."

"I've never had experience with Indians before," Thomas acknowledged.

"Nor have I," Scott added.

"Well, knowing now the little information that I have given you, I need to know if you are still interested in meeting with the governors?" President Hayes questioned.

Scott looked at Jesse and then they both looked at Thomas. They all nodded "yes" at each other and then Jesse confirmed it for the three.

"You bet we are, sir!"

"Well then, we are scheduled to meet with the governors tomorrow morning. We will meet here in my office at 9:00 a.m. sharp if that suits you three OK."

They all agreed that the time and place was just fine.

"Well then gentlemen, you're on your own now in D.C. I have several other meetings scheduled so I'll be seeing you three in the morning. Enjoy the rest of your day."

With that, the three went back to their hotel and then headed for the small saloon inside of the hotel to have a few drinks and discuss the possibilities of their future mission and their plans for the evening.

WASHINGTON, D.C., JANUARY 15, 1881

A fresh layer of snow blanketed the streets of Washington, D.C. during the early morning hours. With the temperature in the teens and the wind howling at twenty miles per hour and gusting to thirty while still snowing, one could almost conclude that they had a virtual blizzard on their hands.

For all parties concerned, it was a cold, wet, and miserable ride in the open carriages from their hotels to the White House. The *Three for Hire* arrived first and were escorted to the president's office. Within fifteen minutes, the two governors and their aides arrived. Governor Freidman brought Andrew Goodson with him and Governor Williams brought along Phil Osborn. These two aides were there to take notes during the meeting.

The president had his office nice and toasty with a blazing fire roaring in the large masonry fireplace that had an ornate oak framed portrait of President George Washington above the large cedar mantel.

On that morning Hayes instructed his staffers to carry a large round table and eight chairs into his office and place them near the fireplace. His intention was to make the meeting as comfortable and informal as possible.

After the introductions were over, Hayes asked everyone to sit around the table, and get comfortable while the White House chef walked around the table and poured each guest a much appreciated hot cup of morning Joe.

Then Hayes started the meeting,

"Gentlemen, I am elated that we were all able to get together on this day. Governors, when we met in August, I told you that I had three men who I thought could help you with your problem. Well, here they are. They are the best in the West," the president said with a smile.

The governors were quite doubtful about the three's ability to help them with their situation. In fact, the governor of New Mexico Territory spoke up and candidly said,

"Sir we'll try anything but tell me how just three men can do what the U.S. Army and our many posse could not accomplish. No disrespect to these three brave men intended."

"I understand your concern governor," President Hayes admitted.

At this point President Hayes took the time to inform the two governors of how these three men had assisted him previously with two of his dangerous projects. Even with that, the governors were still skeptical.

Then President Hayes said,

"Gentlemen, there is not much more that I can do. I have several meetings to attend the rest of the day, so I will leave you seven alone to discuss the mission. You are welcome to use my office all day long if need be. I'll tell the White House chef to bring you lunch at about noon.

You may have noticed that there are several U.S. Army generals and colonels in town; they represent the forts in the Indian Territory and your territories. They also have responsibility for the Indian reservations in those areas. I have asked them to come to D.C. and to update me on the status of conditions in the reservations. However, my personal feeling is that conditions are much improved. I'm also interested to see if they can shed some light on the kidnappings in your areas.

At the end of the day I am planning to introduce all of you to them and ask the officers to give you, Jesse, Scott and Thomas, anything and everything you need to do your job. The cooperation of the U.S. Army could be of key importance to the success of your mission. So that's that.

Another group that I am meeting with is a bunch of ladies from a town in West Virginia. They want me to outlaw liquor in their town. They say their men are becoming too rowdy and they are too hard to control. I think I'll have a few snifters of brandy before I join that meeting. Then I'll carry my bottle of brandy in one hand and a full snifter in the other hand when I walk into the meeting room. Maybe then they'll know what side of the argument I'm on," the president said as he walked out of the room laughing almost uncontrollably.

The seven looked at each other and began laughing as well. That comment seemed to break the ice some. In fact, that was Hayes' purpose for the jest.

Then the meeting began with Jesse speaking up first and taking the lead like he always did.

"Well gentlemen, why don't you two governors tell us about the trouble you're experiencing in your territories and what you think started it and we'll go from there."

"Sounds good," Governor Freidman said. "I'll be more than happy to start. In fact, I'll start from the beginning.

We had six Apache Indian reservations in our two territories. New Mexico had four and Arizona had two."

Then the governor of New Mexico jumped in.

"My four were these: the Tularosa River Reservation which was in place from 1871 – 1874, the Warm Springs (Ojo Caliente) Reservation from 1874 – 1877, the Gila River Reservation established in 1859, and the Mescalero Apache Reservation established in 1873 which is still in operation. Lone Wolf, who is a Mescalero Apache, and his tribe left their reservation several years ago and settled in northeastern New Mexico before Baxter and his troops raided their village."

"Like I said," the governor of Arizona repeated, "I have two in my territory: the San Carlos Apache Indian Reservation which was established in 1871 and is still in existence and the Chiricahua Reservation which was established in 1872 but was closed in 1876."

"Tell us more about Baxter's raid on Lone Wolf's village," Scott insisted.

"Well, from what I heard, it wasn't pretty," Governor Williams said. "In fact, it was downright brutal. Baxter was on the trail of some escaped Kiowa from the Indian Territory and came across the remote Mescalero village. Baxter and his men attacked the village while the Mescalero were still sleeping and killed every warrior in camp and even some women and children. Then they torched the village. This Baxter, he's a tough one. The women and children who survived were marched off to the Indian Territory."

"How did Lone Wolf escape?" Thomas asked.

"He didn't. He was out hunting as were several other groups of warriors. They must have found complete devastation when they returned from their hunt."

"I guess that's what set him off eh?" Scott asked.

"Maybe, I don't know for sure. But if it were me, I think I would want revenge," Williams acknowledged.

"When did the kidnappings begin?" Jesse asked.

"About two years after that raid on Lone Wolf's village," Williams said.

"Two years, well that doesn't make sense," Scott offered. "Why so long after the raid? It seems to me that something else is at work here."

"That's what I always thought," the governor of the Arizona Territory said.

Thomas then changed the subject.

"I don't know much about what goes on in Indian reservations, and why so many are closing."

Governor Williams responded.

"There are a couple of reasons I know of why some of the reservations are closing. First, it's a cost savings measure and secondly, the government is freeing up more land for the influx of whites into these territories. So many people from the east are moving west for new adventures, establishing ranches, and following the gold and silver strikes in the area, amongst other things."

"That's right," the governor of the Arizona Territory confirmed. "The government is congregating so many Indians into the San Carlos Apache Indian Reservation in Arizona that it's getting extremely crowded and disease is running rampant. Plus they are herding many different tribes of Apache together and they do not all get along. And then there's this; I'm not sure they are receiving all the food, clothing and such that they are supposed to be getting from the government."

"What do you mean?" Jesse asked.

"Well, there's a lot of crooked Indian Agents and soldiers running the reservations and they are selling the food and clothing and other supplies for their own profits. Instead of provisions going to the Indians on the reservations, the sales from the goods are lining the pockets of the agents and soldiers. These are the reasons why so many Indians leave the reservations and cause trouble. Geronimo and Victorio are two good examples of that. Because of the horrid conditions in San Carlos, they left the reservation and started up wars with the whites for revenge, killing everyone who came across their paths. You can travel many routes in our territory and find a host of overturned burnt covered wagons and skeletons of bodies picked cleaned by the coyotes and buzzards. It's not a pretty sight."

"But getting back to Lone Wolf, it seems that something else set him off doesn't it?" Jesse asked.

"Yes it does," the governor of Arizona replied. "But the Native Americans have had a lot of reasons to be riled up and for a long time too. I'm sort of a history buff and I know a lot about the plight of the redman if you care to hear about it."

The *Three for Hire* looked at each other and nodded in the affirmative. After all, they were about to spend an undetermined amount of time in the Apache territory and any bit of history relating to the Apache's actions as a whole could help the three understand the reasons why Native Americans acted as they did.

"We have all the time in the world. Go ahead," Scott said.

Thomas stood up and offered, "Since we're gonna be here for a while, I'll throw a few more logs on the fire." And so he did.

Then the governor of Arizona began.

"You know, the Native Americans lived on this continent for centuries, long before the European whites ever set foot on it. There were hundreds of tribes and millions of natives. When whites arrived in the east, there were some who could live amongst the Indians and some who could not.

In the east and southeast there were basically five tribes known as the civilized tribes. They were the Cherokee, Chickasaw, Choctaw, Muscogee-Creek, and the Seminole. They were well established autonomous nations.

George Washington had a vision of how he wanted the white man and natives to get along. It was known as acculturation and it was well underway among the Cherokee and the Choctaw. By the early 1800's the Cherokee had already lost so much land to the whites. But there were many whites sympathetic to the Cherokee and other tribes. Washington's great hope was that their society could be modernized and integrated into the American society of the European whites.

Washington had aspirations and truly believed that with proper example and the support of many, the Native Americans could become social equals to the European whites. He had hopes that they would adopt Christianity, modern techniques of agriculture, become citizens, have property rights and basically all of the cultural traits of the new nation, the United States.

Eventually, government agents were sent to live among the Indian tribes so that they might lead by example. The Cherokee Nation was the tribe that showed great transformation into Washington's dream.

Thomas Jefferson's policy had also been to respect the rights of the Native Americans to their homeland and they could remain east of the Mississippi as long as they remained civilized."

"Well, what changed everything?" Scott asked.

"It wasn't what, it was who. It was President Andrew Jackson who sought a policy of political and military action for the removal of Native Americans from the lands settled by the white man. Some people may call it ethnic cleansing by Andrew Jackson. He advocated enacting a law for Indian removal. I guess he had pressure from politicians who represented people who wanted the Indians evicted, as it were. Southerners especially wanted the valuable growing lands of the Cherokee and the Seminoles. And of course there was the gold rush in north Georgia that started in 1828 that brought more white settlers into Cherokee territory. The prospectors wanted the Indians out of the area so that they would have free rein searching out their fortunes.

And then there was the fact that many of the Indians wanted self-rule. Jackson thought the only way he could accommodate their desire was to resettle them west of the Mississippi River on federal lands. In my opinion, that was one of the excuses he used to move the Indians out west."

The governor of Arizona Territory went on to talk about Andrew Jackson (March 15, 1767 – June 8, 1845) who was the seventh President of the United States from 1829 – 1837.

"I'm going to get off the track for a minute or two and tell you what I know about this character Andrew Jackson. He was nicknamed "Old Hickory", because of his toughness and aggressive personality. Why he even fought in duels of which some were fatal to his opponent. He was also a wealthy slave owner and because of that you can probably guess he was a southern Democrat.

He also expanded the 'spoils system'. Do you know what that means gentlemen?"

"I believe I do," Jesse said. "I'm thinking about getting into politics myself so I'm trying to learn all these terms. It's the practice where a political party, after winning an election, gives a bunch of government jobs to its supporters and even their friends and relatives as an outright reward for working toward victory, and as an incentive to keep them working for their party. I believe the opposite of the 'spoils system' is the 'merit system' in which offices and government work is rewarded based on some measure of merit, independent of some political activity."

"You are exactly right," Governor Friedman said.

"Is that legal?" Thomas asked.

"As sure as buzzards pick bones," Freidman said.

Then Freidman continued,

"Anyway, what followed was the passage of the Indian Removal Act. On April 24, 1830, the Senate passed the bill. Then the House passed it on May 26th. Finally on May 28th, the Indian Removal Act was signed into law by Andrew Jackson. Ole Davy Crockett, a fellow Tennessean of Jackson's, spoke out against the act during the bitter debate of the bill. But even he couldn't stop the momentum of that bill. This new Act authorized Jackson to negotiate treaties to buy tribal lands in the east in exchange for lands further west which eventually became known as the Indian Territory."

"This is really interesting to me," Scott said. "I never heard anything about this before. What happened after the Removal Act was signed?"

"Well it paved the way for the reluctant emigration of about 45,000 Native Americans, during Jackson's administration, from their homeland to west of the Mississippi into what I referred to before as the Indian Territory. After all their treaties were signed, the Indians were removed: the Choctaw were removed first in 1831, then the Seminole in 1832, the Muscogee-Creek went next in 1834, the Chickasaw in 1837, and finally the Cherokee in 1838. Each tribe took a different route to the Indian Territory."

"I heard the term 'Trail of Tears' was used to describe the removal of those tribes," Jesse said.

"You're exactly right Jesse. They say the phrase originated from a description of the removal of the Choctaw Nation in 1831. When they reached Little Rock on their way to the Indian Territory, a Choctaw chief thought to be Nitikechi quoted to the Arkansas Gazette that the removal was a 'trail of tears and death'."

Some people believe the tears came from the onlookers who witnessed the poor Native Americans traveling as many as a thousand miles on foot to their final destination. Many were scantily clothed and some didn't even have shoes or moccasins. Many eyewitnesses said the Indians were quiet and serene during those quasi-death marches.

So many of those poor souls suffered from exposure, disease, and starvation on the route to their destination and so many of them died. I heard as many as 4,000 Cherokee died of the 16,500 who were relocated during the harsh winter of 1838. This event was one of the most heartbreaking events in the history of our young country.

There were other tribes farther north who were also forced to leave their homeland and move west to the Indian Territory. They were: the Wyandot, the Potawatomi, the Shawnee, and the Lenape.

When it was all said and done, Jackson's administration bought and freed up about 100 million acres of Indian land for the European whites.

I don't want to spend too much more time on this subject. However, let me say this. The Removal Act began an avalanche of movement of Indians to reservations. The Sioux, the Comanche, the Apache and many more tribes were forced onto reservations.

Gentlemen, it's as simple as this. The whites wanted more land, the Indians had what the whites wanted, so the government snatched the land and their way of life right out from underneath them.

We treated them like lowlife, no better than animals. Then we placed them on crowded reservations, on land, in many cases, that wasn't fit to survive on. We introduced European diseases to them, starved them, and even killed them for sport. Is there any reason why we shouldn't believe that they would strike back all around this country? Many Americans are facing their retaliation now. That's why Custer and the 7th Cavalry were slaughtered and that's why we are fighting wars now with renegade Apache.

I hope this sheds some light on the subject for you gentlemen."

The *Three for Hire* were silent for a while because they were overwhelmed with much more information about the plight of the American Indian than they expected. However, they found it very interesting and they now had a better idea of what they were up against.

"Thank you for that information Governor Freidman," Scott said, "I personally learned a lot and have a different perspective on things as I'm sure Thomas and Jesse do."

Thomas and Jesse concurred with Scott's assertion.

It was now time for lunch. The White House chef brought in sandwiches at noon just like President Hayes said he would. They spent about forty-five minutes for lunch and took this time to get better acquainted with each other.

After lunch, the governor of New Mexico Territory, Governor Williams, took over and explained to the group that he was fighting a battle on two fronts. Everyone was aware of the Mescalero problem, of course, but not so much of the other problems unrelated to the Apache. It had been consuming a good portion of his time and that's why he was excited that the *Three for Hire* were taking over the Apache problem.

His other challenge was the Lincoln County War and the problem he was having with a ruthless, murdering outlaw by the name of William H. Bonney, born William Henry McCarty, Jr. (November 23, 1859 - July 14, 1881) and better known as Billy the Kid.

The Lincoln County War in New Mexico Territory took place from February 18th to July 19, 1878, just one year before the Mescalero Apache began their raids in New Mexico and Arizona

Territories. It was one of those famous Old West Range Wars between contending factions.

The reason why the Lincoln County War became so notorious was because of the notable figures who were well known, not only in the New Mexico Territory but were making a name for themselves in the entire region. There were names like Billy the Kid, Sheriffs William Brady (August 16, 1829 – April 1, 1878) and Pat Garrett (June 5, 1850 – February 29, 1908), cattle rancher John Chisum (August 15, 1824 – December 23, 1884), lawyer and businessman Alexander McSween (1843 – July 19, 1878), and an organized crime boss by the name of Lawrence Murphy (1831 – October 20, 1878).

Governor Williams began to explain the story of the Lincoln County War to the three.

"Are you sure you have time for me to tell you about our Lincoln County War?" The governor asked.

"We're not going anywhere," Jesse said, "we're snowed in. Since we're gonna be in your part of the country, I want to hear what sidewinders I need to keep my distance from. So, let's hear it."

"Well OK then, here's the deal. It sounds pretty frivolous but this is what started it. The conflict between the two factions came about over the control of the dry goods trade in the county. When you're the only game in town, you can charge exorbitant prices, if you don't have a conscience. That's exactly what Murphy's General Store did. Murphy's was owned by Lawrence Murphy, a shady character, and his business partner James Dolan (May 2, 1848 – February 6, 1898). The townspeople hated them for their price gouging.

We had two young newcomers to Lincoln County; they were John Tunstall (March 6, 1853 – February 18, 1878), an Englishman, and his business partner, Alexander McSween. With the financial backing of a well-to-do cattleman by the name of John Chisum, they were able to open a competing dry goods store in 1876 called, "J. H. Tunstall & Co." and began pricing their products at a more reasonable price than Murphy's.

Both sides began loading up their forces. Murphy and Dolan allied with the Lincoln County sheriff named Brady. They were also supported by the Jesse Evans Gang, the Seven Rivers Warriors, and the John Kinney Gang. Dolan's objective was to goad Tunstall into a fight. But Tunstall showed no interest in fighting.

The Tunstall and McSween faction organized a group of gunmen. Like Murphy and Dolan, Tunstall's group had a lawman on their side by the name of Constable Richard M. Brewer (February 19, 1850 – April 4, 1878).

One of the gangs supporting Murphy began rustling Tunstall's herd of cattle and dispersing them all over the county. However, the main chaos in the county started with the straight up murder of Tunstall by the Evans Gang. On February 18, 1878, while Tunstall was alone, he was shot and killed by Jesse Evans (1853 – ?) and his little known gang members: William Morton, Frank Baker and Tom Hill. I think Dolan gave them the orders to eliminate Tunstall. This event sparked the Lincoln County War.

Of course, Sheriff Brady did nothing about the killing. So Alex McSween organized the Lincoln County Regulators. They were legally deputized and were tasked with the apprehension of Tunstall's murderers. This was a tough group of guys too. The Regulators consisted of Dick Brewer (February 19, 1850 - April 4, 1878), Doc Scurlock (January 11, 1849 - July 25, 1929), Charlie Bowdre (1848 - December 23, 1880), and the infamous Billy the Kid (November 23, 1859 - July 14, 1881).

With Tunstall's death, Lincoln County became a viper's nest. The back-and-forth revenge killings really got out of hand. On March 6th the Regulators captured two of Tunstall's killers, Morton and Baker. On March 9th, the Regulators executed both men.

"Did it end there?" Scott, the retired Texas Ranger, asked.

"Oh no Scott, it got worse. The Regulators continued to avenge the death of Tunstall by murdering Sheriff Brady and Deputy George W. Hindman on April 1, 1878, in cold blood right out in the middle of the street. And then killings continued on both sides for several months.

Then the range war ended, in what some are now calling the Battle of Lincoln County, from July 15 – 19, 1878. It was a vicious four-day gunfight and siege. It resulted in the death of McSween and finally, the scattering of the Regulators.

"Was that the end of all your excitement?" Thomas asked.

"Oh no," Governor Williams said. "There was more. Should I continue?"

"You bet," Scott said. "I was in my last year as a Texas Ranger while this was going on and I heard a little bit about the battles in you territory. I would love to hear how this all ended."

"Well, here's what happened after the Regulators scattered.

A guy by the name of Pat Garrett ran for sheriff of Lincoln County on the pledge that he would run down Billy the Kid and his gang. Well the citizens believed Garrett and elected him sheriff this past November. In early December he got together a posse and set out to arrest Billy. By now, ole Billy had a $500 reward on his head, compliments of yours truly.

I don't know how Garrett did it but he found Billy pretty darn quick. He almost had him caught on December 19th at Fort Sumner. Billy got away but Garrett's posse shot one of the gang members dead. If I remember right his name was Tom O'Folliard.

Four days later, Garrett tracked Billy to an old stone building located in a remote location known as 'Stinking Springs'. What a name, eh? Anyway, Billy and his gang were asleep inside while Garrett and his posse surrounded the building waiting for sunup. Charlie Bowdre was the first one to step outside to feed his horse and he was shot dead by the posse.

Eventually, the outlaws surrendered since they saw no way to escape. Now they are awaiting trial. I assume they'll be hung for their crimes."

"Wow, between the Apache raids and the Regulators, you had your hands quite full, didn't you?" Thomas asked.

"But with Billy out of the way and the Lincoln County War coming to an end, I can now concentrate on bringing these Apache to justice and hopefully getting our wives, mothers, and children back alive."

"Why don't we take a breather and get started again in about twenty minutes?" Jesse suggested.

So they did. The two governors and their aides wandered around the White House while Jesse, Scott and Thomas stayed in the president's office close to the fire. Jesse picked up a couple of logs and threw them on the fire and then stoked up the logs to get a good flame going. Then he turned around and said to Scott and Thomas,

"Well, what do you guys think ?"

"I think we're crazy if we think we can find and then fight a bunch of renegade Apache by ourselves and do something not even the U.S. Army could do," Thomas said.

"What about you, Scott?" Jesse asked.

"You may think my brain is full of buckshot Jesse, but I kinda like the challenge."

"What challenge, to see if we can survive twenty arrows sticking in our chests?" Jesse asked facetiously.

"No, the challenge to see if we can find out why Lone Wolf decided to go on these kidnapping raids in the first place. Something triggered his actions and I would sure like to find out what it was without us getting ourselves stuck, of course like a human pin cushion."

After a while, the other four gentlemen came back into the room and they all sat around the table again. Then the governor of Arizona started the meeting.

"Well I guess you three gentlemen had some conversation about the mission when we left the room. Did you come up with a decision? Do you think you want to go to work for us and join the search for our kidnapped families?"

"This sounds like a tall order, governor. We're interested but we are not sure where to start. Plus, we are really not that familiar with your territories. That's gonna be a challenge for us," Jesse said.

"Actually Jesse, Governor Williams and I talked about that very subject on the train to D.C. What we came up with is that if you gentlemen accepted the job, we would find you an Indian scout who speaks both Apache and English and who knows his way around the Chiricahua Mountains and other mountain ranges where Lone Wolf might be hiding out."

"Where are you gonna find this scout?" Scott asked.

"We're thinking in the San Carlos Apache Indian Reservation," Governor Williams offered.

"That's right," Governor Freidman agreed, "San Carlos has a system that John Clum put in place when he arrived there in 1874 as the Indian Agent. He established the first Indian Tribal Police and Tribal Court, forming a system of Indian self-rule. His Apache Indian police helped to capture Geronimo at Ojo Caliente in the spring of 1877. The Indian police have remained loyal to the cause and one of them, I'm sure, would make an excellent scout for you."

"I don't know much about Indian scouts nor Apache," Thomas admitted. "How do we know we can trust an Apache scout to help us try to find his own kind? I mean, we could have a shootout on the spot with Lone Wolf and his warriors at some point. What's to say that this scout wouldn't turn on us and knife us or unload his repeating rifle in our backs when we're not looking? And what if we get captured by Lone Wolf, is this scout gonna help convince Lone Wolf not to burn us at the stake or tie our arms and feet spread eagle to the ground and let the vultures pick our bones while we're still alive? One of you governors please give us some guarantee why you believe we are safe with an Apache scout."

"I believe I can give you some form of assurance," Governor Freidman said. "Native Americans have been a vital part of U.S. military conflicts for years going all the way back to the Revolutionary War, the War of 1812 and the Civil War. They were a major help to the U.S. Army during the Sioux Wars of 1876 and 1877 as well.

Because of the previous success of the utilization of Indian scouts, the recruitment of Native Americans to be used as scouts for the U.S. Army was authorized on July 28, 1866 by an act of Congress. I know you aren't going to believe this but like I said before, I am a student of Native American history and I can quote the Act verbatim."

"Well bring it on," Jesse said.

"OK, it goes like this:

The president is authorized to enlist and employ in the Territories and Indian country a force of Indians not to exceed one thousand to act as scouts, who shall receive the pay and allowance of cavalry soldiers, and be discharged whenever the necessity for further employment is abated, at the discretion of the department commander."

"Impressive," Jesse said. "But like Thomas, I also have my doubts about their loyalty."

"Look gentlemen, up to now there are no known cases of Indian scouts turning on the U.S. Army. They have been extremely loyal to our cause. They know how to track, they know how to read signs, they know what drumbeats and Indian dances mean and they know how to interpret smoke signals. Plus, no one knows the territories of New Mexico and Arizona better than the Apache. Besides that, an Apache scout will probably be the only one who will be able to find Lone Wolf and our women and children. Now, I suggest you cease worrying about the scout situation and put your efforts toward planning out the mission," Freidman said in a slightly angry tone that seemed to come out of nowhere.

Jesse, Scott and Thomas picked up on the change in tone as things became a little tense, but didn't let that bother them. They knew the frustration these two gentlemen were going through because of the kidnappings and lack of results in solving the problem.

Then Scott spoke,

"Look governor, we understand your outrage over this situation. We are on your side all the way. We just like to know all the facts and what we are up against before we jump into a project feet first. I'm sure you can appreciate that. We are looking forward to the help of an Indian scout."

"I'm sorry, Scott. I didn't mean to let my frustrations show. Now, where do we go from here?"

Then Governor Williams jumped into the conversation,

"Well, why don't you three plan on a date to meet at the San Carlos Apache Indian Reservation to pick up your scout? That would be the best place to start."

The three talked about it for a while. They agreed that they would all travel home and take care of their personal business first. Then they would meet in the San Carlos area on or around February 18th with their rifles, pistols, ammunition, and warm clothing. They would pick up horses, tack, a wagon and supplies for their trip from the trading post at the reservation or from a nearby town.

The governors also talked about how they would bankroll the three and what they would be paid monthly for their efforts. Everyone agreed on the financing part of the mission.

The governors' aides made notes of the entire meeting so that all of the discussions were on record and that there would be no confusion on any of the discourse.

All seven of them sat around the table discussing other topics until President Hayes' advisor came into the room and said,

"President Hayes would now like for me to escort all you to the Red Room of the White House. Contrary to Mrs. Lucy Hayes' wish, the president has set up an open bar for the soldiers and you so that you all can become better acquainted over a few drinks. He would also like for all of you to join him and the soldiers for dinner in the White House tonight."

"Well, I believe we can handle that," Scott said as they all smiled, stood up and followed the president's advisor to the Red Room. The soldiers were already in the room, sipping on some brandy and some of the finest wines imported from France. When the seven walked into the room, President Hayes said out loud,

"Ah, they're here. Gentlemen, may I have your attention please. I would like to introduce to you the governors of your territories and their aides. I know many of you know each other already."

So he did. Then he introduced the *Three for Hire* to the group.

"And finally gentlemen, I would like for you to meet the three whom the governors have hired to help you solve the kidnapping problem in your area. I told you a little about them in our meeting but now you have a chance to meet them personally. These three men are Jesse Caldwell, Scott Johnson, and Thomas O'Brien. They are going to require your full cooperation as they begin their journey to attempt to get your women and children back safely," the president said as he pointed each one out to the group. The three nodded as they were each introduced.

Jesse, Scott, and Thomas could sense that the reception by many of the soldiers was cold as they resented the fact that three civilians were being hired to do something that the U.S. Army was not able to accomplish as of yet.

Then the president added,

"Why don't all of you take a few minutes and get acquainted. Dinner will be served in about 45 minutes. Until then, the bar is open and we have plenty of refreshments available."

The three split up after they received their drinks at the bar and began introducing themselves to the soldiers. The very first person who Jesse introduced himself to was none other than Colonel Baxter of Fort Sill.

Baxter was an arrogant person and easily identifiable by his shoulder length gray hair. However, Jesse was not familiar with his appearance only his reputation about the raid of the Mescalero camp in northeastern New Mexico.

"So you're Baxter, eh?" Jesse said.

"That's Colonel Baxter," Baxter said with a sense of superiority in his tone.

"I heard about your attack on the Mescalero village a few years ago."

"That so?" Baxter said. "Well you can't believe everything you hear."

"How does it feel to kill innocent women and children?" Jesse asked.

"I have no problem with it like apparently you do, Mr. Caldwell. They're all savages and ought to be eliminated off the face of this earth," Baxter said with a smile knowing it would raise Caldwell's ire. Baxter then took a sip of his brandy as Jesse, taken aback by Baxter's callous and rude remark, turned away to go introduce himself to another soldier. Baxter continued to smirk as he knew his comment did not sit well with Jesse. Baxter could care less.

After the dinner was over later that evening, and everyone was leaving the White House, Hayes asked the *Three for Hire* to stay for a few minutes. He wanted to talk to them before they went on their new mission.

When everyone left the White House, Hayes escorted the three to his office and offered up another brandy. They talked a while about the previous mission Hayes had sent them on and then Hayes got very serious.

"Gentlemen, I'm going to be square with you; when you were occupied with the last project for me, I told you to trust no one. Do you remember that?"

"Yes we do," Scott said.

"Well, I'm going to tell you again, even though you aren't being hired by me this time, trust no one as you work this next project."

"Why do you say that?" Jesse asked.

"Because none of this makes sense to me; I'm talking about the Apache kidnapping women and children during a two year period. Something must have really set them off but I have no idea what it was. My gut tells me there's more to this than what we might think. I also perceived that some of those soldiers in my meeting today may have had answers but did not divulge them. They all pretended that everything was going well on the reservations. However, I have my doubts about that. I'm telling you, just stay alert as you travel through Arizona and New Mexico Territories.

By the way, you know that my term is up on March 4th of this year. You also know that your new president-elect is James Garfield. He's a man you can trust."

"I know him well, or know of him well I should say," Thomas said. "Garfield commanded the 20th Brigade of Ohio under Buell at the Battle of Shiloh. I was with him when we arrived on the scene the evening of the first day of the battle when we reinforced Grant's Army."

"That's right Thomas, you were both at Shiloh. It's a small world isn't it?" Hayes remarked. Then he continued,

"Look gentlemen, I will support your cause every step of the way. If you ever want my help with anything, you can count on me. Before I leave office, I will make sure I inform President-elect Garfield how you helped me in some of my endeavors and that you are three men who can be trusted with his life."

"That's very kind of you," Jesse said.

With that, they said their good-byes and Jesse, Scott and Thomas went back to their hotel rooms. The next day they each bought train tickets back to their hometowns: Jesse to Austin, Texas, Scott to Dodge City, Kansas, and Thomas to Scott County, Kentucky.

CHAPTER FOUR:

Hired Assassins

THOMAS O'BRIEN ARRIVES HOME IN SCOTT COUNTY, KENTUCKY

It's getting to seem like a familiar occasion with the O'Brien family: Thomas gets a telegram from the President of the United States, he doesn't think twice and packs for D.C., he accepts a new dangerous assignment, he gives his family the bad news, and he heads out West on a perilous mission with his family wondering if they will ever see Thomas alive again.

Thomas' family met him at the railroad depot once again. Josh and the twin girls Jennie and Jeanie were really excited to welcome their pa home even though he had only been gone for less than a week.

When the locomotive whistle blew and they could see the train coming around the bend one half of a mile down the tracks, the kids began to shout,

"Here he comes ma, here he comes!"

Thomas' coming home was always filled with high elations and today was no exception. The high energy enthusiasm of the children brought a smile to the other people waiting at the depot for their arrivals.

Then as usual, the train pulled into the depot and the familiar steam was released at the wheelbase, making the kids jump with laughter as they were caught right in the middle of the cloud of steam.

When the train came to a complete stop, Thomas was the first one to step off. His kids spotted him right at the get-go and ran up to him as fast as their legs would carry them. They all hugged him and then politely stepped aside for their ma to greet their pa.

"Welcome home dear," Elizabeth said as she gave him a typical wife's peck on the cheek. She then looked Thomas straight in the eyes and already knew the answer to her question.

After being married to Thomas for many years, she could tell by the look on his face without even asking. She knew that Thomas had once again accepted another dangerous mission even though she hoped that maybe this time would be different.

Elizabeth continued to gaze at Thomas while he looked back with a solemn look on his face and then she said, "Oh Thomas, not again."

"We'll discuss it when we get home, Elizabeth," Thomas replied.

After the O'Briens all climbed up into the carriage, Thomas whipped the reins across the hindquarters of the two bay Morgan geldings to begin their thirty minute trip back to their home. The kids looked back as the train's whistle blew, thick black smoke belched out of the smokestack, and the passenger train began pulling slowly away from the Scott County Depot.

The snowstorm which hit Washington, D.C. a few days earlier had first traveled through parts of the Ohio River basin; so their ride to their plantation home was cold, but striking. As they traveled through the beautiful snow covered pines of the Kentucky countryside, they enjoyed the picturesque scene of the late morning sun glistening off the pure white sparkly snow that blanketed the northern Kentucky landscape. It was a sight to behold.

The O'Briens still lived with Elizabeth's parents in the Bannister's large tobacco plantation house. When their carriage rode up in front of the large home with four majestically tall white columns that seemed to reach for the clouds, Mr. and Mrs. Bannister, Elizabeth's parents, were standing at the front door to greet Thomas.

That afternoon, the two families sat in the parlor in front of the large blazing fireplace enjoying the warmth of the toasty heat from the flaming seasoned hickory logs. Everyone was enjoying the family gathering. Mrs. Bannister had just made hot apple cider for everyone and that cinnamon scented aroma filled the kitchen and made its way to the parlor adding to the coziness of the setting.

However, that tranquil and relaxing mood was short lived when Elizabeth, out of the blue, asked Thomas to tell the family about his new assignment. Thomas was a little hesitant at the onset to discuss it right at that moment but then realized it probably was not such a bad time since everyone was together and the feeling was quite placid.

"Well, Jesse, Scott and I have been asked to go on another assignment."

"I hope this one is not as dangerous as your last one," Elizabeth remarked.

"Where are you headed this time pa?" Thomas' son Josh asked.

"I'm headed out West again son, to the New Mexico and Arizona Territories."

"What's your assignment this time Thomas?" Mr. Bannister asked.

"Well, we are working for the two governors of those territories. It seems the Apache, led by an Indian warrior called Lone Wolf and another one named Victorio have been conducting raids out that-a-way and kidnapping the women and children of homesteaders and ranchers."

"You're not telling us that you are planning to fight the likes of those savage Apache, are you Thomas?" Elizabeth questioned.

"I hope not. Our assignment is to find their hideout, parley with them to see what made them start these raids, and try to get those wives, mothers, and children back home safely."

"Oh my," Mrs. Bannister said, "how do you know those poor folks are still alive?"

"We don't, we're just hoping for the best."

"Why don't you leave all of that up to the U.S. Army? That's what they're getting paid to do," Mr. Bannister suggested.

"Well the U.S. Army has been unsuccessful up to now and so has the posse. I believe that if the soldiers came close to finding the raiders anyway, well, they would put all of the hostages in grave danger. There are a lot of soldiers out that way that get their kicks from killing as many Indians as possible with no regards for the likely negative repercussions that would follow. I met one of those soldiers in Washington a couple of days ago. He was proud of the fact that he massacred a village of Mescalero Apache which may have something to do with the subsequent kidnapping raids I spoke about."

Then Jennie, one of Thomas' daughters, ran to her pa and threw her arms around him and said as she began crying,

"Daddy, please don't go this time. I have a bad feeling about this. I couldn't bear it if something would happen to you."

Then Jeanie did the same thing.

"Now girls, nothing's gonna happen to me. I'm gonna be with my two brave friends. We are as tough as they come and can handle ourselves quite well. We have proven that over and over again; so not to worry, my lovely daughters."

Elizabeth and Mrs. Bannister both could not hold back their tears witnessing the fear that was in the hearts of these young girls.

Thomas thought that the mood was getting way too emotional and somber so he decided to make this cozy little gathering come to an end.

"Hey Josh, let's go for a walk outside," Thomas suggested, "I want to discuss a couple of things with you."

"Can Jennie and I go with you daddy?" Jeanie asked.

"Not this time, honey, I want to talk to Josh alone."

Elizabeth, did not like the sound or the tone of that. She knew in her heart that this was going to be a man-to-man talk in the event that the worst would happen out West. She immediately went to the kitchen and made herself busy preparing food for the dinner that night.

Thomas and Josh put on their heavy coats and took along their double barrel shotguns just in case they came across a rabbit or two while they walked through the brush and along the fence lines. Josh was now 15 years old and growing up rapidly. He was very mature for his age.

As they walked along one of the fence lines, Josh asked,

"Pa, can I go with you this time. I'm old enough now and I can shoot right straight and I'm not afraid of no Injuns."

"Son, I know you're not afraid of anything. You have proven that to me over and over again when we took that long journey to Dodge City, Kansas. I was really proud of your bravery and the way you acted like a grown man.

However, I want to be square with you, son. What I am about to tell you, you cannot tell your ma or your sisters or your grandpa and grandma. Can you promise me that, Josh?"

"Yes sir, I can."

"Good, now listen up. Son, this will probably be the most dangerous assignment I have ever been on. The Apache are ruthless killers and most of them hate the white man."

"Why pa, why do they hate us so?"

"It's a long story, son. You and I had nothing to do with it. The government, over time, forced them out of their homelands onto reservations that in some cases weren't fit for animals to live on."

"Why did they do that, pa?"

"For a lot of reasons, son. White men wanted more land for farming, ranching and prospecting. The Indians had it, so the white men took it. The results were wars between the Indians and the whites. Killings begot killings; revenge begot revenge. It was a vicious cycle. Hatred for each continued to escalate and consequently, so many lives were lost including lives of innocent women and children.

But let me get back to what I wanted to tell you. This is gonna be the most hazardous mission I have ever been on and well son, if I don't make it back alive this time, your ma and sisters will be depending on you to take good care of them. Do you understand that?"

"Yes sir, I do; but pa, if it's so risky, why don't you just stay home?"

"Because son, I have always felt I have a duty to my fellow man, just as you do and we all do. If I can help others, then I will do my best to do so. For some reason, these governors and the President of the United States think that Jesse, Scott and I are the best men for this job. If they really believe that, then I can't let them down, no matter what the danger. When you get older son, because of the way you were brought up, you'll understand."

"Pa, I do understand. But I know you'll be back. I just know it pa," Josh said as tears welled up in his eyes, and he quickly turned around so his pa would not see him begin to cry.

On the way back to the house, they jumped two rabbits in the briers. Josh shot both of them and they took them back home for supper that night.

SCOTT JOHNSON RETURNS HOME TO DODGE CITY, KANSAS

Scott first arrived in Dodge City as an aspiring gunsmith on May 30, 1879. It was a booming cow town back then with cattle herds of 1,500 or more longhorns being driven up from Texas via the dust laden Shawnee Trail almost every day from late May to the end of September. Law and order generally went right out the proverbial door when those filthy mangy looken cowboys reached the end of their trail and spent half of their wad in the saloons, brothels, and gaming houses their first couple of days in town.

On Scott's very first day in the Queen of the Cow Towns, being a retired Texas Ranger, he decided to visit the marshal's office first. The marshal at the time was Charlie Bassett and his three deputies were lawmen of great notoriety. It was on that day he met the deputies who would become his friends for life. They were Wyatt Earp, James Earp and James Masterson, Bat's brother.

Scott's main reason for going to Dodge City in 1879 was to open up a gunsmith shop. While in the marshal's office on that first day, Wyatt told him about the one owned by 'Pops' McCarthy who was getting up there in years and would probably be ready to sell his business to the first serious prospect that came along. Well ole Pops was more than willing to sell his business to Scott. However, things didn't quite work out because Scott was always out of town fighting a just cause for President Hayes and his country.

Well on this day in January of 1881 when Scott arrived in town on the Union Pacific railroad line from Washington, D.C., he wanted to stop by and call on ole Pops to purchase a repeating rifle for his new assignment. However, he had a more pressing engagement to take care of first. He had to visit with his girlfriend, Janice, if he knew what was good for him.

Janice worked behind the desk at the local hotel which her father owned. He met her on his first day in town back in '79 and the two hit it off pretty good, right out of the gate. She was quite a looker for a small town girl and Scott went all goo-goo eyes on her at first sight.

After Scott got off the train, he walked over to the hotel where Janice was working. Janice had no idea when he was getting back into town but she was really missing Scott even though he had only been gone for about 10 days.

When he walked into the lobby of the hotel at around 4:30 in the afternoon, he stood in the lobby just watching her doing some book work. Then he faked a cough, she looked up and shouted,

"Scott, you're home!"

"Looks that way don't it," Scott said jokingly.

Janice ran around from behind the counter and gave ole Scott a big hug and a smooch. Scott hugged and smooched her right on back. They were both happy to see each other. They talked for a while and then setup a time for a dinner date for that evening.

Scott walked over to his house at the end of Main Street which he had been renting for almost two years now. His plan was to rest, change clothes and freshen up for an evening dinner with Janice.

When 7:30 rolled around, Scott strapped on his two S&W Schofield six-shooters, not because he had to but because it was a habit he picked up being in the Texas Rangers for a few years. Besides, he did not like to wander the streets of Dodge City at night, unarmed.

Now the law in Dodge City stated that no one was allowed to wear their pistols in town. They had to be checked into the marshal's office first. However, during the cattle drive off-season, the law was not enforced for townspeople.

After Scott was all duded-up for his dinner date, wearing his white collarless shirt, leather vest, red silk neckerchief, rawhide overcoat, Boss of the Plains Stetson and two pearl handle Schofields strapped to his waist, he wandered over to the livery stable to check on his horse to make sure it was being kept well, being there 10 days and all.

Finally, he strolled over to the hotel to escort Janice to a restaurant which was just down the street apiece. It was the fanciest one in town and it was named, The Kansas Steak and Ale House. They would season and fry-up the finest eating Texas beefsteaks in town and had some of the best German wines in the region. Each square table was dressed with a white linen tablecloth and had a lit candle lantern in the center. It was a very nice atmosphere for the likes of a rugged infamous cow town.

Dodge City was fairly calm this time of the year because there were no rowdy Texas cowboys in town to disturb the peace. The only people around were townspeople and a few passers-through of which some were gamblers and some were saddle tramps who may or may not be looking for trouble.

This night seemed peaceful enough. There were about sixteen people eating dinner in the restaurant when Janice and Scott walked in.

Just before Scott walked through the door of the restaurant he glanced across the street and happened to spot two armed strangers leaning up against a post and staring right at him. He stopped, stared back, and then continued to walk into the restaurant.

The lovebirds ordered their meal and a bottle of wine and talked about Scott's new assignment. Janice feared for his life. She heard horror stories about the Indian raids in the 60's on the Santa Fe Trail near what was now Dodge City and she disliked the risks that Scott was always taking. She had settling-down on her mind and Scott was the person she wanted to live with for the rest of her life. She spoke candidly about that during dinner when she found out Scott was heading out on another dangerous mission, this time to Apache country.

During their conversations, Scott told Janice one thing that really bothered him about this mission.

"Before we left Washington, President Hayes told us to trust no one. That worries me more this time than our last mission because we don't have a handle yet on what we are really dealing with."

During their dinner date, ole Scott did not want to worry Janice but he could see out the restaurant window that those two gunslingers were still across the street from the restaurant and seemed to be peering in at him.

When they completed their meal, Scott paid the bill, left a tip and then they walked out of the restaurant into the dark cold night. Scott kept his eyes on those two rascals across the street and told Janice that he would walk her home back to the hotel but that he was very tired from the trip and wanted to get back to his house and hit the sack. He would meet her for breakfast the next morning.

Scott, being the gentleman that he was, walked Janice up to her room, kissed her goodnight and then walked back downstairs. He had a feeling that those two gunslingers were waiting outside for him, but he couldn't figure out why.

Now Scott was fast, fast on the draw and wasn't afraid to meet these guys head on. But he also knew that many lowlife gunmen had no quarrels shooting their prey in the back. So Scott went out the back door of the hotel and quietly snuck around the side to the front like a bobcat stalking a jackrabbit making ready to pounce on its prey. Only the roles were reversed here; the prey was stalking the predators. When he reached the front of the building, those six-gun toting saddle tramps were standing side-by-side with their pistols drawn, facing the front door of the hotel waiting to plug Scott as he walked out of the building.

Scott quietly drew his two Schofields, pointed one at each would-be assassin and said,

"Looking for me you sidewinders?"

The two paused for a second then quickly spun around with their guns ablazing but Scott drilled them both, putting three slugs in each of their chests. One of the gunslingers winged Scott on the side of his head. It was just a small scratch but one inch over to the right, it would have been "lights-out" and Scott would have been another resident of Boot Hill marked by a simple solitary stone with a name and a date.

People started to run out of the buildings onto the street to see what the shooten was all about. Janice was one of them and was taken aback when she found out that her beau was involved.

The marshal came running up the street toting a 10 gauge double barrel shotgun loaded with buckshot and was shocked to see two dead men lying face-down on the boardwalk in front of the hotel.

"What happened here," the marshal asked, "and who are they?"

"I have no idea who they are," Scott said. "Those two snakes had been trailing me ever since Janice and I stepped foot into The Kansas Steak and Ale House."

Janice looked at Scott in disbelief. She had no idea these two gunmen were watching them.

"Then they waited for me outside the hotel while I took Janice to her room. I figured they might be bushwhacking me out here so I took precautions and went out the back door and came around the side. Sure enough, they were waiting there with their guns drawn ready to plug me when I came out of the hotel. I gave them a chance to turn around and was gonna demand that they drop their guns but they had other intentions because they spun around and began firing. Luckily, I was quicker and more accurate."

"Do you know who these guys are?" The marshal asked.

"I have no idea."

"Well, someone go get the undertaker. We'll check them out in the morning and see if they're wanted for anything. In the meantime, everyone clear the streets and go home," the marshal ordered. "It's all over now."

Janice didn't notice the bloody crease on Scott's head because it was quite dark and he sort of hid it with his hat. He sent her back up to her room and then went home and put some iodine on his wound.

Scott had a hard time sleeping. He stared at the ceiling half the night trying to figure out who those hired guns were and why he was targeted to be assassinated.

When morning came around, he slept in until about 8:00 a.m. His first order of business when he awoke was to make himself a strong cup of coffee and then he realized he stood Janice up for breakfast. But instead of looking for Janice and apologizing for his failure, he went straight over to the jailhouse to see if the marshal had found anything out about those two would-be killers.

When he walked into the marshal's office, the marshal said,

"Well, how did you sleep last night Scott?"

"With one eye open and one eye shut. Did you find anything out about those two scalawags yet?"

"Well last night I took a good look at those two men and came right back to the office and went through my stack of 'Wanted' posters. Sure enough, both of these men are wanted, wanted for murder.

One of these guys makes his home in San Antonio."

"San Antonio?" Scott said with a sense of surprise in his voice.

"Does that mean something to you Scott?"

"Well, me and two of my buddies had a run-in with a bunch of assassins in San Antonio last year. But it's probably just a coincidence. What do ya have on the other guy?"

"Here's the other poster. This character is out of the New Mexico Territory."

"What?" Scott asked in disbelief. "Let me see that," Scott insisted as he grabbed the poster out of the marshal's hand. "Dang, two coincidences in one day. If that don't beat all," he said.

"What do you mean?"

"Well, in a few days I'm headed down to New Mexico and Arizona Territories on a mission for the governors of both territories.

But it has to be a coincidence," Scott mumbled to himself.

"What did you say, Scott?"

"Oh, I just said that this has to be a fluke. I don't see how it can have anything to do with why I'm headed down to the Southwest. I'll be dealing with the likes of the Apache when I arrive there."

"There's a reward on their heads for $500 each Scott. I can have it ready for you by this afternoon."

"Give it to Janice, marshal. Then she can buy one of those newfangled catalogue hats from Paris she's always talking about. That should help to calm her down after I stood her up for breakfast this morning," Scott said, as he walked out of the marshal's office still wondering why he had a target on his back.

After he walked over to the hotel and apologized to Janice, he ambled over to the gunsmith shop to say hello to Pops, and to purchase a new rifle for his trip to the Southwest.

Ole Pops was a rugged looking old codger in his 70's, bent over at the shoulders, probably never owned a razor in his life, but as sharp as an Arkansas toothpick.

When Scott opened the door to the gunsmith shop, it jingled a small bell for Pops to hear when he wasn't on the sales floor. Ninety percent of the time, Pops would be working on gun repairs in a small room toward the back of the shop. The front of the shop was for displaying and selling firearms, ammunition, gunpowder kegs, and other related goods.

When the bell rang, Pops looked around the corner and saw Scott.

"You're back, you young whippersnapper. Did you give Hayes a piece of your mind?" Pops asked.

"No Pops, that's not why I went there."

"Well then for what reason?"

"To accept a new mission. I'm headed to Apache country and I need a new rifle."

"Apache country? Why I remember the time when I fought Injuns on the Santa Fe Trail back in the 60's. Those redskins didn't have a chance. Why ten of them came out of nowhere all duded up in war paint and wearing feathers sticking out of their heads. They even painted up their horses. They thought ole Pops was a push over. Instead, they found a rascal, meaner than a rattlesnake. In five minutes, six were eating dust and the rest skedaddled like frightened little prairie dogs."

"I'm sure they did," Scott chuckled.

"Well they did," Pops boasted. "Anyway, what can I do for you today, son?"

"Pops, I need a repeating rifle for my trip. What do you have in stock that I can look at?"

"You're in luck; come on over here sonny and let me show you what just arrived."

Pops reached into a case with glass sliding doors and took out a fancy looking Henry rifle that was manufactured in 1866 and was just like new.

"This will scatter those Injuns here to Sunday," Pops said as he handed Scott the rifle.

"Does it shoot straight?" Scott asked already knowing the answer to that question from its reputation.

"You darn tooten it does. It's one of the best repeating rifles made. Why you can shoot the left wing off a gnat at 100 yards and then back up 50 yards and shoot off the right wing."

"Really?" Scott asked as he chuckled.

"That's right sonny. That's the story I was told."

"Well, give me all the specifics Pops, like only you know how to do."

"Well then listen up good now, ya hear? This is a .44 caliber rimfire, lever-action, breech-loading rifle. It holds 16 fully loaded cartridges. I recommend using brass rimfire cartridges with a 216 grain bullet over 25 grains of gunpowder. That will stop those Apache in their tracks. If Custer had this rifle at the horn, that peacock would be alive today to boast his victory. Back in the War Between the States, some of those Yankees toted these Henry's and whipped those rebels from here to Christmas. Why those rebels called that rifle..."

Just then, Scott and Pops chanted the familiar verse both at the same time.

"That damned Yankee rifle that they load on Sunday and shoot all week!"

"Iffen you know so much about the rifle, why are you asken so dang-blasted many questions?" Pops asked in an irritated voice. Then he laughed and said,

"50 bucks for the Henry and a box of shells. Whatdaya say?"

"You got a deal."

"Say sonny, ya ever gonna settle down, hitch that darlen Janice and buy this here gunsmith shop? Or ya gonna chase bad guys all over tarnation for the rest of your life?"

"Pops, I can't rightly say."

JESSE CALDWELL ARRIVES AT HIS SISTERS' CATTLE RANCH IN AUSTIN, TEXAS

After cattle ranching all of his life and driving his herds since 1866 up trails the likes of the Shawnee, the Chisholm and the Western Trails, to the various railheads in Kansas, ole Jesse wanted out.

Yep, he had enough of inhaling dust behind those filthy Texas longhorns, eating beans for breakfast, lunch and dinner, going two months without a bath, dealing with rustlers, vigilantes, and Indians, rounding up strays after killer stampedes, fighting amongst his drovers, and the vice and lawlessness that awaited the drovers at the end of the trail.

So, before Jesse headed out on his last cattle drive in 1879, which culminated in Dodge City, Kansas, he made a deal to sell his one third share of the family ranch to his two brothers-in-law who were married to his sisters Mary and Ruth.

His sisters' families had built their own homes on the ranch so Jesse made a temporary residence of the old family ranch house with the blessing of his younger sisters.

Even though he now had aspirations to pursue a career in politics, he had yet to make a move in that direction. Actually working for President Hayes on special projects with Scott and Thomas had kept all of them fairly busy for the last fifteen months or thereabouts.

When Jesse arrived at the train depot in Austin after his trip to Washington, D.C. to meet with Hayes and the governors, he walked over to the livery stable to rent a horse to ride back to the family ranch.

Upon arrival at the ranch, he stopped by his two sisters' homes to inform them that he was back home for a few weeks but had another assignment to go on. One of his sisters insisted on a family dinner the next day, Friday evening, so that Jesse could tell them all about his new project. He liked the idea so the plans were made and the dinner party went off as planned. At the dinner that night were his two sisters and his two brothers-in-law. It was after dinner that Jesse informed all of them that he was going on a mission for the governors of Arizona and New Mexico Territories and that he would be dealing with the likes of the Mescalero Apache and possibly some Chiricahua.

Jesse was no stranger to dealing with the Apache because growing up in Texas, he and his family experienced a few forays by the Lipan Apache. However, over in the Southwest, those Apache seemed to be more hostile and malicious than the ones he recollected dealing with in Central Texas.

Naturally, his sisters feared for Jesse's life but they also knew that if anyone could handle himself amongst those savages, being in heated exchanges and all, Jesse certainly was that one.

Every Saturday evening, for as long as Jesse could remember, there had been a tradition on the Caldwell's ranch. It was to have a steak dinner in the old log cabin bunkhouse for all the ranch hands and uncork a few jugs of rye and tequila.

Well the practice continued, even to this day, thanks to Jesse's brothers-in-law. This went a long way in keeping the morale elevated amongst the cowboys and the vaqueros who swapped an honest day's work for an honest day's pay on the ranges dotted with mesquite trees and prickly pear cacti.

It was during this evening that he was actually drilled more with pertinent questions by the ranch hands than he was by his own siblings the night before. While the steaks were being grilled outside over a mesquite fire and the pinto beans, seasoned with fatback for a real Texas down-home flavor, were boiling in the iron pot on cooky's tripod, the questions were two-stepping in, one after another, by the cow punchers who on this day seemed to be getting liquored up a little quicker than normal. However, the foreman kept tabs on the corks and knew when to start plugging the jugs before things got out of hand and "tipsy" became the word of the day.

The bunkhouse was toasty warm with the fire blazing in the old black potbelly stove. There was plenty of firewood stacked up next to the stove to keep it that-a-way all night long.

The bunks were on one side of the building, the potbelly stove was in the middle and a long rectangular wood dinner table that could seat a dozen wranglers or so was on the other side.

There was also a wood burning stove next to the wall about ten feet from the dinner table used to fry up eggs and country ham, stir up some red-eye gravy for dipping, and bake a couple dozen homemade biscuits before first light.

While the Texas cowboys were hearty eaters at first light, the three Mexican vaqueros were light eaters and easy to please. Give them their huevos y tocino (eggs and bacon) in the morning and that's all they needed to make them happy. But when they heard the words, El café que está sobre la mesa es para ti (that coffee on the table is for you), well, that really made their day.

When the cowboys walked into the bunkhouse, they would take off their holster belts and hang them on wood pegs on one side of the door and their wide brim hats and dusty old chaps on pegs on the other side of the door.

Their rifles were placed on a gun rack designed just for that purpose. And if everyone was in the mood, one of the vaqueros would reach down underneath his bed and slide out his guitar and strum a few tunes on it.

Well before dinner was served on this night, most of the cowpokes and Jesse were gathered around the potbelly stove sitting on chairs and shooting the breeze. A couple of the hands were sitting on their bunks nearby.

When they were all situated with drinks in their hands, the questioning began.

"Jesse, it's spreading like a prairie brush fire all over town about those kidnappings in the Southwestern territories, are you involved with that?" one of the ranch hands asked.

"Yep, and somehow, Hayes thinks that me and my other two pards can solve a problem that the U.S. Army hasn't been able to crack for two years."

"Can you?"

"Hell, I haven't the foggiest. As far as I know, all those hostages might be dead and we'll be chasing nothing but ghosts."

"Why did the Apache take to kidnapping so many women and children? I never heard of such a thing," another one of the ranch hands asked.

"Again, you're asking me a question that I do not have an answer for. Somethen ticked them off though and it had to be somethen that really got under their skin. I hear tell that those renegade Apache out there really hate Americans and Mexicans and kill and scalp anyone who crosses their paths. That's a sobering thought, isn't it? I must have been plum loco to take this assignment."

"Well then, why did you?"

Jesse stood up, walked over to the potbelly stove, opened the door and threw another log into the fire as some smoke escaped from the opening. The cowpokes were waiting anxiously for his response. Then he walked back to his chair, sat down, leaned back and said in an unpretentious and sincere tone,

"I guess I was brought up right by my parents and the missionaries at the old Spanish mission, San Xavier. If there is any chance that those women and children are still alive, well I would like to be one of the guys to help get them back home. It's like payback for the good Lord taking care of me and the Caldwell family all these years.

Scott, Thomas and I have been pretty lucky so far handling other projects for the government since we're all pretty straight thinkers and straight shooters. I don't know though, this one has a different feel about it that I just can't wrap my brain around. I just pray that I'm not shipped back to Texas in a pine box."

As the days went on, Jesse hung around the ranch and did typical ranch hand chores: branding calves, mending fences, and breaking horses with the three vaqueros. He was keeping himself busy and his mind off of the upcoming dangerous venture until one day when he received a strange and sobering telegram from Scott that was addressed to both Thomas O'Brien and him.

Thomas O'Brien   *Jesse Caldwell*
Scott County, Kentucky   *Austin, Texas*
One week ago, two men attempted to assassinate me on the streets of Dodge City. Both were wanted for murder and had a price on their heads. One was from San Antonio and the other was from a small town in the New Mexico Territory. Beings I was a Texas Ranger, I thought it could be a revenge killing for me shooting someone's brother. However, you know the dealings we three had in San Antonio and you know where we are headed. Could this be a coincidence or are we being targeted for some reason? Watch your backs and remember what Hayes told us when we left D.C. "Trust no one". See you next month. In the meantime, stay alert!

Scott Johnson
Dodge City, Kansas

CHAPTER FIVE:

Apache Warrior Becomes a Scout

With the receipt of Scott's warning, both Jesse and Thomas joined Scott in being on edge. "Trust no one" had a familiar but chilling ring to it. It was the same message Hayes gave the three men before their previous mission and it proved to be a viable warning.

Even though they knew very little about the kidnappings in the Southwest, they all kept up with Indian affairs around the country, as did most curious and knowledgeable men and women of their day. They made it a point to read their local newspapers and gazettes in towns which they passed through.

Each one of the three made it their business to stay abreast of all current events, not only in their own hometowns, but throughout the entire country since they had now become men of travel and adventure.

Scott had the Ford County Globe in Dodge City, Jesse had the Texas Press in Austin, and Thomas had the Scott County Star in Kentucky. All of them had read articles in the past about the vicious conflicts out West and in the Southwest between the white man and the various Indian tribes in the different regions.

They had all heard stories about Geronimo and his renegades and knew of the Apache brutality based on what they had read. And now the three frontiersmen were about to put themselves right smack in the middle of harm's way by jumping feet first into the deadly viper's nest.

It was nine days before the three's planned meeting date in Arizona. The time had arrived to start sending telegrams to each other and to make arrangements as to which town in Arizona they would initially use as a meeting place. It all depended upon which locality had train service that was closest to San Carlos Apache Indian Reservation. Jesse was the one who did the legwork for the *Three for Hire*.

He discovered that Tucson had just received rail service less than a year ago. The Southern Pacific railroad arrived in Tucson on March 20, 1880. When the railroad arrived, Tucson was already the largest settlement between the west coast and San Antonio with a population approaching 8,000.

With the introduction of the railroad, eastern building materials and construction techniques began arriving almost immediately to transform this dusty adobe town into a thriving modern U.S. city. The railroad brought wealthy entrepreneurs from the East who invested in mining, retailing, ranching and agriculture. It also brought all sorts of supplies to sell and to trade with Mexico.

Oh, it was a great time for this growing new metropolis; but in addition to all the new arrivals to ensure a prosperous future, there was still the morbid past that plagued this growing Southwestern town which could not be ignored and hidden from wealth seekers.

For the outskirts of Tucson was one of the areas raided by the Mescalero renegades in the recent past. So many innocent women and children were taken from their homes, snatched up in the dark of the night, and herded like animals; a treatment the Native Americans themselves were often all too familiar with. The captives were herded to an Apache hideout somewhere in the barren mountainous ranges of Arizona or New Mexico Territories.

Subsequently, amidst all of the excitement of a promising future for Tucson, the railroad was also bringing the *Three for Hire* to endeavor to do something the U.S. Army and local posse had failed to do, that is, find the surreptitious Mescalero Apache encampment and bring home the white hostages safe and sound, assuming of course, they were still alive.

With Jesse's research paying off and Tucson indeed being the perfect location to rendezvous, Jesse saddled up his palomino on this cool and cloudy morning and trotted to town to send off a telegram to both Scott and Thomas. He composed the telegram in the telegraph office and told the operator to send the missive immediately. It read:

Thomas O'Brien   *Scott Johnson*
Scott County, Kentucky   *Dodge City, Kansas*
The time has come. I found a place to meet on or around February 18th. It's Tucson, Arizona. It's a perfect location for these reasons: it has rail service, it is close to San Carlos, and it was one of the towns raided by the Mescalero Apache. Bring your weapons, ammunition and warm clothing. Some of the higher elevations get very cold this time of the year. When you arrive in town, sign into the local hotel closest to the train depot. We will stay there a day or two until we make all of our plans and procure our supplies. See you on February 18th or thereabouts. Don't need to respond unless there is a problem. Vaya con Dios, mi amigos.

Jesse Caldwell
Austin, Texas

Thomas made it a practice to ride into town in his buckboard every other day with his son Josh just to check to see if he had a telegram waiting for him at the telegraph office. On this day, he walked up the two steps and opened the door to the telegraph office and said,

"Good afternoon, Cal, any messages for me today?"

"Yes sir, Mr. O'Brien, I do today. It arrived an hour ago. Here it is," he said as he handed Thomas an envelope.

Thomas quickly opened it and read the telegram. It was the one he had been waiting for, instructions from Jesse.

"Is that the one?" Josh asked.

"Yes son, it is," Thomas replied.

Josh was visibly upset because he knew his pa was about to go on maybe the most dangerous adventure he had ever been on.

In the meantime, Scott too had a telegram waiting for him in Dodge City, Kansas. When Janice was walking down the opposite side of the street from the telegraph office, the operator yelled out from across the street,

"Hey Janice, I believe Scott just received the wire he's been waiting for."

Janice walked over to fetch it for Scott.

Scott was down the street apiece working in the gun shop with Pops. When Janice walked into the gun shop, all she had to do was to hold the telegram in the air and Scott knew what it was.

Scott quickly walked over to Janice, snatched it out of her hand, opened the envelope, and began reading it aloud. Even Pops could hear the words from where he was working, in back of the shop. Scott was visibly excited while Janice was discernibly upset.

Ole Pops came over and said,

"Well sonny, you better start target shooting with that new Henry rifle you bought. You're going to need to shoot straighter than a taut picket line, for sure."

Janice looked at Scott and she could not help but to show a worrisome look on her face. But that seemed to mean very little to Scott because he was now all fired-up to head southwest and take on the Mescalero, side-by-side with Thomas and Jesse, and retrieve those kidnapped women and children. The adventure was about to begin.

Thomas was coming from the farthest distance so he said his good-byes to his family on February 15th, three days before the meeting date of February 18th. Elizabeth and the children took Thomas to the Scott County Train Depot to see him off.

They all pretended that Thomas was just going on another adventurous business trip but in their hearts, they knew that this time was like no other. They were an educated family and read a lot of newspaper articles and books about the dealings with the Native Americans in the West and Southwest; and they especially knew about the brutal activities of the Apache whom Thomas would be facing head on, on their own turf.

The train was already at the station and the engineer was stoking up the fire in the firebox. Elizabeth and the children all hugged Thomas together before he boarded. Then Thomas, being the last one to board, stepped up onto the train car with his baggage in one hand and toting his rifle with the other. He walked into the car and sat down at a window seat.

He was sitting in place for about one minute when the conductor yelled out,

"All aboard!"

The train then began to slowly move away from the depot while the O'Brien family waved good-bye with tears flowing down the cheeks of his twin daughters and his wife. Josh took it like a man.

There was no stopping him now. Thomas was on his way to rendezvous with the Apache.

A few states to the west, Scott was making ready to board the train in Dodge City. He tied up all of his loose ends in town and asked Janice to move into his rental house until he returned, whenever that would be. She lived in the hotel which her father owned but would honor Scott's request because someday she had hoped to be living there permanently with Scott as his wife, and buy that house from the owner.

Janice tagged along to the train depot with Scott as one would expect. However, for the first time ever, Janice's pa and ole Pops went along as well to see Scott off. One can only surmise that Scott's friends did not have a good feeling about this project.

Much farther to the south in Austin, Texas, Jesse was traveling to the train depot in a buckboard with his two sisters and was being escorted on horseback by his two brothers-in-law and three older ranch hands who he had known for many years. They were all going to the train depot to see Jesse off today.

Jesse's two sisters knew better than anyone of the ways of the Apache because they witnessed the horrors and mutilations by Lipan Apache raids on neighboring ranches in Central Texas where they grew up. Plus they knew about Scott's telegram and the attempt on his life.

This was a sad day for Mary and Ruth because they feared, now more than ever, for their brother's life. Oh, they knew that Jesse could handle himself as well as the next guy, but that seemed to offer little comfort on this unusually somber day in Austin, Texas.

Jesse was the first to arrive in Tucson. He was quite surprised to see the progress: how buildings were going up all around town, and the hustle and bustle taking place in the streets of Tucson. This town was aiming to be a booming metropolis situated in one of the last frontiers of the Old West.

The first thing Jesse did when he stepped off the train was to ask the depot manager where the nearest hotel was.

"It's just down Main Street apiece."

"Is it in walking distance from here?"

"You betchya, fella. Walk behind the depot and that there is Main Street. Then look down to the left, and the tallest building you see is the hotel. It's a two story building. The name of the hotel is, 'The Old Pueblo Inn'. It's named after the first residents in this area, the Pueblo Indians. That's your history lesson for today stranger. Now have a great visit and stay clear of the Apache," the depot manager said jokingly as he turned and walked away from Jesse.

Jesse saw no humor in the facetious warning for obvious reasons. He followed the easy directions and signed into the hotel first thing. He told the Mexican hotel clerk,

"I would like for you to save two rooms for my friends. They're due to arrive in town within the next couple of days. Their names are Scott Johnson and Thomas O'Brien."

"How long will you three be staying, señor?"

"Not long, maybe two days or so. Say, is this a fairly peaceful town?" Jesse asked.

"Sure it is. We generally only have uno o dos killings a night over at the saloon. It could be worse," the Mexican hotel clerk replied. "If you go there to drink or gamble, I suggest you pack your smoke wagons if you know what I mean."

"Si te entiendo," Jesse said, meaning he understood. "I'll be packing both of them. Muchas gracias, amigo."

"De nada," the inn clerk replied.

Jesse then took his bags to his room, unpacked and spent the rest of the day roaming around town. It wasn't until the next day that both Thomas and Scott arrived in Tucson. Scott arrived on the morning train and Thomas arrived on the afternoon train. Both signed in at the inn and the three met up in the lobby at five bells and went over to the Longhorn Café to eat dinner.

While at dinner, they made plans for their trip to San Carlos. They figured they needed a covered wagon (Jesse already had that taken care of) to haul their supplies around which consisted of: plenty of extra clothing for the cold nights, food, cooking pots and skillets, a campfire tripod, eating utensils, coffee pot and coffee cups, and plenty of Arbuckle's. Arbuckle's was the coffee of choice for the *Three for Hire.*

Arbuckle's was short for Arbuckle's coffee. The revolutionary concept for this coffee was created by two brothers in the post-Civil War era of the 19th century. They were John and Charles Arbuckle. They were the first ones to develop the idea of selling "roasted" coffee and they did it mainly in one pound packages.

Before their ingenious creation, coffee was sold as "green" coffee beans and had to be roasted in an iron skillet over an open campfire out on the trail or on a wood burning stove in the comforts of home. One thing you could say about the consistency of the flavor of coffee after roasting green coffee beans out on the trail was that the flavor was always inconsistent. One burnt bean would ruin the whole batch.

However, Arbuckle's coffee was perfectly roasted and was of consistently fine quality making the sipping of hot Joe a real pleasure around the open campfire during anytime of the day.

Arbuckle's coffee became famous in the Old West and was a huge hit in cow towns and boomtowns like Dodge City and Tombstone. It truly became known as the Original Cowboy Coffee.

Fresh biscuits made in a Dutch oven, bacon and country ham fried in an iron skillet, pinto beans seasoned with fatback, red-eye gravy for dunking biscuits, topped off with a tin cup of hot Arbuckle's, made a cowboy feel like he was some sort of a special breed of high-class royalty.

After dinner, the three went over to the saloon for a nightcap and then back to the hotel. When they walked into the lobby, the man behind the desk called Jesse over. The other two followed.

The Mexican innkeeper then said in broken English,

"Two men came into the inn while you were all out to eat. They asked to see the sign-in book. One man ran his finger down the names on the page and stopped at each of your names like this."

The innkeeper demonstrated how it was done.

"Did they say who they were?" Jesse asked.

"No señor."

"What did they look like?" Scott inquired.

"Like pistoleros," the innkeeper said.

"Sounds like we're being trailed," Scott suggested.

"Yeah, but by whom, and more importantly, why?" Thomas asked.

"Yeah, and who are they working for?" Scott questioned.

Then Scott looked at Jesse and said,

"I don't like it. I almost got myself killed up in Dodge City last month and I have no idea who those bushwhackers were working for, and why they had intentions to put me down."

"What are we gonna do about it Scott?" Thomas asked. "You were a Texas Ranger, how do we go about protecting ourselves against criminals or assassins we don't know and we don't even see?"

"Hell, I don't know. All I can tell you is to stay vigilant at all times. Don't go anywhere without your guns, don't turn your back on anyone and don't trust a soul. If you're sitting in a saloon or in a café, sit with your back to the wall so you can't take a bullet from behind."

"Wow, I got the feeling this trip is gonna be as much fun as jumping naked on a Texas cactus," Jesse commented in a halfway joking fashion. "Well we can't do anything more tonight. When you hit your bunks, make sure you sleep with one eye open and one finger on the trigger. If you come into my room tonight to borrow my whiskey, you better announce yourself first or you'll be pushing up daisies tomorrow morning on Boot Hill with all those other saddle tramps. Savvy?"

"Yeah, we gotchya Tex," Thomas said flippantly.

All three of the men made sure they locked their doors and windows that night and none of them slept sound due to the circumstances that were bestowed upon them.

When morning arrived, they all met in the inn's café for breakfast. Biscuits and gravy, bacon and eggs and freshly made Arbuckle's sure hit the spot before traveling on their precarious journey to the San Carlos Apache Indian Reservation. Not only did they have to watch for renegade Apache, but now they also had to keep a sharp eye out for would-be gunslinger assassins, lurking in the shadows.

Before Scott and Thomas arrived in town yesterday, Jesse had already purchased a covered wagon and four mules from the livery stable. Mules would be a least likely target by the Apache renegades compared to horses. The wagon was basically set up as a chuck wagon which was perfect for their trip. He also bought three well broke trail horses and all the tack they needed along with saddle scabbards for their rifles.

After breakfast, all three walked over to the livery stable to pick up the wagon, the mules and the horses and purchased several 50 pound sacks of grain for the 7 beasts of burden. They hitched up the four mules, saddled up one trail horse and tethered the other two to the back of the wagon. Scott and Thomas were gonna ride in the wagon and Jesse would take the point on horseback.

The next step was to go to the general store and load up on grub, cooking and other supplies, and extra clothing. It took about forty-five minutes to figure out what they needed and then purchase it. President Hayes bankrolled the three but the territorial governors were to pay the U.S. Government back for the three's advance.

When everything was bought and paid for, a couple of the store clerks helped the three load up the covered wagon and with that, they were off on their dangerous expedition to San Carlos which was just over 100 miles northeast of Tucson.

They figured they could travel it in four days if they rode from sunup to sundown and put in about 27 miles per day. Luckily, there was an established route which they could follow all the way to the reservation.

Since the three had traveled together before, they each had their specific duties and they abided by their strict unwritten rules. Jesse did the cooking since Thomas didn't even know how to boil water. Scott made the coffee because Jesse's coffee tasted like Louisiana swamp water, and Thomas washed the skillets, pots and dishes because being spoiled by his wife, Elizabeth, he didn't know much about nothing, when it came to preparing anything, to be consumed by anyone; except of course for one thing, he knew how to "de-skin a tater".

The trip from Tucson to San Carlos was difficult. It was mighty cold and the days seemed very long and were extremely worrisome. They had to be on their guard at all times watching for renegade Apache warriors and for strangers, the pistolero type, who were out to get them for reasons which were still undefined.

The three reached the San Carlos Apache Indian Reservation on the fourth day of their trip as planned. They were told to meet with the Indian Agent who was J.C. Tiffany. Tiffany was supposed to receive a telegram from the Governor of the Arizona Territory to confirm that Jesse, Scott and Thomas would arrive to pick up an Indian scout who was an Apache police for the reservation.

The three assumed that the correspondence was taken care of and things would be good to go.

When the three rode into the main part of the reservation where there were buildings surrounding a courtyard, they spotted Indian huts, known as wickiups, scattered about the hillside. Most of the Indians walking around in view were thin and the children looked undernourished. Some were coughing and it appeared that they didn't have the proper amount of clothing on to protect them from the cold. It was not what the three expected to see.

They were surrounded by soldiers when they drove up to the building that had a sign above the door that read, "San Carlos Indian Agent". Scott and Thomas jumped off of the wagon and Jesse dismounted his horse and wrapped the reins around the hitching rail. They walked up five steps of the wide stairway and knocked on the door to the agent's office. A soldier opened the door and asked them to state their business.

"I'm Jesse Caldwell and this is Scott Johnson and Thomas O'Brien and we're here on official government business at the request of the Governor of the Arizona Territory."

"We've been expecting you, come on in," came a voice from a man sitting behind a desk on the far side of the room next to the wood burning stove. He then stood up and walked over to the three and shook hands with each one as he said,

"I'm J. C. Tiffany, the new Indian Agent here. Call me J.C. It's a pleasure to meet you. Pull up a few chairs in front of my desk and we'll talk. Corporal, pour these men a cup of coffee. I presume you three all drink coffee, don't ya?"

"Yes sir, we do. Thank you," Jesse said as the other two nodded in agreement.

So the three pulled up chairs as J.C. sat back down at his desk and said,

"I heard about why you were hired, and that you need a scout. We have one picked out for you. He's one of our Apache police here at the reservation, and his name is Meta. He'll make you a good scout."

The Indian agent then took a pipe out of his top drawer and began filling it with tobacco from a pouch he kept on the top of his desk while the three looked on. Then he struck a match and began puffing to light the tobacco. When it was fully lit, he took a big draw, and then blew it up in the air and said with an arrogant tone in his voice which surprisingly came out of nowhere,

"Tell me, what makes everyone think you three guys can do something the Army and the posse were not able to do? What makes you three so special?"

Jesse picked up on the sour tone and dished it right on back.

"They say we're the best in the West, so I guess it must be true."

J. C. snickered and said,

"That so?"

"Yep, that's so!" Jesse said as he took a sip from his coffee cup while Scott and Thomas tried to hide their smiles at Jesse's whimsical comeback. "What else do you wanna know?"

"Nothing," J. C. said, "except, when do you want to meet your scout?"

"The sooner the better," Jesse replied.

"Corporal, go find Meta and meet us in the courtyard. We'll be out there as soon as we see you two."

The corporal opened the door and turned around and said,

"Sir, he's out there now."

"Good, let's go join him," J. C. suggested.

So they all walked out to the courtyard. The three were anxious to meet their new scout. J.C. did the introductions, sort of. He couldn't remember the names of the three or so he pretended as his arrogance seemed to be one step above the egotism of a narcissist.

As Jesse began to do the introductions, Meta spotted a soldier about 50 feet behind Jesse removing his rifle from his saddle scabbard. To Meta, this was very strange and his instincts told him to stay alert. As Meta began shaking hands with the three, he noticed the soldier aiming the rifle directly at Jesse. He quickly pushed Jesse aside and yelled,

"Get down!" just as the gun went off.

The bullet struck Meta in the chest, knocking him down, as the others drew their pistols and ducked for cover.

The shooter then threw down his rifle, quickly mounted his horse and began galloping away at top speed. Another Apache police swiftly ran over to the rifle, picked it up, aimed and fired.

It was a direct hit!

The assassin slumped in the saddle, then fell off his horse and tumbled down the rocky hillside, while the mount continued to gallop away without a rider.

When they saw that the coast was clear and the shooter appeared to be dead, Jesse knelt down beside Meta and checked to see if he was still breathing. He was not.

Jesse looked up at the others, paused and then said, "This man just saved my life."

Scott and Thomas looked on in shock. This had a bigger meaning than what J.C. knew.

There was no doubt now that the *Three for Hire* were being targeted. Their reputation preceded them and for some reason, somebody wanted them dead, every single one of them; but who?

"Corporal, get a couple of men and load that shooter into that buckboard and bring him back here," J.C. ordered, "let's see who he is."

So they did. When they brought the limp and lifeless soldier's body back, they gathered around the wagon.

"Do you know who this soldier is corporal?" J.C. asked. "I don't recognize him."

"Yes sir, he came in last night, after you left the post. He said he was passing through after visiting his family and going back to his fort in the Indian Territory and wanted a place to stay for the night."

"Well, what's his name and where's he from, corporal?" J.C. anxiously asked.

"His name is Sergeant Tyrus Owens sir, out of Fort Sill."

"Fort Sill? Who was his commanding officer?" J. C. inquired.

"Colonel Baxter, sir. At least that's what I think he said."

That name struck a bell with the *Three for Hire* as they looked at each other in disbelief.

"Send a telegram to Baxter and tell him what happened here and see if he can explain this incident," J.C. ordered.

"Yes sir, I'll get right on it."

The corporal immediately went inside and composed a short telegram and gave it to the telegraph operator to send. It read:

Colonel Baxter
Fort Sill
Urgent
Today at the San Carlos Apache Indian Reservation a soldier under your command attempted an assassination on three men working for the territorial governors of New Mexico and Arizona. An Indian scout in the line of fire was shot and killed instead. The assassin's name is Sergeant Tyrus Owens. He has been shot down and did not survive. Can you explain his actions?

> *J. C. Tiffany*
> *Indian Agent*
> *San Carlos*
> *Arizona Territory*

Within five minutes of receipt of the wire, Colonel Baxter fired off a telegram right back. It read:

J. C. Tiffany
Indian Agent
San Carlos
Arizona Territory
I am shocked by this news. I met the three gentlemen you speak of when I was in Washington, D.C. I have no explanation for Owens' actions. He deserted his post four weeks ago. For your information, he has family in Pittsburgh, Pennsylvania. Trust you will notify his kin.

> *Colonel Baxter*
> *Fort Sill*

After the corporal received Baxter's response, he brought it out to J.C. to read. J.C., Jesse, Scott, Thomas, and a few other soldiers were still in the courtyard surrounding the wagon with Owens' body. They also placed the dead Apache scout in the wagon as well.

J.C. read the telegram and then told the corporal and a few other soldiers to bury both bodies in the reservation's cemetery.

Then J.C. said to Jesse, Scott and Thomas,

"We're gonna have to find you another scout. We have only a few Apache left who speak both Apache and English. I don't know how much you know about the different tribes of Apache but we have several here at the reservation and many of them don't get along with each other. Depending on where you intend to look for the kidnappers will determine which tribe will have a potential scout who is familiar with that area. Does that make sense to you?"

"Yes it does," Jesse said. "We're thinking about starting south of Apache Pass in the Chiricahua Mountains."

"Any particular reason?" J. C. asked.

"Well the Mescalero kidnappers need plenty of food to feed their band of renegades and the kidnapped women and children. The governors told us that there's plenty of game up in those mountains," Jesse said. "Plus they told us that there are many small streams up that-a-way which are good water sources."

"How long will it take for you to find a scout, J.C.?" Thomas asked.

"I'm sure we can have one ready for you by tomorrow. I'll have an officer work on it today. In the meantime, we have a guest bunkhouse you three can stay in tonight. It's right over there," J.C. said as he pointed to a small building on the other side of the courtyard. "That's where Owens stayed last night, I would surmise."

"Yes sir, it is," the corporal confirmed.

"In the meantime gentlemen, I recommend that you don't meander around the reservation on your own. It appears that it might be too dangerous based on what just happened here. In fact, I suggest you stay within the confines of that bunkhouse," J.C. advised.

"Don't worry about that, we've had enough excitement for one day," Scott said.

"Well good then, we'll send you some food over at five o'clock for dinner. Till then, enjoy your unscheduled stay, gentlemen. I'll be leaving you on your own now. I have a stack of paperwork waiting for me in my office," J. C. remarked.

With that, the three strolled over to the bunkhouse to check out their sleeping quarters. It was a cozy little one room log cabin with four beds, a square wooden table with four chairs, and a wood burning stove.

The first thing the three did was to gather firewood from a stack outside the cabin and build a roaring fire to warm the place up quickly. Then Thomas went out to their covered wagon to fetch a bottle of tequila, and some jerky to chew on.

While they sat around waiting for time to pass, Jesse found a deck of cards on a shelf and suggested they play some poker to stay busy. However, Thomas wanted to get serious and talk about the unprecedented attempts on their lives.

"Jesse, I'd love to play some poker with you but we have to talk. What the hell is going on? Two men almost wiped out Scott in Dodge City, two pistoleros were checking us out in Tucson and now this today; some soldier from Fort Sill tried to assassinate one of us. I mean, who would want us dead and why? I thought we were here to help. If I knew we were targets, I'm not sure I would have accepted this job."

"Do you want out?" Jesse asked.

"You know better than that Jesse. I don't want out. I want answers. Do any of you guys have an idea of who would wanna make buzzard bait out of us? When Hayes told us to trust no one, he wasn't just whistling Dixie. We even have soldiers shooting at us now. I can't wait to see what our Apache scout tries to pull on us," Thomas said.

"Thomas has a good point Jesse," Scott said. "Where do we go from here?"

"Hell I don't know. What I do know is that there are a lot of wives, mothers, and children depending on somebody to get them back home to their families. That's why we took this job," Jesse reconfirmed.

"Yeah, I know," Thomas remarked, "I just hope I can get back to mine in a vertical position as opposed to a horizontal one."

The other two looked at Thomas and thought the same way. However, after back and forth discussions the rest of the day and throwing doubts on the table like anteing up chips in a poker game, the three agreed to surge on.

When the next morning rolled around, the corporal, whom they met the day before, came over to the guest bunkhouse. He knocked on the door and told the three that they were invited to the mess hall for breakfast with the other soldiers and that they had found a Chiricahua Apache who agreed to scout for them as long as his services were needed.

Well this was good news on both counts. They were mentally ready for a hearty breakfast and they were elated that a scout was found that met their needs.

After breakfast J.C. took the three out to meet their Apache scout. His name was Chato (1854 – August 13, 1934). It wasn't like he came without baggage though. He was once a Chiricahua Apache warrior who carried out raids on settlers in the Arizona Territory in the 1870's. He was also a protégé of the great Apache chief, Cochise. He was with Cochise when he surrendered in 1872 and was with the tribe after Cochise's death when the tribe was moved to San Carlos Apache Indian Reservation here in southern Arizona. In the 70's he had slipped out of the reservation with other warriors including Geronimo once but returned because of the need for food.

Chato was now settling into the realities of living the reservation life. The soldiers and J.C. all felt comfortable that Chato would make the *Three for Hire* a good trusted scout.

Thomas wanted to have a good long talk with the so-called retired Apache warrior before he gave his OK to accepting Chato as their scout. Jesse and Scott thought that was a pretty good idea because all three kept the "trust no one" warning in their minds now more than ever; so the three took the would-be scout into the bunkhouse and asked J.C. and the corporal to join them.

The *Three for Hire* sat at the table with Chato and the other two grabbed two chairs from the corner and did the same.

Chato had the looks of an Apache warrior. He was five feet ten inches tall, had a dark complexion, and wore his hair in the typical Apache warrior style; it was jet black, straight, hung about eight inches below the shoulders and he wore a red cloth that went around his head just above his eyes to hold his hair in place. If you feared the Apache, his looks didn't help any because he was very intimidating looking.

Jesse started the conversation,

"Do you know why we have asked you to be a scout for us Chato?"

"I do not," Chato answered.

"Before I begin to tell you why, I need to know how well you know our language."

"I speak it well," Chato said, "I also read some."

"That's good, we need an interpreter. Well then let me tell you why we need a scout. A group of Mescalero Apache went on the warpath a couple of years ago and kidnapped women and children from various towns in the Arizona and New Mexico Territories. We don't know why and we don't know where they are, or if the hostages are even still alive. The Mescalero Apache were led by Lone Wolf and joined by an Apache named Victorio. Do you know these two Apache?"

"I have heard the name of Lone Wolf, the Mescalero Apache, but I do not know him. I know of Victorio. He was a warrior and chief of the Chihenne band of the Chiricahua. I met him here at San Carlos four years ago. He left and came back and left again due to the bad conditions here. He killed many Americans and Mexicans both. He was also once leader of a band of Chiricahua and Mescalero Apache. I hear he was killed four maybe five moons ago by the Mexican Army in the Tres Castillos Mountains south of El Paso, Texas.

I also hear that Kas-tziden (1800 – 1896), "broken foot" joined up with the Mescalero, Lone Wolf who you speak of. He is an old man now but very mean with a heart full of hate for Americans and Mexicans. This is not good for the captives. Kas-tziden may convince Lone Wolf to kill all the white hostages."

"Oh no, tell us more about him if you can," Thomas insisted.

"He knows Geronimo well. He was married to a sister of Geronimo. He also fought side-by-side with Mangas Coloradas and then Victorio against many Americans and Mexicans. He has killed many white-eyes on both sides on what you call the border of Mexico and America. He particularly hates blue bellies.

The Mexicans call him Nana because of his age. In your language it means "grandma". But Nana is not like an old woman, but more like an older mountain lion and ten times as mean. Hear me well. Even at his age, it is told that he has the courage, cruelty and strength of a young warrior. This I believe, and this does not hold well for your people, the captives."

After that revelation, Jesse, Scott and Thomas stared at each other with an uneasy look and began really wondering if they were in fact, going out on a ghost hunt.

They all were impressed at the knowledge of Chato about the other Apache leaders but needed to hear more information about him yet, before they could even begin to trust him as their scout.

"Tell us more about yourself, Chato," Scott requested.

"Not much more to tell. I was with Cochise for years. I became friends with his two sons Taza (1843 – September 26, 1876) and Naiche (1857 – 1919)."

"What were they like?" Thomas asked.

"Taza was the oldest son of Cochise. He taught me and Naiche to ride and hunt. Taza became chief of the Chiricahuas when Cochise died. Taza died visiting Washington, D.C. in 1876 of sickness the white man calls pneumonia.

Naiche then became chief of the Chiricahua. He did not want to live on the reservation so he joined up with Geronimo in Mexico."

"How do you know this information?" Scott asked.

Then J.C. jumped in and said,

"Many Indians that leave the reservation end up returning because they can't find enough food to survive when they're continuously dodging U. S. and Mexican soldiers. So they come back before they die of starvation or getting themselves shot and killed for being renegades. When they do return, they bring with them stories of other Apache traveling outside of the reservations."

At this point, Jesse thought that they learned enough about Chato's background and decided to wind up the questioning. He then leaned forward, looked Chato squarely in his eyes, and said,

"OK Chato, here's the deal. We need your help to find Lone Wolf and the white hostages. We want to get them back alive with no one getting injured or killed. We also need to find out why Lone Wolf conducted those raids in the first place. We think something or someone set him off and we want to find out who or what it was. We're getting word that he is hiding out in the Chiricahua Mountains. We want your help to find Lone Wolf and the renegades and get the hostages back safely. Of course, that includes us too. So the question is, are you willing to help us, Chato?"

Chato stood up, walked over to the closed door, then turned around and said,

"I will help you on one condition."

"What's that?" Scott asked.

"I will tell you three, not these two," Chato said, meaning he didn't want J. C. and the corporal to hear his demand.

J.C. was not happy with Chato's comment but the two left the cabin at Jesse's request.

"Now, what is it Chato?" Jesse asked.

"I will go with you if you promise that you will tell the father in Washington to treat the Apache on the reservation with more respect. We are treated like dogs and we are not dogs. We are no different than you. The white-eyes took away our freedom and our horses and weapons to hunt our own food yet food is scarce. We also need white man's medicine for our sick. We only ask that we be treated as they would treat the white man. Can you do this for my people?"

"You have my word on it, Chato," Jesse committed.

"Well then, when do we leave?" Chato asked.

"We leave as soon as we get packed. Get your things together and load them into our covered wagon out front. We'll purchase a horse from the soldiers for you and we'll give you a weapon when the time comes that you need one," Jesse promised.

Within an hour, they were all packed and ready to go. J.C. came outside to see them off but didn't say much being suspicious of Chato's private conversation with the three. Jesse thanked J.C. for his hospitality and help in finding a scout. Then they all shook hands and J. C. said,

"Good luck men, you're gonna need it."

CHAPTER SIX:

The Search for the Renegade Apache

On February 2, 1881, a new county was created in the Arizona Territory. The *Three for Hire* read about it in the *Weekly Arizona Citizen, Tucson Pima County Arizona Territory*, while in Tucson, but they paid it no mind. It appeared with no fanfare and was in the fifth column under the heading "The Legislature". About halfway down the column, there was just one sentence that read, "The Governor has signed the bill creating the county of Cochise".

Cochise County was created out of the eastern portion of the district known as Pima County. The new region took its name from the legendary chief of the Chiricahua Apache, Cochise. With the formation of this new province, came the formation of a new county seat. It was one of the last real boomtowns of the Old West. It was Tombstone, Arizona, which was founded in 1879 by Ed Schieffelin and was incorporated in 1881. Tombstone would remain the county seat until 1929. In that year Bisbee became the new county seat.

The first sheriff of the new Cochise County was Johnny Behan (October 24, 1844 - June 7, 1912) who was one of the main observers on that infamous day on October 26, 1881 when the Earps and Doc Holliday took on their lawless and cattle rustling adversaries at the O.K. Corral.

Cochise County was the area in which Jesse, Scott, Thomas and their Indian scout Chato would search for Lone Wolf and his captives. When they were in San Carlos, the three spent no time developing search plans. They just wanted to high-tail out of there, faster than a mule deer being chased by a hungry cougar, fearing that there might be another attempt on their lives by someone who had a bellyache with them for reasons unknown. So they headed southeast at the suggestion of their scout.

After traveling for about six hours, they spotted a small adobe structure about 300 yards or thereabouts in front of them near the base of a mountain range. Chato agreed to check it out while the others waited in place. They were close enough to watch every move Chato made. Chato rode up to the building and circled it. Then he jumped off his horse, cautiously peered through the open door and cased the place. It was all clear so he waved the three in.

The building was abandoned and from the chaotic looks of the inside, it had fallen prey to an Apache raid sometime in the past. The table and chairs were turned over and tossed around, cooking pots and various kitchen utensils were thrown off the shelves and scattered about the floor. The place was in shambles.

There were noticeable bloodstains on the floor, probably shed by the victims of the raid. Thomas discovered and picked up a doll on the floor in the corner that probably belonged to a helpless little girl and he couldn't help but to think of his own two lovely daughters. It strengthened his resolve to do everything in his power to find the kidnapped women and children and return them to their homes, safe and sound.

Jesse surmised that their bodies were buried in those three fresh graves marked with piles of rocks about 100 feet from the adobe structure. The burial place gave the appearance that it was a family of three that was slain of which one was indeed a small child, considering the length of the grave. Soldiers must have found the remains and hopefully buried them before the coyotes braved their way through the front door and feasted off the decaying cadavers.

As morbid as it may have seemed, this was a great place for the four searchers to spend the night and make their plans for their upcoming journey. There was plenty of firewood on hand, which would keep the adobe structure nice and toasty on this very cold night in late February.

Ole Thomas was quietly hoping that they would find more abandoned settlements along the way (not because of the same reason, mind you) since he was the one least excited about bedding down outside next to the dying embers of a burnt out campfire underneath the stars on insufferably cold, bone-chilling nights.

Thomas' wish would probably come true because the entire territories of New Mexico and Arizona were flecked with old quaint "adobe" structures which were vacated due to decades of numerous vicious attacks by renegade Apache.

The word "adobe", meaning "mud brick" has been around 4,000 years and can actually be traced back to a Middle Egyptians' word meaning the same. The English language borrowed the word "adobe" from the Spaniards in the early 1800's.

Adobe is a natural building material made from sand, clay, water and fibrous or organic material which could be sticks, straw or even animal manure. The builders would shape the mixture into bricks by using frames and then allow the bricks to dry in the sun. Adobe mortar was used to set the bricks.

These structures were very durable and were extremely long lasting. They were built by indigenous people of the Americas in the southwestern United States and regions of South America and Mesoamerica (a region and cultural area extending approximately from central Mexico to northern Costa Rico) for several thousand years.

The Pueblo people built their structures with handfuls and basketfuls of adobe material until the Spanish taught them how to make bricks from the same substance. Spaniards made adobe bricks dating all the way back to the eighth century B.C.

While the rescue party was spending the night in this old abandoned adobe house, not far from them in the new county seat of Cochise County, the boomtown of Tombstone was in the process of constructing a two story adobe building that would continue to be the largest standing adobe structure in existence in the southwestern United States all the way into the twenty-first century.

It was called the Schieffelin Hall and was built in 1881 by Albert Schieffelin (July 26, 1849 – October 13, 1885), the brother of Tombstone's founder, Ed Schieffelin, and by a man by the name of William Harwood of whom not much is known.

The Schieffelin Hall was a first class opera house, theater, recital hall and meeting place for Tombstone citizens. It was constructed on the corner of Freemont Street and Fourth Street and opened on June 8, 1881. It seated 450 people on the floor and 125 people in the gallery.

When it opened, it was said to be, "The largest most elaborate theater between El Paso, Texas and San Francisco, California."

After the *Three for Hire* determined that this was a safe location to spend the night, one of the first things they did was to gather firewood and strike up a roaring fire in the large adobe fireplace to take the biting chill out of the air in their temporary living quarters. Then they unpacked their bedrolls and some of their food, along with their weapons and ammunition from their covered wagon. They loaded their weapons and kept them close at hand because one could never be too vigilant since they were in a region where Apache raids were too often realistic and not just a fabricated tale from an eastern dime novel.

Thomas straightened up the place while Scott put on a pot of Arbuckle's and Jesse prepared dinner. Chato wanted to stay outside and keep a watchful eye on the place until nightfall. The three thought it was a good idea because they were unaware if renegades were still in the area. However, Chato's motive for staying on the alert was because he knew something the other three did not; for on this particular night, it was not a band of renegade Apache he was apprehensive about.

After dinner that night, with just the dim light from the flaming logs in the fireplace, the four sat around the table and began laying out their plans over the last few cups of Arbuckle's left in the coffee pot.

Jesse, Scott and Thomas had to rely solely on Chato's discretion on where to begin the search for Lone Wolf and his captives and how much territory to cover.

Jesse was the first to begin the discussion.

"Chato, where do you think we should start the search for Lone Wolf and the hostages?"

"Do you mean all four of us, or all six of us?"

"What do you mean all six of us?" Scott asked as the other two appeared to look as confused as Scott about Chato's strange and unexpected inquiry.

"Two men have been following us for several miles now," Chato said. "Are they with us?"

"No they're not with us, when did you spot them?" Scott asked.

"About two miles outside of San Carlos. I did not know if they were with us or not."

Scott then looked at Jesse and said, "Those must be the two pistoleros who were checking us out in Tucson."

"If that's true," Thomas said anxiously as he stood up and looked out the window into the dark of the night. "What the hell do they want with us?"

"Well if that doesn't beat all," Scott said, "we have Apache in front of us and pistol toting gunslingers behind us. Nothing like getting caught up in crossfire, eh guys?"

"Chato, you just continue to look for the renegades and we'll keep a sharp eye out for those two saddle tramps behind us," Jesse said. "In the meantime, where do you suggest we begin our search?"

"We should begin just south of here by two suns, in the Dos Cabezas Mountains (the name means 'two heads' in English for the twin granite peaks, Dos Cabezas peaks). This is the mountain range on the north side of Apache Pass," Chato said as he went on to convincingly explain the reasons why.

"There are many good places for Lone Wolf to hide out and camp. There are several natural springs and an abundance of wildlife for food. Plus there are fertile canyon floors for growing, along with many sources of nuts and wild berries to eat. From high on top of the mountains, you can see a great distance into Sulphur Springs Valley in the direction the sun sets in the evening and into San Simon Valley in the direction the sun rises in the morning."

"That sounds like a good place to start. How well do you know the mountains, Chato?" Scott asked.

"I know these mountains well. I traveled through them while in hunting parties. There are trails where a wagon can go and there are other places where it cannot. In many places we will need to make camp and leave our wagon there and travel on horseback. We should travel in a large circle pattern and continue to a small circle pattern to be sure we make a good sweep," Chato suggested as he drew imaginary circles on the table with his forefinger while explaining his strategy.

"How long will it take to cover this mountain range?" Jesse inquired.

"Several moons."

"That's no good," Scott countered, "the hostages may not survive that long."

"They may already be dead but even if not, there is no other choice," Chato insisted, "although, I will make sure we search only the land that the Apache and hostages can survive on."

After the plans were made and the strategy was laid out, Jesse suggested that they bolt the door, hit the bunks and try to get a good night's sleep because tomorrow, like all the other future days ahead were bound to be very arduous and difficult. Scott, Jesse, and Thomas, each laid rights to a bed while Chato, after throwing more wood on the fire, claimed a spot on the floor next to the fireplace. He slept on an "Euklisia rug" that Jesse picked up in Tucson. It paid Chato no mind sleeping on the floor, because that's all he knew.

The warmth from the intense fire, the sound of the crackling bark of the seasoned pine logs, and the faint distant songs of the howling coyotes, aided the *Three for Hire* in the drifting from a worn-out semi-consciousness state, to a welcomed deep sleep. It was just what the proverbial doctor ordered.

First light came by too quickly to suit the three frontiersmen but rise and shine was greeted by a nice warm fire that Chato kept stoking throughout the night. Like most Apache, he was a light sleeper and heard every sound nature and the surroundings threw at him. His main concern was that no one made off with the mules and the trail horses during the night. That would spell disaster.

Before coffee and breakfast, Chato was the first to go outside and scout things out to make sure those two gunslingers trailing them did not move in closer during the night for the kill. Chato jumped on his horse and made a 200 yard circle around the adobe house but saw no signs of the pistoleros. That was good news to Jesse, Scott and Thomas.

After breakfast, they put out the fire, packed their gear, hitched up the mules, saddled a horse while tethering two to the back of the wagon, and headed south toward the first location to search in the Dos Cabezas Mountains. Chato took the point and scouted about 200 yards out ahead of them while Jesse kept an eye out for those two gunslingers shadowing them. Thomas was the teamster on the covered wagon, while Scott rode shotgun.

After traveling about four miles, Chato loped back to the wagon and told the three that it was time to start a search. He instructed Thomas to move the wagon to the base of the mountain range in front of them and then saddle up the horses. There was a trampled down horse trail up one side of the mountain which would lead them to another trail overlooking a box canyon which could be a potential hideout for Lone Wolf.

The guys did what Chato suggested and they rode upward for thirty minutes to just short of the peak of the mountain range. They then jumped off their horses. Thomas held onto the reins while Chato, Scott and Jesse ran bent over, up to ten feet of the peak, and then they sort of crawled the last few yards to the top to capture a view of the canyon below.

Sure enough, they saw the smoke from two campfires. As Scott, Jesse, and Chato looked down, Chato knew right away that they needed to get out of Dodge quickly before they were spotted because below in the canyon was a raiding party of about fifteen Apache. This band was too small to be Lone Wolf's renegades but large enough to wipe out their search party; so it was best to high-tail out of there, pronto. So they quietly backed up and then turned around and ran to Thomas and the horses.

"What did you see?" Thomas anxiously asked with his eyes wide open the size of wild turkey eggs. He knew that something no good was up by the way the three were dashing back to the horses.

"There's a band of about fifteen renegade Apache in the canyon. They could be the ones who killed off the family where we stayed last night. Geronimo might even be with them. We best make ourselves scarce as water in a dry hole and burn the breeze," Jesse insisted, "before they get on the move and spot our dust."

The four mounted their steeds and galloped back down the trail to the covered wagon faster than you could say "scallywag". No grass was growing under their horses' hooves today.

When they reached the wagon, Thomas tied his horse to the back, climbed into the driver's seat, grabbed the reins, leaned forward in the seat and whipped the leather across the backside of the mules, while the other three galloped on their horses beside him.

Chato scouted in front of them about 300 yards out until they reached the next encampment possibility, about two hours down the range. It was along a shallow winding stream in a flat wooded area on a high elevation. The aroma of the pines was invigorating; it was like a hidden paradise. They even chased up a few healthy looking, well-fed rabbits in the tall clover when they rode through it. Ole Jesse was tempted to plug a couple of those plump critters for dinner but he knew that one shot could bring in a swarm of Apache as thick as flies on a buffalo's hindquarters.

This time they searched in a specific pattern with the wagon being the home base and a virtual hub. They went out in a radius of about three miles from the wagon and rode in a circular pattern making the loop smaller and smaller until it eventually ended back at their starting position. They all went in different directions but met back at camp each night. It took them three days to make a clean quiet sweep of the area; but once again they came up empty handed.

And the search continued on in the same fashion through the Dos Cabezas Mountains for days and then for weeks. It got to the point that the three had no idea what day of the week or week of the month it was.

However, they did know that on March 5th, whatever day that was, their friend in the White House, President Hayes had completed his four year term and now James Abram Garfield (November 19, 1831 – September 19, 1881) assumed his new post as the 20th President of the United States of America after serving nine consecutive terms in the United States House of Representatives (1862 – 1878).

Hayes and Garfield had many things in common: they were both born in Ohio, they both served in the Union Army during the Civil War, they were both Republicans, and they both even sported a full length beard.

During the Civil War, Garfield fought at the Battle of Middle Creek (January 10, 1862, in eastern Kentucky), the Battle of Shiloh (fought April 6–7, 1862, in southwestern Tennessee), the Siege of Corinth (fought from April 29 to May 30, 1862, in Corinth, Mississippi), and the Battle of Chickamauga (fought from September 19–20, 1863 in Catoosa County and Walker County, Georgia). Garfield, a brave soldier who demonstrated great leadership abilities during battle, reached the rank of major general during the Civil War.

Hayes had promised the *Three for Hire* that he would talk to Garfield about the heroic roles they played for the government and promised he would convince Garfield to commit to helping the three if the situation warranted such.

After Hayes left office, he and his wife moved to their estate named Spiegel Grove in Fremont, Ohio. Spiegel is the German and Dutch word for "mirror". The story goes that Hayes' uncle named the place Spiegel Grove for the reflective pools of water that collected on the property after a rainstorm.

The house that Hayes and his wife lived in on the site was built around 1860. It was a two story brick mansion featuring many bedrooms and a wrap-around porch. In 1880, the house was expanded to include five new rooms and a massive staircase that led all the way up to the 4th floor. It was quite a sight to behold.

Finally, Hayes had "Old Whitey" buried on the property in 1879. Old Whitey was a war horse that belonged to Hayes and served him during the Civil War. He became the mascot of the 23rd Ohio Volunteer Infantry. The grave marker reads, "Old Whitey A Hero of Nineteen Battles 1861 – 1865".

Jesse, Scott, and Thomas knew that Hayes was the one man they could always rely on if times became tough and things began to unravel for them.

It was well into April now. They had combed possible encampment areas of the mountain range north of Apache Pass with no success. They were running very low on rations and the bad news was that Chato continued to spot those two hombres trailing them while they journeyed through the Dos Cabezas Mountains.

But what was of urgent need now was to find a place to procure supplies. Chato knew the location of a trading post in a small mining camp town at the base of the Dos Cabezas Mountains. It was basically a tent city with a couple of wood buildings in construction. The city consisted of a trading post, blacksmith shop, saloon, clothing store and tents for living quarters.

It was a town with no name, as of yet, and a town with no law officers to keep the peace. Gunfights could explode at any time quicker than a mason jar of nitro falling off a shelf after igniting too much dynamite during a "fire in the hole" in a silver mine.

The name of the establishment was Apache Pass Trading Post. Before they entered the small little mining camp, Scott insisted that Chato put on his blue U.S. Army shirt so that the persnickety prospectors knew he was a scout and not some sort of renegade Injun on the prowl.

All four stayed close together and kept their eyes peeled as they rode into town. They had no idea what to expect. The plan was to load up on supplies at the trading post, go over to the saloon and bend the elbows a couple of times and then head directly south to the Chiricahua Mountain Range getting out of that lawless place faster than you could say "I have a hankering to piddle around".

When they entered the trading post they were elated to see that there was a wide variety of food and vittles to choose from. They loaded up with salted sowbelly, flour, Arbuckle's, pinto beans, lard, potatoes, carrots, salt, sugar, jerky, country ham, and such. They found just about everything they needed and enough to last them another month on the trail. They even picked up a newspaper out of Tucson to read later in the mountains when sitting around the campfire one evening.

Then they walked over to the saloon for couple of swigs of rye hoping that the quality was a few grades higher than the typical rotgut made from alcohol, burnt sugar and chewing tobacco added for color, found in these types of temporary establishments.

The saloon was packed with miners, drifters, saddle tramps and probably a few fugitives from the law. It was obvious that soap was scarce in this part of the country by the looks and smell of this place.

"Let's get a couple of quick drinks and then let's get the hell out of here," Thomas remarked, "We could catch dysentery in here just by breathing the air."

"I'm with you on that one," Jesse confirmed as did Scott.

Jesse bought a bottle from the barkeep and Thomas carried three glasses to an empty table. Chato sat at a separate table on the other side of the room with his back to the wall. He was drinking nothing, just chewing on a piece of jerky. He was trying to stay away from trouble.

As Jesse was pouring the second round, two gunmen walked through the swinging doors. They were toting two .44's and wearing two cartridge belts each. They looked like killing machines.

Chato noticed them the minute they stepped into the saloon but the *Three for Hire* paid them no mind until the two walked over to their table and stood there and said,

"We finally caught up with you yellow-bellied scumbags."

They all looked up and Jesse said,

"You are obviously mistaking us for somebody else."

"You three were in San Antonio last year weren't you?"

"Shadow Assassins!" Scott shouted as he grabbed the table and flipped it over for cover in one quick motion.

Everyone drew their pistols and began firing away. Bullets were flying in both directions. But the three were in cover behind the table and the two gunslingers were standing right smack out in the open with both guns ablazing. Jesse and Thomas were faster on the draw and more accurate than the two gunslingers and drilled them before anyone else in the saloon had a chance to hit the deck.

When the smoke cleared, the two pistoleros were lying dead on the floor in pools of their own blood. Chato came over as did everyone else in the saloon to get a good look at the two would-be assassins.

Then Jesse looked at Chato and said,

"Well, I guess we finished off the two who've been following us since San Carlos, right Chato?"

Chato looked at the two lying dead on the floor and then at Jesse and said nothing.

"Well Chato?" Scott asked waiting for confirmation to Jesse's question.

Chato looked at the three and then said,

"These are not the two who have been tracking us."

"What, are you sure about that, Chato?" Thomas asked.

"As sure as I'm Apache."

Now the three were really puzzled.

"Let's get out of here," Jesse insisted.

Thomas walked over to the barkeep and threw a few $10 gold pieces on the bar and said, "Give those guys a coward's burial, would you?"

Then they rode out of town as quickly as you could say "skedaddle". And they rode and rode until they and their horses and wagon mules were plum tuckered out. When they found a place to make camp, they didn't say much. They were still in shock from the event back at the mining camp. They built a fire, put on a pot of coffee and just sat around quiet for a while. Then Thomas spoke up,

"I can't believe we just killed two men back there."

"What do you mean? It was self-defense. It was either them or us," Jesse said.

"Jesse's right Thomas, we had every right to put them down," Scott added.

"I know, I guess I'm just getting tired of all this gun play it seems we're always involved in."

Then Chato, who was brushing down the horses, walked over and asked,

"One of you shouted *Shadow Assassins* before the shooting began. What did that mean?"

"We had a run-in with a group of killers in San Antonio last year who were known as the *Shadow Assassins*. When one of them asked if we were in San Antonio last year, well, I didn't have to think twice. With their reputation, my instincts told me to act fast or we would be pushing up daisies instead of them."

"Say, how did those guys find us anyway, and why now?" Jesse asked.

"What I wanna know is who hired them to kill us? Do you think that maybe the guy who hired that Tyrus Owens character is the same guy who hired those two *Shadow Assassins,* and those two guys who tried to kill me in Dodge City? All of these assassination attempts didn't start up until we took this job. What is it that somebody is trying to keep us from doing or finding out?" Scott asked as he stood up and threw his half full cup of coffee out on the ground in an agitated gesture.

"Let's not forget too, according to Chato, we still have two men on our tail," Thomas reminded everybody.

"Yeah, and a band of renegade Apache somewhere on our point," Jesse added.

Then Jesse stood up and said,

"I don't know about you guys, but I'm ready to chow down. I'll cook up something for supper."

Thomas walked over to the wagon and grabbed the newspaper from Tucson that they picked up at the trading post and began reading it next to the campfire for light since the sun had already gone over the Dragoon Mountain Range to the west.

"Well what do you know about that. It says here that the law captured that McCarty guy who was in that Lincoln County War that the governor of the New Mexico Territory was telling us about when we were in D.C."

"Who did you say?" Scott asked.

"You know, that reprobate they call Billy the Kid. He was captured by Pat Garrett and it says here that he was on trial for two days for killing Sheriff Brady and was found guilty of murder on April 13th. He was sentenced by Judge Warren Bristol to hang on May 13th. That should bring an end to all those senseless killings in Lincoln County."

"Unless that no-good polecat escapes again; he's like a slippery little weasel that seems to get out of every predicament he finds himself in," Scott said.

"Yep that boy is harder to hold than a hand full of yellow jackets," Jesse remarked.

After supper that night, they sat around the campfire and laid out their plans for the next few days. Chato told the men that their search of the Dos Cabezas Mountains was over because there were no more possible encampment areas that he knew of. It was time to cross Apache Pass and head for the Chiricahua Mountains where he felt that Lone Wolf, in all probability, was hiding out with his captives.

Chato knew the Chiricahua Mountains like the back of his hands since he lived there as a young boy and also a young warrior with Cochise and his band of Chiricahua Apache. But there was one problem. The area was vast and there were so many places to look. It would be like desperately searching for one lone Arizona Sycamore in a 21 mile wide and 35 mile long Ponderosa pine forest; and worst of all, they believed time was not on their side.

Scott, Jesse and Thomas' concerns were if the hostages could endure the elements of the extremely cold winter weather in the high elevations of the Chiricahua Mountains, and if the Apache could find enough food for the small children and their mothers to eat and stay alive during their captivity.

These questions and many more could be answered in the days or weeks to follow.

CHAPTER SEVEN:

Risky Parley Attempt

It was now time to cross Apache Pass. At times this could be a precarious venture with renegades the likes of Geronimo, Naiche, and Kas-tziden (Broken Foot) who were off the reservation and willing to kill any white man who crossed their paths.

It was important to be on the alert at all times. They began to cross the Pass at a little after first sunlight thinking that if they started then, they would clear the Pass early enough to be safe from a renegade attack. However, right at the spot they chose to cross there was a problem. Apache renegades had already attacked a three party wagon train. The covered wagons were burnt down to the axles along with the owners' belongings on the inside of the wagons. There were no signs of women and children but three men with several arrows in them lay dead and were all scalped. They were Mexican men probably traveling from South Texas to California.

Apache hated the Mexicans and it appeared that these poor souls didn't have a chance. Chato looked around and determined that there were about twenty horses in the renegade band. Chato said they best get out of the area pronto because this raid had happened just about an hour ago. The wagons were still smoldering and the manure left from the horses was still fresh.

Jesse noticed the Christian cross on a chain that one of the slain men was wearing around his neck and said,

"We can't just leave them lie here to become buzzard bait. We need to bury them. There's a shovel in this wagon."

"If you think we need to bury these Mexicans, we better do it fast," Scott said.

Chato agreed.

"That's right; chances are those renegades are still in the area."

So they went to work quickly and got the job done. Then they galloped out of the area faster than a dust storm whipping across the flatlands of Kansas. They rode around the west side of the foothills of the Chiricahua Mountains until they came across an old wagon trail that led to a higher elevation where prospectors mined about a decade ago.

When they arrived in what appeared to be a desolate location with many large boulders scattered about, three rapid shots rang out and bullets buzzed over their heads but close enough to knock Jesse's wide brim Stetson right off his head. They swiftly jumped off their horses, drew their pistols, and scattered to hide behind some large rocks.

"Who's shooting at us?" Jesse shouted out to Scott and Thomas.

"I don't know. I didn't see anyone," Scott yelled.

"Me neither," Thomas shouted back.

While the three were yelling at each other back and forth, Chato was sneaking around the rocks to try to ambush the shooters from behind. A couple more shots rang out from the bushwhackers then it became very quiet. Before you knew it, Chato yelled for Jesse, Thomas and Scott to come up; he had the two shooters captured.

Jesse walked over to pick up his hat and stuck his finger in the bullet hole and told Scott,

"This here is the closest I ever came to getting my brains blown out."

"Today's your lucky day, cowpoke. Hopefully you'll have many more."

Then they walked up the hill with their pistols still drawn and were surprised at what they saw. Chato had his rifle pointed at two filthy looking bearded old codgers standing in front of a cave. They were prospecting for any kind of precious metals they could find. They weren't choosy. They were digging for gold, copper and silver. To their left were two pack mules tied up to a picket line stretched between two large pines.

"What's your reason for shooting at us?" Jesse asked. "You damn near shot off my head."

"Thought you were claim jumpers," one of the old men said.

"What's your names?" Thomas demanded to know.

"I'm Jed Kincaid and this here is my brother, Willy Kincaid. I came from the East to join him about five years ago. Ole Willy's been out here prospecting in these hills for thirty years or more.

"Dats rite you whippersnappers. Say, your Injun's got sand fer shore, and saved your bacon, fellas," Willy said.

Thomas looked at Jed and asked, "What did he say?"

Jed kinda laughed and said, "I'm always interpreting my brother's words. He said your scout has guts and saved you lives."

At this point, the three holstered their six-shooters because these two old timers really meant no harm.

"Say fellas, let's quit jawing. Do you blatherskites have any tornado juice on ya? I haven't been fuddled in six moons. I also have a hankering for some real chuck. I'm plum tuckered out of eaten whistle berries every day," Willy said as he spit juice from his chew to the side and then wiped his mouth with his filthy tobacco stained shirt sleeve.

Thomas looked at Jed and said, "What did he just say?" At this point Jesse and Scott began laughing. Chato thought Willy was just peculiar.

"Willy wants to know if you have any whiskey. He says he hasn't been drunk in six months. He also wanted to know if you have any real food with you. Says he's tired of eating beans every day, you know, whistle berries," Jed said as he too began to laugh.

"We can spare a meal," Jesse said, "but first we want to ask you a question. Did you happen to see any Apache with white women and children come by here in the last eighteen months or so. There was a rash of killings and raids by Apache in some towns in the New Mexico and Arizona Territories and they kidnapped women and children for some unknown reason. We're trying to locate the renegades and see if we can reason with them to get the hostages back."

"Reason with Apache? I reckon you'll have better luck reasoning with a South Texas badger. Yes, we saw several wagons of whites with Apache on horseback heading south deeper into the Chiricahua Mountains a little over a year ago. The hostages could be in Mexico by now and sold as slaves or they could all be dead. Your chances of finding them alive and in one piece are slim to none.

"Don't agree," Chato said. I don't believe the Mescalero known as Lone Wolf would kill them."

"What about the one the Mexicans call, 'Nana'?" Scott asked.

"That's a different matter," Chato confirmed.

"Well, at least it seems like we're heading in the right direction. Let's break out some grub and then head south," Jesse suggested. So they did.

After chowing down and before they left, Ole Willy said,

"Say, iffen you bellyachers ever go piddling around in Tucson, look up my old darlen and tell her ole Willy is still a kicken. Her name is Josephine. She's a songbird at the Cattlemen's Palace and twice as pretty and serene as the sunset over the Rockies. She was much better looken than some of those old mares in that place that looked like they were rode hard and put up wet. Oh, she could git mean as lightning mind you and put up a fuss, but we had a hankering for each other. Scuttlebutt was true; I even brung her a bookay of Arazonie wild cactus flowers once, when I was all soaked up from rotgut, of course. Brunging flowers to a pretty gal was not an everyday type currance for this old rooster. Know what ah mean?"

"We know what you mean, Willy," Jesse said as the three of them laughed while they made ready to hit the trail again. Even Chato cracked a rare smile thinking that maybe ole Willy was just a wee bit touched.

They left the two old timers to their futile prospecting adventure and rode south, through the Chiricahua Mountain range. They traversed and searched both the rich grassy and sometimes desert covered lowlands, plus the Ponderosa pine and Douglas fir forests of the highlands.

While they were camping one night, after six weeks of following trails that seemed to lead to nowhere, they finally felt that they might be getting closer to the Apache stronghold based on Chato's premonition. Because of this it was time to start discussing and get dead serious about what they would do when they came upon Lone Wolf's encampment.

"We can't fight them. We are just a few against many. And we don't want to get the hostages killed if they are still alive," Chato said, "What is your plan?"

"Our only hope is to reason with them," Scott suggested.

"You will find it hard to reason with Nana, maybe Lone Wolf, not Nana," Chato insisted.

"Anybody have any ideas on how to reason with Lone Wolf?" Scott asked.

Then Jesse made this suggestion,

"I say we ride into their camp underneath a white flag to show we come in peace. Then we parley with Lone Wolf and ask him what event caused him to kidnap the hostages. We must convince him that we mean no harm, and that we are not trying to get them to go back to the reservation. We'll tell him that we just want the hostages freed and we will give him our word that we will do our best to resolve whatever issue caused them to take such drastic actions. What do you think, Chato?"

"I think your chances of getting out of there alive are like the great buffalo herd surviving another ten years on the Great Plains. But there is no other way to turn. You have to risk everything if you intend to get the white captives back. If bluecoats try, the hostages will die. You are their only hope."

"Well, what do you guys think?" Jesse asked Thomas and Scott.

"I think we have lost our minds. Other than that, we have no other choice," Thomas said.

Then Scott jumped in,

"I agree, we have no other alternative. But let me say this, if things go haywire, I just want you guys to know that it's been an honor and an adventure being with you these last couple of years. Maybe the three guys known as the *Three for Hire* will be written up in those dime novels out east; and then again, maybe not. Anyway, I'm ready to get this job done and go home to Dodge. Chato, how close do you think we really are to finding the Apache village?"

"I believe just two suns away."

Chato was correct because two days later, while they were traveling through a lowland grassy area, Chato spotted smoke signals. They were coming from an Apache lookout point and being sent to a high point near the Apache hideout.

Smoke signals were used by Native Americans to quickly communicate visual messages over long distances. The rudimentary messages were delivered by columns of intermittent puffs or clouds of smoke.

The Apache used smoke signals to convey many different types of messages: warnings and alarms, help needed, news, and a host of other things determined by the sender and the receiver of the signals.

There was not one set meaning for the signals otherwise enemy tribes could pick up and interpret the messages. Sometimes they used just simple codes. Other times they used more complicated ones. Simple signals would be: one puff of smoke might mean, "attention"; two puffs may have signaled, "all's well"; three puffs might signal, "danger"; and four puffs could signal, "strangers are approaching".

Preparing and then sending a smoke signal was a fairly simple process. The first thing the Apache did was to select an area that could be seen from great distances. The Chiricahua Mountains offered many opportunities for this prerequisite with many high points scattered along and throughout the lowlands.

They then gathered fuel for the fire that gave them a dense dark smoke. Wood material produced a tan or brown smoke and sometimes animal dung was added to produce a darker smoke. The addition of other materials like damp leaves or green grass would produce a thick smoke. With a dark thick smoke, the signal could be seen for miles.

Two Apache would hold a blanket over the fire to keep the smoke from rising. When a lot of smoke accumulated under the blanket, the blanket was raised to allow a puff or cloud of smoke to escape. The blanket was then lowered and placed over the fire again to accumulate more smoke for the next puff.

On this day, Chato figured that the smoke signals being sent were to warn the encampment that strangers were approaching. He was correct. That's exactly what they were doing.

Now everyone knew that they were getting close to the Apache village. Certain danger was most likely right around the corner.

Chato suggested that they not go any further until he scouted out the village to get an idea of what they were facing and if in fact, they came upon the right village. If they did not have the right encampment and stumbled across Geronimo and his band of savages instead, well that would certainly spell "certain doom" for the search party. And if it in fact was the right encampment, who's to say that it too wouldn't spell lethal danger for the three, including their Apache scout, Chato.

Since the smoke signals gave away the fact that they were spotted, the four backtracked into a wooded area. At nightfall, Chato proceeded forward around boulders and through wooded areas. He followed a trail through a pine forest to a slightly higher elevation. Then he tethered his horse to a tree and walked the rest of the way up the trail. A Comanche moon provided the light for him to travel through the woods at night. But it also allowed the other Apache sentries to see just as well, so he had to be extra cautious.

When he arrived at the top of a cliff, he peered over it and there it was at long last. The Apache village they were looking for. He saw many wickiups and campfires and if his eyes were not deceiving him, he thought he could see white women and children walking around. He could tell that those women and children were white by the color of their hair and the way they wore it.

However, what he also saw was disturbing and made him question in his own mind whether it was safe to approach the encampment even under the universal connotation of a white flag. He would leave that decision up to the *Three for Hire.*

After watching the encampment for about fifteen minutes, he decided he better get back to the other three since the place was crawling with Apache warriors. He traveled a different route back for safety reasons just in case any Apache picked up his trail.

When he arrived at the place where the three were hiding out, he told them not to build a campfire this night because they were too close to the Apache stronghold.

"You found it then," Jesse said.

"Yes I did."

"Could you see the hostages, the white women and children?" Scott anxiously asked.

"Yes, I saw many walking and sitting around campfires. There are many wickiups in this village and many ponies. That means there are many warriors."

"Could you see Lone Wolf or Nana?" Thomas inquired.

"No, but Nana is in the village."

"How do you know that?"

"I saw signs of his torture and killing techniques in the camp."

Chato went on to describe to the three the savagery he saw and what it meant. This really put to light the question of their own safety. But being the brave and committed frontiersmen that they were, they all agreed that there was no turning back now.

On that night, none of them got much sleep thinking and wondering about what sunup would bring when they rode into the hostile Apache camp, if in fact, they would even get that far.

When morning arrived, Jesse built a small fire, just large enough to make a pot of Arbuckle's and cook up some beans and rice for breakfast. They did not want to head into the Apache camp on an empty stomach. When they were finished eating and packed, Jesse suggested this,

"Men, when I used to go on cattle drives, I would offer up a prayer every evening for our safety the next day. If you don't mind, I would like to say a prayer now."

"Please do," Thomas requested, "I have the feeling we're going to need it."

"Bow your heads. Dear Father, we are about to enter a time and place we know nothing about. We fear that not only our lives are in danger but also the lives of innocent women and children. We pray that today you give us the courage and fortitude to see this challenge through and that you protect us as we bargain for the safe release of the hostages. We ask this in Jesus' name. Amen."

"Amen," repeated Thomas and Scott.

Jesse then grabbed a long stick he found the night before and tied a white cloth to it and attached it to the covered wagon so the flag was about five feet above the top of the wagon in plain view. Thomas climbed up into the wagon while the other three mounted their horses.

"Lead the way, Chato," Jesse said as he sat brave and tall in his saddle on his stout Palomino. They then rode out into plain sight. Chato lead the way with Thomas being flanked by both Jesse and Scott.

Out of nowhere, Apache with rifles started appearing standing on top of boulders and the mountains that protruded around the flat passageway that lead to the Apache village. They were high on the right and they were high on the left. Then about twenty Apache on horseback rode out with their rifles held high in the air in one hand while they gave out shouts and battle yells as they surrounded the four. The four men just kept moving forward and tried to ignore the warriors.

Finally, the warriors ceased the yelling and just rode beside the four into the Apache village. It appeared to the four searchers that the first step was accomplished, that is, they made it to the camp with their scalps still intact. At this point, they saw no white hostages.

But what happened next was horrifying; for they arrived just in time to witness an execution of Mexican captives, Apache style.

But before the execution, they were swarmed by Apache renegades and dragged off their horses and Thomas was pulled off of the wagon. The fear in their eyes was telling. Several of the Indians tied the hands of the four behind their backs with pieces of leather. Then they were forced to watch the executions.

There were ten, eight-foot tall posts in the ground about six feet apart from each other. Tied to each post was a Mexican soldier with their shirts ripped down. Their bare chests were already sliced up with knife wounds but they were all still alive, bleeding and moaning.

Then out of the nearest wickiup came an old warrior.

"Nana," Chato said loud enough for Scott, Thomas and Jesse to hear.

The three looked on and wondered what was about to happen.

Then ten warriors mounted their horses and rode over to the other side of the camp and they each pulled up a spear that was sticking in the ground. Now they rode up to about 50 yards from the tied up Mexicans and positioned themselves side-by-side.

When they were in position facing the Mexican soldiers, they paused and looked at Chief Nana. Nana raised his hand, waited and then lowered it. That was the signal for the warriors to charge. So with their spears in the throwing position and yelling an Apache battle cry, they rode hard and fast toward the Mexicans and thrust their spears into the chests of the captives as they rode by the execution posts.

Thomas turned his head while Scott, Jessie and Chato looked on. This was a nightmare. Were they next? Several Apache untied the dead Mexicans from the posts and dragged their bodies to the side.

Then Nana ordered his braves to rip the shirts off of Thomas, Scott, and Jesse and tie them to the execution posts. Chato started shouting out frantically in Apache language to see Lone Wolf.

As the Apache warriors were tying the three to their posts, a tall slim but muscular warrior came out of another wickiup and walked over to Chato and said in Apache,

"I am Lone Wolf. Why do you bring these white-eyes to our camp?"

"They come in peace under a white flag. They are not wearing guns. The guns are in their wagon. They want to parley with you about the hostages and discuss with you their release and find out what caused you to begin kidnapping innocent women and children. They come representing the governors of the Arizona and New Mexico Territories. They mean no one harm and harm should not come to them."

"Nana has other ideas for the three you brought. It will be hard to convince him otherwise," Lone Wolf said.

"You must stop Nana and let the three speak," Chato pleaded.

"I will see what I can do."

Lone Wolf walked over to Nana and said in a firm voice,

"These four came to parley with me, they are my prisoners. Have your warriors release them to my men."

Nana was not pleased with the request but honored it anyway. Nana's men backed off and Lone Wolf's men moved in and untied the three from the posts. Lone Wolf then instructed the three to pick up their shirts and follow him to his wickiup. As they walked through the small village they noticed that there were several wickiups being guarded by Apache warriors. The three figured that was where the hostages were being held. They wouldn't know for sure though until they saw them firsthand.

When they entered the wickiup, they sat in a circle around the fire pit that was built in the middle of the Apache living quarters. Just by the brief conversation as they walked to the wickiup, they could tell that Lone Wolf spoke good English. This was a major plus since they didn't have to talk through an interpreter.

Lone Wolf spoke first,

"Why did you come to our village and who do you represent?"

Jesse spoke their intentions after he first introduced everyone to Lone Wolf.

"We represent the governors of the Arizona and New Mexico Territories, Governors James Freidman and Lawrence Williams. First and foremost we come in peace and ask for the release of the hostages, the women and children that you took from their homes; assuming of course, they are still alive and all in this camp. Secondly, we want to know why you took them and killed many men and what it was that made you do this. We want to know so we can work with the great father in Washington to get the problem resolved."

"My warriors killed no one. That was my order to them," Lone Wolf said.

Love Wolf paused, thought about it a while, and then said out loud,

"Victorio!"

"What about Victorio?" Scott asked.

"Victorio must be the one you are speaking of. He joined my band to kidnap hostages. He went his way; I went my way, both with the same objective. I should have known better. Victorio had a killing streak in him unlike me. He won't kill anymore. He's gone to the spirit world now. However, Nana, who you already met, is many times the killer Victorio was. He hates all whites, Mexicans and Americans. The hate is strong in his heart.

All I want is justice for the bluecoat murderers who massacred my family in our Mescalero village in the northeast New Mexico Territory and who killed my family and people in the Fort Sill area. When justice is served, I will release the hostages."

"Fort Sill area? What are you talking about Lone Wolf?" Jesse asked in surprise. "We heard about Baxter's men raiding your encampment in the New Mexico Territory but we don't know about any Apache being killed in the Fort Sill area. You better tell us what you know."

The four were astonished at the revelation about the Fort Sill events. They had not heard any stories about that from anyone, yet it sounded as though this was one of the major reasons for Lone Wolf's actions.

Then Lone Wolf told his side of the story.

"It was about four years ago that Long Gray Hair, the one you call Baxter, and his blue bellies raided our peaceful Mescalero village and massacred my people and some of my family and then drove many to Fort Sill like cattle.

My father Red Feather led my people to that land. We did not want to live on the Mescalero Reservation because living conditions were not good although maybe not as bad as San Carlos and Fort Sill.

My father was a peaceful man. He knew many great Apache chiefs and warriors like Geronimo, Mangas Coloradas, Victorio, Cochise, and Juh. But my father was not like them.

I am Mescalero like my father and his father before him and his father before him. We are proud people. Prior to moving to the reservation life, the Mescalero people were nomadic hunters and gatherers of food that grew in nature all around us: on bushes, trees, and roots of plants. We found nourishment in these things and many of them were healing aids and medicine to us. Nature provided us with everything we needed to survive. We didn't only survive in nature, we were one with nature.

The men of the villages were excellent horsemen and brave warriors and did not fear death. They were also hunters and providers of meat while the women harvested and prepared food from many different plant sources.

We were always Apache but white Spanish trespassers on our land gave us the name Mescalero because where we roamed and lived, the mescal plant was plentiful and it became our main food source during good times and bad.

Things we know we learned from our tribe elders. We do not have books like white-eyes. Our lives were shaped according to stories that were passed down to us. Our grandparents often spoke of a faraway place called White Mountain. It was there that the creator gave us life. It is a special place for all Apache. It was on White Mountain that a White Painted Woman gave birth to two sons, a Child of Water and a Killer of Enemies. They were born during a turbulent rainstorm when thunder and lightning came from the sky. From then on, Apache learned how to survive with nature and defeat its enemies.

I tell you these stories so you know my people. I was in part raised by a woman named Golden Sun. She was white but became part of our tribe before reservation life, during it and after it. She taught me how to speak your language and taught me about your Christian religion. Her religious teachings have made me think differently than many of my Apache brothers. Those who are close to me are similar to me.

After my father led many from the reservation to be free with nature once more, my tribe was happy. Then this long gray haired man you call Baxter came and massacred my village when we were out hunting. From the top of the mesa, I saw dead lying in their blood, my village burnt and women and children herded away like cattle to Fort Sill, not the Mescalero Reservation for reasons I do not know.

My head wanted revenge only on blue bellies but my heart told me to pray to the Great Spirit for counsel. I joined up with Geronimo for a while, went on raids against blue bellies and Mexicans but Geronimo wanted to kill all white-eyes so we parted ways. Me and my people wandered around in the wilderness with no purpose. After time, I was still torn between revenge and no revenge. Then I chose no revenge until one day when three Apache escaped from the reservation in the Fort Sill area and told me about what happened there."

Now the three were listening attentively and anxious to hear what Lone Wolf was about to tell them.

"The three brought me news that started a raging fire in me I could not control. They said that the government stopped food supplies and medicine to the Apache and the women and children were starving to death. Somehow many Indians received new repeating rifles and ammunition and there was an uprising amongst the Lipan Apache, Kiowa, and Comanche in the area, young and old. Fights broke out and soldiers tortured and killed many of our people.

My mother and my wife died of starvation. My sister died of white man disease because there was no medicine. And I recently got word that my only son is now dead. He was tortured and killed by Baxter's men."

Lone Wolf then stood up and said in an angry voice,

"This is the reason why I took your women and children from their homes. I want the white man to feel the pain me and my people have felt."

Lone Wolf then stormed out of his wickiup. Jesse, Scott, Thomas, and Chato sat there quietly in disbelief looking at each other and were ashamed and could not believe what they just heard. If all of this was true, there was no wonder why Lone Wolf sought revenge.

"Something is not right at Fort Sill," Jesse said.

"Well, that's an understatement," Scott replied. "But what do we do now?"

"We need to see the hostages and make sure they are all OK and being taken care of. Then after we inform the governors about what we found out, we better meet with President Garfield since this seems like a federal issue and not a territorial issue," Thomas proposed.

Scott and Jesse both agreed.

Then Thomas added,

"You guys don't think we can fight our way out of here and take the hostages with us, do you?"

"Are you out of your mind? Do you want to end up like those Mexicans out there? We're outnumbered ten to one," Jesse said.

"OK so what do we do right this instant?" Scott asked.

"You three stay here. I will go talk to Lone Wolf and ask to see the hostages," Chato said.

Within minutes Chato returned and said,

"Jesse and I can see but not talk to the hostages, you other two must remain in this wickiup for now."

Jesse and Chato were escorted by two Apache warriors. They went from wickiup to wickiup only looking through the opening which was exposed when an Apache warrior lifted and held the blanket door to the side.

When Chato and Jesse looked in, they saw the hostages. It appeared that the mothers were in the same wickiups as their children. The children had drawn and sad faces. It seemed they were not starving but they were not being served an abundance of food either. The mothers looked to be healthy but they had worried and defeated looks on their faces. They weren't sure what to think when one white man stared in at them. The hostages didn't know whether he came to rescue them or to buy them and sell them in Mexico as slaves.

After Jesse and Chato verified that the hostages were in camp, they were taken back to Lone Wolf's wickiup where they were told to wait.

"Did you see them?" Scott anxiously asked.

"Yes we did. I guess we saw them all but we can't be sure," Jesse remarked.

"What did they look like?" Thomas asked.

"Like frightened little rabbits looking for a few more meals and a safe passage home, I suppose," Jesse said.

"Now what happens?" Thomas inquired.

"We wait. We wait until Lone Wolf decides what to do with us. There are two Apache sentries outside. We can't go anywhere until Lone Wolf says so," Chato answered.

Then about one hour later, Lone Wolf entered the wickiup and sat down and said,

"Hear me. You will go to your father in Washington and tell of the tragedies at Fort Sill and seek white man justice and punishment for those who killed my people. The hostages will not be released until you prove to me that justice is served. If white man justice is not served, then there will be Apache justice. When you are gone and many suns come and go and we do not hear from you, we might move our village to a hideout which whites will not find. If justice is served, we will let our hideout be known and the hostages will be released."

155

"We will go Lone Wolf, and do our best to ensure justice. But if harm comes to these hostages, I can tell you that the ones you call blue bellies will swarm these mountains like locusts and bring down wrath upon your people the likes you have never seen before. This is not a threat. This is just fact," Jesse responded.

Jesse thought it wise to answer a demand with a strong assertion. To Apache, it was important to show strength, when Apache showed strength.

Thomas leaned over and whispered to Jesse,

"Do we smoke a peace pipe now or something?"

Lone Wolf heard Thomas and said,

"Apache don't smoke peace pipes like the northern Plains tribes, the Cheyenne and the Sioux. My word is your truth. You must believe in my word as I must believe in yours."

Lone Wolf then stood up and said, "Now you are free to go."

They then stood up and walked out of the wickiup and prepared to ride out. They were happy to get out of that place with their scalps still attached.

For the first two miles, they were surrounded by Apache who escorted them out of the area and then in a flash the Apache turned their horses around and galloped back to their village.

The four rode about five more hours and then made camp next to one of the streams flowing in a low area. Jesse cooked the meal while Scott made the coffee after Thomas and Chato gathered wood and built a campfire. After supper, they talked about where to go and what to do next.

"Here's what I think," Jesse said. "I see no reason to meet with the two territorial governors. I think we just send them a wire and tell them we found the hostages and they are safe but Lone Wolf has demands. We'll tell them we are planning to meet with President Garfield because resolution will be more of a federal issue than a territorial issue. Do you guys agree with that?"

"I do," Scott said.

"I agree with that too," Thomas added. "Why don't we head back to Tucson now and catch a train to Washington. Chato, we'll buy you clothes like ours to wear when we're in Tucson because we will need you with us during this whole project. Don't you guys agree?"

They all did, even Chato.

"I have never traveled on a train before and never been out of the Arizona Territory much. Will I see the great white father?"

"You'll not only see him, you'll speak to him," Jesse said as he grinned along with Thomas and Scott. "Now let's get some shut-eye and get up early tomorrow and head west to Tucson after breakfast. We have some long days ahead of us."

CHAPTER EIGHT:

Gold of a Different Color

It was just over a one hundred mile trip from their location in the Chiricahua Mountains to their destination, Tucson, Arizona. It took a little longer than normal because of the bumpy wagon ride over the rocky paths of the Chiricahua mountain range. If you traveled the trail too fast, you could break a wheel or even worse, an axle.

They finally arrived in Tucson on the seventh day of their journey. They were extremely worn out and agreed to stay in Tucson for two days to catch up on their rest. They knew that the hostages' lives were not in immediate danger so they felt OK with their decision.

Jesse suggested they get four hotel rooms first and then go get a bath and a shave. Everyone agreed. However, when they signed into the hotel, the proprietor did not want to allow Chato to have a room since he was an Apache Indian. So the proprietor made up a story and told Jesse that the hotel was full.

Now Jesse had a pretty good sense of humor and a quick wit. Plus, he was too tired to argue a point so he asked the hotel clerk,

"You say you are sold out of rooms, eh?"

"Yes sir we are."

"Well, let me ask you this question," Jesse responded, "If President Garfield would walk right through your front door, right this instant, would you have a room for him?"

"Of course I would," the hotel clerk responded.

"Well, I happen to know that President Garfield will be spending the night in Washington, D.C. so I highly suggest you give this here Apache scout, who was hired by the government to assist us in getting back white women and children hostages from renegade Apache, a nice comfortable room," Jesse said as he unholstered his six-shooter and twirled the cylinder to see if it was fully loaded.

The nervous looking skinny hotel clerk asked Chato to make his mark in the book and take room number 201. Scott and Thomas turned their heads to hide their grins.

All four of them, including Chato, went to the bath house and the barber. While Thomas and Chato were each sitting in a tub of hot soapy water taking a much needed bath in the backroom, Jesse was sitting in the barber's chair while Scott was waiting his turn and reading some old Tucson newspapers lying around. One article especially was of interest to him.

"Hey Jesse, remember when we read that Billy the Kid was captured and sentenced to be hung?"

"Yep, I remember."

"Well that little weasel escaped."

"How in Sam Hill did he do that?" Jesse asked.

"Well it says here that he was held under guard by two of Garrett's deputies, a guy by the name of James Bell and another one by the name of Robert Ollinger. He was being held on the top floor of the town courthouse. On April 28th, while Garrett was out of town, the Kid killed both the guards and escaped."

"How in the blazes did he do that?" Jesse asked.

"According to this, the speculation is that one of the Kid's friends put a six-shooter in the privy that the Kid was permitted to use under guard. Ole Billy retrieved the gun, and turned it on Bell at the top of the stairs when they came back from the privy. He shot Bell and then grabbed Ollinger's 10-gauge double barrel shotgun which was standing against the wall. Both barrels were loaded with buckshot. Ollinger was across the street at the time. Billy knew he would come a running as soon as he heard the shot so Billy waited at an open window for Ollinger to cross the street. When he did, Billy pointed the double barrel shotgun at Ollinger and yelled out, 'Hello Bob' and unloaded both barrels into the deputy. It says it took the Kid about one hour to get the irons off but when he did, the Kid rode out of town on a stolen horse, reportedly singing."

Then the barber added,

"Rumor has it that the Kid rode off to Old Mexico. You can bet a shave and a haircut that Ole Garrett will be on his tail like a chicken hawk on a rooster."

"You think?" Jesse responded.

When Jesse's shave and a haircut were completed, Scott traded places with him. And then later, Scott and Jesse traded places with Thomas and Chato. Of course, Jesse and Scott demanded that clean water be put in the tubs.

After the three were all clean shaven, and the four washed up and smelling as pretty as a bouquet of marigolds, they went over to the train depot to pick up their tickets to Washington, D.C. They would be leaving the day after next.

At this point, Jesse suggested they go to the telegraph office and send off two telegrams. The first one was to the governors of Arizona and New Mexico Territories. It read:

Governors Lawrence Williams and James Freidman
Be advised that we found Lone Wolf and the hostages. All hostages are alive. To protect the safety of the hostages, we cannot tell you of their location. There are demands from Lone Wolf that must be met first in order to free the hostages. There is a federal issue involved which will necessitate having a meeting with President Garfield. We will be heading to Washington in two days to meet with the president. We will keep you posted. You should consider this top secret for now. We do not want to endanger the hostages any further.
                                   Jesse Caldwell, et al.

Then Jesse composed a telegram to President Garfield that read:

President Garfield
Washington, D.C.
President Hayes informed you of our project to find the women and children who were kidnapped by the Apache and taken from their homes in the New Mexico and Arizona Territories. We have found them but there are demands by the Apache which must be met by the federal government before the hostages are released. We are taking a train to Washington and will be there in about 5 days to meet with you. We are in Tucson, Arizona Territory now. Would you please acknowledge receipt of this and let us know when you can meet with us.
                                   Jesse Caldwell
                                   Scott Johnson
                                   Thomas O'Brien

After they sent the telegrams off, all four went to the saloon for a drink and told the telegraph operator that if a response came back within the hour, to bring it over to the saloon, otherwise, take it to the hotel where they were staying.

The response from President Garfield came within 30 minutes. The young telegraph operator was so excited to receive a telegram from the President of the United States that he wasted no time rushing it over to the saloon.

He swung open the saloon doors, quickly glanced around, spotted Jesse, Scott and Thomas, waved the telegram high in the air and shouted,

"Here it is, here it is, from the President of the United States himself."

Everyone in the saloon looked his way when he said "president".

Jesse grabbed the telegram in an agitated state of mind and said in an angered tone,

"Why don't you blab it to the whole world, fella? Thanks, here's your money, now skedaddle out of here before the wrath of my Apache friend comes down on you."

The young telegraph operator looked at Chato, slowly backed off, then turned and ran out of the saloon faster than a dog being chased by a twelve-foot long Louisiana swamp gator.

Jesse read the telegram to the other three very quietly so no one else in the saloon could hear. It read:

Jesse Caldwell
Scott Johnson
Thomas O'Brien
I am in receipt of your telegram. I will plan to meet with you immediately upon your arrival and will do all in my power to help. President Hayes has told me many things about your good works. We will arrange transportation and rooms when you arrive. Have a safe trip.

President Garfield

"Well, he seems to be a man of few words," Thomas remarked.

"That's fine, let's just hope that he gives us the support we need to get the job done. Do you think he will, Jesse?" Scott asked.

"I believe he will."

THE *THREE FOR HIRE* AND CHATO MEET PRESIDENT GARFIELD

When the four arrived at the Washington, D.C. Train Depot around 11:30 a.m., they were picked up by a special presidential carriage as promised. Jesse had sent a telegram to the president at the last stop before Washington, D.C. and informed him of their expected time of arrival.

The carriage first delivered them to the hotel to sign in, drop off their luggage, and clean up. Since they did not have breakfast on the train, they decided to get a bite to eat at the hotel's café.

At about 2:00 p.m., they departed for the White House which was only about one mile away. President Garfield was looking out of the window when the carriage drove up to the White House. The four walked up the steps and Jesse said to Chato,

"Why don't you knock on the door?"

"What do you mean, knock on the door?"

"Like this," Jesse said as he held his fist up and simulated knocking into the air.

So Chato did and immediatedly a man answered the door and said,

"Come on in, gentlemen."

"We are here to see President Garfield," Jesse announced.

"Well, you are looking right at him," Garfield said as he smiled.

They introduced themselves and then President Garfield took them to his office. After about fifteen minutes of getting to know each other, they got right down to business.

"Jesse, your telegram stated that you located the hostages and there were demands that only the federal government could satisfy. Explain what you meant and most importantly, are the hostages in danger?"

"Sir, we found the hostages in the Chiricahua Mountains. A Mescalero Apache by the name of Lone Wolf is holding them. Right now, Lone Wolf will not harm them but he does have demands. But I must tell you that there is another Apache leader in camp with him. His name is Nana. Even though he is an old man, he has hatred for whites in his heart the likes I haven't seen before. He and his warriors brutally murdered some Mexican soldiers when we arrived at their camp. We witnessed it. It was barbaric. If it weren't for Chato, the coyotes would be cleaning the meat off our bones right now too. I think it's time to start acting with a sense of urgency if we want to get these hostages back alive."

"OK then, tell me about his demands," Garfield insisted.

"Well first of all, let me tell you what Lone Wolf told us about what's happening around the Fort Sill reservation area."

"What does Fort Sill have to do with Lone Wolf taking hostages?" Garfield asked.

Then Scott jumped in,

"Everything sir, absolutely everything. Lone Wolf told us about the raid and senseless massacre of tribal men, women, and children by Baxter on their village in the northeastern New Mexico Territory and how they marched off the surviving women, children and old men to Fort Sill."

"Yes, Hayes told me about that episode. Go on."

"Well sir, later, Lone Wolf received word that the government cut way back on food, supplies and money for the Indians in the Fort Sill area and even discontinued sending medicine for the sick."

"That's absurd!" President Garfield asserted.

"Please let me finish," Scott insisted. "Lone Wolf also said that Indians in the Fort Sill area have received repeating rifles from somewhere and someone in order to fight back. But what really set Lone Wolf off was that he found out that many of his family and tribal members died of starvation, and from lack of medicine. He also said his only son was tortured and killed."

Garfield was a man of action. By now he had heard enough, he stood up in anger and called in his aide and told him to immediately summon the Secretary of the Interior Samuel Jordan Kirkwood (December 20, 1813 – September 1, 1894) and Hiram Price (January 10, 1814 – May 30, 1901) who was the Commissioner of Indian Affairs and reported to Kirkwood. Both men were new on their jobs and recently appointed by Garfield. Garfield did not jump to any conclusions yet but wanted to search out answers and to see if his appointees had any information regarding the happenings around Fort Sill and if in fact they were true.

He also sent for his Vice President, Chester Alan Arthur (October 5, 1829 – November 18, 1886) despite the fact that he and Arthur were not on good terms at this time. He wanted Arthur involved just in case he needed to delegate authority to him regarding this project. Garfield's wife, Lucretia, had become very sick in May and contracted malaria and possibly spinal meningitis. Her health was deteriorating rapidly and she was thought by some to be very near to death. The president didn't discuss her sickness with the *Three for Hire* but obviously, Arthur was well aware of her health issues. She eventually would recover but Garfield would not want to leave her side at any time during the next couple of months.

It didn't take long for the three gentlemen to arrive at President Garfield's office. Garfield introduced the three Washington men to the *Three for Hire* and Chato and then had Jesse and Scott once more explain the whole situation to Arthur, Kirkwood and Price, from Lone Wolf's terms to the happenings around the Fort Sill area.

"What do you know about this?" Garfield asked both Kirkwood and Price.

"Nothing," Kirkwood responded.

"This is the first time I'm hearing about it also," Price commented. "Food, medicine, clothing, and money are constantly being shipped to all of the reservations throughout the country including the Indian Territory. There are three tribes in the Fort Sill area right now: the Kiowa, Apache and Comanche. Whites are not supposed to enter the area except for government men and soldiers. Although, we do allow cattle to be driven up from Texas, through the Indian Territory, and up to the cow towns in Kansas. The forts in the Indian Territory are to protect the whites and the Indians alike.

"Well if there is some type of corruption going on in Fort Sill, I intend to get to the bottom of it and quickly," Garfield avowed. "Who's the commanding officer there?"

"Baxter, Colonel Baxter, sir," Kirkwood responded.

"Ah, Baxter, from what I hear, he has an intemperate anger when it comes to his feelings about Indians. He has quite a reputation in that regards. We need to bring him to D.C. immediately," Garfield demanded.

"Sir, if I may offer something up, please."

"Go ahead Thomas, what is it?"

"Mr. President, I think we could get to the bottom of things quickly if you allow Jesse, Scott, Chato and me to do some snooping around down by Fort Sill. I'm afraid if you inform Baxter and whoever may be working with him about the investigation, you may never find the answers you're looking for. We might be able to expose something more devious going on than we could ever dream of."

"I like that idea too," Jesse confirmed. "You could let us know when wagons of food, supplies and medicine are being dispatched to Fort Sill and we could follow the shipment at a distance to see what happens to it and where it ends up. It's not unusual for supplies meant for the Indian reservations to be sold by corrupt soldiers and Indian agents to line their own pockets. We've heard rumors about such things and that's what might be going on here."

That sounds like a plan. I suggest that the subjects we talked about here today do not leave this room. Let's keep it to ourselves until we get some answers," Garfield insisted. Then he added,

"Say, that reminds me. I have a bill on my desk to be signed that passed the House and Senate. It's the 'Fort Sill Indian Reservation Consolidation Bill of 1881'. It cites San Carlos Apache Indian Reservation as the precedent and states that it wants to move the Fort Sill Indians to a different location in the Indian Territory for economic reasons and because the Indians in that area are becoming difficult to handle. It also states that the move would open up more land for white expansion. I think I will just put this bill on the back burner until we find out about the happenings at Fort Sill. This bill may have some relevance to the deplorable activities going on there. Who knows, maybe someone discovered gold or other precious metals we don't know about."

"Maybe sir," Jesse agreed, "Whatever it is, we'll do our best to find out for you."

Then Hiram Price offered this information to the group.

"This may be relevant sir; there in fact are new rumors floating around that there may be gold on the east side of the Wichita Mountains which are just west of Fort Sill. If so, well everyone knows what happened in the Black Hills in the Dakota Territory."

"You just keep that rumor to yourself, Hiram. I don't want a surge of gold seekers flocking the Fort Sill area," Garfield ordered. "That will just complicate things even further and start up a war between the local Indians and the white intruders."

Garfield, a man of decisiveness, then directed the Secretary and the Commissioner to do the following:

"Kirkwood and Price, I want you to find out when the next shipment of supplies for the Indians is headed to the Fort Sill area and where they are being shipped from. Then I want you to give that information to these four gentlemen so they can follow the wagons to their destination."

"Mr. President, I already know where supplies are being shipped from for Fort Sill. They are dispatched from Fort Worth, Texas which is directly south of Fort Sill," Price said.

"That's perfect," Scott remarked. We can stay at my parents' ranch near Fort Worth and wait for your telegram there, Mr. Price. We'll catch a train to Fort Worth tomorrow so we can be ready to start trailing the supplies as soon as they are shipped."

"Splendid! Now is there anything else we need to talk about?" Garfield asked.

"Well, there is just one more thing," Scott offered. "For some reason, and ever since we started this project, there have been multiple assassination attempts on our lives."

Garfield's eyes almost popped out of his head while Arthur, Price and Kirkwood, quickly turned their heads toward Scott.

"Assassination attempts? By all means, tell me more," Garfield demanded.

"Well after we took on this mission, two men tried to gun me down in Dodge City. Then a U.S. Army deserter from Fort Sill shot at Jesse in San Carlos. After that, two men tried to kill us in Arizona; and there have been two gunslingers trailing us since Tucson when we all three met to begin the search for the hostages."

"That is extraordinary," Garfield said in disbelief. "Have you discussed these happenings with the two governors whom you're working for?"

"No sir, we haven't. There's nothing they can do about it anyway. We'll just continue to stay on our guard and trust that Chato can sniff these guys out before they snuff us out," Scott said halfway jokingly.

"OK then, everybody knows what to do from here on out. Godspeed to you all. I'll say a prayer for your safety," Garfield promised. "After all, you'll be trailing supply wagons through the Indian Territory where there seems to be a warranted hostile revolt."

Garfield's comment about offering up a prayer for them wasn't just an idle remark. He was the only President of the United States who had actually been a clergyman. He was a minister for the Disciples of Christ but resigned from the clergy when he was elected president, saying that, "I resign the highest office in the land to become President of the United States."

ON TO FORT WORTH, TEXAS

It was now onward to Fort Worth, Texas by rail where they knew they could get three hearty squares for a few days at least, compliments of Scott's mother, Mrs. Johnson. It would be a waiting game for a telegram from either Price, the Commissioner of Indian Affairs or Kirkwood, the Secretary of the Interior, informing them about a supply shipment to the Fort Sill area for the Indians.

When the four arrived at the Fort Worth Train Depot, they split up for a few minutes. Scott went over to talk to his old friend at the telegraph office to inform him that they were expecting a top secret telegram from Kirkwood or Price out of Washington, D.C. He told him it was an urgent matter; so as soon as it came, he should bring it out to his parents' ranch.

In the meantime, the others went over to the livery stable to purchase five horses. One would be used as a packhorse. They had sold their other horses, mules, and wagon in Tucson before they headed to Washington, D.C. for their meeting with President Garfield. Since they would be tailing the supply wagons, they had to pack light and go without a wagon on this trip.

A few days went by after their arrival in Fort Worth. They wondered how long they would have to wait before they heard from D.C. Well it wasn't long. While eating lunch in the Johnsons' home on the fifth day back, they heard a horse galloping up to the cabin and then immediately there was a knock on the door. Scott got up, walked over to the window, and slowly moved the curtain aside to see who it was. At this point, the four could not allow themselves to throw caution to the wind. They knew that there were two gunslingers possibly still out there who had remained unaccounted for. However, this time it was the telegraph operator, so he let him in.

"This is the message you've been waiting for," he said as he handed the telegram to Scott.

"Come on in."

Scott began to read the telegram aloud while everybody anxiously looked on. It read:

Scott Johnson, Jesse Caldwell, Thomas O'Brien
Be advised. Large shipment of supplies leaving for Fort Sill area on Thursday
from Fort Worth. They are being picked up at T. Kiefer's General Store.
Good luck.

> *Samuel Jordan Kirkwood*
> *Secretary of the Interior*

Mrs. Johnson asked the telegraph operator to stay for lunch but he said that he needed to get back to work quickly since he was the only one on duty that day. When he left, Scott sat down at the table and passed the telegram around and said,

"Well, this is it guys. We begin phase two of the project. We'll either solve the puzzle or get ourselves killed."

"I vote for solving the puzzle," Thomas said.

"I'm with Thomas," Jesse added.

Chato remained quiet and saw no humor in the subject probably because he was more aware of the potential lethal dangers that lurked in the uncertain future.

The four left the ranch early on Thursday morning to head for Fort Worth. When they arrived in town, sure enough, there were six wagons in front of T. Kiefer's General Store being loaded with supplies. Five wagons were loaded for the Indians in the Fort Sill area and one was loaded with food supplies for the teamsters, plus hay and grain for the horses.

Jesse and the other three kept their distance down the street so as not to be noticed as they watched the drivers complete their loading and then throw a tarp over their supplies and tie the tarp ropes down to the sides of the wagons.

It wasn't but a few minutes later that the teamsters climbed up into their wagons and began heading north on their 185 mile grueling long journey to Fort Sill. Since the supply wagons were heavily loaded down, the drivers were lucky if they could travel 10 miles per day.

It was June 6th now and the Southwest was in the middle of a nasty drought with temperatures well above normal for that time of the year; so the trail to the Indian Territory was hot and grubby with the wagon wheels churning up an unprecedented dust storm that was almost unbearable to the teamsters riding the wagons on the back end of the caravan. If you were the unfortunate one to be riding the drag, why it was so dusty and your mouth was so dry, you couldn't spit even if you had to.

However, what was a detriment to the teamsters was a benefit to the *Three for Hire* and Chato because all they had to do was to follow the exploding dust cloud, which enabled them to trail at quite a distance behind the wagon train, which kept them from being spotted.

On about the tenth day of the journey, the wagons unexpectedly made a detour to the west to a trading post that was about a mile off of the main trail. At first Jesse surmised that it was probably a stop to procure more food for the teamsters or maybe it was to unlawfully offload food and medicine and sell it for dirty money. Instead, what they saw through their binoculars from a distance was the men loading up fifteen cases of what appeared to be crates of rifles into the sixth hay, grain, and food wagon.

"Well would you looky here," Scott said as he peered through his binoculars, "I believe there are rifles in those crates. I seen crates like those when I was in the Texas Rangers. We may have just found the source of the Indians' rifles. When the wagons pull out, let's make a quick stop at the trading post to see what gives."

"We can do that but we have to be sure we don't blow our cover," Thomas added.

"Wait a minute," Scott said as he continued looking through his binoculars, "here come four soldiers out of the post. It looks like those rifles are going to get an Army escort. Maybe the guns are on the up and up."

"Maybe, but maybe not," Jesse remarked. "We'll know soon enough. But listen, when we stop at the post, let's have Chato continue to follow the wagons so we don't lose sight of them."

They all agreed and that's exactly what they did. When the caravan pulled out, Chato kept his distance while dogging them as the wagons and their escorts took an alternate path back to the main trail and continued their northward bound journey.

The *Three for Hire* waited about fifteen minutes before they rode up to the trading post. When they walked into the building, there was only one man inside. When they questioned him, being as vague but as stern as possible, they found out that this guy thought he was just acting as a middleman between a gun manufacturer and the U.S. Army. That was his story and the *Three for Hire* believed him because he was very forthcoming with the details. He told the three that there had been numerous rifle pickups over the last year or so. He figured that the Army was equipping itself with the newest repeating rifles on the market.

Scott asked him why the rifles were being delivered to him from the manufacturer and not being delivered directly to Fort Sill.

"I have no idea," the proprietor responded, "I really gave it no thought since it was easy money in my pocket for handling the rifles."

"How do they pay you?" Scott asked.

"In gold coins. The same four soldiers who escort the wagons are the ones who pay me for handling the crates. Say, is there some kind of a problem I don't know about and who are you guys anyway?" the proprietor asked.

"We're just saddle bums trying to make a living," Jesse replied as they said "Adios" and went on their way.

The three took the path leading north and could easily follow the wagon wheel tracks in the dusty dirt road. Not long after that, they set up camp for the night knowing the routine of the teamsters who habitually made camp about two hours before sundown.

When the sun completely vanished from the western skyline, Chato rode into camp with some telling information.

"The wagons reached a fork in the road. One sign pointed north, two miles to Fort Sill and the other sign pointed to the Wichita Mountains. At that point, the wagons split up."

"Whatta ya mean?" Jesse asked.

"Two wagons took the trail to Fort Sill and the other four with the bluecoats headed into the sunset."

"Headed west?" Jesse sort of questioned in surprise. "Which way did the wagon with the guns go?"

"It followed the sunset," Chato replied, "toward the mountains."

Now the three really became suspicious. None of this made any sense unless of course there were some shady dealings going on which wouldn't surprise them one bit.

"What do we do now?" Thomas asked. "Should we split up and follow both trails?"

"No need to go to Fort Sill," Scott insisted. "I say that it's a sure bet, if we follow the four wagons west, the soldiers are gonna inadvertently expose their hands and we're gonna get ourselves some answers."

They all agreed, and since they felt like they were onto something big, they used a different trailing strategy the next day. They wanted to be sure they would not be spotted which would certainly jeopardize the whole mission; so they sent Chato out ahead to follow the wagons. The three waited until Chato and the caravan were well ahead of them before they continued to follow the wagon wheel tracks in the dusty dirt path.

But now, here came a danger they were hoping to avoid. A small band of six revengeful renegade Comanche spotted them from a distance and as the three expected, but hoped would not be true, the hostiles were armed with repeating rifles.

Being fierce warriors and fed up with their people dying of European diseases they were not immune to, starvation in the reservations, and horrible reservation conditions in general that were wrought upon them by the "government", this Comanche band decided to kill and scalp every white man that came across their path.

Instead of running, the three quickly jumped off their horses and took cover behind some large boulders. The Comanche came charging in, yelling with their rifles aimed at the three and firing away. Comanche were excellent horsemen and could control the movement of the horses with the use of their legs. They fired one round after another and their bullets ricocheted off boulders the three took shelter behind.

Jesse and the other two waited until the Comanche were about 75-yards away, and then they took dead aim and opened fire. The hostiles didn't have a chance. They were wide open targets and the *Three for Hire* were all sharpshooters of the highest caliber. With the first three shots, three Comanche fell off their horses and bit the dust. Then with a sense of courage, confidence and a little carelessness, the *Three for Hire* stood up to finish off the remaining renegades and began a series of rapid fire.

Volley after volley went in both directions. Then one of the Comanche bullets nicked Thomas in the arm and he fell backwards down behind the boulder but Jesse and Scott continued their barrage of bullets aimed at the fearless warriors. Within just a few seconds, the other three Comanche were riddled with bullets and fell to the ground as their horses galloped off at top speeds in the opposite direction.

Jesse and Scott both ran to Thomas' aid to see the extent of his wound. Luckily he was just grazed in the arm and it was nothing serious. As the three collected themselves, they realized that they now had a more pressing concern. Did the soldiers and the teamsters hear the gunfire from the impromptu skirmish with the warring Comanche?

It was just blind luck. When the wagons reached the south foothills of the highlands, they then turned north directly adjacent to the west side of the Wichita Mountains. The towering mountain range, along with the low pressure winds out of the west that day, blocked the sounds of the gunfire.

In the meantime, Chato continued to keep his distance behind the wagons while the *Three for Hire* began following the wagon wheel tracks in the dust. About five miles up from the southern tip of the mountain range, another unexpected move happened. The wagons made a sharp turn into a narrow passageway that led into a hidden canyon.

Just before Chato reached the turnoff, he dismounted his horse and climbed up a cliff to peer down into the canyon. What he saw was a well hidden box canyon and he came across a discovery that he could not explain. He thought he better climb down from the peak and go back and apprise the other three of his findings.

When Chato met up with the three, he quickly informed them of his discovery. However, there were some questions that Chato was not able to immediately answer so Jesse suggested that they all four go back to the box canyon, but wait until nightfall to keep from being spotted. They decided to stay out of sight and off the road until sunset because they had no desire to run into the four soldiers who may be headed back to Fort Sill. Even after sunset, there could be a risk involved.

Sure enough, when the sun was sinking below the pinkish western skyline, Chato heard four horses trotting down the road. He had positioned himself closest to the path and acted as a lookout while the other three were well off the route. He stayed low but he could see that in fact, it was those four escort soldiers and they appeared to be heading back to Fort Sill. Chato waited about ten minutes to make sure they cleared the area. Then he went and summoned Jesse, Scott and Thomas.

Immediately, all four of them headed north and by the time they reached a few hundred feet just before the turnoff into the box canyon, daylight became scarce. There was a narrow trail which was passable on horseback which Chato previously discovered that would lead them to a point overlooking the box canyon. They quietly rode that trail and dismounted their horses before they reached the peak.

Within seconds after crawling up to the peak, and looking down from what Chato called a crow's nest, they witnessed about twenty Indians riding into the canyon. There were several lanterns spread around the campsite that shed light on the area. The four guys, Chato, Jesse, Scott, and Thomas were stooping down and lined up in that order watching the Indians ride in. Scott was looking through his binoculars but could not distinguish if they were Lipan Apache, Kiowa, or Comanche so he passed the binoculars to Chato. Chato took about a minute then whispered,

"Mostly Kiowa, some Lipan Apache, some Comanche."

"Now what's going to happen?" Jesse asked. "As if I don't know."

After the Indians slid off their horses, they all walked over to the wagon where the rifles were stowed. One civilian guard untied the canvas ropes from the wagon and unveiled the crates of rifles. Several of the Indians grabbed the rope handles on the ends of the crates and pulled a few to the ground and busted them open with their tomahawks. Sure enough, they were full of repeating rifles. From the looks of the shiny brass plates at the breeches, they were brand new Henry rifles.

The Indians gave them a good looking over. Then one civilian guard handed out a rifle to each Indian. Lastly, it appeared that each band of Indians brought a travois with them. They split up the crates and loaded them onto the travois and tied the crates down. It was readily apparent that money was exchanged for the rifles. When the Indians rode out of the canyon, the three tribes separated and rode off in different directions.

"Well, we now have a second piece of the puzzle," Scott said.

"What do you mean?" Jesse inquired.

"Well, we already know why Lone Wolf kidnapped the women and children. He told us so himself, remember? Now we know how the Indians are being armed."

"Still need more answers," Thomas whispered, "like what's that small building for down there and what are they going to use all that heavy lumber for, and why are they guarding that water hole like there's a buried treasure in that small little pond? I wonder if that's a secret entrance or a flooded shaft into a gold mine."

"Chato, when those civilian guards bed down, you think you can sneak down there without being spotted and get a closer look-see?" Scott asked.

"Yes, I'm Apache. I can be as quiet as a bobcat. I'll get answers."

After waiting several hours and watching the campfires below slowly burn out and the logs turn to cinder, Chato made his move. He cautiously climbed down the cliff on the backside of the canyon close to the wagons. When he reached the canyon floor, he snuck behind one of the wagons and waited a few minutes to be sure that everyone was sleeping. They were; so he looked around and saw a pile of spoiled food. He then crawled on his belly over to the small pond. It looked strange to him so he lowered his cupped hand in it and pulled out a handful of gook. Not knowing what it was, he took the scarf off from around his forehead, dipped it in the pond and then went back up the hill to show the other three.

When he reached the top, Jesse asked what he saw.

"This," Chato said as he handed Jesse the soiled scarf.

Jesse took the scarf, ran his fingers through it, smelled it and said,

"Well stoke up the fire and put on a possum, those guys discovered a petroleum seep."

"A what?" Thomas asked.

"A petroleum seep, you know, oil. They call it 'black gold' or 'gold of a different color' up north because it's a liquid gold mine," Jesse said.

"Oil in the Indian Territory?" Scott asked in disbelief. "Well whatta ya know about that!"

"Wow, that opens up the door to a pile of puzzle pieces," Jesse remarked.

"Now that you mention it, it sure does," Thomas agreed.

"What are we gonna to do now?" Scott asked.

"Let's get out of here right quick before sunup and start heading back to Fort Worth. If we get caught in this place, we won't make it out of here alive. There seems to be a lot of irons in this fire. Greedy hands can be mighty deadly. We found that out last year with those *Shadow Assassins*," Jesse said with anxiety in his voice.

So the four grabbed the reins of their horses and quietly walked down the narrow rocky mountain pass. There wasn't a full blown Comanche moon that night but the three quarters moon in the cloudless starlit sky gave them enough light to negotiate their way. When they reached ground level, they mounted up and galloped out of there faster than loose sage brushes blowing across the open prairie in a hurricane-like windstorm.

THE PETROLEUM SEEP EFFECT

To put it in simple terms, a petroleum seep was the result of a seal above a reservoir of raw petroleum being breached by underlying pressure causing the substance to come to the surface and sometimes causing a small pool. Oil seeps throughout certain parts of North America were not that uncommon.

The discovery of petroleum in the United States changed so many things. A new light source was created by using a distillation process on petroleum which created a product known as kerosene. Before kerosene was produced from petroleum and used mainly for lamps and eventually for heating, whale oil was widely used in oil lamps. Whale oil was obtained by simply boiling strips of blubber harvested from whales. The process was branded "trying-out". On deep-sea whaling expeditions, the trying-out was done right on the whaling ships so the remaining carcasses could be thrown overboard.

Baleen whales were the main source of whale oil. They were very common and very large. These whales are in the Baleen family: Blue whale, Fin whale, Bowhead whale, Right whale, Humpback whale, Gray whale and Minke whale. Baleen whales are edentulous whales meaning they are toothless whales. Instead of teeth, they have baleen plates for filtering food from water. Their main source of food are Krill which is a Norwegian word that means "young fry or young fish".

Whale oil was initially used as a cheap illuminant although it was not very popular because of the strong odor it produced. In the last half of the 19th century it was eventually replaced by a cheaper, more efficient, and longer lasting product known as kerosene, a product of petroleum. Kerosene played a major role in stepping up the economy in the north and the east because factories now had an economical light source available which enabled them to produce goods longer into the night hours.

Generally, where oil seeps were discovered, oil wells would eventually follow. The very first oil well in North America was dug in Oil Springs, Ontario, Canada in 1858. It was dug by a man named James Miller Williams (September 14, 1818 – November 25, 1890). Born in Camden, New Jersey, and moving to Canada in 1840 with his family, he became a businessman and political figure in Ontario, Canada. He is often viewed as the "father of the petroleum industry" in Canada. Williams partnered in business manufacturing carriages and then bought out his partner and expanded into manufacturing vehicles for public transit, and also railway cars.

In 1855 he switched professions and took over the International Mining and Manufacturing Company. It was operating a 150 gallon per day oil gum bed well from a petroleum seep, used to produce asphalt, paints, and resins, in the Village of Oil Springs. During a drought in 1858, Williams set out to dig a water well downslope from the seep. However, instead of finding water, he hit liquid gold, free flowing oil. He thus became the first person to produce a commercial oil well in North America. He also set up Canada's first refinery of crude oil to produce kerosene.

Just one year after the Canadian oil strike, the oil rush began in the United States. It became known as the Pennsylvania oil rush. The potential for discovering oil in western Pennsylvania was great because of the numerous amounts of oil seeps in the area.

A man by the name of Edwin Drake (March 29, 1819 – November 9, 1880), was the first person to drill and hit oil. The well produced twenty-five barrels a day. Drake became president of the Seneca Oil Company and they began drilling in Titusville, Pennsylvania. Many of the company's drilling sites produced very little results and the company ran out of capital. However, Drake had a strong feeling that there was liquid gold underneath the Pennsylvania topsoil so he took out a personal line of credit for his company to continue the digging.

On August 27, 1859, Drake struck oil at 69 feet, just before the funds dried up. This discovery changed everything in western Pennsylvania and his drilling was considered the first large-scale commercial extraction of petroleum in the U.S.

Drake's personal success did not last though: the well yielded only minor returns, he did not purchase any extra land in the region while the oil industry exploded around his well, and he was eventually fired as president of Seneca Oil Company.

The oil boom in Pennsylvania lasted from 1859 to the early 1870's and is said to parallel in many ways to the gold rush in California in 1849, just ten years earlier than the discovery of oil in Pennsylvania. Towns like Titusville, Oil City and Pithole became oil boomtowns and population in those cities exploded just like they did in the silver and gold mining towns out West.

Before European whites put petroleum to use, Native Americans in Pennsylvania, California and in other parts of the United States were putting oil seeps to good utilization for centuries. North American tribes collected the oil from the seeps and employed it as ointments, insect repellents, skin coloring and even for some religious ceremonies.

Ironically, about the same time Drake's oil well came in, oil was discovered in the Indian Territory by accident. Lewis Ross who was a brother of Chief John Ross (October 3, 1790–August 1, 1866), of the Cherokee Indians was manufacturing salt at the Grand Saline, on the Grand River, in what later became Mayes County, Oklahoma in the northwest Indian Territory.

In an attempt to produce more salt, he sank a deep water well and by happenstance, struck a vein of oil which flowed about ten barrels a day for a year until it went dry.

Even before this discovery, oil springs in the Indian Territory were attracting considerable attention as they were thought by many to be remedies for all chronic types of diseases like rheumatism, dropsy and just about anything that ailed you.

So there could be some conniving and corrupt soldiers and civilians, who were overcome with greed and trying to strike it rich quick by eventually putting a claim on land that housed a hidden petroleum seep in a box canyon in the Wichita Mountains. They could be the ones who created the conditions that eventually set Lone Wolf on a kidnapping rage in the New Mexico and Arizona Territories. At least, that would become Jesse's theory.

AFTER DISCOVERING THE BOX CANYON

Jesse, Scott, Thomas and Chato were now on their way back to Scott's parents' ranch in Fort Worth to make plans for their next move. After about three days on the trail though, they became plum tuckered out. It was then they decided to make a one day stop in Wichita Falls, just south of the Red River and about 115 miles northwest of Fort Worth.

The Choctaw Indians settled the area of Wichita Falls in the early 18th century. White settlers arrived there in the 1860's to establish cattle ranches because of the vast grazing land it offered. On September 27, 1872, the area was officially titled, Wichita Falls.

This was a great stopping off place to rest, get a shave, a bath, and get three squares. The town buildings were fairly new and it had a nice hotel to stay in. The hotel was a combination, hotel and café and it was just a few buildings down and across the street from a small saloon.

The four signed into the hotel, cleaned up and then met for dinner at 6:00 p.m. After a hearty steak and potato meal, they leisurely strolled over to the nearly empty saloon at 7:30, where they imbibed in what was labeled "Tennessee's Finest Sour Mash" but probably distilled in the backroom of the saloon the day before. They sipped whiskey and discussed until 9:00 p.m. what their next moves would be.

Jesse felt that the time was right to send a telegram to the two governors and inform them of what they had discovered so far.

"Jesse, I agree with you but I would like to wait until we get to Fort Worth where I know we can trust the telegraph operator," Scott recommended. "He's a good friend and I've known him for years."

"Don't you think we ought to notify President Garfield too?" Thomas asked.

"I say yes, but let's again wait until we get to Fort Worth," Scott again advised. "In fact, Thomas, it's none of my business but you probably wanna notify your family where you are and that you are safe. I wanna do the same, you know, sending a message to Janice in Dodge City. She probably thinks by now that I deserted her. But we can do all of that in Fort Worth. Agree?"

They did. Then Jesse proposed,

"You know, that's a long trip to D.C. to talk to the president about what we discovered. Do you think we can get him to meet us in St. Louis like we did with President Hayes last year?"

"The worst he can do is say no," Scott said.

"OK, then, when we get to Fort Worth, we'll wear the telegraph operator out and send everyone we know a telegram," Jesse said as he laughed and concluded by saying, "Why don't we head to our rooms now and get the best night's sleep we have had in a long time. I'm looking forward to peace and quiet lying in that feather bed tonight, looking up at a ceiling for a change instead of gazing at a sky full of stars and listening to those wailing coyotes."

Then Thomas said,

"Wait, there's still a little more whiskey in this bottle. Here, let me pour you one more for the road and let's toast to what looks to be a successful venture."

So they all stood up, smiled, held up their glasses, toasted, and down the hatch the whiskey flowed. They set their glasses down on the table, laughed and started walking out of the saloon with Chato leading the way. As he swung the two hanging saloon doors outward, a barrage of shots rang out from across the street and a bullet struck Chato in the part of his leg just above his knee knocking him backwards to the floor. The *Three for Hire* ducked back inside quickly as a volley of bullets came flying through the saloon windows. The barkeep and the other saddle tramps hanging out in the saloon also ducked for cover. Chato laid on the floor bleeding profusely while the three drew their pistols, broke out panes in the front windows with their gun barrels and began firing blindly back across the street, hoping to hit someone they couldn't even see.

Then from out of nowhere, two men with their pistols drawn, rode up on horseback like bushwhackers out of the past from a scene on the Missouri border during the days of Quantrill's raiders. They took aim at the three men who were shooting into the saloon and killed the would-be assassins with the precision of highly skilled marksmen. They then galloped out of town as quickly as they rode in. Their faces were never seen by the *Three for Hire*.

"Who the hell were they?" Scott yelled.

"The shooters across the street or the shooters on horseback?" Jesse shouted back.

While Jesse and Scott were trying to momentarily figure out what just happened, Thomas was stooping over looking at Chato's wound while he was stretched out on the floor writhing in agony.

"Get me a towel from the bar, Chato's been hit in his leg and he's bleeding pretty bad," Thomas shouted.

The barkeep ran over with a towel and gave it to Thomas. Thomas immediately made it into a tourniquet to stop the bleeding. There was no exit wound so the bullet was lodged in his leg.

"Is there a doctor in this town?" Thomas asked the barkeep.

"Yes, three doors down to your right. He lives upstairs from his office. I would go around the side, upstairs and knock on the door. I'm sure he'll go down and open his office for you. Tell him I sent you over."

Scott and Thomas helped Chato to his feet and began to walk him out of the saloon when the sheriff arrived on the scene and directly started asking questions.

"I'll talk to the sheriff; you two take Chato to the doctor's office and get that dang bullet out of him," Jesse said.

Luckily the doctor was home and allowed Chato, Scott and Thomas to come into his examining room. Thomas and Scott felt good that they were able to see the doctor so quickly, that is until the doctor began asking strange questions.

"What kind of Indian is he?" The doctor inquired.

"He's a government Indian scout," Scott answered.

"No, I mean from what tribe?"

"He's an Apache. Why is that important?"

"Because I don't treat Apache," the doctor brazenly remarked.

Scott looked at the doctor in disbelief, and then he pulled out his .45 Smith & Wesson Schofield revolver, stuck the end of the barrel into the doctor's right cheek, slowly pulled back the hammer with his thumb and said,

"You do tonight, fella."

There was a pause for about a minute. Then the doctor spoke with a quivering voice,

"Yes, I guess I do," the doctor said as nervous sweat immediately began flowing down his forehead to his eyebrows and he got religion real quick like. With the point of the barrel still sunken into the doctor's cheek, Scott slowly lowered the hammer on his six-shooter when he heard the words he was patiently waiting for; then he holstered his pistol and let the doctor go to work.

It took about forty minutes but the doctor finally removed the bullet, medicated the wound, and bandaged the leg. In the meantime, Jesse came over and told Scott and Thomas that he squared everything with the sheriff. Since there were cowboys in the saloon who witnessed the whole incident, the sheriff had no reason to hold or question the *Three for Hire* and Chato any further.

They told the doctor about their plans to travel to Fort Worth tomorrow and asked if it was OK to transport Chato in a wagon. The doctor suggested,

"Why don't you wait until tomorrow afternoon and allow me to look at the wound one more time, medicate it and rebandage it. Then I recommend that as soon as you arrive in Fort Worth, you take him to a doctor and have him look at the wound and rebandage it again. You want to make sure an infection doesn't set in."

"We'll bring him by at one o'clock tomorrow. Thanks for your service doc," Scott said.

"My, uh, my pleasure, sir," the doc answered back as he turned around, picked up a half pint of whiskey off the counter and took a big ole swig, relieved that this little episode just came to an end.

When they left the doctor's office, they all went back to the hotel. Chato was able to limp back on his own although they had to help him up the stairs to his room. When the three made certain that Chato was comfortable, Scott asked Jesse and Thomas to come over to his room and talk for a few minutes before they hit the sack. So they all did.

Scott sat on his bed while the other two pulled up a chair in front of him. He lowered his head into the palms of his hand, rubbed his face, then looked up and said in frustration,

"What the hell happened here tonight? Does anyone have a clue?"

"Yeah, I have a theory," Jesse said. "Somebody has a plan, we're getting in their way, so they want us dead. It's as simple as that."

"OK, I'll buy into that. Now, who has that plan, what is it, and who wants us dead?" Scott quickly shot back.

"Yeah, and who the Sam Hill were those two bushwhackers that came storming in like knights in shining armor and put lights out on those three men like they were picking off wingless ducks in a pond?" Thomas asked. "And by the way, who the heck hired them?"

"Too many unanswered questions guys. I don't like it. I feel like our lives are in more danger with this mission than any others we've been on. We have to get answers quickly. The walls are closing in on us. And let's not forget about all those innocent women and children Lone Wolf is holding," Scott reminded the other two.

"I'm convinced we'll get the answers we're looking for," Jesse said. "It's just gonna take a little more time than we figured. Don't get discouraged if we just take small steps. Let's just make sure we're taking all the right steps. That's all we can do. We talked about it before, we'll send a telegram to Garfield and the others when we get to Fort Worth. Right now, let's focus on getting Chato and ourselves safely back to Texas."

"Good idea Jesse," Scott confirmed. "Tonight is not too early to begin focusing. I recommend we lock our doors and sleep with our pistols underneath our pillows."

"You know pards, I don't think we're getting paid enough for this project. Say Jesse, I always wondered about this. You and your drovers experienced a lot of trouble with Indians and vigilante groups driving your cattle north to Kansas. What did you pay those guys for their troubles?" Thomas asked.

"More than enough, three dollars a day and found. Most other drovers were paying their cowboys one dollar and found."

"Three dollars a day and found? Found what?"

Scott looked at Jesse too wondering himself what that meant.

Jesse laughed and said, "What found meant was that I would supply the food at the work place, on the trail, where the cowboys could be found for me to give them their next orders. If they strayed like wandering cattle and couldn't be found, then I fired their sorry backsides."

"Well you can 'found' me in my room, I'm hitting the sack," Scott said. "See ya tomorrow morning."

Even with all the excitement that day, they got a pretty good night's sleep because they all felt like they were dragged around the rugged countryside with one foot stuck in a stirrup. They were beaten down and just plum worn out.

After a late breakfast the next morning, Jesse went over to the livery to purchase a buckboard with a two-horse team to haul Chato back to Fort Worth. Chato was feeling pretty rough from ole sawbones digging out that slug last night. Jesse then rode the wagon over to Kincaid's General Store to load up on some food and Arbuckle's for the trip.

However, before heading to Fort Worth, they did what the doctor suggested. They took Chato to doc's office for one more look-see and to get the leg wound medicated and rebandaged. Since there was no infection present, doc gave them the "go ahead" to travel to Fort Worth; but he gave Scott some extra bandages and medication so they could change Chato's bandage at least once on the trail.

It was not an easy trip. They had 115 miles left to travel on a bumpy, dusty cattle drive trail with the south wind in their faces, hauling a wounded scout in an old nearly broken-down buckboard, and trying to make up for lost time in summer temperatures that were hot enough to fry an egg on a flat rock. Thomas drove the wagon with his horse tethered behind the buckboard while Scott and Jesse flanked him on either side. With a lot of determination and grit, they arrived at Scott's parents' ranch just outside of Fort Worth on the fourth day. They unloaded some of the things and then headed to the doctor's office in town to have Chato looked at.

They all walked into the doctor's office together to make sure there wouldn't be any trouble like what they experienced in Wichita Falls. There wasn't, so Thomas stayed with Chato while Scott and Jesse walked over to the telegraph office to send messages to President Garfield and the two governors.

The message that Scott and Jesse sent to Garfield on this day of June 26th read:

President Garfield

Urgent! We must meet with you regarding our top secret findings near Fort Sill. We discovered what appear to be some criminal activities with hostiles involving U.S. Army soldiers. We witnessed activities serious enough to warrant court-martials, in our humble opinions. We wondered if we could meet you at a halfway location like St. Louis to expedite the project since we still need to consider the fate of hostages at the hands of Lone Wolf. Also request, of course with your permission, a commanding officer to be in our meeting so we know how to allocate responsibilities on future follow-up activities. Lastly, we will notify the two governors of our progress in general terms. Please inform us the date, time and place we can meet.

Jesse Caldwell
Scott Johnson
Thomas O'Brien

After sending a telegram to the president, Jesse and Scott wrote a telegram to the two governors being a bit more general and to just notify them that they were making good progress. They felt like they needed to inform the two governors that what they discovered, which had possible connections to the cause of the hostage taking, necessitated interaction with the federal government.

It wasn't until two days later, June 28th, that Jesse, Scott, and Thomas received an answer from the president regarding the requested meeting details. When they read the president's telegram, they were surprised with the dignitaries joining the president. The message read:

Jesse Caldwell
Scott Johnson
Thomas O'Brien
Either I or Vice President Arthur will meet you there in St. Louis on July 9th. Also in attendance will be the Secretary of the Interior, and the Commissioner of Indian Affairs. You met these two gentlemen in D.C. Also traveling with us will be General William Tecumseh Sherman and a lawyer from the Justice Department since you mentioned "court-martial" in your communications. Transit from D.C. will be on the president's train which will be used as the meeting place. Look for engine number 112. We trust this meeting will yield good results and future direction.

President Garfield

CHAPTER NINE:

Corruption in the Ranks

After receiving President Garfield's telegram, the *Three for Hire* made their travel plans to meet with Garfield et al. However, Chato became extremely adamant with a suggestion he offered. Since they had no contact with Lone Wolf coming up on three months now, he pleaded that he and one of the three go with him to inform Lone Wolf of their progress. He thought this was essential for the safety of the hostages.

The three discussed it and thought that Chato's suggestion had merit. Without hesitation, Thomas offered to take the trip with Chato. They all agreed upon the message that Garfield needed to hear and the information that should be shared with Lone Wolf. Thomas' plan was to leave with Chato on July 5th for the Arizona Territory, a couple of days before Jesse and Scott would leave for St. Louis to meet with President Garfield.

Then out of nowhere, on Sunday evening right at dinner time on the Johnson ranch, there was a frantic knock on the door. It was the telegraph operator. He didn't bring a telegram with him this time but instead a copy of the Dallas Daily Herald dated Sunday, July 3, 1881.

"Garfield's been shot! Garfield's been shot!" He yelled.

Scott jumped up from the dinner table and opened the door.

"What did you say?" Scott anxiously asked. Oh, he heard it alright. He just couldn't believe his ears. Neither could the others.

"President Garfield's been shot. Here, it's in today's Dallas Daily Herald."

Scott snatched the newspaper out of his hand and began reading it. The headline read "A DASTARDLY DEED, Attempt on the Life of the president".

"Is he dead?" Jesse asked as Thomas and the others looked on in utter disbelief.

"I don't know yet," Scott replied as he began skimming through the article.

"I think he's in serious condition but still alive," the telegraph operator offered.

Scott then began reading excerpts from the article. "It says here,

The president was shot at 9:28 a.m. as he was entering the Baltimore and Potomac depot to take a train for Long Branch. As they reached the ladies' waiting room, a man who stood on the right of the president raised his arm and deliberately fired two shots from a revolver exclaiming as he did so,

'Now we will have Arthur for president'. The first shot struck the president in the right arm…After the first shot the assassin immediately fired again. When the shot took effect in the president's side…he sank to the floor."

Scott continued to scan the article, almost in a panic mode. "It says that,

The president is conscious and does not complain of great suffering. It is impossible to say as yet what the result will be."

"Does it say who shot him?" Jesse inquired.

"Yes, it says here,

His name is Charles Guiteau, he is about thirty years old and supposed to be of French descent. He is about 5 feet 5 inches in height, sandy complexion, and is light but not weighing more than 125 pounds. He wears a moustache and has whiskers and has sunken cheeks and eyes, far apart of which gives him a sullen or, as officials describe, a loony appearance."

"It sounds like they caught the lowlife cur," Thomas said.

Scott skimmed further down the article and read,

"The assassin was seized by those standing near, and would have been torn to pieces but for the police.

Listen to this. Here's a letter they pulled out of this guy's pocket:

The president's tragic death was a sad necessity, but it will unite the republican party and save the republic. Life is a flimsy stream, and it matters little when one goes. A human life is of small value. During the war thousands of brave boys went down without a tear. I presume the president was a Christian, and that he will be happier in Paradise than here. It will be no worse for Mrs. Garfield, dear soul, to part with her husband this way than by natural death. He is liable to go at any time, anyway. I had no ill will toward the president. His death was a political necessity. I am a lawyer, a theologian and a politician. I am a stalwart of the stalwarts. I was with General Grant and the rest of our men in New York during the canvass. I have some papers for the press, which I shall leave with Byron Andrews and his co-journalists, 1420 New York avenue, where all the reporters can see them. I am going to jail. signed, Charles Guiteau

That's about it. Oh wait, here's something else. What's this all about? It reads here,

He writes a letter to General Sherman. The following letter was found on the street shortly after Guiteau's arrest. The envelope was unsealed and addressed to General Sherman or his field assistant in charge of the war department.

To General Sherman:
I have just shot the president. I have shot him several times as I wished him to go as easily as possible. I am a lawyer, a theologian, a politician. I am a stalwart of the stalwarts. I was with General Grant and the rest of our men in New York during the canvass. I am going to jail. Please take possession of the jail. Very Respectfully, Charles Guiteau."

"What a tragedy! Garfield shot by a lunatic. I sure hope he pulls through. These sorts of things just don't make sense. He was in the same battle with me in Shiloh during the War, one of the bloodiest of the War, and he made it through without a scratch. Then some half-brain idiot ambushes him in a train depot where he doesn't have a chance. Talk about a raw deal," Thomas remarked.

"What are you boys going to do now?" Scott's father asked. "You still have the safety of women and children hostages to worry about."

Jesse was considering that also while Scott was reading passages from the newspaper. He was trying to think things out logically.

"Here's what I think we should do. Thomas and Chato should leave for the Chiricahua Mountains tomorrow. Let's be up front with Lone Wolf and inform him that the president has been shot and if he dies, we know his replacement will follow through with making the right decisions regarding the prosecution of the guilty parties. We met the vice president and we trust this to be true. We must convince Lone Wolf of this.

Then I suggest we send a telegram to Secretary Kirkwood and ask him to talk to Arthur and see if he will meet with us on Garfield's behalf on the date and in the place agreed upon. I know this seems a little callous to push the issue now but like your father said, Scott, 'We have the lives of the hostages to think about'."

Everyone was in concurrence with Jesse. It only took a day for Secretary Kirkwood to respond back with a wire. Vice President Arthur was scheduled to make the trip anyway and with the president's health in a stable condition, the July 9th meeting date held. The *Three for Hire* were encouraged that things were moving as planned.

So when the time came for Scott and Jesse to head for St. Louis, Chato and Thomas traveled by rail to Tucson and then planned to backtrack on horseback to Lone Wolf's hideout in the Chiricahua Mountains. Chato could now ride with his leg wound with no problem. It was healing nicely.

Scott and Jesse reached St. Louis many days before Chato and Thomas reached Lone Wolf and they beat Vice President Arthur's train by several hours. Waiting around at the train depot on a sultry July summer afternoon in St. Louis was like sticking your head in a fired-up wood burning stove. That's what those humid July days felt like in river towns along Old Man River, the mighty Mississippi.

Before Arthur's train arrived, Scott told Jesse that he would be somewhat intimidated by the presence of General Sherman. And who wouldn't be, especially if you were fighting on the other side during the Civil War like Scott did in the Texas Confederate Army.

William Tecumseh Sherman (February 8, 1820 - February 14, 1891) was considered an outstanding military strategist. Perhaps the name Tecumseh was the inspiring motivational force behind his success. Sherman wrote in his memoirs that his father gave him the name, Tecumseh because he greatly admired the Shawnee Chief Tecumseh for his bravery and leadership skills.

Tecumseh (March, 1768 - October 5, 1813) had become known as an iconic folk hero in America, Aboriginal and Canadian history. He was born near what is now Springfield, Ohio. He fought against the United States in the early 1800's and attempted to organize a confederation of various Native American tribes to resist white European settlements. In the War of 1812, he and his followers joined the British forces to battle the United States. Later Tecumseh was killed in the Battle of the Thames in Canada on October 5, 1813 and died a warrior's death.

Maybe the proud and patriotic Sherman met the enemy head on with abandonment and unprecedented courage because he was inspired by these words of Tecumseh, "When it comes your time to die, be not like those whose lives are filled with the fear of death, so that when time comes they weep and pray for a little more time to live their lives over again in a different way. Sing your death song and die like a hero going home."

Sherman held many ranks in the U.S. Army and eventually climbed to the highest rank in the country.

Second Lieutenant, USA - July 1840
First Lieutenant, USA - November 1841
Captain, USA - September 1850
Colonel, USA - May 14, 1861
Brigadier General of Volunteers - May 17, 1861
Major General of Volunteers - May 1, 1862
Brigadier General, USA - July 4, 1863
Major General, USA - August 12, 1864
Lieutenant General, USA - July 25, 1866
General, USA - March 4, 1869

Sherman served underneath Grant in the Battles of Shiloh (April 6 - 7, 1862) and Vicksburg (May 18 – July 4, 1863) but made his permanent mark on history in his "March to the Sea" (November 15 to December 21, 1864) which is said to be the event that helped get Lincoln elected to his second term. With 60,000 men, he relentlessly and some say without conscience, ripped through the southern state of Georgia leaving a 60-mile-wide path of total destruction. "Total war" (destroy everything) was his strategy to break the South's will to fight. Four months later, Lee surrendered and the War came to an end.

When Grant assumed his position as the president of the United States in 1869, Sherman succeeded him as the Commanding General of the entire U.S. Army from 1869 to 1883. After the Civil War, Sherman's new focus was the Indian Wars out West.

For progress and industrial development to move forward in the new frontier, the railroad had to be built to connect all parts of the country, especially the East to the West; so one of Sherman's main duties was to protect construction of the railroads from brutal attacks by renegade and hostile Indians. Doing what he saw necessary to achieve the country's goal, he ordered total destruction of warring Indian tribes who got in the way of progress.

Sherman was not afraid to put in writing to Grant how he felt about Native Americans impeding the progress of constructing a cross-country railroad. After the 1866 Fetterman Massacre, he wrote that "We must act with vindictive earnestness against the Sioux, even to their extermination, men, women, and children."

In 1867 he wrote to Grant, "We are not going to let a few thieving, ragged Indians check and stop the progress of the railroad."

Outraged at Custer's defeat at the Battle of the Little Bighorn, Sherman wrote that "hostile savages like Sitting Bull and his band of outlaw Sioux...must feel the superior power of the Government." He further added that "During an assault, the soldiers cannot pause to distinguish between male and female, or even discriminate as to age."

Even with his harsh feelings and treatment toward the warring tribes, Sherman unpredictably spoke out against the unfair treatment and unscrupulous practices of government agents toward Indians within the reservations.

Even though Sherman's son confirmed that Sherman was a Catholic before the Civil War, Sherman did not adhere to any organized religion during the latter part of his adult life; so maybe some of his moral fabric toward the treatment of Indians on the reservations came from the influences of his wife Ellen Ewing Sherman (October 4, 1824 - November 28, 1888) who was a devout Catholic and organizer of the Catholic Indian Missionary Association (raising money for Catholic missions and schools on Indian reservations) and their son Thomas Sherman (October 12, 1856 - April 29, 1933) who was a Catholic Jesuit priest. Or just maybe he was able to reach deep into his past and was able to do some serious moral soul searching.

Sooner or later, General Sherman became war weary like many others. He coined a famous phrase that would be repeated for generations.

"I am tired and sick of war. Its glory is all moonshine. It is only those, who have neither fired a shot nor heard the shrieks and groans of the wounded, who cry aloud for blood, for vengeance, for desolation. War is hell."

Yes, Scott actually feared meeting Sherman. However, that fear would soon change to favor as he would learn that Sherman wanted to get down to the business of discovering: who was responsible for the harsh treatment of the Native Americans around Fort Sill, who was supplying rifles to the Indians, and finally, what were their reasons for doing so.

A few hours after Scott and Jesse arrived at the St. Louis Train Depot, engine number 112 pulled up to the station. Besides the engine and the fuel car, there were three other cars attached: the meeting car, a passenger car for soldiers guarding Arthur and the others, and a caboose. Scott and Jesse walked out onto the boardwalk to meet it.

When the train came to a complete stop, a lieutenant of the U.S. Army stepped off the train, asked Scott and Jesse to identify themselves, and then the soldier introduced himself and asked the two to step aboard. When they did, the train moved forward onto a spur and then stopped again.

Both Jesse and Scott's hearts were racing faster than any one of the fifteen thoroughbreds who ran in the first Kentucky Derby on May 17, 1875 in front of a crowd of about 10,000 people. Even though they met three of these gentlemen in Washington, D.C., it was in a formal setting and there wasn't much said between them. Most of the conversation was with President Garfield. However, it wasn't the first time they were dealing with Washington elite so they knew how to carry themselves in such company.

When they entered what was the president's car, everything looked familiar, as well it should. This was the same car Jesse, Scott and Thomas met President Hayes in when during the year before, they discussed the findings of a secret society who hired the *Shadow Assassins* who created havoc around the country.

The car was still set up like a plush hotel room except it lacked a bed. The windows were draped, the beautiful wood floor was adorned with Oriental area rugs and the car contained custom made leather furniture. It still had a well-stocked bar and of course, a round meeting table with six chairs for discussing things of a serious nature or playing a few hands of draw poker during transit.

The first order of business was for Arthur to introduce General Sherman to Scott and Jesse. Then Arthur introduced the lawyer in the room to the two. The attorney from the Justice Department was James Brent, a lawyer originally from Pennsylvania. Of course, the other gentlemen on board were the Secretary of the Interior Samuel Kirkwood and the Commissioner of Indian Affairs Hiram Price.

Before Arthur began the meeting, he offered everyone a snifter of brandy and they toasted to the full recovery of President Garfield.

"Here, here," they all said as they lifted their glasses to Garfield.

"I pray that he will recover," Arthur continued, "but he is not out of the woods yet."

Then Arthur began the meeting,

"Scott and Jesse, you informed us that you have made much progress with this project. Share with us what you know."

Jesse was the one who spoke first.

"First let me tell you that Chato and Thomas are headed to the Chiricahua Mountains to update Lone Wolf of the progress of our investigation with the purpose to keep the hostages alive."

"If we know where the hostages are, why don't we just send a force of 500 soldiers with ordnance and wipe out the Apache and rescue the hostages?" Sherman asked. "Surely we can handle that small band of renegades."

"With all due respect General, Nana would like nothing better. That would give him an excuse to kill all the hostages. They can see you coming over two miles away from their location. Every one of those women and children would be slain and mutilated before your first shot rang out. No sir, we have to do this our way and we'd like for you to back our play," Jesse insisted.

Sherman took a puff from his cigar that he just lit up and then said, "OK, go on."

"We followed the supply wagons from Fort Worth just like we all planned. About an hour or two after we crossed the Red River into the Indian Territory, the supply wagons turned onto a path that led straight to an old trading post."

"Is that where they unloaded and stole the supplies?" Arthur asked.

"No sir, that's where they loaded up a bunch of crates of new rifles, Henry repeating rifles we reckoned. We watched through our binoculars from a hillside and could see everything."

Then Scott jumped into the conversation,

"After the rifles were loaded into the wagons, four uniformed soldiers came out to escort the wagons away. When they left, we found out that the gun manufacturer had been dropping off rifles at that location for quite a while instead of Fort Sill. The owner of the post was very free with that information."

"Well that doesn't make sense," Sherman insisted. "Why didn't the manufacturer just drop them off at Fort Sill?"

"Because they weren't destined to go to Fort Sill," Scott said.

"I don't understand," Arthur replied. "Didn't you suggest that the shipment of rifles had a military escort?"

"Oh they had a military escort all right," Scott said. "Those four soldiers escorted the rifles right to a band of Comanche, Kiowa, and Apache."

"Good grief!" Arthur shouted as he grabbed a cigar in a nervous gesture and lit it up. "We have traitors in our military. For heaven's sake, what in the Sam Hill is their motive for selling rifles to the Indians and creating all this turmoil? Is it to line their pockets?"

"No sir, there seems to be much more than that. Let me backtrack a minute. After the six wagons left the trading post, only two wagons headed to Fort Sill while the soldiers and the other four wagons headed west to the Wichita Mountains."

"Wait a minute," Sherman said as he unrolled a map of the area like a military general and strategist loved to do. "Show me everything on here, Scott."

"Yes sir, this is the trading post right about here. The wagons headed west to the southern tip of the Wichita Mountains and then turned north on the west side of the mountain range. There's a box canyon that they turned into, right about here. That's where the wagons stopped. The soldiers met up with several civilians there, talked for a while and then left. It wasn't too much longer that the Indians showed up and then left with all of the rifles."

The anger on Sherman's face became so apparent that it was almost frightening. In fact, Arthur, Kirkwood, and Price were all fuming by now as well. However, the motive for the soldiers selling the rifles to the Indians was still not clearly apparent to them.

"Are you sure it just wasn't for gold pieces and a get rich quick scheme?" Arthur asked.

"If it was simply for money," Jesse offered, "this case would be halfway solved. No sir, there's more to it than that. What we didn't tell you yet was that the civilians were guarding a large pond, well that's what we first thought, until Chato snuck down there at night and found out that the pond was really a large petroleum seep."

Then James Brent, the attorney from Pennsylvania spoke up,

"If I might jump in here for one minute gentlemen, that explains a lot. Being from Pennsylvania, I'm very familiar with petroleum seeps. Generally speaking, where there are seeps, there's oil under the surface fairly close. Back home, we called oil, 'gold of a different color', or 'liquid gold'. Whoever brings in an oil well is monetarily set for life and likewise, his family members for generations to come. Gentlemen, I think if you put two and two together, you will find your motive for these traitors and those civilians selling rifles to the Indians and creating chaos. I think we can get to all of the answers in depositions and a court-martial."

Scott and Jesse shared everything else they knew with the group that day.

Arthur then proposed a question to Attorney Brent,

"In your opinion James, where should we proceed from here? Do we have enough to arrest these four soldiers?"

"I would say yes. It sounds to me like we can get their names from the trading post proprietor."

"What about the civilians?" Arthur asked. "What do we do about them?"

"I would proceed with warrants for their arrests after we get convictions on the soldiers."

"Do you think the commander of Fort Sill is involved?" Arthur inquired. "What's his name? It escapes me."

"Colonel Baxter," Sherman responded.

"The only way we will be able to get to all of the answers we need is to find a traitor amongst the traitors," Brent said. "In other words, we need one of them to turn state's evidence before the trial and give up the others and their scheme."

"Explain what you mean by state's evidence, Mr. Brent," Jesse said.

"The definition of turning state's evidence is for an accused or convicted criminal, in this case one of those soldiers, to testify as a witness for the state against his accomplices. This generally happens when one of the alleged guilty parties has a change of heart or a feeling of guilt he finds hard to live with. However, most of the time it's done in response to a generous offer from the prosecution, such as a reduced sentence or even complete immunity from serving time. There can be other considerations also. I have experience in these matters and I can say with some certainty that I will probably be able to convince one of these varmints to squeal like a stuck pig. And I dare say, knowing what I know now, when the answers begin to come to light, I think we are not going to like what we find. When it comes to greed, corruption has a way to find its way up the proverbial ladder."

"Well, nothing will surprise, Jesse or me," Scott said, "we've seen so many unbelievable things, the last two years, that it would make your head spin."

"Well, what do you need from us now, Mr. Arthur?" Jesse asked.

"I think you should notify your employers, the two governors, of where we are in this investigation. They have a right to know. Then tell them to inform the hostages' families that the federal government is working on the terms which the kidnappers have demanded for the release of the hostages. We feel certain that the men will be with their wives and children soon."

"You will also be required to give depositions and be witnesses for the state during the court-martial," Brent added.

Then General Sherman threw in his two cents,

"Scott and Jesse, you guys did a splendid job with your investigation. The military will handle the arrests from here. We'll also get those rifles back from the renegade Indians around Fort Sill. It's a shame it came to this because of the greed of a few who have caused the grief and hardship of many. I promise you, justice will be served."

"I believe it will, sir. That's good to hear you say General, because it's justice that will set those hostages free in the Chiricahua Mountains and get them back to their grieving families where they belong," Scott replied. "You can reach us by telegram in Fort Worth when you need us."

With that, Arthur poured one more brandy in everyone's snifter for the road and then afterwards, Arthur's train traveled back to Washington, D.C. and Scott and Jesse headed back to Fort Worth catching the next train available.

When Scott and Jesse arrived in Fort Worth, they had to sit around Scott's family ranch for days wondering how Thomas and Chato were making out. Thomas and his scout were heading into renegade country again and the question was, would they be accepted as neutral negotiators as before?

After days and days of traveling, Chato and Thomas were finally approaching the Mescalero encampment. In fact, they were close enough to be looking for smoke signals being sent by the Apache sentries to the Apache village. But today, they saw no smoke signals. Then they waited for Apache sentries to approach and escort them to the Apache stronghold. But today there were no escorts. Something was wrong and Chato did not like the looks of it.

Finally, when they rode up to the Apache village, what they found was disturbing. The village was abandoned and the tracks indicated that the band of renegades had moved the hostages further south just as Lone Wolf warned he would do if too many suns passed with no word of justice. Their fear was that the Mescalero had taken them across the border into Mexico.

Chato looked at Thomas and said, "This is not a good sign, my friend."

Just then, five Apache rode in with their rifles held high in the air while yelling battle cries and quickly surrounded the two. There was no time for the two to draw their guns and protect themselves. What they didn't know was that if they would have skinned their smoke wagons, they would have been shot down like dogs.

The long wait for a message from the *Three for Hire* troubled Lone Wolf and Nana so they moved their encampment further south. One of the five Apache surrounding Thomas and Chato spoke English and asked Thomas,

"What message do you wish to give to Lone Wolf?"

Thomas decided to keep the message short and sweet since he was not speaking directly to Lone Wolf. His instincts also told him to convey a very positive message.

"Tell Lone Wolf that great progress has been made. We are arresting the guilty and they will be tried. Justice will be served. We trust that Lone Wolf is a man of his word and will not harm the hostages."

"I will give Lone Wolf that message."

"How will we be able to find you when justice is served and the hostages can be released?" Thomas asked.

"Have your Apache scout go to the highest point of that mountain range over there, toward the rising sun, and send a smoke signal. Send up three blankets. Then come to this abandoned camp and wait for us to appear. We will take you to Lone Wolf's camp. Lone Wolf insists that you bring proof of justice before hostages are released. If there is no proof of justice then there will be no more talk, only blood. Do you understand?"

Thomas was infuriated with that reckless remark but dared not show his ire because the Apache had the upper hand.

"Yes, I understand. Now you tell me, how is the health of the hostages?"

"They are tired and thin. Food is scarce. Word of justice needs to come quick."

The message was clear. The hostages were exhausted and famished. Time was running out.

The five renegade Mescalero turned their horses and rode off as fast as they rode in. Thomas looked at Chato and said, "Let's head back to Tucson, quickly. Time is now of the essence."

During the time Thomas and Chato were traveling in Arizona, news was being made out of Fort Sumner, New Mexico Territory and echoing around the country, spreading faster than a pat of butter over a hot Dutch oven biscuit. Billy the Kid had been ambushed, shot and killed by Pat Garrett.

Fort Sumner was a military fort named after the military governor of New Mexico Territory, Edwin Vose Sumner (January 30, 1797 – March 21, 1863). He held that position from 1851-1853. While serving in the Mexican-American War, he earned the nickname "Bull Head" because supposedly a musket ball bounced off his head during battle.

During that time period there were also two civilian governors of New Mexico Territory who were Whig party members and assigned by President Fillmore: 1851 – 1852, James S. Calhoun (1802 – July 2, 1852); and 1852 – 1853, William Carr Lane (December 1, 1789 – January 6, 1863). Incidentally, Lane was the first mayor of St. Louis, Missouri and held that position between 1823 and 1829 and again from 1837 to 1840.

The fort was located in east central New Mexico Territory and charged with the duties of the internment of nearby Navajo and Mescalero Apache populations from 1863 to 1868. The United States Government closed the fort in 1868 and sold its buildings in 1870 to Lucien Maxwell (September 14, 1818 – July 25, 1875) who was a prominent New Mexico landowner. Lucien was a rancher and entrepreneur who at one point owned 1,714,765 acres of land making him one of the largest private landowners in United States history.

On July 14, 1881, the infamous outlaw, William Henry McCarty, Jr., (a.k.a. William H. Bonney and Henry Antrim) better known as Billy the Kid, was gunned down by Patrick Garrett at Maxwell's Fort Sumner home which was then owned by Pete Maxwell, the son of Lucien Maxwell. The Kid was later buried just a few feet from Lucien Maxwell in Fort Sumner, New Mexico.

Newspapers all around the country were running various headlines for several weeks proclaiming with similar banners, "Billy the Kid was shot and killed". The Dodge City Times on July 21, 1881 ran a story on the front page in the fourth column about three quarters of the way down. The actual story read:

THE KID KILLED

The Las Vegas Gazette has positive information that Billy the Kid, the notorious murderer and outlaw who for several years has been the terror of New Mexico cattlemen, was on the 14th killed by Pat Garrett of Denver, Colo. Garrett had been on his trail for some time, and on the 14th overhauled him in a cabin at Fort Sumner and shot him dead. The Kid is a native of New York. His real name is McCarty.

The Las Vegas they speak of is Las Vegas, New Mexico.

In the same newspaper, The Dodge City Times dated July 21, 1881, another story was run and it appeared directly following the "The Kid Killed" story. There was no title to the story but it read this way:

The train robbery at Winston, Missouri in which Conductor Westfall was brutally murdered, was one of the most atrocious affairs of the kind in the annals of crime in this country. The stage and train robber has been hitherto considered the most chivalrous of the profession, but this crime had in it no redeeming features. It was cowardly and brutal to the last degree.

This story was actually about an event that happened on July 15, 1881, the exact day after Billy the Kid was shot and killed. Frank and Jesse James committed what was said to be one of the most appalling crimes ever. A Chicago, Rock Island & Pacific train left the Winston, Missouri station on July 15th. As the train was just a bit down the tracks, Jesse and Frank James, and Wood Hite jumped on board into one of the passenger cars. Simultaneously, two other gang members by the name of Dick Liddil and Clarence Hite jumped into the express car.

The James boys were after conductor William Westfall, whom Frank and Jesse believed was in charge of the train that delivered some Pinkerton agents to their mother's house back in 1875 the night that she lost an arm, and their half-brother, Archie Peyton Samuel (July 26, 1866 – January 26, 1875) was killed. The Pinkerton detectives threw what was thought to be a bomb through a window; Archie, who was thought to have some mental disabilities, believed the bomb was a log, so he picked it up and threw it into the fireplace. It exploded, killing him instantly and wounding his mother.

Now whether the James boys were out to rob the train, out to get Westfall, or both is anybody's guess. The fact is, they achieved both.

Jesse spotted Westfall standing in the passenger car with his back turned toward him and Frank. Jesse quickly drew his pistol and shot Westfall in the back without warning. Westfall immediately fell to the ground and Jesse ran up to him and shot him in the head to finish him off. A passenger by the name of Frank McMillan somehow got involved, possibly trying to stop Jesse from shooting Westfall. He in turn was shot and killed by Frank James.

In the meantime, the other two outlaws robbed the safe in the express car. In frustration, they knocked the agent out with a pistol butt when they discovered that the money wasn't the amount they were expecting. They jumped off the train where they previously left their horses and divided the loot, only $650. Then they split up and rode off.

While Jesse Caldwell and Scott Johnson were awaiting the return of Thomas and Chato from their parley with the Apache, plus awaiting word from D.C. on how to proceed in the future, General Sherman made plans for the immediate arrest of the four soldiers involved in the illegal activities of selling stolen rifles to the Indians on the reservations and the theft of food, supplies and medicine from the U.S. Government. These would be the preliminary charges with undoubtedly more to follow.

On Sherman's arrival back to Washington, he wasted no time. He selected General Sheridan to ramrod this case.

ABOUT GENERAL PHILIP SHERIDAN

Sheridan (March 6, 1831 – August 5, 1888) made a career out of serving in the United States Army as an officer and was a successful Union General in the Civil War leaving his mark on more than ten battle fronts; especially in 1865 when his cavalry pursued General Robert E. Lee and was instrumental in forcing the Confederate General to surrender to General Grant at Appomattox Court House, Virginia on April 9, 1865.

Whereas General William Tecumseh Sherman was right at six foot in height, General Sheridan was quite short. Fully grown, he stood only five foot five inches tall, a height that led to his nickname, "Little Phil".

Abraham Lincoln is credited with an anecdote which humorously described Sheridan's appearance: "A brown, chunky little chap, with a long body, short legs, not enough neck to hang him, and such long arms that if his ankles itch, he can scratch them without stooping."

Lincoln probably called him chunky because even though he was thin in his youth, the short general grew to be 200 pounds, quite "chunky" for a man of small stature.

Sheridan had a dislike for soldiers and officers profiteering from stolen goods. An incident came up in 1862 when he refused to pay soldiers for horses they stole from civilians but then he confiscated the horses for Army use. When Sheridan's commanding officer, Major General Samuel Curtis ordered Sheridan to pay the officers for the stolen horses, Sheridan retorted, "No authority can compel me to Jayhawk or steal." Curtis had Sheridan arrested for insubordination but no formal proceedings followed.

After the Civil War, attention turned toward the Indians of the Great Plains. Indian wars began breaking out as settlers moved westward overtaking lands occupied by many Native American tribes. Treaties were broken on both sides and Indians were leaving the reservations for numerous reasons.

In August 1867, Grant appointed General Sheridan as head of the Department of Missouri, encompassing many states and territories, to make peace in the Plains. So the battles began but his troops were spread too thin. They fought the Cheyenne, Kiowa, and Comanche tribes in their winter quarters in 1868-1869, stripping the Indians of their supplies and livestock and killing those who resisted and refused to go back to the reservations.

Sheridan knew that if there were no buffalo, the Indians could not survive off the reservations. So when professional hunters trespassed on Indian land and killed over four million buffalo by 1874, Sheridan applauded them and said, "Let them kill, skin and sell until the buffalo is exterminated". Eventually, many Indians returned to their reservations. But there was more work to be done. Sheridan's department conducted the Red River War, the Ute War and the Great Sioux Wars of 1876-77 which were infamous for Custer's Last Stand at the Battle of the Little Bighorn, the bloodiest of all the battles of the Great Sioux Wars.

There's a story that Sheridan seemed to deny that ever happened but nevertheless, he has gone down in history as being the one credited with coining a phrase that has echoed in this country for generations, not because people agreed with the assertion, but because of the cruelty of the soul it purported.

There was a Comanche chief named Chief Tosawi who allegedly told Sheridan in 1869, "Me Tosawi; me good Injun". Sheridan supposedly replied, "The only good Indians I ever saw were dead." The statement was also rephrased, "The only good Indian is a dead Indian." Sheridan denied ever making either statement.

SHERMAN MOVES FORWARD

Sherman summoned General Philip Sheridan to D.C. for a meeting with himself, Kirkwood, Price and Attorney James Brent from the Justice Department. Sherman and the others filled in Sheridan on all of the details of the case. It was now up to Attorney Brent to establish criminal culpability and what type of charges to file and to prosecute. Unfortunately, this would take some time to ensure warranted verdicts and appropriate sentences. Then there was time needed to: identify and gather witnesses, take depositions, and finally build a strong case against the defendants. In addition, the most important aspect of the case was to convince one soldier to turn state's evidence without the other accused soldiers or anyone else knowing. The state's witness would need to be kept quiet or his life would certainly be in danger before the trial ever began. Paid assassins seemed to be a dime a dozen in the Old West.

The only order that Baxter received from Washington, specifically, the office of General Sherman, was to cease all future orders for rifles. It was necessary to do this because Sherman did not want any more rifles being sold to the Indians. Sherman made it appear to be a direct order to all forts so suspicions would not be aroused. He also sent a formal letter to every gun manufacturer stating that all orders for weapons were to be temporarily suspended and shipments halted. He addressed it as a fiscal issue.

During the months of August, September, and October of 1881, while the government's case was being built, things were not quiet around the country. Headlines were being made from the east coast to the west coast and ricocheting around the rest of the country from the remote points of the majestic northern pine forests to the most southern tip of the grassy Great Plains.

THE BATTLE OF CIBECUE CREEK

On August 30, 1881, there was an Apache uprising that became known as the Battle of Cibecue Creek. The battle was fought between the United States Cavalry and the White Mountain Apache in the eastern Arizona Territory at Cibecue Creek on the Fort Apache Indian Reservation. As seemed to be a story that had a resounding and reoccurring echo about it, Apache were fed up with the unhealthy conditions which were a result of corruption in the ranks and amongst some Indian Agents.

Because of the deteriorating reservation conditions, an Apache medicine man by the name of Nock-ay-det-klinne, who had counseled Apache leaders like Cochise and Geronimo, began holding ceremonies known as ghost dances. These ceremonies included heavy drinking and the use of many hallucinogenic plants, especially one known as peyote. Native Americans are said to have used peyote for at least 5,500 years. It was a cactus plant native to southwestern Texas and Mexico and found among scrub where there was limestone. The top or crown of the cactus consisted of disc-shaped buttons that were sometimes dried. They were generally chewed or boiled in water to produce the psychoactive tea affecting the mind. Generally nausea from consumption preceded the psychoactive effects.

With permission, the Indian Army scouts often joined the dances. Overtime, the scouts' attitudes began to change and many soldiers began to lose trust in these scouts. Settlers feared the dances would turn into Indian wars. So the soldiers investigated and removed the medicine man from his followers. During the removal, fights broke out, the medicine man was killed, the Army Indian scouts turned on the soldiers, and lives were lost on both sides. This is the only documented case where Army Indian scouts turned on the U.S soldiers. This affair touched off a regional

Apache uprising. Chiricahua and Warm Spring Apache leading warriors like Naiche (son of Cochise) and Juh (1825 – November, 1883) left the reservation and joined Geronimo on a war against the white man that lasted about two years.

PRESIDENT GARFIELD DIES FROM HIS BULLET WOUNDS

On September 19, 1881, President Garfield succumbed to the gunshot wounds inflicted on July 2, 1881 by Charles J. Guiteau. His presidency only lasted 200 days. The country was deeply saddened. He was the second president to be assassinated within only a 16 year period.

Once Garfield died, the assassin was officially charged with murder. He was formally indicted for murder on October 14, 1881, went to trial on November 14, 1881, found guilty on January 25, 1882, and hung on June 30, 1882.

VICE PRESIDENT CHESTER A. ARTHUR BECOMES PRESIDENT

In what could be construed as showing respect, Arthur was reluctant to be seen acting as president while Garfield was struggling to survive. So for two months there was a void in the executive office. Through that time period, Arthur did not travel to Washington. He was in his Lexington Avenue home on the East Side of the borough of Manhattan in New York City when he learned that Garfield had died.

Judge John R. Brady of the New York Supreme Court administered the oath of office in Arthur's home in the wee hours of the next morning at 2:15. Two days later, Arthur boarded a train to Washington. On his arrival the day of September 22nd, Arthur's oath of office was replicated by Chief Justice Morrison R. Waite, to assure procedural compliance.

He retired at the end of his first and only term due to poor health. A journalist by the name of Alexander McClure later wrote, "No man ever entered the Presidency so profoundly and widely distrusted as Chester Alan Arthur, and no one ever retired... more generally respected, alike by political friend and foe". Arthur earned praise for his solid performance while in office.

Accolades came after his death in 1886: The New York World stated, "No duty was neglected in his administration and no adventurous project alarmed the nation". Mark Twain wrote, "It would be hard indeed to better President Arthur's administration".

SHOOTOUT AT THE O.K. CORRAL

The date was October 26, 1881. The place was Tombstone, Arizona. The headline in the WEEKLY ARIZONA CITIZEN out of Tucson, Arizona Territory in Pima County on Sunday, October 30th read simply: *A Desperate Street Fight.* The article appeared on page 3 in the 7th column. The subtopic read:

Marshal Virgil Earp, Morgan and Wyatt Earp and Doc Holliday Meet the Cowboys – Three Men Killed and Two Wounded, one seriously – Origin of the Trouble and its Tragical Termination.

What was posted next in the article was the whole story from the Tombstone Nugget, October 27, 1881 edition. The first paragraph read:

The 26th of October, 1881, will always be marked as one of the crimson days in the annals of Tombstone, a day when blood flowed as water, and human life was held as a shuttlecock, a day always to be remembered as witnessing the bloodiest and deadliest street fight that has ever occurred in this place, or probably in the Territory.

... *The firing altogether didn't occupy more than twenty-five seconds, during which time fully thirty shots were fired.*

The gunfight at the O.K. Corral was fought by the three Earp brothers and Doc Holliday against outlaw cowboys Billy Claiborne, Tom and Frank McLaury, and Ike and Billy Clanton. Ike Clanton and Billy Claiborne ran from the fight unharmed. Ike's brother Billy Clanton was killed, along with both Tom and Frank McLaury. Virgil and Morgan were both wounded. Doc and Wyatt were unharmed.

Scott Johnson knew ole Wyatt up in Dodge City back in '79 before Wyatt and his brothers left for Tombstone. In '80, Scott and Jesse met in Tombstone with Wyatt regarding another project they were on for President Hayes concerning a secret society.

Needless to say, Scott and Jesse were very interested in this story about the shootout at the O.K. Corral. After reading it, Scott sent his concerns by telegram to the Earp family in Tombstone.

JESSE AND FRANK GO UNDERGROUND AND LIVE UNDER ALIASES

After the July 15th robbery and killing on the Chicago, Rock Island & Pacific train at Winston, Missouri, Jesse and Frank went underground. Frank headed east to Virginia which he thought was a safer territory. He went by the name of Ben J. Woodson. Jesse headed to St. Joseph, Missouri where he went by the alias of Thomas Howard. Unbeknownst to Jesse or anyone else, his days were numbered. On April 3, 1882, Bob Ford shot Jesse in the back of his head while Jesse was either dusting off or straightening a picture in his home. "A coward shot Mr. Howard".

ARRESTS ARE MADE IN FORT SILL

By early November, the facts were gathered, charges were determined, targets for arrests were verified and General Sheridan and ten soldiers traveled by train and then horseback to Fort Sill. There was no announcement of the visit. It was to be a complete surprise. Sherman and Sheridan knew that Baxter had to be involved with the corruption but wanted more proof before they arrested him. They were hoping the proof would come from a traitor amongst the traitors.

About 10:00 a.m. on November 8th, what appeared to be a small Army platoon approached Fort Sill. The sentry recognized the stars on Sheridan's coat and promptly ordered a private to open the gates. Soldiers in the courtyard were shocked to see General Sheridan ride in with a squad of ten cavalry soldiers.

A sergeant immediately ran into Colonel Baxter's office to inform him of the unexpected visit by the general. Baxter's eyes almost popped out of his head at the announcement. He quickly buttoned up his uniform, brushed his hair, and straightened up the top of his desk. He even hurriedly put out his half-smoked cigar and threw it into his wastebasket.

As he heard the soldiers walking up the wooden steps toward his front door, his heart rate soared to levels he never experienced before, even in the heat of battle. A guilty conscience will do that to you. He put a fake smile on his face and a cheerful tone in his voice when he opened the door and asked General Sheridan to come in. All ten of the general's soldiers entered as well.

Baxter saluted the general and then said,

"General Sheridan sir, it is my honor to meet you. To what do I owe the pleasure of this visit?"

Sheridan wasn't amused at the phony greeting and got right to the point. He removed a piece of paper from his shirt pocket and said as he read from what appeared to be an official document,

"Order your aide to escort the following four soldiers to this office immediately: Sergeant Jake Miller, Corporal Josh Taylor, Corporal Ben Allen, and Corporal James Pendergast."

"Yes sir, but can I ask you for what reason?"

"You will know soon enough when they arrive here."

Sheridan then turned his back on Baxter in a demeaning sort of gesture and began whispering to his lieutenant. Baxter became extremely uncomfortable and the mood was very subdued.

It took about ten minutes, but it seemed like an eternity to Baxter, before the aide came back with the four soldiers. When they all walked into Baxter's office and saw the general and his ten soldiers, they had a pretty good inkling of what was about to happen. Baxter knew too but his main concern was his own hide.

Sheridan's lieutenant then said, "Stand at attention soldiers."

Sheridan handed the legal document to his lieutenant to read while Baxter looked on with a "pale face". The lieutenant stood at attention in front of the four soldiers and read,

"Sergeant Jake Miller, Corporal Josh Taylor, Corporal Ben Allen and Corporal James Pendergast, you are all under arrest for corruption and conspiracy to defraud the United States Government, stealing government ordnance, supplying and selling arms to the reservation tribes, pilfering government supplies, food and medicine and desertion of posts while doing so.

You will immediately be escorted to Fort Reno where you will be incarcerated for an indefinite period of time wherein you will be given an attorney and then attend your court-martial in the courthouse at Fort Reno."

"You are innocent until proven guilty but as far as I am concerned, you are a disgrace to the uniform," Sheridan said.

As the charges were being read, all four defendants looked at Baxter as if to say, "Well boss, what are you going to do about this?"

Baxter refused to look at the four, yet the four had no intention to give Baxter up. Loyalty to the end, right? Well, at least for today. Other than that, well it remained to be seen.

At this point, Sheridan asked his lieutenant and his men to lead the four prisoners to their bunkhouse to collect their clothing and personal belongings and to be ready in thirty minutes to depart for Fort Reno.

Sheridan stayed for a few minutes with Baxter and asked Baxter's aide to leave the office. When the aide shut the door behind him, Sheridan didn't hold back telling Baxter how he felt about him.

"Colonel Baxter, I'm going to be blunt with you. You are under investigation, as well. You are ordered to stay within the confines of this fort. You or no one in your command will be allowed to visit that box canyon in the Wichita Mountain Range. Let me repeat. It is off limits to you and everyone under your command. Is that understood?"

"Yes sir."

"Furthermore, if you abandon your post for any reason, I mean any reason at all, even if it's just to pick wild daisies outside the fort for your dinner table, it will be treated as an admittance of guilt and you will be hunted down, court-martialed, and executed like any other deserter. Is that understood Colonel?"

"Yes sir."

"Lastly, General Sherman has ordered that new shipments of food and medicine be transported here for immediate distribution to the reservation tribes. I trust that 100% of these supplies will be distributed in the proper fashion. Is that understood Colonel?"

"Yes sir."

"We will be in touch," Sheridan said as he turned around, opened the door and walked out of Baxter's office without saluting Baxter and without even closing the door. Baxter walked over to the door, slowly closed it and looked out the window as he watched General Sheridan, his platoon, and the four prisoners ride off to Fort Reno.

When the gates were closed, Baxter walked over to his desk with his head hanging low, sat down in a despondent state, opened the top drawer to his desk, removed a pistol, cocked it, placed it on top of his desk in front of him, and stared at the trigger.

CHAPTER TEN:

I Would Like to Call...

A few days after the arrest at Fort Sill, Secretary of the Interior Kirkwood was instructed by General Sherman to send a wire to the *Three for Hire* directing them to return to the box canyon in the Wichita Mountains to look for more clues, especially in the small office building that was on site.

Scott saw the events as good news for the hostages. Before they returned to the Fort Sill area, Scott quickly fired off a telegram to the governors of Arizona and New Mexico Territories to inform them that arrests had been made, things were moving along quickly and justice would soon be served.

By this time, word about the arrests spread around the Indian Territory like a smallpox outbreak. Many were in shock, yet to some, the treatment of the reservation Indians was like an old story being rehashed.

The civilians at the site of the petroleum seep received word of the arrests when they picked up supplies at the very trading post where the rifles arrived from the gun manufacturer and were taken to the canyon to be sold to the Indians. So they packed up and headed back north to Pennsylvania fearing legal action would be taken against them.

The foreman in charge whose name was Will Franklin was especially vulnerable to a criminal indictment. He would become a key person of interest because he most likely took orders from someone other than Baxter, someone who in all likelihood was ramrodding this entire "get rich quick" scheme. Franklin might be the key player in this investigation, even more so than one of the soldiers who the government had hoped to turn state's evidence.

Now several things were taking place simultaneously: the *Three for Hire* were trying to find more evidence of criminal involvement at the box canyon, Attorney James Brent was staying at Fort Reno endeavoring to cleverly get one of the four prisoners to turn state's evidence, Baxter was under criminal investigation, the hostages were short on food and the Mescalero renegade kidnappers were growing short on patience.

It would be easy to get a conviction of the four soldiers. But that wasn't enough. The government needed more. There was corruption in the ranks, but was there corruption even higher up? Attorney James Brent was the key player at this point and everyone knew it. It was up to his expertise to get one of the prisoners to turn on the others before trial and spill his guts.

After spending about four weeks with the prisoners and taking depositions, there was a break in the case. Brent sent a telegram to General Sherman. It read:

General Sherman

Arrest Colonel Baxter on the same charges as the four soldiers from Fort Sill. You can begin court-martial proceedings in one month to include Baxter and the four prisoners. I will continue to live at Fort Reno to build the government's case. Also, arrest a gentleman by the name of Will Franklin of Pennsylvania for conspiracy to defraud the government and being an accomplice in illegal activities on an Indian reservation. That's just for starters. Keep me informed on the date of the court-martial. I will have the Department of Justice build a civilian criminal case against Franklin.

Attorney James Brent
Department of Justice

When Jesse, Scott, Thomas and Chato arrived at the box canyon in the Wichita Mountains, they found the place deserted. The first order of business was to tear that office building apart. Their objective was to see if they could find clues as to who were some of the co-conspirators with Baxter and his cronies and to see if there was anything else that would connect this area with a petroleum seep to the kidnappings in Arizona and New Mexico Territories. They were searching for a possible cause and effect relationship.

A rock must strike a glass before the glass breaks.

The question was, "What had to happen before the barrels flowed out of or around this seep?" That was the real question and that was the point that would hopefully come out in the court-martial because it appeared that there were not any obvious answers lying around.

Unlike the previous mission they were on last year for President Hayes, they could not find any clues on site that pointed to criminal culpability. However, what they did find were piles of spoiled food and unused medicine supplies that were obviously originally meant for Indians on the reservation. It was clear that there was no intention of profiteering from the sale of these stolen goods. Therefore there had to be another motive for pilfering them from the government and keeping them out of the hands of the reservation tribes.

Scott thought this information was relevant to the criminal case so he forwarded their findings by wire to Attorney Brent in Fort Reno. Brent indeed saw the importance of this discovery in developing his prosecution case.

Scott, Jesse, Thomas and Chato temporarily went back to Fort Worth to await word from Attorney Brent on the date of the court-martial. Then word came. The court-martial was to begin on January 6, 1882. The timing allowed Thomas and Jesse to visit their families at Christmas time and return in plenty of time for the trial. Chato stayed with Scott's family.

Thomas walked into a buzz saw at home. His wife was fed up with his adventurous spirit and dangerous activities. She had enough of him being gone most of the year with very little communications on his whereabouts or anything that referred to missing his family. His marriage was in jeopardy.

What should have been a happy occasion, being at home with his family during Christmas, turned into an ultimatum; either give up these projects or move out. It was as simple as that. His wife was tired of him being a part-time husband and father. Plus, she could no longer take the agony of not knowing whether she was going to see him arriving home, standing up or returning in a pine box. Thomas certainly had some soul searching to do.

After Christmas, wires were sent out and all essential parties headed for Fort Reno for the military trial. When the *Three for Hire* arrived a few days early, they were asked to give depositions because they most likely would be called to the stand to testify.

Fort Reno was a perfect place to hold the court-martial. It was established as a permanent post in July of 1875 so the facilities were still fairly new. The fort was located near the Darlington Indian Agency on the old Cheyenne-Arapaho Indian Tribal Reservation in the Indian Territory.

The fort was named for General Jesse L. Reno (April 20, 1823 - September 14, 1862) who was killed at the Battle of South Mountain which was fought on September 14, 1862, as part of the Maryland Campaign of the Civil War. Three battles were fought for possession of three South Mountain passes. The passes were named: Crampton's Gap, Turner's Gap and Fox's Gap.

Reno was shot in the chest by a Confederate sharpshooter as he stood in front of his troops watching the enemy advance up the road at Fox's Gap. He was carried by stretcher to Brigadier General

Samuel Davis Sturgis's (June 11, 1822 – September 28, 1889) command post and he said in a clear voice, "Hello Sam, I'm dead". General Sturgis was a long-time friend of Reno and fellow member of the West Point class of 1846. Sturgis thought that Reno sounded so natural that he was sure Reno was joking and told him he hoped it was not as bad as all of that. Reno then replied, "Yes, yes, I'm dead - good-bye". He died a few minutes later.

THE GENERAL COURT-MARTIAL, JANUARY 6, 1882

The scene was now set. The research was complete. The charges were perfectly clear. The prosecutor was ready for trial.

It was a cold wintry morning in the Indian Territory. There was no snow on the ground, no sleet falling, and no clouds in the sky. It was just chilling to the bone as most January days were in the Indian Territory. However, in the courthouse at Fort Reno today, a fire would be lit shedding light and exposing the truth in heated exchanges and burning stares that were hot enough to start a brush fire on even a wet prairie.

The time was 9:30 a.m. The Fort Reno courtroom quickly turned from an empty, dark and cold lifeless room into a crowded, noisy, lit up quasi-Wild West show.

In attendance were soldiers, government civilian workers, Indian Agents, squatters in the unclaimed area of the Indian Territory, and some onlookers from northern Texas towns just south of the Red River.

However, most importantly, in attendance were the *Three for Hire* and Chato, the aides representing the governors of the Arizona and New Mexico Territories, families of kidnapped victims from those territories, and attorneys from the United States Department of Justice.

At precisely 10:00 a.m., a U.S. soldier stood up in front of the courtroom and shouted,

"Quiet in the courtroom, all rise!"

Just then, a door to the left opened and five uniformed U. S. Army officers entered the room and lined up behind a long wooden table in front of the courtroom. They were the panel of court-martial members of which one presided as the judge. Directly in front of the panel in the middle of the room was a witness chair. To the right were chairs and a table for the defendants and defense counsel and to the left were chairs and a table for the trial counsel, the prosecuting attorneys.

Before a case goes to a court-martial, there is a pretrial investigation under Article 32 of the Uniform Code of Military Justice to determine if in fact the case is worthy of a trial. However, the accused have the right to waive this provision. Baxter and the four accused waived their right to a pretrial.

Then the judge banged a wooden gavel to a block and said,

"Quiet please, the court is in session."

When all were standing and it was quiet to where you could hear a squirrel bark in the next county, the judge said,

"Bring in the accused."

Just then, the back door opened and heads turned to watch as the five accused walked in with a military escort down the middle aisle and subsequently took their places behind their table.

Then the judge stated,

"The purpose of this court-martial is to seek the truth and administer justice.

Since the accused have agreed to be co-defendants and tried jointly, trial counsel, please read the charges and specifications of the accused."

The trial counsel remained standing and began reading,

"The charges are: attempted murder, manslaughter, theft of government property, sale of stolen U.S. Government ordnance to reservation Indians, mistreatment of reservation Indians, conspiracy to maliciously create war and break the peace treaty between the U.S. Government and reservation Indians for their own greed, and desertion of their posts and dereliction of duty.

The specifications are: between the years of 1878 and 1880, your mistreatment of reservation Indians by pilfering their food and medicine, caused not only sickness and death of reservation Indians, but was also the catalyst that initiated the killing of white men and the kidnapping of women and children in the New Mexico and Arizona Territories. In addition, you obstructed the government investigation of the said events by attempting to murder the three individuals and their scout who were employed by the territorial governors of New Mexico and Arizona. Their names are Jesse Caldwell, Scott Johnson, Thomas O'Brien and Chato, Apache scout for the U.S. Government. Lastly, your illegal actions of supplying government purchased ordnance to reservation

Indians of the Comanche, Kiowa and Apache tribes, endangered lives on both sides, and created the environment for broken peace treaties.

You five accused have heard the charges and the specifications. I will ask each of you how you plead.

Colonel Baxter, how do you say to the charges, guilty or not guilty?"

"Not guilty."

"To the specifications?"

"Not guilty."

Sergeant Jake Miller, how do you say to the charges, guilty or not guilty?"

"Not guilty."

"To the specifications?"

"Not guilty."

"Corporal Josh Taylor, how do you say to the charges, guilty or not guilty?"

"Not guilty."

"To the specifications?"

"Not guilty."

"Corporal James Pendergast, how do you say to the charges, guilty or not guilty?"

"Not guilty."

"To the specifications?"

"Not guilty."

"Corporal Ben Allen, how do you say to the charges, guilty or not guilty?"

"Guilty sir."

"Would you repeat that for the court, Corporal Ben Allen?"

"Yes sir, I plead guilty to the charges."

"How do you plead to the specifications?"

"Guilty sir."

"Would you repeat that for the court, Corporal Ben Allen?"

"Yes sir, I plead guilty to the specifications."

When Corporal Ben Allen pleaded guilty, the silence ceased to exist in the courtroom amongst the spectators and the noise level rose by several decibels as no one expected a guilty plea from any of the defendants.

The other four accused looked at Ben Allen in disbelief. They had an agreement with each other that they would all plead "not guilty". They were confused as to why Ben Allen changed his mind regarding his plea right there in the courtroom. Baxter, who was more educated than the others on such matters, began to figure it out and became notably perturbed and then concerned with Allen's decision.

After the pleads, the trial counsel gave his opening statement.

"Gentlemen, in this court-martial of the accused, the prosecution will prove without a shadow of a doubt, that the deplorable, despicable and illegal activities of the accused directly caused and influenced the horrid deaths and the kidnappings of innocent homesteaders and settlers, men, women and little children, in the New Mexico and Arizona Territories by the Mescalero Apache, who prior to said activities by the accused, were peaceful and were simply satisfied to live with nature as their ancestors did for thousands of years in the Americas. The homesteaders wanted nothing more than to fulfill their dream of establishing new roots on the virgin frontier. Those dreams were destroyed and shattered by the actions of the accused.

We will also present undeniable evidence that the said accused attempted to commit murder, murder I say, of the very individuals who sought to negotiate the release of the hostages for the grieving families and the two territorial governors.

Lastly, we will prove without a shadow of a doubt that the illegal activities, the theft of government property, and the unprecedented mistreatment of Indians on the reservation were a result of the greedy intentions of the accused with blatant disregard for human life.

When the facts of the case are presented with undeniable supporting evidence and credible collaborating witnesses and testimonies, we trust you will bring down a guilty verdict and sentence that is warranted of the crimes committed by these accused," the trial lawyer said as he raised his voice while pointing to Baxter and his cronies.

When the trial lawyer completed his opening statement, the judge looked at the defendants' attorney for his opening statement. Their attorney kept it short,

"Gentlemen, we will prove that the charges brought forth against the accused are fallacious and without merit. We will also establish that the state's number one witness lacks integrity and therefore his testimony weighs in with the absence of credibility. Thank you."

The defendants' attorney had just found out before the court began that one of the accused turned state's evidence. However, he did not know who it was at this point.

The judge then directed the trial counsel, the prosecuting attorney,

"You may call your first witness."

"I would like to call Scott Johnson please."

Scott walked up to the witness chair and was approached by the bailiff who said,

"Place your left hand on the Bible and raise your right hand. Do you swear that the evidence you shall give in the case now in hearing, shall be the truth, the whole truth, and nothing but the truth, so help you God?"

"I do."

Scott then sat down and the questioning began.

He told the court his name, talked about his background as a retired Texas Ranger, and his work on projects for President Hayes, Garfield and Arthur. Then he became very specific about the three and Chato being hired by the two governors to help locate the kidnapped women and children and then their subsequent parley with Lone Wolf.

He also cited all the assassination attempts on their lives. However, what was of key interest were the words of Lone Wolf, that he had kidnapped the women and children as a direct result of the treatment of his family and other members of his tribe in the Fort Sill area which caused the death of many of his family and his people. Lone Wolf said that his tribal members were not given enough food, there was no medicine for the sick and some Indians were beaten and tortured to death, one being his only son.

"Objection!" yelled the defendants' attorney. "This is hearsay evidence."

"Objection overruled," the judge replied.

The trial attorney continued,

"Scott, tell the court about the box canyon discovery in the Wichita Mountains."

Scott went on to describe the events they saw at the canyon without offering any opinions. He just stated the facts like you would expect a lawman to do: they saw the four soldiers escort the wagons of rifles from the trading post to the canyon, piles of spoiled food and unused medicine, the purchase of rifles by Indians from civilians, civilians guarding a petroleum seep...

Just then, when Scott mentioned a petroleum seep, spectators began talking loudly with their neighbors. The noise level of the conversations became so deafening that the judge had to pound the gavel three times and demand,

"Order in the court!"

This was the first time anyone mentioned or even heard of a petroleum seep in the Wichita Mountains. Some people in the courtroom were now thinking motive; but still couldn't put the entire puzzle together even though pieces were beginning to fit into place.

After about one hour of questioning and testimony, the cross-examination began:

"Do you know who hired the assassins to kill you?"

"No sir."

"Did you actually see these accused or did you see civilians hand over the rifles to the Indians?"

"Civilians sir, but..."

"I didn't ask you to explain, did I Mr. Johnson?"

"No sir."

"How close were you when you spotted the soldiers at the trading post?"

"We were about 150 yards up on a hillside."

"And at 150 yards you can without hesitation say that without any doubt whatsoever, that the soldiers you saw from that hillside were these four accused?"

"We had binoculars sir, and we could plainly see their faces."

"Is that a fact?"

"Yes sir, that's a fact."

"No further questions your honor."

It was now 11:30 a.m. and instead of calling the next witness to the stand, the judge called for a one hour recess and lunch break. At that point, the trial lawyer asked the judge in a sidebar to separate Corporal Ben Allen from the other accused. The judge agreed to do so, and Allen was escorted out a different door than the other prisoners. It was for his personal safety.

During the recess, the four accused who pleaded "not guilty" talked about Ben Allen's guilty plea.

"Why would he plead guilty?" Corporal Taylor questioned Baxter.

"You mean you really don't know?" Baxter asked.

"No sir."

"They got to him. He was the first one the Department of Justice interviewed a few weeks ago and evidently, they made a deal with him and that slimeball is gonna rat on us."

"Why, why would he do that?" Sergeant Miller asked.

"Do I have to spell it out for you, you idiot," Baxter said, "As a reward for spilling his guts, he's getting off free or some sort of reduced sentence. We're finished boys, it looks like we're finished."

The court-martial resumed at exactly 12:30 p.m. as ordered by the judge.

"Call your next witness," the judge ordered the prosecution.

"Your honor, I would like to call the accused, Ben Allen to the stand."

At this point, Ben Allen stood up, refused to look at the other accused and walked to the chair. He wasn't smiling, he wasn't frowning, he had a neutral expression on his face and a feeling of mixed emotions since he was about to hang his friends up to dry, right smack in front of them.

However, he agreed to tell the truth and admit guilt because it was the first step toward personal redemption. But there was no denying it; he was helped up the first step with the offer of a reduced sentence for turning state's evidence.

After Ben Allen was sworn in, the prosecuting attorney directed his announcement to the panel of five.

"Your honor and officers of the court, at this time I would like to submit for the court's record that the accused Corporal Ben Allen has turned state's evidence in return for a reduced sentence which will be determined by the court based on his testimony."

Baxter looked at the other three accused sitting next to him and whispered, "I'll kill that traitor if I ever get out of here."

The other three wanted to crawl underneath a rock, but not Baxter. He had the stare of a catamount ready to pounce on his prey and rip the flesh off its bones.

"State your name, rank and your place of birth for the court record," the trial counsel requested.

"My name is Corporal Ben Allen. I was born and raised in Hydetown, Pennsylvania in Crawford County."

"Are you familiar with a town called Titusville, Pennsylvania?"

"Yes sir, it is only about four miles from where I grew up."

"Do you know what Titusville is famous for?"

"Yes sir. It was the site of the first oil well in Pennsylvania."

"Objection," yelled the defendants' attorney. "This has no relevance whatsoever to the charges of the case."

"Objection overruled," ordered the judge. "Continue counsel."

"Mr. Allen, would you say you were close friends or just mere acquaintances of the four accused sitting at that table?"

"We were all very close friends, all being from Pennsylvania and fighting for the Union in the War. We spent a lot of leisure time together in the late 1870's splitting a bottle of rye and playing poker in Colonel Baxter's tent when we were on the road, or in his quarters at the fort."

"Do you know which one of the accused grew up in Titusville and are you familiar with his father's business and to whom and what his father supplied in Titusville?"

"Yes sir, Colonel Baxter is from Titusville. His father owned a sawmill there. They made large beams for oil well drilling rigs in the area."

"Now, let's move on," the trial counsel said. "Would you please tell the court how the petroleum seep was discovered in that box canyon in the Wichita Mountains?"

"Yes sir. It all started when we went on a reconnaissance mission in the Wichita Mountains in early 1876. We stumbled across a passageway on the west side of the mountain range. Colonel Baxter ordered Sergeant Tyrus Owens, Corporal Josh Taylor, Sergeant Jake Miller, Corporal James Pendergast and myself to ride through the passageway and check it out. The narrow corridor opened into a box canyon. It was there we discovered a large oil seep. I knew exactly what it was and its financial potential because I had seen many of them in and around Titusville."

"What did you do then?"

"Well, all five of us talked about it and saw dollar signs in front of our eyes and agreed to tell only Colonel Baxter about our findings when we rode out of the canyon. That's exactly what we did. Baxter told us to keep it quiet and he would know what to do from there on out. He contacted an old friend from Titusville and before you knew it, we became a tight knit group who were paid off in gold pieces to keep our mouths shut about the findings. In addition, we were also told by Colonel Baxter that our reward for keeping this secret would be financial benefits from the seep."

"Do you know the name of the person who Colonel Baxter contacted in Titusville?"

"Yes sir. It was Will Franklin, an oil magnate with a lot of political clout."

Then the counsel looked at the judge and offered, "For the record, Will Franklin has been arrested for similar charges as the accused in this court."

The trial counsel then asked Corporal Allen to continue. This is where Allen became extremely somber and almost demonstrated shame as he gave further testimony.

"Colonel Baxter and Will Franklin came up with a scheme with the objective of getting their hands on the land where the seep was located."

"A scheme you say?"

"Objection, mere speculation and inflammatory language!" the defending attorney yelled out.

"Objection overruled, continue counsel."

"You said a scheme, Corporal Allen, explain to the court what you meant."

"Colonel Baxter believed that the only way we could get our hands on that land was to have it freed up by the government and removed from the reservation by establishing a new treaty. He referred to the Black Hills Gold Rush where they took the areas around the towns of Lead and Deadwood away from the Sioux and opened the doors to white settlers and prospectors."

"Just how did he plan to do that?"

"Create an uprising amongst the Comanche, Kiowa, and the Apache on the reservation."

"How does one create an uprising on a reservation, Corporal Allen?"

"Baxter had us divert food and medicine which were destined for reservation Indians and take them to the box canyon and dump them there. He figured that the lack of food would starve the Indians. Plus without medicine, the sick would die. His scheme was to make the Indians so mad by depriving them of food and medicine that they would rebel. He then figured they needed weapons to put up an adequate rebellion so he bought rifles from a gun manufacturer with government money and then sold the guns to the Indians so that they could create havoc."

"But how would this ensure he would be able to acquire the land around the canyon?"

"He said there was a precedent set at the San Carlos Apache Indian Reservation, a precedent of consolidating Indians to another reservation for economic reasons and because the Indians became too hard to handle in their present location. They would be much easier to handle if they were consolidated to another location. He said he and Will Franklin had people in places that could take care of the political side of the scheme."

"Did Baxter specifically mention who he was talking about?"

"No sir, he never mentioned that. However, I was always under the impression that he and Will Franklin were receiving their orders from someone else."

"Explain why you would have thought that."

"Well, when Colonel Baxter came back from a meeting in Washington, D.C., he mentioned that he had met three men who could spoil their whole plan."

"Are those three men in this courtroom today, do you know their names, and can you point them out?"

"I only know their names sir, because Colonel Baxter told us, on a number of occasions, that it was necessary to assassinate the three because they were hot on our trail and could spoil everything. Their names are Jesse Caldwell, Scott Johnson, and Thomas O'Brien. Baxter said he was told by his contact to assassinate Johnson in Dodge City, and Caldwell in San Carlos. When all those attempts backfired, he arranged to have all three killed in a small mining camp at the southern base of the Dos Cabezas Mountains just north of Apache Pass. When that failed, he tried again at Wichita Falls, Texas. He even wanted their scout killed."

With this revelation, the noise level once again got out of hand.

"Order in the court!" the judge demanded as he pounded the gavel on the block.

When the spectators became quiet again, the judge asked the prosecution to continue.

"Did Baxter suspect that his depriving the reservation Indians of food and medicine caused the kidnappings by the Mescalero Apache in the New Mexico and Arizona Territories?"

"Yes sir. The day he read about the kidnappings in the paper he laughed and said that he knew those Mescalero Apache who left the reservation would go running to Geronimo or somebody and then cause havoc in the territories."

"So Baxter himself thought that there was a direct cause and effect relationship to his actions?"

"Yes sir he did. He said as much. That's why he was very concerned about those three guys hired by the governors of the two territories spoiling his get-rich-quick scheme. That's why he wanted them dead and out of the picture."

"Now I understand that you were close friends with Sergeant Tyrus Owens. Would you like to clear up something in court about him today?"

"Yes sir. Sergeant Tyrus Owens was killed in the San Carlos Apache Indian Reservation trying to assassinate Jesse Caldwell. When the Indian Agent there sent a telegram to Colonel Baxter and asked him if he could shed some light on the subject, Baxter said no, that Tyrus was a deserter. That was a downright lie. Baxter sent Tyrus to kill Jesse Caldwell and instead, Tyrus got himself killed. Then Baxter shamed Tyrus' name by calling him a deserter."

At this point, court etiquette went right out the proverbial window as the noise level once again exploded like a dropped jar of nitro as everyone began talking loudly to their neighbor. Now Jesse, Scott and Thomas had a clear picture about why they were being shot at. So many times they were targeted to die; so many times they miraculously escaped unscathed.

While the whole story was rapidly unfolding before the eyes of the court, the accused were squirming in their chairs like the sidewinders they were and people began seeing Baxter as cold blooded as a rattler in winter.

Jesse leaned over to whisper to Scott, "I have a question for you. Who do you think was giving the orders to Baxter to wipe us out?"

"I don't know but when this trial ends today, let's backtrack over a few drinks tonight and see if we can skin a skunk."

When the prosecution completed the questioning of Allen's lucid testimony and the whole story was laid out on the table for everyone to view, the defense attorney cross-examined Allen with the intent to discredit his testimony stating he could not be trusted:

he was a criminal himself, and he would say anything to get off the hook and save his own bacon.

However, the defendants' attorney did not get far with his assertion and futile attempt to discredit. What Allen had going for him was collaborating testimony from Scott Johnson. In addition, later that day, the trial counsel called the trading post proprietor to the stand to identify the four soldiers who always paid him gold pieces for handling the rifles and who escorted the wagon of rifles away.

He also called to the stand one of the teamsters out of Fort Worth, Texas who took food and medicine to the box canyon and unloaded the supplies there on many occasions. In addition, rifle orders to the manufacturer signed by Baxter were produced in evidence and they were compared to inventories of ordnance at the fort.

The result was painfully obvious for the disbelievers when evidence was presented in court that there was a major shortage of rifle inventory in relationship to the amount charged by the manufacturer and OK'd to be paid for by Baxter.

And then there was this; the *Three for Hire's* discovery of the stockpile of spoiled food along with piled-up unused medicine supplies at the canyon spoke volumes in support of Allen's testimony.

The prosecution closed its case and the judge called for an end to the day. He asked the defense to be ready to present their case tomorrow morning at 9 o'clock. Most of the spectators came in wagons and were able to pitch tents on the grounds at Fort Reno. The *Three for Hire* and Chato were given special quarters to stay in as were the attorneys and witnesses for the prosecution and the defense.

There was a mess hall in the fort where anyone and everyone could eat. The Army expected a multitude of diners from the trial so they were well prepared for the large crowd that evening.

After dinner, Jesse, Scott, and Thomas met in Jesse's room. Chato went right to his room to be alone. These three knew more about this whole case than anyone because they were there from the very beginning. They figured Baxter was more or less a puppet or a pawn just like the other four accused. There had to be someone else who was calling the shots; but who, that was the question.

The three started from the beginning, backtracking out loud from the time they went to Washington, D.C. to this very day.

Then it hit Jesse like a flying hoof from a wild mustang into an unsuspecting cranium.

"Say, do you guys remember when we were in that meeting with President Garfield, Vice President Arthur, Secretary Kirkwood and Commissioner Price discussing everything we knew up to that point about the mission and why Lone Wolf kidnapped those folks?"

"Yeah, so?" Thomas questioned.

"Oh my Lord," Scott said. "I know where you're going with this."

"Well would somebody please deal me in?" Thomas retorted.

"Remember when we were just about to conclude the meeting, Garfield said he received a bill to sign that was passed by the House and the Senate. It was called the, uhh, uhh.."

Then Thomas jumped in,

"I remember it. It was called the Fort Sill Indian Reservation Consolidation Bill of 1881."

"That's it!" Jesse said. "The bill was designed to move the Fort Sill Indians to another reservation because they were becoming too hard to handle. Plus if I remember right, it cited San Carlos as the precedent for consolidating Indians for economic reasons plus the move would open the doors for white settler expansion. In fact, that's what came out in the trial."

"OK, what does all of that mean?" Thomas asked.

"Here's what I think. I think that bill may present us with a new set of suspects," Jesse said convincingly. "It just might be that whoever sponsored that bill might be pards in crime with Baxter and the others. Maybe they're the ones calling the shots. We've seen it before. Like they say, politicians can be as crooked as a dog's hind leg."

"If my memory serves me right," Scott added, "Garfield put that bill in his top drawer for future consideration until we got answers. Arthur was there with us. Let's hope he still has that bill on hold."

"Let's keep this to ourselves until after the trial," Jesse suggested. "Muddying the water now could distort the trial and slow up the proceedings. Anyway, the other question I have is, if there were politicians involved, who were they taking orders from, this guy Will Franklin who's going to trial in Amarillo next week?"

"Could be, he's no doubt the money man and the guy who knows how to get oil out of the ground, so I hear," Thomas remarked. "We may find out firsthand since we were ordered to appear in court as witnesses for the prosecution in Franklin's trial."

When the trial started the next morning at 9 o'clock sharp, the courtroom was once again filled up with onlookers. The defense was asked to bring forth their witnesses and the questionings and the cross-examinations began. Most of the witnesses for the defense were soldiers who were praising the characters of the five accused. Some were Civil War comrades of the defendants acknowledging the bravery and worth the five contributed to the cause.

But what was clearly lacking was any evidence that could counter the corruption and lawless assertions of the prosecution. Bottom line was that the defense had a very weak case and they knew it. That's why none of the accused testified.

The defense rested their case before noon. The judge suggested that the case be put to bed tomorrow morning. He asked both sides to present their closing arguments first thing in the morning starting with the prosecution at 9:00 a.m. The defense would follow. After the closing arguments, the court would make a determination of guilt and then if warranted, sentences would be issued.

The evidence was overwhelming for the prosecution so that afternoon, the judge and his panel had a preliminary meeting and discussed the evidence. They would not make a final decision though until the closing arguments were heard.

After closing arguments the next morning, the judge and the panel left the room for about an hour and then reconvened court.

At precisely 11:10 a.m. an officer of the court stood up and shouted, "All rise!" The judge and his panel entered the room and sat down. Everyone else did as well. Then the judge said,

"Would the defendants, excluding Mr. Allen, please stand. We have listened to the opening arguments, witnesses for both sides, cross-examination of witnesses, closing arguments and weighed the evidence. It is the judgment of this panel that the evidence for all charges is overwhelming against the accused. Therefore, we find the accused 'Guilty' on all counts. As of this date, you are stripped of your ranks and will receive a dishonorable discharge.

In addition, all of the persons found guilty are hereby ordered by this court-martial to serve no less than twenty years each in the military penitentiary in Leavenworth, Kansas. You will remain under guard at Fort Reno until arrangements are made for your transport.

Baxter showed no emotion but the other three guilty soldiers were visibly upset. "Why Allen, why did you rat on us?" Pendergast shouted, as the four were escorted out of the room.

Allen put his head down and did not respond.

After the four guilty parties exited the courtroom, the judge ordered Corporal Ben Allen to rise for his conviction and sentence. Then the judge spoke,

"All of the evidence collected against the soldiers who were just found guilty is relevant to your case. Since you have turned state's evidence and enabled this trial to move swiftly forward with a fair and accurate judgment by the court against the four previously accused and now judged, we have decided to bring this judgment forward on you.

The court finds Corporal Ben Allen guilty on all counts. You are hereby stripped of your rank and will receive a dishonorable discharge as of this date. However, because of the significant role you played in this case favoring the prosecution and aiding in the conviction of the disgraced, you will receive a reduced sentence of three years in prison. You will serve your three years in the Arizona Territorial Penitentiary in Yuma. Your term is to commence immediately.

Court dismissed."

CHAPTER ELEVEN:

The Last War Paint

Baxter and his cronies were convicted and justice was served. But was this enough for Lone Wolf to release the hostages? Thomas thought so but Jesse and Scott had second thoughts. Chato too felt that if Lone Wolf knew that Baxter answered to someone else, he would not be satisfied until that someone else received justice as well.

The sometimes uncontrollable and overpowering appetite for greed could be found in places and people one would never suspect. The *Three for Hire* witnessed that realism firsthand when they battled the *Shadow Assassins*, et al, back in 1880. And they beheld the horrifying results travel to places, beyond the scope of credence, which shocked not only themselves but the entire country.

Now that the trial was over, it seemed like the less difficult part was done. It's always easy to trap and catch the snakes crawling in the short grasses; it's the ones hiding in the caves that are always hard to snag. The question was, which cave do you build a fire in front of to smoke out the slippery sidewinders. The answer to that question wasn't readily apparent. There was still much work to be done.

The *Three for Hire* along with Chato were anxious to get on the road and head to Amarillo for Will Franklin's trial. They began thinking that this guy could hold the key to unlocking the door that would enable the courts to walk the yet to be determined criminals right into their jail cells.

However, there was another issue pressing. Somehow, they had to get word to President Arthur and find out if that bill in his top drawer was still there or if he had already signed it. Then they had to find out who sponsored it and endeavor to determine if the sponsors were guilty of malfeasance and instigated direction to Baxter on all of his illicit activities. Who to send a telegram to was the question.

Luck had it though that General Sheridan was on the grounds the day of the sentencing. He was there to witness the judgment. Afterwards he was scheduled to travel to Fort Sill to appoint a new commanding officer there now that Baxter was a convicted felon. After the appointment, he had plans to head back to D.C. He was the one who could carry the message to President Arthur. The *Three for Hire* asked for an audience with Sheridan and he agreed to give them one right there at the courthouse after everyone vacated the premises.

The *Three for Hire* explained their theory to General Sheridan and asked him to carry their message to President Arthur. He was more than happy to. They discussed a few other issues about the three's future plans regarding the case and the release of the hostages and asked Sheridan to convey those things to President Arthur as well.

After their meeting with Sheridan, they were anxious to go to the telegraph office on the fort's premises and shoot off a quick wire to the governors of the New Mexico and Arizona Territories. The three knew that this would be welcome news to the governors and that the release of the hostages was now closer than ever, so they thought. The message to the governors read:

Governor Lawrence Williams
Governor James Freidman
Good news today! Baxter and his co-conspirators were found guilty at their court-martial and have been sentenced to twenty years each. We will take proof of the convictions and sentences to Lone Wolf which means, if he is a man of his word, the hostages will be released soon. Chato and Thomas O'Brien will deliver the news and keep us informed of the outcome. We will inform you when and where the hostages will be released. It's a great day for the families of the victims!

> *Scott Johnson,*
> *Jesse Caldwell,*
> *Thomas O'Brien*

On receipt of the wonderful news, each governor responded back quickly with a message of delight for the trial outcome and the most likely release of the hostages. They also expressed their sincere gratitude to the *Three for Hire* for their excellent detective-type work and their tenacity and dedication to the case.

After meeting with Sheridan and sending their telegrams, the four wasted no time. They packed up their limited gear, saddled up their horses and rode directly west for Amarillo, Texas. It would not be an easy trip. Amarillo, Texas was about 230 miles away by the way the crows fly. If they could travel a little more than thirty miles a day, they could make it in about a week and be there in time for the trial.

Actually, they had no choice but to get there as quickly as possible because Scott and Jesse were star witnesses for the prosecution. Thomas and Chato did not stop in Amarillo. They went on to Tombstone, Arizona and waited there for a telegram from Scott and Jesse to see if there would be any relevant information coming out of Franklin's trial which would give Thomas and Chato more ammunition that would convince Lone Wolf to finally give up the hostages.

Will Franklin's trial only lasted three days. He was found guilty as charged and sentenced to ten years in prison for selling rifles to the Indians, stealing government property and being instrumental in causing the peace treaty to be broken. He was not charged with manslaughter like Baxter and his cronies. Franklin was ordered by the court to serve out his sentence in the Yuma, Arizona Penitentiary.

During the trial, Jesse and Scott discovered through their own interpretation of the evidence that Franklin did indeed hold the key to the question, "Who was the number one man giving the orders to Baxter?"

President Arthur sent them a classified and somewhat coded telegram stating that there were two senators who sponsored the bill which was still in his top drawer. They were the senators from Pennsylvania and Texas. Pennsylvania made sense, Texas, not so much, except for one thing; the presence of natural petroleum seeps in Texas had been known for hundreds of years. They were scattered throughout the state and the science from the Pennsylvania oilmen was required to extract oil from those areas. So connecting the dots put the senators in a shady location, not necessarily under a willow tree.

Arthur wrote that the two denied any involvement in the matter but they were being investigated and relieved of their duties while the investigation was ongoing.

However, Arthur was convinced that these two senators were pawns similar to Baxter and were taking their orders and being paid off financially by someone else. A slip of the tongue by the Pennsylvania senator seemed to throw the ball back into Franklin's court.

Franklin wasn't giving up anyone; he didn't before the trial and he certainly did not during the trial. Who was he protecting and why? Things seemed to be at an impasse. That was until Scott came up with a creative but hair brained idea that could in fact land the *Three for Hire* in the slammer. He told Jesse about it to which Jesse replied, "I like it. Let's do it."

Scott sent a message back to President Arthur and asked him to send a telegram to the marshal of Amarillo, instructing him to deputize both Jesse and Scott in order that the two might escort Franklin to the Yuma Penitentiary. Arthur had no idea what Scott and Jesse were up to but he trusted the two like no others, so he sent the authorization as requested. What helped with Arthur's decision to go forward with the request was that Scott was a retired Texas Ranger and knew the ins and outs of being a lawman. President Arthur also sent a telegram to Scott and told him that the wire was sent to the marshal.

When Scott received Arthur's telegram, he said,

"Well Jesse, you're about to become a lawman."

They walked over to the marshal's office to get sworn in and make plans for their long journey to Yuma, Arizona Territory. It would be a straight shot across Texas, New Mexico Territory and all the way to the southwest corner of the Arizona Territory. Only what no one knew, but for Jesse and Scott, there was to be an unscheduled detour to the Chiricahua Mountains.

When they arrived at the marshal's office, they introduced themselves and Scott showed the marshal his telegram from President Arthur. Then they all sat down and drank a cup of Arbuckle's that was freshly made. Scott told the marshal that they would be leaving first thing in the morning. They needed to buy a covered wagon and two draft horses. Plus they needed to stop at the general store and buy supplies for the long journey. The marshal supplied the shackles for the prisoner. When they were done drinking their coffee and laying out their plans, the marshal said,

"It's time to swear you in boys. Stand up, raise your right hand and repeat after me."

Marshal: "I accept the responsibility of the United States Deputy Marshal."

Scott and Jesse: "I accept the responsibility of the United States Deputy Marshal."

Marshal: "And I do solemnly swear to uphold and defend the honor and respect of the law in the discharge of my duties."

Scott and Jesse: "And I do solemnly swear to uphold and defend the honor and respect of the law in the discharge of my duties."

Marshal: "So help me God."

Scott and Jesse: "So help me God."

Marshal: "Congratulations, you are now deputy marshals."

Jesse: "Is there some type of badge that goes along with this?"

The marshal smiled, went over to his desk, opened his top drawer and grabbed two badges and handed them to Jesse and Scott. Jesse proudly pinned the badge on his chest and said,

"Well looky here, I'm legal."

Scott looked at Jesse, smiled and said,

"Congratulations Mr. Lawman, now let's go buy some slabs of bacon for our journey."

Thomas and Chato were hanging out in Tombstone waiting for word from Jesse and Scott on how to proceed. After Scott and Jesse purchased everything they needed for the long trip, Scott fired off a wire to Thomas and Chato and told them to sit tight, that they were on their way to Tombstone with a guest of the state. Thomas did not understand Scott's telegram in full but he did understand the part about, sitting tight. Scott also told Thomas to check the telegraph office twice a day in case there was a change in plans.

Well when the sun came up in Amarillo the next morning, Scott and Jesse met at the Panhandle Café for a hearty flapjacks, eggs and bacon breakfast. They were already packed and ready to go. While eating, Jesse asked Scott,

"Do you think your scheme can break Franklin?"

"Like breaking a 35 year old nag with bad hooves, I reckon," Scott confirmed.

"Look, this Franklin is not a hard-nose gunslinger or westerner. He's an eastern oil businessman who was just after a quick buck. He probably never fired a pistol in his life. Even if he did, he probably couldn't hit the side of a cattle car at point blank range. Yeah, I think my scheme will work but we best keep it quiet for now or else we may not get a chance to use it."

After breakfast at the Panhandle Café, Jesse and Scott went over to collect Franklin. They put him in shackles and made him climb into the rear of the covered wagon. Scott tethered their two saddle horses to the back of the prairie schooner and then jumped into it to guard Franklin. Jesse climbed onto the driver's seat then whipped the long leather reins across the powerful hindquarters of the muscular draft horses and away they went following the sun in the western sky.

The journey to Tombstone was about 650 miles, give or take a few. They were determined to make it in two weeks, but they had to ride hard to do it, traveling from the break of dawn to the setting sun.

When they arrived in a town in south central New Mexico by the name of Las Cruces, also known as "The City of the Crosses", Scott thought that they could save time by having Thomas and Chato meet them at a place closer to the Chiricahua Mountains. So he sent a telegram to Thomas in Tombstone which read:

Thomas O'Brien

A change in plans. To save time, we are changing the meeting place. Leave now. Meet us at the old San Simon Station of the Butterfield Overland Mail on the San Simon River between Apache Pass and Stein's Peak Station. From there we will all travel to the Chiricahua Mountains together.

Scott Johnson

Scott assumed that Thomas would get the message so they didn't wait around for a reply. Instead, they continued to head west. Thomas and Chato did receive the message and began their eastern journey immediately not aware of what Scott and Jesse's plans were.

Jesse and Scott had the longest distance to go yet, about 152 miles. They made it in four days riding hard and fast through the rocky and dusty terrain of the Southwest. Thomas and Chato were already there waiting for them. Will Franklin had no idea what was in store for him so he patiently just sat around thinking that this was just another stop on their long journey to Yuma.

When Scott and Jesse took Chato and Thomas aside and told them Scott's scheme, Thomas said, "Have you lost your mind? That can't be legal!"

"Legal has nothing to do with it," Scott said. "I'm after the mastermind no matter what it takes; I'm talking about the ringleader who gave the orders to murder all of us. I think we can get Franklin to talk if we can scare the hide off his backside. Jesse and I questioned the little weasel all the way from Amarillo but he refused to talk. When our friends get through with him in the Chiricahua's, I suspect he'll sing like a canary."

"I suspect so," Thomas replied as he began laughing while he visualized the unprecedented and truly unlawful stratagem.

It was time now to head to the Chiricahua Mountains and locate Lone Wolf. They took the trail to the pre-arranged spot where Chato and Thomas knew there would be sentry Apache. Now Franklin knew something was up and asked the question,

"Why are we in the mountains? This isn't the way to Yuma."

"We're taking you to church service to get religion," Scott said as he smiled kind of devilish like.

"What do you mean get religion?" Franklin asked.

"Let me put it this way my Yankee friend. If you don't get religion, you may be shaking hands with Cochise in the spirit world, savvy?" Scott replied.

Franklin started to sweat bullets. "Cochise" meant Indians, "in the spirit world" meant death, "Yankee friend" meant that Scott sounded like a vindictive southerner, and being in a remote area in the Chiricahua Mountains could mean, "Never found again, alive". Scott could see that a little intimidation on this weasel might have the makings of a sweet little songbird about to turn rat on a comrade. Franklin was afraid to say anything else and just sat in the wagon not so much enjoying neither the bumpy ride nor the nerve-wracking threats.

Down the road apiece, the men were met by several Apache warriors. They were the same ones who met Chato and Thomas before. Chato spoke Apache with them. He told them that they had good news of justice on Baxter, the one Lone Wolf called Long Gray Hair; but they needed Lone Wolf and his warriors to help obtain information out of a prisoner they brought with them.

The Apache warriors escorted the group to Lone Wolf's stronghold. Chato and Thomas were surprised to see that the Apache renegades had moved back to their original encampment. They did that because there was more wild game in the area for meat and they were closer to wild mescal which they could harvest for food and drink.

They rode to the middle of the camp and were immediately surrounded by many warriors with repeating rifles in hand. Chato and Thomas dismounted and Jesse, Scott and Franklin climbed down from the wagon. Franklin looked at Scott and asked,

"What are we doing here?"

"We came for a party, a war party," Scott replied. "You should feel privileged. You're the main guest. Now you just keep your mouth shut, there will be plenty of time for you to speak, I assure you."

Franklin looked like he was just two heartbeats away from a coronary.

Chato told a warrior that Jesse, Scott and Thomas wanted to parley once again with Lone Wolf and that they were bearers of good news. The warrior walked to a wickiup in the center of the camp and went in. A few minutes later, Lone Wolf came out and told the *Three for Hire* to enter his abode.

After they sat down, the conversation began,

"You are welcome in my camp," Lone Wolf said. "I trust you brought me good news of justice for Long Gray Hair."

"Yes we have," Scott confirmed. "He has been tried and convicted in white man's court. His punishment is 20 years in prison."

"Why was he not put to death for his crimes against the Mescalero?"

"I can't answer that. I can only tell you that he will be behind bars for a long time."

"Where is he now?"

"He's at Fort Reno in the Indian Territory and will be there for quite a while until they move him to a prison in Kansas."

"You brought someone with you. He is shackled. Why is he here and why shackles?"

"We need your help to get him to talk. We suspect he knows who the real leader is, the person who Baxter answers to. If we can identify him, we'll bring him to justice as well. We're as anxious to get that character, as you were to get Baxter."

"If Baxter gets orders from him, then we want him punished too," Lone Wolf insisted.

"So do we Lone Wolf," Jesse said. "It was he who gave the orders to kill Scott, Thomas, and me. We want him identified and caught as much as you do."

"What do you want from me?"

"We want you to scare that polecat out of his hide to get him to talk. But you can't actually harm him," Jesse said.

"I can do that. We will tie him to Nana's death post. I will begin in about one hour. In the meantime you can visit with the hostages. You will find they are in good health. We will put your prisoner in an empty wickiup until we are ready to get the answer out of him. Tell Chato to stand guard. I promise you, he will talk."

Lone Wolf called ten of his strongest and fiercest warriors together and laid out a plan as if they were going into battle. He instructed them all to smear on war paint.

ABOUT WAR PAINT

War paint was used as a non-verbal form of communication. Each Native American tribe throughout North America had its own designs and painted their bodies and faces: for rituals, dances and for battle. Painting their horses was also a tribal practice before going into combat.

Sometimes the designs were thought to hold magical powers for protection while engaging in rival encounters. War paint was used to intimidate their enemies in battle; thus the term, war paint. Colors and images were used to make warriors look more ferocious.

Symbols and colors all had meaning. A hand on the body, face or horse meant that the warrior had been successful in hand combat. A zig-zag line across the forehead that looked like lightning was believed to add power and speed to the warrior.

Colors had great significance and could vary by tribe. However, the most universal meanings for colors were these:

Red – meant war, blood, strength, energy, power and success during warfare. It might also symbolize happiness and beauty in face paint.

Black – was worn in preparation for war. It was a very aggressive color. It meant strength and that the wearer was a very powerful warrior. It also was used to symbolize victory and would be put on before returning home after a battle.

White – symbolized mourning. Also a color of peace when placed on the face.

Blue – symbolized wisdom and confidence.

Yellow – symbolized the color of death. It also indicated the wearer was heroic, had led a good life, and was willing to fight to the death.

Green – symbolized endurance. Associated with harmony and represented a great healing power and improved vision.

Colors were developed from the resources available in nature that could be used to make different colored dyes and pigments. In its simplest form, paint consisted of ground up pigment suspended in some sort of liquid, or binder such as urine, spit, egg yolks, animal fat or blood.

The Native Americans dried and stored the paint as powder in deerskin pouches; in that way they could easily travel with the substance and apply it when they saw fit. Generally they would first rub their bodies with buffalo or deer fat and then rub on the paint. War paint was applied using many different methods: fingers, animal bones, sticks, and grasses. The Indians that roamed the Plains used a spongy bone from the knee joint of the buffalo which held paint just as a bird quill did which was used to sign the Declaration of Independence.

THE FINAL DAYS AND HOURS

Now the ten warriors were ready for battle and the intimidation was about to begin. They all removed their buckskin shirts and smeared war paint all over their bodies. Franklin was sitting in a wickiup by himself while Chato stood guard outside. Franklin had no idea that he was about to become a tethered rooster in an Apache game known as "spear the chicken".

Three painted-up ferocious looking warriors came yelling and charging into the wickiup, grabbed Franklin and pulled him outside, dragging him like he was a sack of grain. He began kicking and squirming and shouting obscenities. They ripped off his shirt and pulled him over to one of Nana's death posts. There were ten posts lined up in a row. The posts were about six feet apart from each other and stood about eight feet tall. They all still had blood stains on them from the Mexicans who were tied to the posts and were tortured, butchered, and eventually speared by Nana's warriors.

They tied Franklin's hands behind the last post on the right. One of the Indians had a large hard squash shell which held red dye in a liquid form. He started at the post farthest away and one-by-one drew a heart on each post with his finger that was dipped in the red dye. When he got to Franklin, he likewise drew a heart, right in the middle of Franklin's chest. Franklin was shouting frantically,

"What are you doing? What are you doing?"

Then the ten warriors jumped on their horses and rode over to an area where there were ten spears stuck in the ground. Each warrior yanked up a spear and raised it into the air and began yelling Apache battle cries.

Then the warriors all lined up side-by-side, each facing a post which was about 50-yards directly in front of them. Scott walked over to Franklin, who by now looked like he was about to lose his lunch, and said,

"You have one last chance to tell me who the mastermind is behind all of the criminal activities relating to the petroleum seep in the Wichita Mountains."

"You're crazy," Franklin said. "I have no idea what you're talking about."

"Suit yourself pard," Scott said.

Scott then turned around, raised his hand in the air, then lowered it and quickly stepped aside.

The first warrior came charging and yelling with the spear held high in a throwing position and then rode toward the far post and hurled the spear as he rode up to and past the post. The spear hit its mark, and stuck right smack in the middle of the heart drawn on the post. Immediately the next warrior came charging and yelling and threw his spear and hit the mark on the next post. Then the next and the next and the next until there was only one post left, the one Franklin was tied to. The last warrior, twirled his horse around in a circle, reared it high in the air and began to charge, yelling and screaming toward Franklin. Franklin started shouting and yelling frantically,

"Stop! Stop! I'll talk!" as the spear was thrown and landed in the post, just above his scalp and nearly parting his hair at the roots.

"It's my half-brother," he shouted, "my half-brother."

Then he shouted out the name; and he shouted it out again.

Everybody became still. Jesse's, Scott's, and Thomas' faces became pale as if they just saw a ghost. Scott walked up to Franklin and put his hand around Franklin's throat and said,

"If you're lying to us, I'll snap your neck faster than a Chinese cook can ring the neck of a chicken."

"I'm not lying. I promise you. I'm speaking the truth. He's the mastermind behind all of it and we all received our directions and orders from him, even Colonel Baxter and the senators up in Washington. He's the one that ordered you three to be assassinated."

Scott, Jesse and Thomas gathered together while Lone Wolf walked over and cut the leather which was binding Franklin's hands. Two warriors took Franklin back to the wickiup. Lone Wolf told the *Three for Hire* to follow him to his wickiup.

When they arrived, Lone Wolf told them to sit and then he said, "When this white man leader is arrested, me and my warriors will bring the hostages to the Mescalero Reservation and there we will release them and give ourselves up and live on that reservation. However, before I do this, I must be with you when you arrest this white man."

"You can be there, but that is all. If you cause trouble, we cannot guarantee your safety, understood?"

"Understood."

"I visited with the hostages," Thomas said. "They look healthy. That's good. I told them they are very close to going home."

"They will go home when final justice is served," Lone Wolf stated.

Scott then suggested that Lone Wolf travel to Tucson with all of them. From Tucson, they would send a telegram and ask either Sherman or Sheridan to assist them in the arrest of the ringleader. Scott and Jesse were deputies so by law, they could make the arrest. However, so could Sherman or Sheridan.

After traveling for several days, they arrived in Tucson. Thomas, Chato, Franklin, and Lone Wolf camped outside of town to prevent Lone Wolf from being captured and hung by vigilantes. Scott sent a telegram to President Arthur and informed him of their discovery but did not name names and asked for assistance from Generals Sherman or Sheridan.

It just so happened that Sherman was investigating corruption in the San Carlos Apache Indian Reservation so he was close by. Arthur sent a telegram to Sherman so he rode out immediately for Tucson with a patrol of fifteen soldiers.

When Sherman arrived in town, Jesse and Scott escorted Sherman out of town where they met Thomas and the others.

Thomas introduced Lone Wolf to Sherman and explained why he was there. It was very obvious that Sherman was giving Lone Wolf the cold shoulder and was not about to greet him as a friend but more as a criminal and kidnapper and an Indian who belonged on the reservation no matter how high up he was in his tribe.

Sherman was told the identity of the mastermind. His only comment was, "It's hard to believe but I must tell you, nothing surprises me anymore. When do you want to make the arrest?"

"We are ready when you are," Scott said.

"Well then let's go get it done."

"By the way General, we're taking Franklin with us, he's the half-brother that ratted on the ringleader. There should be some interesting conversations at that arrest, don't you think?"

It took them a few days to arrive at the place of the apprehension. When they awoke in their camp the morning of the arrest, Lone Wolf was already awake and decked out in war paint along with his horse. He was ready to go but was warned by Sherman to only be an observer, or pay the consequences.

Jesse kicked dirt on the campfire, Scott removed the shackles from around Franklin's ankles, and then they all saddled up. This time they all rode horses. Scott sold the wagon in Tucson. They really had no intention from the start to take Franklin all the way to Yuma. They would rely on a town marshal down the road somewhere to do that for them with a little shove from Washington, D.C.

Then they rode, all sitting tall in their saddles: Jesse, Scott, Thomas, Chato, Lone Wolf, General Sherman and fifteen cavalry soldiers. Franklin, not so much, more like slumping. They were approaching the east side of town with their destination being on the west side.

When they were spotted at a distance in the east, a lone citizen figured out what was going down. He quickly ran into the telegraph office, snatched up a piece of paper, grabbed a pencil and wrote down two words. Then he jumped on his horse and rode as quickly as he could to warn the ringleader. He was just in front of Jesse and the others.

When the man arrived at his destination, he quickly dismounted, ran up the stone steps, and frantically knocked on the door. A butler opened the door and the man said,

"Give this note to the governor. Hurry!"

The butler ran up the steps to the governor's office, knocked on the door and then walked quickly into the office and said,

"Here's an urgent note for you, sir."

The governor opened up the folded letter and it read,

"THEY KNOW!"

The governor looked out of the second story window and there, walking up the steps was General Sherman, Scott, Jesse, Thomas, Chato and Lone Wolf, who was shirtless, and holding a long battle spear and wearing war paint all over his chest and face. Franklin was trailing behind.

The governor had been tortured with a migraine for several days now. He knew this day would eventually come. Sherman knocked on the front door. The butler opened it.

"Where is he?" Sherman asked.

"He's upstairs, sir."

Then they all began marching up the steps. When they got to the top, a gunshot rang out and echoed through the halls of the governor's mansion. Jesse and Scott broke down the locked office door and when they entered, they found the Governor of the Arizona Territory lying in a pool of his own blood from a self-inflicted gunshot wound to his head. They all stood there and said nothing. Then Scott looked at Franklin with a question in his eyes and Franklin acknowledged,

"Yes, that's my half-brother."

The job was done. It didn't quite end the way everyone expected but it was over nonetheless. Now all that was left was for Lone Wolf to honor his promise and release the hostages to their families.

Sherman wanted to follow Lone Wolf back to his camp but Jesse and Scott talked him out of it. They trusted Lone Wolf's word. So Sherman and his troops along with the *Three for Hire* headed to the Mescalero Reservation in the south central New Mexico Territory.

The Indians had several wagons stashed away to carry the hostages to the reservation. Townspeople were notified by telegraph to start heading to the Mescalero Reservation to reunite with their family members. They were instructed to bring covered wagons and tents to stay in, not knowing how long they would be waiting for the return of their wives and children.

Chato rode side-by-side for a while with Lone Wolf until they split up and went different directions. However, before they parted, Chato asked Lone Wolf if he had intended to kill the Governor of the Arizona Territory when they entered his mansion. After all, he was wearing war paint and carried a spear. Lone Wolf said,

"Yes, I think so but I cannot say for sure. When I walked through the doors of the governor's mansion with my spear in hand, I remembered the words of my father after we moved from the Mescalero Reservation to that hidden village in northeast New Mexico Territory. He said if war and killing was going to cease between the white man and the redman, it needed to begin with the one with the most courage to do so. That's why my father and our people moved to the north and didn't fight even with bad conditions on the reservation. Father wanted peace. I heeded those words and fed the good wolf knowing that my revenge would come at the hands of the white man bringing down justice on the governor. I have tried to force the evil wolf to flee to the mountains where it would starve and be no more. But I watched Long Gray Hair kill my people and family in cold blood. There is a struggle inside of me that I find hard to control. I fear that someday soon, both wolves will die."

Chato understood the words of his fellow Apache and said nothing. He knew what Lone Wolf had in his heart and no one but Lone Wolf could resolve the struggle.

The reservation had a bunkhouse where the soldiers and Chato, Jesse, Scott and Thomas could stay as they waited for Lone Wolf and his band of renegades to return with the hostages. Even the Governor of New Mexico Territory had arrived early to greet everyone as only politicians know how.

Chato delivered a request to the governor from Lone Wolf. Lone Wolf was afraid of retaliation on his people when they returned to the reservation so he requested that the governor talk retaliation down and talk up peace. The governor said,

"I will tell the settlers not to fan the flames of discontent toward the Mescalero. Rather, put their bitter and odious feelings aside and thank the good Lord for the safe return of their wives, sons, and daughters."

Chato was pleased with that response.

The day that the Mescalero Indians rode in with the hostages was almost biblical. It was quite overcast but when the settlers could see the clouds of dust from the wagons rolling in with the women and children, the clouds in the sky parted and the warm rays of the brilliant sun shone through. The only thing missing was the angels appearing and blowing their trumpets in celebration. Shouts of joy and happiness rang out amongst the settlers. The *Three for Hire* and Chato were as delighted as the settlers and even more so because they were the ones who made this day come to fruition. Even Gen. Sherman had a untypical big grin on his face.

The anticipation built as the wagons came closer and closer and finally, they arrived. The women and children jumped out of the wagons while the settlers ran up, finding their loved ones and hugging them like they would not allow their families to be separated again. There were tears of joy and smiles and laughter. It was one big celebration.

The Mescalero Indians were solemn. They had nothing to be elated about. Their way of life and running free as the deer was over. Sherman's troopers took their knives and rifles and asked them to dismount from their horses. They were home now too but it wasn't the loving home that the hostages were going to.

Scott, Jesse, Thomas and Chato were all on their horses observing the reunion. Scott looked around and then asked the other three,

"Where's Lone Wolf? Do any of you see Lone Wolf?"

Scott then rode up to one of the Apache he knew who spoke English and asked,

"Where is Lone Wolf?"

"Lone Wolf is not here. Today his evil wolf takes him to the spirit world."

Scott looked at Chato and asked, "What does he mean Chato?"

Chato looked at Scott and said nothing. Scott once again repeated his question but this time yelled at Chato, "What does he mean Chato?"

Chato looked at Scott and said, "He's going after Baxter. He seeks revenge and is willing to die for it."

"Oh no," Jesse shouted. "He's going to get himself killed."

"How far ahead is he?" Scott asked the Mescalero.

"He is about one half sun ahead. He rides hard because he knows you will follow."

Chato interpreted, "One half day ahead."

Scott told Sherman the circumstances and then Jesse, Scott, Thomas, and Chato, whipped and kicked their horses and rode east like the wind creating a dust cloud that would rival a Great Plains dust storm. No one thought about sending a telegram of warning.

It was a long ride to Fort Reno, about 440 miles. It would take about eight to ten days to get there. Lone Wolf was determined to get there as quickly as possible and the *Three for Hire* and Chato were determined to catch up with Lone Wolf. The question was, who was more determined? That question could only be answered at the end of the trail.

Long days and short nights were the norm for both parties. Wearing out horses after riding hard was also an obvious reality. Lone Wolf rode with two other Apache warriors because they were necessary to work his plan. They stole and swapped horses from ranchers and settlers along the way while Jesse and his group traded with ranchers and trading posts for fresh stock.

They rode through Texas panhandle towns that would later become known as Bovina, Friona, and Hereford. Lone Wolf stayed south of Amarillo but then rode east to the Indian Territory and north of the Wichita Mountains and onward to Fort Reno.

When the Mescalero arrived near the fort, they were greeted by a few friendly Lipan Apache who were caught up in the earlier reservation corruption and knew of the starvation and tortures by Baxter, who became known by all Apache as Long Gray Hair. They also knew the area quite well because they were free to roam around the open fort since it was a reservation territory.

Lone Wolf trusted the Lipan Apache and informed them of his plan. They were more than willing to give him information that would aid him in carrying out his deadly plot. The military post did not have a prison and Baxter and his cronies were free to roam outside of their quarters while they were closely guarded by three sentries. The Lipan knew it and informed Lone Wolf of this. It was still a few weeks before the convicted felons would be escorted to Leavenworth.

But time was running out. Jesse and the other three were riding hard and fast. They were hot on Lone Wolf's trail, and he sensed it.

As the Lipan predicted, two privates rode out of the fort in a buckboard to collect firewood for cooking and heating. Lone Wolf, the two Mescalero, and the two Lipan lay low until the wagon was full. Then they ambushed and jumped the two troopers. The two Mescalero traded clothes with the soldiers to disguise themselves so they could easily ride the wagon into the confines of the fort.

Lone Wolf had no intention of killing the two soldiers so he told the two Lipan to guard the troopers. In the meantime, Lone Wolf removed his shirt in preparation for battle and went through a short spiritual ceremony and applied deer fat followed by war paint which he brought with him to smear all over his chest and face.

This time the color was yellow, signifying death, his and Baxter's death. Yellow also indicated that the wearer was heroic, had led a good life, and was willing to fight to the death. He also used the color red to signify strength, energy and blood.

It was now time. Lone Wolf crawled into the back of the wagon grasping his battle spear. The two Mescalero, dressed in military uniforms, covered him with brush and sticks and then climbed into the driver's seat and whipped the horses to go forward. They were just ten minutes out from the boundaries of the fort. Lone Wolf told the drivers to stop and shout out an Apache battle cry when they saw Long Gray Hair. That would be Lone Wolf's signal to jump up and attack Baxter.

As they rode into the fort, the two drivers spotted Baxter. One of the Mescalero whispered back to Lone Wolf, "Make ready, Long Gray Hair is in the courtyard." Just then the sun appeared from behind the clouds and one of the Mescalero said, "It is a good day to die."

The wagon rode in a circular pattern, once around, and approached Baxter and stopped. Then the two Mescalero stood up and yelled out an Apache battle cry with their fists to the sky. Lone Wolf jumped from underneath the brush, out of the wagon, ran toward Baxter and hurled his battle spear right through Baxter's heart. The three guards instinctively fired multiple rounds from their repeating rifles at Lone Wolf, killing him instantly and then they turned their weapons on Lone Wolf's unarmed two Mescalero companions, killing them as well.

Soldiers came running from every direction to find the unthinkable, an Indian attack right in the confines of Fort Reno. Baxter lay dead with a spear through his heart and Lone Wolf laid next to him riddled with holes in his war painted chest. The other two Mescalero lay dead next to the wagon.

It wasn't but five minutes later that Jesse, Scott, Thomas and Chato came riding in with horses sweating profusely and about to collapse. But they were too late. Lone Wolf got his revenge and paid for it with his life.

Jesse and his group dismounted and slowly walked over to the lifeless bodies as the other soldiers surrounded the slain as well.

Scott looked down at Lone Wolf and Baxter and said,

"Greed killed Baxter and revenge killed Lone Wolf."

There was a fort minister standing nearby with his Bible that never left his side. He asked Scott, "Did you say greed and revenge?"

"Yes sir, I did."

The preacher remarked, "This Wild West is full of greed and revenge. These two sins seem to always create another sin, murder. Murder runs rampant out here in the new frontier. I have seen it too many times."

"Not now," Scott said. "We're not in the mood."

Then Jesse said, "Let him speak his piece, it may do all of us some good."

The preacher opened up his Bible and read,

"As for greed it is stated in the good book in Timothy 6:10, 'For the love of money is a root of all kinds of evils. It is through this craving that some have wandered away from the faith and pierced themselves with many pangs'.

As for revenge it is stated in Romans 12:17-21, 'Repay no one evil for evil, but give thought to do what is honorable in the sight of all. If possible, so far as it depends on you, live peaceably with all. Beloved, never avenge yourselves, but leave it to the wrath of God, for it is written, vengeance is mine, I will repay, says the Lord. To the contrary, if your enemy is hungry, feed him; if he is thirsty, give him something to drink; for by so doing you will heap burning coals on his head. Do not be overcome by evil, but overcome evil with good'."

Chato looked at Lone Wolf's body and said,

"Lone Wolf's prediction was true. Both wolves, which struggled in him, are now dead. He so respected his father because his father was a peaceful and honorable man. Lone Wolf was not like his father."

THE END

Epilogue

While the *Three for Hire* and Chato were standing near the wagon, watching the soldiers collect the dead bodies, two riders who appeared to be gunslingers rode in and dismounted their horses. Chato recognized them right away and told Scott, Jesse, and Thomas,

"Those are the two pistoleros who followed us in the Arizona and New Mexico Territories. All three put their hands on their holstered six-shooters. When the two pistoleros saw the three's reaction, they both stretched their arms out in front of them and yelled,

"Whoa, don't shoot; we're on your side."

"Explain," Scott demanded.

One of the pistoleros offered this explanation,

"It seemed you fell into favor with President Hayes. He hired us to be your personal bodyguards but didn't want you to know about us. We've been following you since you first traveled to Tucson on your mission for the governors. He's paying us out of his own pocket. Now that it looks like your job is complete, I guess ours is as well."

"Well if that don't beat all," Thomas remarked.

"Well, what now?" Jesse asked.

"I guess we're done and we can go home," Thomas said. "I think I'm hanging up my adventurous spirit before my wife kicks me out of the house."

"I think I'll go back to Dodge City and ask Janice to become my bride. I think that ole Pops, who owns that gunsmith shop is ready to sell it to me," Scott said. "What about you Jesse? Where are you headed from here?"

"Well, I guess I'll go back to Austin to visit my sisters then take a trip out east and see if I can locate my friend Lilly and see if we can start up a relationship again. While I'm in the East I'll stop in D.C. and cue in President Arthur on everything and say adios from all of us. What about you Chato, what are you going to do?"

"I want to continue to be a scout for the U.S. Army, so I will stay here and see if the commanding officer of Fort Reno will have me."

"I'm sure he will," Jesse said. "You are one of the best and a man of integrity who can be trusted."

Chato smiled.

"Well my friends, Thomas and Scott, this is it. I think we made a difference like patriots are supposed to. I wish you all the best. It's been a privilege riding with you," Jesse said as they all shook hands. "Let's find a way to keep in touch."

The *Three for Hire* mounted their horses and rode out about 100 feet, turned around and waved to Chato. Then they all rode out about two hundred yards and veered off in different directions. About one hundred yards further, they all turned their horses around, took off their hats and waved them to each other and said good-bye with their Stetsons for the very last time.

The efforts of the *Three for Hire* which resulted in the exposure of the corruption in the reservations and the successful convictions for the first time ever, set the stage for a government crackdown on conditions on the Indian reservations around the country. This was the way Scott, Jesse, and Thomas fulfilled their promise to Chato that they would take an active role in getting the government to treat Native Americans on the reservations with more respect.

In 1882, a grand jury in Tucson, Arizona Territory investigated the corruption of San Carlos Indian Agent J. C. Tiffany. This report of the Federal Grand Jury of the Arizona Territory, investigating the Apache Agent J. C. Tiffany, appeared in the Tucson Star on October 24, 1882:

"The investigations of the Grand Jury have brought to light a course of procedure at the San Carlos Apache Reservation ... which is a disgrace to the civilization of the age and a foul blot upon the national escutcheon.... We feel it our duty ... to express our utter abhorrence of the conduct of Agent Tiffany and that class of speculators who have ... caused more misery and loss of life (in Arizona) than all other causes combined.... The management of the Indian Reservations in Arizona was a fraud upon the Government.... The constantly recurring outbreaks of the Indians and their consequent devastations were due to the criminal neglect or apathy of the Indian agent at San Carlos.... Fraud, speculation, conspiracy, larceny, plots and counter plots, seem to be the rule of action upon this reservation."

The clean-up begins!

Actual Article of the Shootout at the O.K. Corral Published October 27, 1881

This is the actual article, obtained from the Library of Congress, that appeared in the WEEKLY ARIZONA CITIZEN, TUCSON, PIMA COUNTY, ARIZONA TERRITORY, SUNDAY, OCTOBER 30, 1881. It was obtained by the ARIZONA CITIZEN from the Tombstone Nugget which ran on October 27, 1881, in Tombstone, Arizona Territory. Therefore, it is the actual article that was run in Tombstone, Arizona Territory the day after the shootout at the O.K. Corral.

NOTE: This article includes errors in punctuation, grammar, and spelling because it is exactly how it was printed in the Arizona Citizen. The article appeared on page three the best I can determine and in column seven. It read:

A Desperate Street Fight

Marshal Virgil Earp, Morgan and Wyatt Earp and Doc Holliday Meet the Cowboys - Three Men Killed and Two Wounded, One Seriously - Origins of the Trouble and its Tragic Termination.

[Tombstone Nugget, Oct. 27.]

The 26th of October will always be marked as one of the crimson days in the annals of Tombstone, a day when blood flowed as water and human life was held as a shuttlecock, a day always to be remembered as witnessing the bloodiest and deadliest street fight that has ever occurred in this place, or probably in the Territory.

THE ORIGIN OF THE TROUBLE

Dates back to the first arrest of Stilwell and Spencer for the robbery of the Bisbee stage. The co-operation of the Earps with the Sheriff and his deputies in the arrest causing a number of the cowboys to, it is said, threaten the lives of all interested in the capture. Still, nothing occurred to indicate that any such threats would be carried into execution. But Tuesday night Ike Clanton and Doc Holliday had some difficulty in the Alhambra saloon. Hard words passed between them, and when they parted it was generally understood that the feeling between the two men was that of intense hatred. Yesterday morning Clanton came on the street armed with a rifle and revolver, but was almost immediately arrested by Marshal Earp, disarmed and fined by Justice Wallace for carrying concealed weapons. While in the Court room Wyatt Earp told him that as he had made threats against his life he wanted him to make his fight, to say how, when and where he would fight, and to get his crowd, and he (Wyatt) would be on hand.

In reply Clanton said:

FOUR FEET OF GROUND

Is enough for me to fight on, and I'll be there." A short time after this William Clanton and Frank McLowry came in town, and as Thomas McLowry was already here the feeling soon became general that a fight would ensue before the day was over, and crowds of expectant men stood on the corner of Allen and Fourth streets awaiting the coming conflict.

It was now about two o'clock, and at this time Sheriff Behan appeared upon the scene and told Marshal Earp that if he disarmed his posse, composed of Morgan and Wyatt Earp, and Doc. Holliday, he would go down to the O.K. Corral, where Ike and James Clanton and Frank and Tom McLowry were and disarm them. The Marshal did not desire to do this until assured that there was no danger of an attack from the other party. The Sheriff went to the corral and told the cowboys that they must put their arms away and not have any trouble. Ike Clanton and Tom McLowry said they were not armed, and Frank McLowry said he would not lay his aside. In the meantime the Marshal had concluded to go and, if possible, end the matter by disarming them, and as he and his posse came down Fremont street towards the corral, the Sheriff stepped out and said:

"HOLD UP BOYS.

Don't go down there or there will be trouble; I have been down there to disarm them." But they passed on, and when within a few feet of them the Marshal said to the Clantons and McLowrys: "Throw up your hands, boys, I intend to disarm you."

As he spoke Frank McLowry made a motion to draw his revolver, when Wyatt Earp pulled his and shot him, the ball striking on the right side of his abdomen. About the same time Doc Holliday shot Tom McLowry in the right side. using a short shotgun, such as is carried by Wells, Fargo & Co,'s messengers. In the meantime Billy Clanton had shot at Morgan Earp, the ball passing through the point of the left shoulder blade across his back, just grazing the backbone and coming out at the shoulder, the ball remaining inside of his shirt. He fell to the ground, but in an instant gathered himself, and raising in a sitting position fired at Frank McLowry as he crossed Freemont street, and at the same instant Doc Holliday shot at him, both balls taking effect, either of which would have proved fatal, as one struck him in the right temple and the other in the left breast. As he started across the street, however, he pulled his gun down on Holliday saying, "I've got you now." "Blaze away! You're a daisy if you have," replied Doc. This shot of McLowry's passed through Holliday's pistol pocket, just grazing the skin.

While this was going on

BILLY CLANTON HAD SHOT

Virgil Earp in the right leg, the ball passing through the calf, inflicting a severe flesh wound. In turn he had been shot by Morg Earp in the right side of the abdomen, and twice by Virgil Earp, once in the right wrist and once in the left breast. Soon after the shooting commenced Ike Clanton ran through the O.K. Corral, across Allen street into Kellogg's saloon, and thence into Toughnut street, where he was arrested and taken to the county jail. The firing altogether didn't occupy more than twenty-five seconds, during which time fully thirty shots were fired. After the fight was over Billy Clanton, who, with wonderful vitality, survived his wounds for fully an hour, was carried by the editor and foreman of the Nugget into a house near where he lay, and everything possible done to make his last moments easy. He was "game" to the last, never uttering a word of complaint, and just before breathing his last he said, "Goodbye, boys; go away and let me die." The wounded were taken to their houses, and at three o'clock this morning were resting comfortably. The dead bodies were taken in charge by the Coroner, and an inquest will be held upon them at 10 o'clock to-day. Upon the person of Thomas McLowry was found between $300 and $400, and checks and certificates of deposit to the amount of nearly $3000.

DURING THE SHOOTING

Sheriff Behan was standing nearby commanding the contestants to cease firing but was powerless to prevent it. Several parties who were in the vicinity of the shooting had narrow escapes from being shot. One man who had lately arrived from the east had a ball pass through his pants. He left for home this morning. A person called "the Kid," who shot Hicks at Charleston recently, was also grazed by a ball. When the Vizina whistle gave the signal that there was a conflict between the officers and cowboys, the mines on the hill shut down and the miners were brought to the surface. From the Contention mine a number of men, fully armed, were sent to town in a four-horse carriage. At the request of the Sheriff the "vigilantes," or Committee of Safety, were called from the streets by a few sharp toots from the Vizina whistle. During the early part of the evening there was a rumor that a mob would attempt to take Ike Clanton from the jail and lynch him, and to prevent any such unlawful proceedings a strong guard of deputtes was placed around that building, and will be so continued until all danger is past.

At 8 o'clock last evening, Finn Clanton, a brother of Billy and Ike, came in town, and placing himself under the guard of the Sheriff, visited the morgue to see the remains of one brother, and then passed the night in jail in company with the other.

OMINOUS SOUNDS.

Shortly after the shooting ceased the whistle at the Vizina mine sounded a few short toots, and almost simultaneously a large number of citizens appeared on the streets, armed with rifles and a belt of cartridges around their waists. These men formed in line and offered their services to the peace officers to preserve order, in case any attempt at disturbance was made, or any interference offered to the authorities of the law. However, no hostile move was made by anyone, and quiet and order was fully restored, and in a short time the excitement died away.

AT THE MORGUE.

The bodies of the three slain cowboys lay side by side, covered with a sheet. Very little blood appeared on their clothing, and only on the face of young Billy Clanton was there any distortion of the features or evidence of pain in dying. The features of the two McLowry boys looked as calm and placid in death, as if they had died peaceably, surrounded by loving friends and sorrowing relatives. No unkind remarks were made by anyone, but a feeling of unusual sorrow seemed to prevail at the sad occurrence. Of the McLowry brothers we could learn nothing of their previous history before coming to Arizona. The two brothers owned quite an extensive ranch on the lower San Pedro, some seventy or eighty miles from this city, to which they had removed their band of cattle since the recent Mexican and Indian troubles. They did not bear the reputation of being of a quarrelsome disposition, but were known as fighting men, and have gener-conducted themselves in a quiet and orderly manner when in Tombstone.

Bibliography

Native American Calendar
http://www.native-net.org/na/native-american-calendar.html

Mescalero Apache
http://en.wikipedia.org/w/index.php?title=Mescalero&oldid=570
023888

Mescalero Apache
http://www.mescaleroapache.com/area/history_and_cul.htm

Cochise
http://en.wikipedia.org/w/index.php?title=Cochise&oldid=59448
0188

Apache Pass
http://en.wikipedia.org/w/index.php?title=Apache_Pass&oldid=5
94496640

Geronimo
http://en.wikipedia.org/w/index.php?title=Geronimo&oldid=594
265902

Victorio
http://en.wikipedia.org/w/index.php?title=Victorio&oldid=57815
8198

Mangas Coloradas
http://en.wikipedia.org/w/index.php?title=Mangas_Coloradas&ol
did=594259673

Apache
http://en.wikipedia.org/w/index.php?title=Apache&oldid=59417
9309

Victorio's War
http://en.wikipedia.org/w/index.php?title=Victorio%27s_War&ol
did=590494227

Trail of Tears
http://en.wikipedia.org/w/index.php?title=Trail_of_Tears&oldid
=594745849

Indian Removal Act
http://en.wikipedia.org/w/index.php?title=Indian_Removal_Act
&oldid=594399833

Henry Rifle
http://en.wikipedia.org/w/index.php?title=Henry_rifle&oldid=59
4591801

John Clum
http://en.wikipedia.org/w/index.php?title=John_Clum&oldid=56
9117660

United States Army Indian Scouts
http://en.wikipedia.org/w/index.php?title=United_States_Army_I
ndian_Scouts&oldid=560389391

Wickiup, wigwam, wetu
http://en.wikipedia.org/w/index.php?title=Wigwam&oldid=5918
07691

Tepee
http://en.wikipedia.org/w/index.php?title=Tipi&oldid=59451641
7

Chiricahua Mountains
http://en.wikipedia.org/w/index.php?title=Chiricahua_Mountains
&oldid=583252640

Dos Cabezas Mountains
http://en.wikipedia.org/w/index.php?title=Dos_Cabezas_Mounta
ins&oldid=564329406

Sooners
http://en.wikipedia.org/w/index.php?title=Sooners&oldid=58427
4752

Naiche
http://en.wikipedia.org/w/index.php?title=Naiche&oldid=573735
774

Nana
http://en.wikipedia.org/w/index.php?title=Nana_(chief)&oldid=5
95349429

Ed Schieffelin
http://en.wikipedia.org/w/index.php?title=Ed_Schieffelin&oldid
=589270725

Albert E. Schieffelin
http://www.findagrave.com/cgi-
bin/fg.cgi?page=gr&GRid=77523716

Schieffelin Hall
http://en.wikipedia.org/w/index.php?title=Schieffelin_Hall&oldid
=593361298

Chato
http://en.wikipedia.org/w/index.php?title=Chato_(Apache)&oldi
d=555721483

Adobe
http://en.wikipedia.org/w/index.php?title=Adobe&oldid=594721
334

Kiowa people
http://en.wikipedia.org/w/index.php?title=Kiowa_people&oldid=
590486784

Battle of Cibecue Creek
http://en.wikipedia.org/w/index.php?title=Battle_of_Cibecue_Cr
eek&oldid=549224723

Billy the Kid
http://en.wikipedia.org/w/index.php?title=Billy_the_Kid&oldid=
595466595

John Kinney (outlaw)
http://en.wikipedia.org/w/index.php?title=John_Kinney_(outlaw)&oldid=514108856

Dan Tucker (lawman)
http://en.wikipedia.org/w/index.php?title=Dan_Tucker_(lawman)&oldid=573932853

William Tecumseh Sherman
http://en.wikipedia.org/w/index.php?title=William_Tecumseh_Sherman&oldid=592360458

Tecumseh
http://en.wikipedia.org/w/index.php?title=Tecumseh&oldid=594728626

Ellen Ewing Sherman
http://en.wikipedia.org/w/index.php?title=Ellen_Ewing_Sherman&oldid=566769551

Thomas Ewing Sherman
http://en.wikipedia.org/w/index.php?title=Thomas_Ewing_Sherman&oldid=548793604

Edwin Vose Sumner
http://en.wikipedia.org/w/index.php?title=Edwin_Vose_Sumner&oldid=580825048

Pat Garrett
http://en.wikipedia.org/w/index.php?title=Pat_Garrett&oldid=586754149

Philip Sheridan
http://en.wikipedia.org/w/index.php?title=Philip_Sheridan&oldid=595374346

Pennsylvania Oil Rush
http://en.wikipedia.org/w/index.php?title=Pennsylvania_oil_rush&oldid=592762973

Petroleum seep
http://en.wikipedia.org/w/index.php?title=Petroleum_seep&oldid=590636243

Travois
http://en.wikipedia.org/w/index.php?title=Travois&oldid=578845593

Whale oil
http://en.wikipedia.org/w/index.php?title=Whale_oil&oldid=594701844

James Garfield
http://en.wikipedia.org/w/index.php?title=James_A._Garfield&oldid=595475614

Charles J. Guiteau
http://en.wikipedia.org/w/index.php?title=Charles_J._Guiteau&oldid=595512794

President Arthur
http://en.wikipedia.org/w/index.php?title=Chester_A._Arthur&oldid=595533122

Apache Wars
http://en.wikipedia.org/w/index.php?title=Apache_Wars&oldid=592587078

Chief Seattle
http://en.wikipedia.org/w/index.php?title=Chief_Seattle&oldid=595340268

Indian Territory
http://en.wikipedia.org/w/index.php?title=Indian_Territory&oldid=593723901

Fort Sill
http://en.wikipedia.org/w/index.php?title=Fort_Sill&oldid=594199687

Fort Stanton
http://en.wikipedia.org/w/index.php?title=Fort_Stanton&oldid=5
91351834

Spiegel Grove
http://en.wikipedia.org/w/index.php?title=Spiegel_Grove&oldid
=587661928

Great Fire of Pittsburgh
http://en.wikipedia.org/w/index.php?title=Great_Fire_of_Pittsbu
rgh&oldid=592601644

Mescal
http://en.wikipedia.org/w/index.php?title=Mezcal&oldid=595548
190

San Carlos Apache Indian Reservation
http://en.wikipedia.org/w/index.php?title=San_Carlos_Apache_I
ndian_Reservation&oldid=585290744

Court-Martial Procedures Manual
http://www.google.com/url?sa=t&rct=j&q=&esrc=s&frm=1&so
urce=web&cd=1&ved=0CCQQFjAA&url=http%3A%2F%2Fww
w.loc.gov%2Frr%2Ffrd%2FMilitary_Law%2Fpdf%2Fmanual-
1918.pdf&ei=W7j_UuLODYbOyAGRiYHwCg&usg=AFQjCNH
bnEJIDqe5wsbLmAclsi6Pykp-9w

The Dallas Daily Herald, 1881
http://chroniclingamerica.loc.gov/lccn/sn83025733/1881-07-
03/ed-1/seq-
1/#date1=1881&index=0&rows=20&words=president+President
+shot&searchType=basic&sequence=0&state=Texas&date2=188
1&proxtext=President+shot&y=10&x=18&dateFilterType=yearR
ange&page=1

Winston, Missouri Train Robbery by the James Gang
http://www.angelfire.com/mi2/jamesyoungergang/winston.html

Oil in Oklahoma
http://digital.library.okstate.edu/chronicles/v004/v004p322.html

William Carr Lane
http://en.wikipedia.org/w/index.php?title=William_Carr_Lane&o
ldid=559769847

O.K. Corral The Nugget and the Weekly Arizona Citizen, 1881
http://chroniclingamerica.loc.gov/lccn/sn82015133/1881-10-
30/ed-1/seq-3/

Arbuckle's Coffee
http://www.arbucklecoffee.com/category-s/1848.htm

Lozen
http://en.wikipedia.org/w/index.php?title=Lozen&oldid=595054
355

Smoke Signals
http://www.warpaths2peacepipes.com/native-american-
culture/smoke-signals.htm

War Paint
http://www.warpaths2peacepipes.com/native-american-
culture/war-paint.htm

Harrisburg, Pennsylvania
http://en.wikipedia.org/w/index.php?title=Harrisburg,_Pennsylva
nia&oldid=595229160

Hydetown, Pennsylvania
http://en.wikipedia.org/w/index.php?title=Hydetown,_Pennsylva
nia&oldid=589016191

Titusville, Pennsylvania
http://en.wikipedia.org/w/index.php?title=Titusville,_Pennsylvani
a&oldid=595545666

Lincoln County War
http://en.wikipedia.org/w/index.php?title=Lincoln_County_War
&oldid=594962247

J.C. Tiffany
http://www.zoominfo.com/p/J.-Tiffany/1593869629

Turn State's Evidence
http://en.wikipedia.org/w/index.php?title=Turn state%27s evide
nce&oldid=583201135

Peyote
http://en.wikipedia.org/w/index.php?title=Peyote&oldid=595548
069

General Jesse L. Reno
http://en.wikipedia.org/w/index.php?title=Jesse L. Reno&oldid
=578434311

Lucien Maxwell
http://en.wikipedia.org/w/index.php?title=Lucien Maxwell&oldi
d=581285934

Chief Seattle's letter
http://www.barefootsworld.net/seattle.html

Chief Seattle
http://en.wikipedia.org/w/index.php?title=Chief Seattle&oldid=5
95340268

Silver City
http://en.wikipedia.org/w/index.php?title=Silver City, New
 Mexico&oldid=597122448

Gnadenhutten massacre
http://en.wikipedia.org/w/index.php?title=Gnadenhutten massac
re&oldid=595771886